. . . UNTO THE FOURTH GENERATION

. . . UNTO THE FOURTH GENERATION

Margaret Potter

GUILD PUBLISHING
LONDON

Phototypeset by Sunrise Setting, Torquay, Devon
Printed and bound in Great Britain by
The Garden City Press Ltd, Letchworth, Herts

This edition published 1986 by
Book Club Associates
by arrangement with W.H. Allen & Co Plc

. . . UNTO THE FOURTH GENERATION

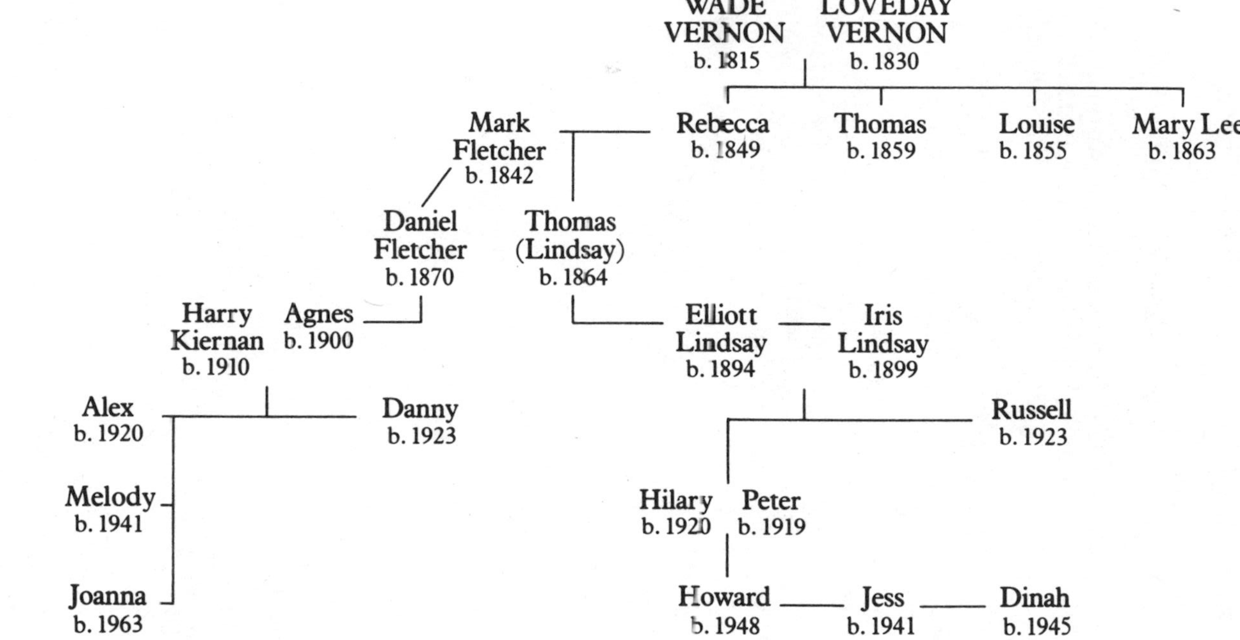

WADE VERNON b. 1815
LOVEDAY VERNON b. 1830
Mark Fletcher b. 1842
Rebecca b. 1849
Thomas b. 1859
Louise b. 1855
Mary Lee b. 1863
Daniel Fletcher b. 1870
Thomas (Lindsay) b. 1864
Harry Kiernan b. 1910
Agnes b. 1900
Elliott Lindsay b. 1894
Iris Lindsay b. 1899
Alex b. 1920
Danny b. 1923
Russell b. 1923
Melody b. 1941
Hilary b. 1920
Peter b. 1919
Joanna b. 1963
Howard b. 1948
Jess b. 1941
Dinah b. 1945

CONTENTS

EPISODE ONE

1863

A Crime

1

Where was Rebecca? Fretfully, because he had been abandoned, and guiltily, because he had been told to stay in his room, three-year-old Thomas Vernon stepped out on to the veranda and began to call his sister's name. He was uneasy as well as unhappy; there was something wrong about the day. Thomas was old enough to recognize when he wasn't being told the truth, although still too young to work out for himself what was happening. He understood only that there were secrets in the air which he was not allowed to share. No one but his sister could provide the comfort that he needed now. There was no reassurance to be found in the house. He had to call it his home because he had no other, but it didn't have the safe, friendly feeling of a real home. It was too big and too empty. Thomas was always frightened when he was left there alone.

The Round House stood on the high eastern bank of the Mississippi, a little downriver from the cluster of palatial houses in the middle of Natchez. In the easy-spending days of peace and prosperity, when cotton was king, Wade Vernon – Thomas's father – had determined that his town house should be completely surrounded by its own generous parkland; he needed more space than remained in the centre of a community reputed already to contain a greater concentration of millionaires than any other spot on the American continent.

The outbreak of the war between the states had put an end to Wade's plans for landscaping the grounds and taming them into rose gardens and terraces and bowers, with a statue at the end of each vista and a gazebo on the bluff. Except for the clearing in which the house had been built, the land was still as he had found it: a wilderness, its tall pines and cypresses and magnolias smothered by a rampant liana which no one now left on the estate had the strength to control. The vine transformed the forest areas into a city of green walls and towers, as though the ruins of some lost civilization waited behind it to be discovered by an explorer. To slash through the leafy screen was to step into a dappled silence in which any sound could be made only by a snake or a spy. The quietness was shiversome, and not just because of the shade provided by the trees and their unwanted shroud. Nothing good had had time to happen here. Even the children, who had not yet encountered evil, were reluctant to enter the wilderness alone.

Certainly Thomas, on this steamy Mississippi afternoon in the July of 1863, was not prepared to leave the security of his home to search for his sister. Instead, he wandered forlornly along the veranda, calling her name. 'Rebecca! Rebecca, where you gone?'

There was no answer – no sound at all in the still air. The day was so hot that even the birds were silent within the jungle of trees; so hot that the outline of the sun had melted into the angry yellow sky. There would be thunder soon. Thomas could feel the air gathering itself together, ready to explode above his head. He was frightened of thunder. Where was Rebecca?

The corners of his mouth turned down sulkily as he climbed into his mother's rocking chair, without the energy to set it into motion. Although he was not quite four years old, he knew how his own time-table was supposed to run. Someone ought to have given him something to eat now, when the sun was high in the middle of the day. But Rebecca had made him lie down on his trundle bed instead, telling him that it was time for his rest and he was to be a good boy. Being a good boy always meant doing things that only suited other people.

Rebecca was supposed to be looking after him today. He had heard their mother tell her before she went into Natchez. It wasn't right for her to leave him alone. Well, Thomas did recognize that he was not entirely alone, because he could hear Louise practising her scales. But everyone knew that when Louise was playing the piano nothing less than the house burning down would attract her attention. She would be cross if he interrupted her and asked her to play. Everyone in the family was out of sorts today. Thomas himself was cross because he was hot and hungry and nobody was taking notice of him. He didn't know what had got into the others.

He began to rock himself in the chair, gently at first, but gradually working it up into a fury. Then a sound on the other side of the house caused him to slide off the seat with a thud and keep still, listening. Someone was coming up the long drive.

It couldn't be his mother, for she had driven herself and the baby off in the buggy that morning, and what he could hear now was not the patient plod of Captain Jack's hooves and the rattling of wheels over the potholes, but the slow shuffle of tired footsteps. Thomas made his way round to the front of the house to see who was approaching.

It *was* his mother after all – and if she had walked all the way home from the centre of Natchez, carrying Mary Lee, it was not surprising that she looked worn out. But there was something more than tiredness to be seen in the pallor of her face. There must have been an accident. Perhaps something had happened to Captain Jack. Thomas jumped down from the veranda and ran barefoot towards her, ready to comfort her and to be loved a little in return.

His mother walked straight past him. She didn't stop to give him her usual hug. She didn't even smile. Only when he tugged at her skirt to hold her back did she look down at him.

'Tomorrow, Thomas,' she said, and went on by, into the house. With one arm pressing the baby tightly against her shoulder, she used the other hand to pull herself up the steep ladder which led to her den. Thomas was strictly forbidden to climb even a single rung of that ladder. The little cubicle to which his mother retreated when she wanted to write letters had holes in the floor and gaps in the wall; it was so unsafe, she said, that not even Rebecca could be allowed inside: certainly not Thomas.

'Mama!' he called up to her, his voice breaking with a tearful resentment, but she didn't seem to hear. He could just see her up there, hugging Mary Lee so tightly that the baby began to whimper. Thomas turned away disconsolately. On the floor below, Louise had finished with her scales and was practising a minuet, playing the same few difficult bars over and over. And there was still no sign of his eldest sister. Hungry and desolate, Thomas sat down on the edge of the veranda, his chubby legs dangling down towards the ground. When would Rebecca remember about him and come back?

2

The grounds of The Round House extended down to the swirling water of the Mississippi River. At their lowest level they embraced the Old River Lake, which once upon a time had been part of the river bed. Changing its course at some moment in its long and twisting history, the Mississippi had taken a short cut across the neck of a bend, leaving it to stagnate behind a bank of silt. A bayou, fed by the river water at its open end, pointed towards the curved sausage shape of the Old River Lake but no longer made contact with it. The land beside the bayou was swampy, a breeding ground for mosquitoes, and even around the lake the air was too steamy to be comfortable. Wade Vernon had chosen to build his palace on the bluff which rose two hundred feet above the river. Between the woodland and the cliff was a narrow ribbon of rock too bare for any vegetation to colonize, and this part of their land had been placed out of bounds to the children before he went to the war. It was dangerous, he told them. Although it had the appearance of a track, the open area was too close to the verge and the powerful river current below was perpetually undermining the cliff.

Deliberately now, because she was not a child any longer, Rebecca Vernon was sitting on the very edge. Her feet, dangling over the cliff, drummed angrily into the bank. If the ground were to crumble and throw her into the Mississippi thousands of feet below, she wouldn't care. Perhaps people would be sorry when she was dead and wish they'd paid more attention to her when she was still alive. She wanted to cry, but she was grown now, too old for childish tears.

She had known that she was grown as soon as she awoke that morning to find the stains on her nightdress and sheet. Her mother had warned her a year ago about what was going to happen to her; but Rebecca had been sure that she would be different from everyone else, and then she had forgotten, and anyway she hadn't expected it to feel so dirty. Ashamed of the mess, she had sneaked out of the room she shared with Louise first thing, to wash the sheet before her eight-year-old sister learned of her disgrace. That was how she came to be awake when their nearest neighbour came running to The Round House before dawn. Miss Emily Price had battered at the jalousies instead of tugging at the long bell pull; and yet when Mrs Vernon rushed out to see what the matter was, she seemed unable to open her mouth.

In the long silence which followed, Rebecca watched the colour draining from her mother's face until she was as pale as her neighbour. All that Miss Emily was able to say, in the end, was a single sentence. 'The new lists from Gettysburg are coming through on the wire.' Within half an hour both women had left the house, taking Mary Lee with them. Thee was no one left to whom Rebecca could talk. Holding her secret filled the morning with loneliness, cutting her off from her brother and sister. A year ago she could have run to Molly for reassurance. But Molly had run off with the field slaves as the Yankee army approached the Vernons' plantation, not caring that little Thomas would weep inconsolably and that Rebecca and Louise, abandoned by someone who had been their second mother, would feel betrayed.

Rebecca understood why her mother needed to hurry down to the telegraph office. But her understanding could not prevent her from feeling neglected and miserable as she kicked away at the face of the cliff. The stained sheet had been one indication that she was no longer a child, but there was another. Today was her fourteenth birthday. And nobody had remembered. Not one single person. She could not have expected her father, after months away from home with the army in the east, to interrupt his fighting in order to go to a store and arrange for a gift to travel such a great distance and arrive on exactly the right day. Mary Lee was just a baby and even Thomas was perhaps too young to know one day from another. But Louise was eight and had been working for weeks on a patchwork cushion which was supposed to be a surprise. What had happened to that?

And her mother – how could a mother forget the birthday of her eldest daughter? They might be too poor now to enjoy the extravagant, frivolous presents of their plantation days, but surely Mama must have noticed that she was bursting out of all her clothes. Even something as trifling as a new ribbon for her hair would have cheered up the day. There should have been a parcel waiting by her pillow when she woke up that morning. But there had not been the smallest token. Not even a word.

Rebecca's attempt to turn misery into indignation did not deceive even herself. Her dismay at what was happening to her body was genuine enough, and so was her disappointment that her birthday was being treated as a day just like any other. But between these two layers of unsettlement churned a deeper and more terrible emotion. She understood the fear she had seen in her mother's eyes, because she felt it herself. What if the news were bad? For two years they had been sure that nothing could destroy their happy family group. But three of Rebecca's closest friends, who had felt equally proud of their fathers or brothers, and equally sure of their invulnerability, were now wearing black. As a child, Rebecca feared the loss of the man she loved most in all the world. As an adult she feared the future: if Papa dies, who will look after us all?

The huge question sparked off a smaller unease. She was supposed to be looking after Thomas. But he could not come to any harm, sleeping peacefully in his own bed. Totally absorbed in her own unhappiness, she dismissed from her mind the thought of her little brother.

Two hundred feet below Rebecca's drumming heels the swirling brown water of the Mississippi eddied with a sudden intensity and erupted in a boil. There was a rock hidden below the surface which often produced this effect, startling even the watchful pilots of the river boats. It meant that there was a storm higher up the river and that a sudden deluge had caused a surge of extra water. Rebecca raised her eyes. To the north of Natchez the river curved in such a wide bend that the expanse of water looked as wide and limitless as the ocean must be. Above it now, still far away, a single heavy cloud sent a shaft of rain slanting down towards the earth. Surrounded and outlined by sunlight, it looked as solid as one of the columns of The Round House and pointed as deliberately and firmly as the pencil with which Rebecca wrote her lessons. But within a few moments, as she watched, it reached the bend of the river and revealed itself as not narrow at all, but a wide wall of water, sweeping down the Mississippi like an army relentlessly advancing. So clear was the line between rain and sunshine that if Rebecca were to raise her feet in front of her there would be a second in which her boots would be soaked and her face still burning.

She waited, indulging her self-pity. There was an unfamiliar pain in her stomach and her head throbbed beneath the pressure of the heavy air. In the past ten minutes she had persuaded herself that her father must be dead. She told herself that she was only pretending, making up one of the stories which she was accustomed to tell Thomas, so that when the good news arrived from the battlefield she could experience all the delight of surprise. But her throat was choked with the need to sob aloud. When the rain reaches me, she thought, when it touches my eyes, I can let the tears burst out and nobody will be able to tell.

'Thomas is crying.'

So startled was Rebecca by Louise's voice that she very nearly fulfilled her father's worst fear and toppled over the bluff and into the river. And when she scrambled to her feet, her sun-beaten head was so dizzy that for a moment she did not know which way to step and was for a second time on the point of falling. Louise, obeying orders, was standing back beneath the trees.

'You shouldn't startle people like that, creeping up,' Rebecca accused, made angry by guilt as well as shock. She knew very well that she ought not to have left Thomas in the care of an eight-year-old. 'And I told you to stay nearby. He's not to be by himself in the house.'

'Mama's back.'

Rebecca stood still while the ground rocked around her. If their mother was home, she must have had some news. 'How did she look?'

'She wouldn't say anything. She went up into the den with Mary Lee and she wouldn't talk to me and she wouldn't talk to Thomas. So now he's yowling and I can't make him stop.'

Something cold and heavy sank slowly to the bottom of Rebecca's stomach, weighing her down so that for a moment she was unable to move. And then, with a single terrifying crash of thunder immediately overhead, the storm arrived. Rain swooshed over the surface of the river and battered fiercely against the trees and their roof of creepers. It slapped Rebecca in the face just as she had expected, but she could no longer allow herself the indulgence of tears. Awkwardly, because of the clumsy cloth between her legs, she stepped forward to clutch Louise's hands. With their heads bent down against the deluge, the two sisters ran towards the house.

Thomas was sitting at the top of the steps, between two of the huge white columns which had been part of their father's grand design for his town house. The scale of the portico dwarfed the little boy, making him look even younger than his three-and-three-quarter years. The sound of his misery was more subdued now than Louise had described it, as though he had cried himself into exhaustion. Rocking himself from side to side, he sucked at the rag which had once been part of his cradle blanket. He looked appealingly up at Rebecca, his face smudged with the tears rubbed in with dirty hands.

'I want my mama. She's in there with Mary Lee and she won't let me come too. I want my mama.'

Rebecca shook off the rain and stretched out her arms as her heart swelled with love for her little brother. Already in his short life he had said goodbye to his father without understanding why. He had woken up one morning to find that his mammy had disappeared. He had been snatched away from his plantation home to live in an unfamiliar house which was not even finished. And just as he was used to his cramped nursery, he had been turned out of it again to make room for a baby who demanded too much of his mother's time. It was no wonder that he felt even more neglected and lonely than Rebecca herself, for she at least could understand what was happening.

'Come and love Rebecca,' she said. She sat down on the step beside him and took him on to her lap, hugging him close as she rocked him from side to side. 'I'll look after you, Thomas. I'll be your mama and love you for ever and ever.'

'You won't go away?' said Thomas, burrowing his head into her neck. Rebecca bent to kiss his forehead. 'No,' she promised. 'I won't ever go away.'

3

At five o'clock the next morning Loveday Vernon climbed stiffly down from the barely-furnished cubicle in the beams of The Round House which she called her den. The baby, unsatisfied after her morning feed, continued to cry after she was set back in her cradle, but Loveday left her there all the same and let herself quietly out of the house. Only at this hour of a summer morning was the air cool. The white mist which now hovered just above the ground would soon invade the atmosphere to make it steamy and oppressive. Loveday breathed deeply, filling her lungs in the hope that the fresh dawn air would restore her strength.

For a day and a night she had mourned the death of her husband in battle. Now, however bitterly she might cry alone at night, she knew that for the sake of the children, so vulnerable to the new dangers which surrounded them, she must appear to be strong. But the prospect was daunting. The burning of the plantation had deprived the family of its only income. She had been able to carry away with her some of the proceeds of last year's cotton crop, but her hidden store of money was vanishing fast. By now the effects of the Northern blockade were making themselves felt not only in the complete disappearance of some foods but in the inflated prices demanded for those which remained. It was months since she had tasted either tea or coffee. Well, she could do without those if she must, but every day which passed made it more difficult to provide the children with a healthy diet.

At least they had a roof over their heads – but Loveday could not resist a bitter laugh as she gazed at the huge domed building which stood so proudly in the midst of the wilderness. Wade Vernon had promised to build his wife a palace. As a young man he had travelled in Europe and was able to present his architect with a sketch which combined the elegance of a Palladian villa with the domed grandeur of St Peter's in Rome. Only by the addition of wide verandas did he make any concession to local needs.

He had lived to see at least the shell of his dream completed. The negroes brought from Netherlee to work on the new house perhaps murmured to each other at night about the rumours spreading from Richmond or Washington as war between the states grew more and more inevitable and at last erupted into bloodshed. But during the first year of the war they remained outwardly respectful, working with a slow deliberation which was normal rather than insolent. The supervisor appointed by the architect had provided craftsmen to undertake the special challenge of the dome, and on her regular visits to check the progress of the work, Loveday had watched in admiration as the timber infrastructure was clad in wood, which had been patiently bent into shape with the help of water and sunshine and then ridged and tiled to glisten, a perfect shape, beneath the Mississippi sun. By the time that Wade left after his last furlough to rejoin the army in the east, the grand portico with its four pairs of huge white pillars had been added, so that from outside the house appeared to be complete: a dream come true.

The reality was different. The central core of the house was a perfect circle, although this was obscured by the high portico at the front and by rectangular extensions of what had been planned as the spacious entertaining rooms. There should have been a marble-floored entrance hall with a railed open circle in the centre to give a view of a tiled pool in the semi-basement below. Above the entertaining rooms the architect's drawing showed another gallery round the base of the dome, acting as a circular corridor from which all the bedrooms would lead. But none of these plans had been put into effect.

The lowest floor of the house, half sunken into the ground and half above it, was the only layer to have been completed; and this was never intended to be luxurious. It was to contain a billiard room, a smoking room, a play area for the children and smaller spaces set apart for domestic tasks. The timber for the entrance hall had been fixed in place, providing a ceiling for all but the centre of the basement area; but it had never received its marble covering, and none of the other floors had even been laid. For it was at that stage of the construction that the civilization of the South began to crumble and collapse. Here, as on the plantation, the slaves proved disloyal, creeping away to join the flight towards freedom.

Even more disastrous was an early effect of the Northern blockade. Loveday sadly recalled the excited happiness with which she and Wade had made their plans for the embellishment and furnishing of the new house before there was any thought of war. They had sent out orders for Italian marble and English panelling, French furniture, Belgian carpets, Dutch tiles, Bohemian crystal; but they had waited in vain for their treasures to arrive. Only the grand piano had made its way safely from Germany to New Orleans before the blockading ships tightened their stranglehold on the Southern ports. Its place should have been upon polished parquet in a ballroom; but the rooms designed for entertaining possessed neither any ceiling nor a finished floor. Instead, the piano stood in the open centre of the basement.

Finished or not, The Round House was now the only home which the Vernons owned. In company with their neighbours they had packed up their belongings and moved south from their main plantation as the Union army approached, and before long had heard that Netherlee had been burned to the ground. At first – pregnant, and exhausted by the move – Loveday had settled her young family into the slave quarters which the negroes had built for themselves while they were working on the house. But the wooden huts were damp and invaded by bugs and mosquitoes. On the morning that she found a rat gnawing at Thomas's mattress she moved into the basement of The Round House, closing her ears to the children's complaints as she allocated the bleak rooms amongst them.

In the whole of the edifice which towered so hugely above, the only other habitable area was a tiny cubicle boarded into the space between the beams which should have supported the dining room floor. The supervisor had roughly enclosed it to serve as an office for himself. Reached by a vertical ladder, it had been placed out of bounds to the children partly to keep them out of danger but mainly so that Loveday herself could have just one small private place.

Life in The Round House had not proved easy for any of them. The children, just as much as Loveday herself, had always taken it for granted that someone would wait on them. They continued to drop their clothes on the floor as though an invisible hand would spirit them away to be washed and ironed and silently returned. Their hair was untidy because they expected someone to brush it for them and their beds would have remained unmade all day if Loveday had not become a nagging mother. Loveday herself, in those early days, was as much at a loss as the children. She could sew and paint and play the piano and transform an armful of flowers into a work of art; but she had never been taught to cook.

Well, she had learned, and with rugs and drapes and pictures and love had made the basement into a home. She had never lacked courage and understood that during her husband's absence she must accept temporary responsibility for the welfare of the family. Now that responsibility was total. She would have to be father as well as mother to her four children. Her neighbours and friends would certainly provide support, but they were all in much the same insecure situation. She could rely on no one but herself.

That was not quite true, she thought, watching the eastern clouds flush with the sunrise. She could rely on her eldest daughter. Rebecca was thirteen – but no, she remembered with a start: fourteen. Yesterday had been her birthday, but the gift already sewn and wrapped still lay unpresented in the den. Well, Rebecca would understand and forgive. Thomas was too young to be sensible and Louise, although she was eight, easily distracted from any task except that of playing the piano – which was not a chore for her but a passion. Rebecca, though, was intelligent and affectionate and steady. She had rebelled for a time against some of the domestic tasks which she thought of as negroes' work. But whenever she was given a reasonable explanation of a request, she did what she was asked.

She appeared at that moment through the low door which led directly from the basement. Perhaps she had been awakened by Mary Lee's crying. Loveday had been forced to feed her fourth baby herself, but the shock of seeing her husband's name on the list of dead had robbed her of her milk. That, however, was one of the few problems which could be quickly solved.

In the cool morning air Rebecca yawned and stretched herself, not knowing that she was being watched. Her nightgown – like all her clothes – had become too tight in these last few months when she seemed to be growing visibly in every direction at once. Her stretching strained the gown across her chest, revealing the two points of her swelling breasts. Loveday felt a prick of unease at the thought of another danger, another responsibility. But that one must wait its turn. She stood up and began to walk towards the house.

Rebecca came running towards her as soon as the movement caught her eye, and for a moment the two women stood locked in each other's arms.

'You know?' asked Loveday when at last her daughter's passionate hug relaxed.

'Is Papa dead?' Yes, Rebecca knew. She was expecting only confirmation.

Loveday nodded, and felt the tears swelling in her eyes, defying her resolve to be brave. 'Will you tell Thomas and Louise for me, gently?' she asked. 'I'll comfort them when they know, and say a prayer with them, but I somehow can't seem to pronounce the words.'

It was Rebecca's turn to nod, and Loveday was able to pull herself together again. 'We'll allow them time to cry a little,' she said. 'It doesn't do to pretend that everything's going on the same. But this afternoon we'll have the birthday party that should have happened yesterday. It will be a sign that we have to go on with our lives, just the five of us.'

'You remembered, then!'

Loveday understood from Rebecca's relief the disappointment she had felt and hugged her again, in love this time and not in grief. 'Did you think I could forget? It was just that I couldn't have made myself smile yesterday, not even for you. But I had a cake baked already, and a gift waiting. We'll celebrate fourteen-years-and-a-day and do our best to be happy. But before that, Rebecca, there's something important I must tell you.' She led the way to the steps so that they could sit down together. As long as she could be businesslike, the desire to weep would be kept at bay. 'Have you heard what happened at Vicksburg?'

Rebecca shook her head. 'I thought Miss Emily said the battle was at Gettysburg.'

'That was where your father . . . yes. The day after that, though, Vicksburg surrendered. Twenty thousand of our men have been taken prisoner. The news came faster because it's so close. It means that the Yankees control the river now. If they press on south, there's nothing to stop them from reaching Natchez. It's not more than a few days' march. They're burning as they move. We could find ourselves without a home again. And food will be short. There are black days ahead, dearest. But I have a secret. I want to tell you, but no one else must know. We have a cow.'

Rebecca stared at her with an astonishment which on any other day would have made her laugh. 'How did you come by that?'

'The Morgans are moving east to their folk in Alabama. They saw me outside the telegraph office in the buggy yesterday and asked for a trade. The buggy, to help them leave, in exchange for their cow, Bella. She'll have been brought to the shed in the slave quarters by now. We must find a place where she can graze and not be seen from the house or the river. And then I want you to be in charge of her, Rebecca, to milk her night and morning. She calved two weeks ago, so there's plenty of milk.' She saw the distaste on her daughter's face and went quickly on. 'Mary Lee's life could depend on it, 'Becca, and the time may come when the rest of us will only eat if we have something to sell or barter. Etta Morgan showed you once how to do it, didn't she?'

She waited anxiously for an answer; the task must be done willingly if it were not to be sometimes forgotten. Rebecca agreed only with reluctance, but Loveday knew that she always kept her promises.

'What do I tell Thomas, though?' asked Rebecca. 'The milking will be at the times when you're giving Mary Lee her morning and evening feeds, and Thomas always hangs round my skirts when you're with the baby. He'll want to know and he'll want to come. And Louise can't stand to be left out of a secret either.'

Loveday considered the problem for a moment in silence. 'We must keep it from Louise,' she said at last. 'She chatters away with no sense of what's important and what's not. I'll ask her to play the piano for me whenever I'm feeding, to soothe the baby.'

It was a good solution. The grand piano had been ordered for the pleasure of Loveday herself – who had little leisure in which to play it. But from the first time Louise was lifted on to a piano stool stacked high with cushions she had explored the notes with a kind of awe, demanding at once to be taught how to make a tune and how to read the notes on the music. She practised her scales and exercises and pieces until the repetition drove the rest of the family to distraction, although in every other part of her life she was undisciplined, abandoning a task whenever the fancy took her to try something different. After even such a short time it was clear that she had a talent for music and that her greatest pleasure lay in exercising it. There was no such easy answer for the three-year-old.

But Rebecca – although she had raised the question herself – said now, 'I can deal with Thomas. I'll take him along when I go to milk Bella. It can be a secret, just between him and me. I'll make him feel that he's stepping into a different world whenever he comes, with terrible things that will happen if he tells. Besides, he's so little that if he babbles by mistake, we can make out he's talking about a toy. Leave Thomas to me.'

'Darling!' It was not just because a practical difficulty could be solved that Loveday opened her arms to embrace her daughter again. It was the relief of having someone in whom she could confide – another adult to share the strain of what was to come.

Later that day, however, the harmony of their shared adulthood was broken when the delayed birthday party at last took place. The occasion started happily enough. Thomas, already forgetting that he had cried for a father he could hardly recall, jumped up and down with excitement as Rebecca unwrapped the necklace he had threaded from nuts polished and bored by his mother. Louise's patchwork cushion was pronounced too fine to sit on – and then everyone took turns to bounce on it and acclaim it as stuffed to perfection. But there was a moment of sadness when it was time to hand over the gold locket which Wade had left behind for his eldest daughter so many months ago. Loveday had painted the miniature inside it herself and could hardly hold back her tears as she remembered the calm, happy afternoons when her husband had sat for her.

Then she produced her own gift: a new dress, made of the finest lawn in a pale, cool shade of blue. As she sewed it, Loveday had poured all her love into the tiny stitches and delicate embroidery. There was a deep blue sash and sprigs of the same blue around the hem and in the high collar. She waited proudly to be kissed and thanked; but instead saw that Rebecca was staring at the dress in disappointment.

'What's the matter, dearest?' she asked, dismayed. 'Don't you like it?'

'It's a child's dress.' Rebecca spoke through clenched teeth as though she could hardly force the words out. She picked up the dress and held it against her body to show how short it was. 'I've grown up, Mama. Don't you *realize*? I need long dresses now, and a hooped petticoat. This would look fine on a little girl, but . . .'

'Next year. . .' began Loveday; but Rebecca interrupted her.

'I'm fourteen years old. Now, not next year. You expect me to *behave* as though I'm as old as you. So how can you ask me to wear . . .' Her voice faded away, choked into silence by resentment. Loveday stood up, gripping her eldest daughter's wrist almost roughly – because she too was disappointed by the failure of her gift – to pull her away from the younger children. 'Look after Thomas, Louise,' she called over her shoulder. Only when they were out of earshot did she begin her explanation.

'I don't want the little ones to be frightened, Rebecca,' she said. 'But I can tell you the truth, and you must believe me. Very soon, I'm afraid, the Yankees will occupy Natchez. They may destroy it and move on, or they may camp here for a while. Either way we can't expect good treatment from them. You've heard the stories about their looting and burning. You know what happened to Netherlee. And they have no respect for women. Now hear me, Rebecca. A moment ago, when you were angry, I saw you as a beautiful young woman. If a Yankee soldier sees you like that . . .' She paused, wondering how much she dare say to convince her daughter without terrifying her. 'You'll be one of the enemy in his eyes, you see. He won't care how he treats you. He might try to kiss you, and be rough – you wouldn't like that, would you? But if he sees you as a child, he'll maybe remember his own children at home and be kind. *I* know that you're a woman, dearest. But if you dress as one and appear in the world as one, I shall never have a moment's peace until we've won the war.'

'And how long will that be? Shall I still be in short skirts until I'm eighteen?'

'Of course not. We can't pretend for ever. But just for one more year. Please, Rebecca.'

She had never been the sort of mother to bully her

children into compliance. In the old days there had been no need. The negroes spoiled the children and she had smiled to see them doing it. Now, she supposed, unable to use even the name of their father to support her wishes, she must learn to be firmer. But she needed Rebecca on her side, not against her. Her voice contained only an appeal; not a demand.

For what seemed a very long time Rebecca stared her out. Then she turned away, making no pretence of being pleased but accepting the situation by her retreat from further argument.

'I'll go and look out a place to hide Bella while I'm still wearing my old dress,' she said. Loveday looked after her sadly as she ran off into the forested grounds. The day was spoiled. What should have been a happy birthday occasion had become yet another casualty of war.

4

Four days after the Union army marched into Natchez an officer dressed in the detestable blue uniform strode briskly up the steps of The Round House and tugged at the bell pull. The four men with him spread themselves in a row in front of the house with their hands on their rifles as though they expected a defending army suddenly to leap from the dome.

The jangling of the bell brought Rebecca to the window of her basement room to see who was there. Then she hurried up the stairs to the true entrance floor and opened the huge pine door which none of the family ever used. For a moment, as she faced the enemy, she stiffened her back proudly, ready to resist any demands. Then she remembered her mother's instructions. Deliberately but unobtrusively she set herself to act the part of a child, shrinking her body until it seemed small and fragile. The shame which she felt at the foolishness of her expression would quickly be conquered by pride if she succeeded in deceiving a hated Yankee.

The act worked just as her mother had promised it would. She saw the young officer's own expression change from one of wary aggression to something softer. His voice was brisk, but not unfriendly. 'Where's your father?'

'Dead.'

'Your mother, then.'

'She's out at Miss Emily's, rolling bandages. What do you want?'

'I want this house.' The officer stepped inside without being invited.

'You can't have it.' Rebecca's voice rose in shrill indignation. 'It's ours. We live here.'

'Think yourself lucky we don't plan to burn it down. We need hospitals for our wounded. This looks okay for size.' But by now he was right inside the entrance hall and looking upwards in disbelief. 'God in hell, what's this!'

Rebecca's eyes followed his gaze through the gaps between the joists above her head, past the huge beams which should have supported the galleried bedrooms, up and up into the empty dome. She was so used to the echoing space that she had forgotten how startling it must seem to anyone who had studied only the grand exterior of the building. 'It wasn't ever finished,' she said.

'But you said you lived here.'

'In the cellar.' All the children had called the basement of The Round House the cellar when they first grumpily moved in, until their mother told them sharply that this was their home and they must learn to like it. Rebecca used the word again now deliberately, knowing the impression it would leave – and added, untruthfully, for good measure, 'It's damp and dirty and dark and there are rats, but we don't have any other place to live because you burned our plantation house.'

The indignation in her voice brought Thomas running up to her side to see if anything was wrong, but produced the desired effect on the Yankee, who began to turn away.

Probably, if he was only looking for hospital space, he had already found enough in the large houses clustered in the centre of Natchez. The Round House was too far removed from the others to be convenient, and the long approach was rough in dry weather and slippery with mud when it rained.

Standing between the columns of the portico, the officer turned back abruptly. 'Any livestock here?'

Thomas had slipped his hand into Rebecca's when he came to join her. She gripped it now tightly, pressing one finger into his soft palm until it almost hurt. It was a signal that he must not say anything, anything at all – they had arranged that between them as part of the elaborate protection of their secret. Probably Thomas did not know what the word livestock meant, but Rebecca was taking no chances. 'No,' she said shortly.

The officer gave a disbelieving grunt. 'Never met a rebel household yet that didn't have a horse or two stashed away somewhere.'

'My father took the saddle horses with him two years ago. I expect you killed them at Gettysburg. We had to sell the carriage horses, and we gave the pony away to a neighbour who was taking her chattels east. After the plantation was burned, we couldn't afford to feed them, anyway. We've no pasture here.'

The officer glanced at the wilderness of trees and scrub that surrounded The Round House and must have been convinced. Unfortunately, though, his eye was caught by a movement round by the back of the house. He gestured to two of his men. 'Go get them.' Within a few minutes the men were back, each clutching the legs of two hens which squawked, heads down, in panic. 'No livestock, hey?'

'I didn't know chickens were livestock. You can't take those. We need the eggs. We don't have hardly anything else to eat. And there's my baby sister and Louise as well as Thomas and me and Mama.'

'Don't rate against more'n a thousand sick men depending on me for their strength and comfort. How many fowl you folk keep here?'

'Just the four,' said Rebecca, hoping desperately that the cock would keep quiet and that Jemima and Trish would not choose this moment to come fussing round. 'You're taking them all!'

'Sure hope so. You can tell your mother that Captain Fletcher presents his compliments and will be back in his good time to see if she has any more generous contributions to make.' He turned away more finally this time and ran down the steps with the slightly bowed legs of a cavalryman.

'I don't like that man,' said Thomas. 'Is he going to kill our chickens?'

'No, he wouldn't do that. That would be plain stupid. Laying fowls are tough as old boots to eat. He'll keep them for the eggs, just like we did.' Rebecca kept on talking in order that Thomas should forget that he had been frightened. But as she closed the heavy door her mind was on what they still held, not on what they had lost. Any reluctance she might originally have felt at being made to dress as a child and work as a milkmaid had disappeared during the brief doorstep encounter. Now she understood one of her mother's warnings. The time might come – and was perhaps very near – when the hours she spent in the most secret part of the grounds would provide a lifeline for the whole family. At all costs Captain Fletcher must be prevented from discovering Bella's existence.

5

In the fall of 1863 visitors arrived unexpectedly at The Round House. Thomas, helping his mother in the patch of ground which she had cleared from the wilderness to serve as a vegetable plot, was the first to notice them. He saw a girl two or three years older than himself appear round the side of the house and then turn to call over her shoulder. 'Mother! This way.'

His own mother straightened herself at the sound, wiping the sweat from her forehead with the sleeve of the old dress which she kept for her work in the garden. Then the tiredness vanished from her eyes and her mouth opened in a wide smile. 'Beth Lindsay! Gracious, who would have thought it!'

Thomas watched with interest as the two women hugged and kissed each other. It was a long time since he had seen his mother smile in quite that way. When she kissed him goodnight at bedtime she had a special kind of loving smile for him, and he had noticed that she smiled in a different, sadder way when she rocked Mary Lee, who these days seemed to wail almost the whole day. But it was only Rebecca who laughed happily as she played with him in the way that his mother was laughing now. He looked questioningly at the girl, who had come to stand beside him.

'I'm Alma Lindsay,' she said.

Thomas considered how to respond. Rebecca had given him so many warnings about not talking to strangers that he found it safest to keep quiet except in her company. But it did seem that the two callers were friends. 'My name's Thomas Wade Vernon and I'm just four years old,' he said.

Alma stretched out her hand and Thomas shook it politely. 'My mother and your mother were at school together,' she told him. 'Then my grandmother died and my mother was sent away to school in the east. She got married there and I was born and we live in Massachusetts.'

This last statement was delivered with a firmness which made Thomas understand that some reaction was expected, but he had no idea what it implied. 'Where's Massachusetts?' he asked.

'In the north,' said Alma. 'It's part of the Union.'

This time she did not have to wait for Thomas's understanding. 'You mean you're a damn Yankee?' he demanded.

'Mother says that we must all love all our fellow human beings,' began Alma, but she was interrupted.

'Thomas, how often do I have to tell you not to use that

phrase!' His mother's voice sounded severe, but he could not be sure that she meant it. 'I can't think where you picked it up.'

'Rebecca says it all the time.' But perhaps it was sneaking to tell on her. Ashamed, he retreated into silence again while the first chatter of reunion spent itself and there was a movement towards the shade of the veranda. His mother disappeared inside to wash the dirt off her hands and face while Mrs Lindsay, relaxing in a rocking chair, felt in the bag she was carrying.

'Do you like candy, Thomas?' She held out a long twisted stick, as hard as glass and as golden as wild honey. Thomas took it curiously and then looked up at Mrs Lindsay to see what he should do with it.

'It's a barley sugar stick,' she explained. 'If you crack it with your teeth it will soon be gone, but if you lick it or suck it slowly it will last almost for ever.'

Thomas put out his tongue and tentatively licked the top of the stick. The taste was sweet, with a little tingle in it. He could hardly remember when he had last tasted anything so sweet. Wide-eyed with pleasure, he looked again at Mrs Lindsay. 'All of it for me?'

'Yes indeed. I've something else for your sisters.'

Thomas put one end of the stick into his mouth. His lips formed a kiss around it while his tongue explored the spiral curve. From time to time he took it out to study its shape and calculate whether it was diminishing. He was content to sit on a cushion at the back of the veranda and listen to the two adults talking. His mother had carried out a tray with a jug of the home-made wine which she produced on special occasions.

'The only kind of coffee we have now is made from burnt corn,' she said. 'Will you try this instead? It's my own making.'

Thomas watched as Mrs Lindsay sipped at her glass. He guessed that she didn't care for it, but she smiled and pretended. 'My, but you're adventurous, Loveday. I can't seem to . . .'

'It's made from the weeds in the grounds.' Thomas saw the smile fade from his mother's face and for a moment she looked tired again. 'Who would have thought, Beth, when you and I were learning about the plants of the fields, that one day I'd need to look out my notebooks and see what leaves hold poison and what can be boiled and mashed into soup – and think myself lucky that I have the land to search. There are poor folk in town who'll be starving before winter is over – unless it's true what I hear, that the North is losing stomach for the fight.'

Mrs Lindsay shook her head. Now, Thomas guessed, all the conversation would be about the war. Ladies never talked about anything but food and the war these days. Thomas was not interested in what they said, but he listened all the same while the dug out the dirt beneath his fingernails with a splinter of wood from the veranda floor and from time to time stroked the barley sugar stick with his tongue. The subject had changed to that of Mrs Lindsay's plans when he raised his head to listen in a different direction.

Yes, Rebecca and Louise were approaching on their way home from school. He could hear them – although it was mainly Louise – chattering as they trudged up the long drive which was fast narrowing to a footpath now that there were no hooves or wheels to flatten the encroaching weeds. He pushed the stick of candy into his pocket, jumped down from the veranda and ran towards his sisters, flinging himself into Rebecca's arms so that she could toss him into the air if she chose, or throw him to he ground to be tickled until he squirmed with delight. Only when this daily ritual was at an end did he warn her that something unusual had occurred.

'There's folk visiting with us from the North,' he said, nodding knowingly at his sisters' surprise. He clutched Rebecca's hand and they ran together towards the house.

6

As soon as she saw the old dress that her mother was wearing, Rebecca guessed that Mrs Lindsay and Alma must have arrived at The Round House without warning. In the old plantation days, which she could remember, that was how visits always happened, with friends knowing for sure that there would be a welcome waiting whenever they happened to drop by and however long they cared to stay; there were plenty of house slaves to set an extra place at table and put fresh linen on a bed. These days, though, with food so scarce, even close friends took pains to call only at a time which would impose no obligation to offer refreshment. So Rebecca found it easy to interpret the thoughts going through her mother's mind as she introduced her two eldest daughters to the Lindsays and at once suggested that Louise should entertain them on the piano. That would give the opportunity for beds to be made up for the visitors. There was no guest bedroom in the basement of The Round House, so no doubt Mrs Vernon would move in with Thomas for a night or two.

Rebecca expected to help in the preparations – but her mother, leaving Louise to show the way to the piano, held her back outside. 'Will you go down to Bella now?' she asked.

'It's too early.' Rebecca's objection was not on her own account, but as guardian of Bella's daily timetable.

'I know that, dearest. But what am I to set before Beth tonight? I doubt she's used to seeing a dish of vegetables as her entire meal. But you could gather some nuts and berries on your way. And if you were quick coming back, I could make a rennet from some of the milk while it's still warm.'

Rebecca prepared to do as she was asked. She made the secret sign to Thomas which meant that he should slip away from the house and meet her at the old slave quarters. This was the place where Rebecca kept her forage knife. In order that Bella should remain hidden it was necessary to keep her on a tether, so on each evening journey Rebecca cut armfuls of extra fodder to carry down with her. Two buckets, put back by her mother as soon as they had been emptied and scalded, were ready in the shed as well. The children had a long walk to reach Bella before the milking could even begin, for it had been necessary to choose a place for her which was level enough to provide some pasture but could not be seen from either river or house. The way back was steep as well as long, so Rebecca found it easiest to divide the load. On the way down, though, Thomas usually carried both the empty buckets while Rebecca slashed with the knife at the undergrowth.

'Why don't Mama ever let us have milk to drink?' Thomas asked, watching as Rebecca drew the hooked knife from its hiding place and tested the sharpness of its blade against her thumb. 'She gives some to Mary Lee, but you and me's the ones who do all the work and we don't get hardly a drop.'

'Mary Lee's a baby and babies can't take anything but milk; so if she didn't have that, she'd starve.'

'But she can't drink as much as we carry.'

Rebecca hesitated. Thomas ought perhaps not to be told any more secrets. But in the weeks since the arrangement began, he had shown himself unusually discreet for such a little boy. Her warnings, it seemed, had so greatly impressed him that he hardly opened his mouth to anyone else nowadays. To make up for that, he chattered non-stop to Rebecca when they were alone.

'We trade it, Thomas,' she told him as they set off. 'Money's no use these days. Everyone has to find something else to pay with instead. The Rendalls have their fruit trees and the Dukes have kept a sow hidden, and Mrs Frank Whitty has stashed away every suit of clothes her four sons ever owned, from the cradle. Your new breeches were paid for with milk. And three days a week Mama carries some over to the Dukes so that we can have a piglet to fatten when it's old enough to leave its mother. If there's any left when all the trading's done, you have it. You know that.'

'It's always turned by then,' Thomas objected. But he

was in a happy mood and skipped along cheerfully as they made their way through a grove of live oaks gracefully draped with grey Spanish moss.

'Tell me about Mrs Lindsay,' asked Rebecca. She had been hustled away too quickly after the first introductions to find out who the visitors were or why they had come.

'She was at school with Mama and then she married a damn Yankee and now she's come to see her Daddy because he's old, old, old – and Mama, because they're dearest friends – an' then she's going to be a mishunry. What's a mishunry, 'Becca?'

Rebecca told him. Her explanation only briefly interrupted his flow of words.

'Well now, Mama s'posed that Mrs Lindsay would be sailing round the Horn, an' I don't know what that means, but Mrs Lindsay said no, she was terr-i-fied to think of the storms an' all that rocking and pitching an' then she went whispering an' thought I couldn't hear, but I could, an' said that anyway she was going to have a baby an' it wouldn't do the baby a mite of good if she was sick all the time an' besides it might be born on the ship because she'd have to be on board perhaps six months an' the baby was coming in five so she'd rather take the risk of going through Injun territory because then she'd likely come to San Francisco in time an' if she didn't she could stop a few days, on dry land, while the baby came.' He paused for breath, triumphant at his feat of memory, and then frowned briefly in puzzlement. 'You'd think she'd wait till she'd met up with her husband and settled in a house before she went out to get the baby, wouldn't you?'

'My!' exclaimed Rebecca,laughing. 'What big ears the little pitcher has!' She didn't answer his last question. Knowing about babies was one of the things which made her an adult and different in every kind of way from Thomas. This was a secret she was not about to share. But if Mrs Lindsay was expecting a baby that was a good reason why she should be offered milk with her supper. Without asking any further questions Rebecca paused beneath a willow tree. She held down one of its branches and cut off an armful of the drooping leaves for Bella to enjoy. Then she moved down the hill again at a faster pace.

As a general rule she played a secret game with Thomas as they made their way to the place where Bella was concealed; they were scouts, prospecting a trail through Indian territory, and must move silently in single file between the tall pines and cypresses, not drawing attention to themselves by conversation or quick movement. But today was so unusual that she as well as Thomas forgot to take the usual precautions. It was not just the excitement of having visitors but the earliness of the hour which made the day sparkle with adventure. With the sun still bright it was impossible to believe that there could be any danger concealed in their own familiar territory. Together, laughing, Rebecca and Thomas skipped and ran through the woods and towards the Old River Lake.

7

It was not with any intention of spying on the Vernon family that Captain Mark Fletcher had climbed up to the bluff which formed the highest part of their land that afternoon. He felt no sense of trespass, because with Natchez firmly under Union control, no one had any rights that the Federal army didn't concede and he wouldn't hesitate for a moment to rob the Vernons of the whole of their property if that would serve any useful purpose. But he didn't propose to harry a family of young children just for the hell of it. General Grant, on his recent tour of inspection, had given instructions that the citizens of Natchez were to be treated with propriety as long as they continued to co-operate in providing billets and medical facilities for the army, and Captain Fletcher was punctilious about obeying orders. He was satisfied that the Vernons were as poor as they claimed to be and that the cellar of The Round House was their only home. It served them right for being rebels, but they could keep it. It was no use to the wounded men for whom he was detailed to find shelter and food.

So his intrusion into their grounds on this occasion had no purpose more sinister than exercise which would give him a breath of fresh air and a view of the Mississippi. Captain Fletcher had been born and raised on a farm near the Mettawee. He had fished in the river as a boy and on its banks he had courted Dorothy, who would one day be his wife. Whenever he had a free hour in this place so far from home, he liked to calm his spirits by watching the Mississippi water sweep down towards the gulf. The nearest point to his billet was the landing stage at Natchez-under-the-hill, but the atmosphere there was too oppressive to be relaxing. Coming from Vermont, he was unaccustomed to the steamy heat of Mississippi, which robbed his lungs of air and his body of energy. He wouldn't go so far as to allow that their appalling climate gave these southern Johnnies the right to own other human beings and work them to death, but he could understand how they had come to be so lazy.

The search for a breeze and an illusion of coolness was enough to drive him on to the highest point of the bluff, approaching it not past The Round House but by a steep climb up from the landing stage. He was standing now at the head of a small peninsula. As he looked down, the wide water of the curving Mississippi was in front of him and also on his right, whilst on the left the stub of a bayou cut a little way into the land. The area was wild and neglected – it was hard to realize that less than half a mile away the soldiers of the garrison and the nurses from the Sanitary Commission were moving busily about their well-ordered affairs. He sat down on the edge of the bluff and leaned backwards on his arms, savouring the silence.

The sound of laughter attracted his attention. Somewhere in the woods below him twigs were snapping under running feet while mocking-birds, disturbed, rose into the air with a startled flapping of their wings. Curious, Captain Fletcher pulled himself to his feet and turned away from the river. His eyes searched to see who was crashing down the slope. But the trees, and the lianas which shrouded them, formed a jungle rather than a forest, so that from above it was not possible to distinguish a path. Captain Fletcher was just about to turn away when two children emerged into the more open ground which surrounded the bayou.

He recognized them as the two he had seen on his first visit to The Round House – the girl who had been so upset at the loss of the family's chickens and the frightened little boy who had clung to her skirts. They were each now holding a bucket which – to judge by their light-hearted swinging of it – was empty. No doubt they had been sent out by their mother to gather pecans or hickories or whatever else might be growing wild in their patch of forest.

As he watched the two children make their way, more carefully now, across the swampy land at the end of the bayou, Captain Fletcher smiled to himself. He could have been spiteful, waiting until they had collected whatever crop they were seeking and then confiscating it for his own use. But instead his heart warmed to their innocent light-heartedness. He had young brothers and sisters of his own at home. It was many months since he had last seen them – so long that he felt a sudden hatred for the army life which had cut him off from any kind of happy relationship with children. If he were to follow these two, and smile, they would not smile back. They were more likely to scream and run away. So he would leave them alone to glean whatever they could from their land.

Below him, the children reached the edge of the woodland on the far side of the bayou and came to a standstill. The girl picked up a stick and began to beat the lower branches of the tree, and then to throw the stick at the higher branches. They were collecting black walnuts. The little boy scurried about, picking up the nuts and stowing them in a pouch slung across his shoulder. There was more laughter as his sister raced him to collect the last few nuts. Then she took hold of his hand, imposing on him what could be recognized even at this distance as a change of mood. They reclaimed the buckets which they had set down, but no longer swung them gaily as they moved on in the direction of the river. Instead, their behaviour became what could only be described as furtive. Captain Fletcher watched as they turned with their backs to the woodland and began to look round as though to check that they were not observed. With the swift reaction of a soldier he dropped to the ground and continued to watch them.

The girl was holding some kind of sickle in her hand. Once she was satisfied that the coast was clear, she turned back towards the trees, which there also were covered by a screen of the rampant climbing vines. She moved the blade through the leaves with an ease which made it clear that she did not need to cut an opening but was probing for an entrance already made. After one last look behind, she lifted a large flap of the tangled creeper so that her little brother could pass through in front of her. Following him, she allowed the natural green curtain to fall back behind her.

Captain Fletcher rose slowly to his feet again, brushed the dust off his trousers and tugged his jacket down. His eyes fixed intently on the spot where the children had disappeared as he mentally noted the features which would identify it when he came close. Suspicion rather than mere curiosity led him to make his way rapidly down the steep slope towards the bayou. What he had just observed gave the impression of being something more than a childish game. Those rebel kids had something hidden away there that they wouldn't want him to see; and so he was going to see it.

8

It was Thomas who had come across the hut to start with, and he was very proud of it. He wouldn't allow Rebecca ever to call it anything but 'Thomas's place' even though it was Bella who lived in it. On that first day when they went exploring, he hadn't even known what it was that they were looking for. All the same, he was the one who had pushed his way through the tangle of creepers and called to his sister to see what he had found.

This was the perfect spot for Bella. The hut which offered shelter to Rebecca at milking time was close to the Old River Lake; and the land round the lake, screened by trees, was flat. At some quite recent time it had been cleared and cultivated, but by the time Thomas found it there were no signs of crops growing; instead, a long lush grass had taken possession. Rebecca had guessed that probably their negroes had built the hut and cleared the patch in order to grow extra food for themselves while they were working on the construction of The Round House. The patch was an awful long way from the house, but Thomas didn't mind. He felt important and proud that Rebecca had chosen him to be the one to keep guard for her while she was milking, and to keep the secret safe.

Bella was grazing contentedly at the end of her tether when they arrived today. She must have been surprised to see them come so early, and Thomas wondered whether she would allow herself to be milked. He was lifted up by Rebecca into the loft which the slaves had fixed at the back of the wooden hut to dry or store the vegetables they grew. He sat on the edge with his legs dangling down. This was where he always stayed while Rebecca was milking. It kept him safe from Bella, who was inclined to kick out with her back hooves. It also gave him a good view of anyone who might approach, because the back wall of the hut between the loft and the roof had either fallen down or else had never been fixed in the first place. But of course nobody ever did come near. This was a secret spot.

As usual, Rebecca put the forage knife carefully up beside Thomas. He knew that he was not allowed to touch it. She brought Bella into the hut, tied her securely, lifted down the little milking stool, set the first bucket in place and sat down. Thomas pulled his barley sugar stick out of the pocket in which he had stowed it for safety and began a thorough licking to clear off all the bits of dirt and fluff which its stickiness had attracted. While he licked, he listened in fascination as the milk began to hiss and tinkle into the bucket. He was too high up to see how milking was done and the one time he had been allowed to try for himself, with Rebecca's hands over his own, nothing had happened at all. But he was sure that if he watched and listened very hard he would learn the secret one day.

After a little while Rebecca moved round to Bella's other side and Thomas remembered guiltily that he was supposed to be on guard duty. Leaning forward as far as he could without falling, he looked around Bella's patch of ground. Nobody there. Twisting his feet up on to the loft he crawled towards the back so that he could stare in that direction as well. There was nobody, but then he dropped the barley sugar in alarm. Someone was coming through the trees.

It was a soldier. A Fed. And not any old Fed, but the one who had come to their house a few weeks back to steal their chickens. Thomas had been frightened of him then and was even more frightened now. He opened his mouth to call out a warning to Rebecca, but no sound would come out. There wouldn't have been anything he could do, in any case, because the soldier had started to run and would see her long before she had time to undo Bella's halter rope. With a movement that he had not made since his fourth birthday, Thomas put his thumb between his teeth and began to chew on it. He pressed himself flat against the wall of the hut, near to the back of the loft. Now he was invisible, and safe. But what was going to happen to Rebecca?

9

Captain Fletcher's shadow reached the door of the wooden hut before him. He saw the girl look up from her milking, startled and afraid. Her jerk of alarm must have frightened the cow, which backed away and kicked over the milk bucket. The girl groaned to see the spilt milk as though that were the greatest of her troubles. She surely did not think that she would be allowed to keep the cow.

'Reckon you made a right fool of me,' he said, staring coldly down at her. 'No livestock, heh?' He gestured towards the rope which held the cow's head steady. 'Untie that and bring her outside.'

The girl stood up slowly and faced him without speaking. She was a pretty little thing, with wide-set hazel eyes and long wavy brown hair, reaching almost to her waist and caught into a bunch by a ribbon at the back of her neck. Shock had paled her complexion beneath its freckles, emphasizing the rosiness of her mouth. He guessed that she was just about to make some kind of appeal to his pity and spoke roughly to prevent it. 'Get going.'

Still she did not move her feet, but pulled the rope towards herself, clutching it to her chest. Keeping his eyes fixed on her, Captain Fletcher bent down and set a light to the layer of dry brushwood which had been cut and spread over the floor of the hut. The flame ran for a foot or two and then died in a column of smoke. Captain Fletcher lit the brushwood again.

Made uneasy by the smoke, the cow mooed, tossing her head, and tried to back out of the shed. The girl came round from behind and stepped towards him. She was taller than he had remembered from their first meeting: her legs – stockingless, and scratched by brambles – were long and well-shaped. He just had time to notice that and then she was upon him, flailing at his chest with her fists.

'Bella's ours. You can't have her. You're no better than a thief, trying to make off with other people's property. And if our baby doesn't have milk she'll die and then you'll be a murderer, d'you hear? Thief and murderer. Thief and murderer.'

She was not strong enough to hurt him with her blows. He laughed at her fury as he gripped both of her wrists and held them away from himself. Struggling to break free, she twisted away. His arm stretched across her chest and he felt her breasts, small and firm, pressing against his wrists. No longer laughing, he jerked her hard towards him and changed his grip to pinion her arms behind her back. Her chin jerked up in defiance as she tried to lean away from him.

'How old are you, then?' he demanded. 'Not quite such a little girl as you try to pretend, hey?' Five months had passed since he had said goodbye to his Dorothy in Vermont. They were promised to each other, but she had sent him away with no more than a tender kiss to remember her by. The memory of that disappointment surged now into a rage of frustration. This was a *sekesh* girl, a girl of no importance, a girl who had lied to him and who deserved what was coming to her. Pushing her in front of him, he took two quick steps forward to be out of the way of the frantic cow. The girl had already lost her balance before he flung her to the ground and hurled himself on top of her, tearing at her skirts. She began to scream.

10

In his hiding place at the back of the loft Thomas heard Rebecca scream for help. He crawled forward to find out what was happening. It was difficult to see through the smoke, which by now was rising thickly from the burning brushwood, but he could just make out that Rebecca was lying on the ground and the soldier was on top of her. Was he trying to strangle her? Thomas knew that he must do something to save his sister. Using both hands, he picked up the hooked knife which Rebecca had set beside him in the loft. Although he had been strictly forbidden to touch it, this must be an emergency great enough to override ordinary rules. He was frightened, though, that if he threw it he might hit his sister instead of the soldier, because they were so close together. As he hesitated, a thick swirl of smoke filled his lungs. Although he tried as hard as he could to control it, he could not prevent himself from coughing.

The man heard the sound and twisted away from Rebecca to stare upwards. From the way in which his eyes were moving, it looked as though he could not see who was behind the curtain of smoke. More clearly than anything he had ever known in his life before, Thomas understood that he must kill the soldier in order to save Rebecca. He lifted the knife above his head and flung it down.

There was a roar of pain and anger. Thomas's four-year-old muscles were not very strong, but the height of his perch added force to the throw. He had not taken any special aim, but the point of the knife must have caught the soldier in the face, for he was clutching at one eye with his hand, and blood was flooding between his fingers. With the other hand he groped for the knife, picked it up, and held it high like an axe raised for chopping.

'You vicious little vixen!' he shouted. He must have thought that it was Rebecca who had stabbed him. He was going to kill her; Thomas felt sure of that – yet instead of running away she was lying on the ground, crying.

'Run, Rebecca!' shouted Thomas, and she must have heard him, for she began to move. It was more of a crawl than a run, as though she were not strong enough to get to her feet. The knife began to slash downwards – but instead of lunging after Rebecca, the soldier made an abrupt half turn and cut Bella's throat instead.

Suddenly there was blood everywhere. Trumpeting in agony, Bella made one last attempt to break the rope which still tethered her to a beam. Then her front legs buckled under her and she slipped gradually to the ground, jerking around for what seemed a long time before she became still. Even after that the blood continued to spurt from her neck, hissing as it touched the flames which by now had a strong grip on the wooden walls of the hut. It was all so horrible that Thomas, unable to take his eyes off the dying cow, was sick.

By the time he had finished retching the smoke was so thick that he could not see through it at all and, on the other side of the dense grey curtain, a silence more sinister even than Rebecca's sobs or Bella's death agonies fed his fears. Had the soldier died from the wound in his face? If so, what would happen to Thomas himself when other soldiers found out what he had done? And had Rebecca managed to escape, or had she been killed by the soldier before he collapsed? Would Thomas be to blame for that as well, because he had not kept watch well enough to call out a warning? He began to cry loudly and bitterly, calling for his sister. But no one answered. The only sound was an angry crackling as flames devoured the wooden walls of the hut.

Thomas stopped crying to listen, and for the first time understood his own danger. The front of the hut was blazing, making it impossible to escape that way. He crawled along the high storage ledge which had given him a hiding place, grateful now for the missing sections of wood at the back of the hut, which would allow him to escape. But when he reached the gap he hesitated, still on all fours. Should he stand up and jump down to the hard ground? Or should he lower himself to hang by his hands and then let go? Either way, the drop was frightening. He was still trying to choose what to do when the walls of the hut collapsed, tipping him without warning forward and down.

11

The clanging of the bell beside the great front door disturbed Thomas at a time when he ought not to have been asleep. As he struggled into wakefulness he could tell from the patch of sunlight on the wall that it was late in the afternoon and not early morning. That was not the only unusual feature of his awakening. His head ached and his mouth was dry and he was too hot. The hotness was not surprising, because somebody had piled far too many covers on top of him. Thomas threw them off. His sister Louise promptly piled them back on again.

He had not seen that she was sitting beside him, for his head hurt if he turned it, but now he tried to push her away.

'Mama says you're to be kept warm,' Louise said. 'You've got a fever.'

Thomas considered this statement. He could remember having a fever once before, and it hadn't felt like this at all. That time, the heat had all been inside his body, fighting to get out. But today, it seemed to him, he was really quite cold and shivery and only felt too hot because of all the bedclothes. He would have called his mother, but he could hear her talking to the callers above his head.

'Is that Mrs Lindsay?' he asked, remembering the previous day's visitor.

'No. It's the Feds come back again.'

'What do they want?'

'They're going round asking questions. One of their officers was attacked yesterday. He's unconscious, and if he dies they're going to shoot someone for murdering him. They came to school this morning and we all had to say what we were doing yesterday. Maybe they want to ask you what *you* were doing. Mama's going to tell them that you're too little for it to matter. But if they do ask you, you had a fever yesterday as well, remember. Go back to sleep. Or pretend to, anyway. You're to keep your eyes tight shut until they've gone away and we say you can open them.'

'Where's Rebecca?'

'Go to *sleep*!' hissed Louise. Thomas did not as a rule take orders from someone who was only four and a half years older than himself, but today he recognized that she was frightened, and that made him feel frightened as well. He screwed his eyes shut, listening to the angry voices above, until the heavy door closed again.

Only when he felt a hand on his forehead did he open his eyes. Louise had gone away and his mother was sitting beside the bed instead. She looked tired and unhappy. There were big black shadows round her eyes and her forehead was creased with worry lines that he had never noticed before. With one arm she cradled the baby, who looked pale and peaky and had a sour smell to her. 'What's the matter with Mary Lee?' he asked.

'She's sick. And she's hungry. I'm discovering a lot of things that she doesn't care to eat, but nothing that she can keep down.'

'Why can't she have her ordinary milk?'

'We aren't going to get any more milk,' his mother told him. 'Bella died when the hut burned down yesterday. Don't you remember?'

'Louise said I had a fever yesterday.'

'That's what you're to tell any soldiers who ask you questions.'

'You mean it isn't true? I'm supposed to tell lies?' Thomas was shocked.

'No, it's true,' his mother assured him. 'But before you had the fever, do you remember what happened?'

Thomas thought hard. Was it yesterday that Mrs Lindsay had come to visit? She had given him a barley sugar stick. Then Rebecca had taken him down to milk Bella, just as usual, except for being early. He could remember running down to the Old River Lake with her and being lifted up to his usual place in the milking hut. He could see himself sitting on the edge of the loft, with his legs dangling over, and he could remember the taste of the barley sugar as his tongue explored its twists. Something had happened while he was licking it. He was sure that there was something to be remembered, and yet he could not remember. It was as though he was looking down at a book which he knew to be bright with pictures, but was unable to see them because his eyes were blindfolded. For a few moments the eyes of his memory struggled to pierce through the barrier. They found one tiny gap. 'I dropped my barley sugar stick,' he said, aghast at his loss.

'And that's all? You don't recall the fire?'

Thomas shook his head and groaned with the movement. 'My head hurts,' he said.

'You fell out of the hut and gave it a bad bump,' his mother told him. 'We had to carry you back here last night. So it's true you were ill then. But it would be best if you didn't tell the soldiers that you were near the hut. You could pretend that you didn't even know about Bella. That was Rebecca's secret, not yours. It's only a very little lie.'

To Thomas it seemed a large matter. It was his mother who had taught him that he must always tell the truth. But something else worried him even more. 'Where's Rebecca?' he asked for a second time.

12

Halfway down the hill, one of the Federal soldiers came to a standstill.

'Changed my mind,' he said. 'Reckon we'd best have a word with the *sekesh* kid after all. Check for ourselves that he's sick. The lieutenant said everyone on the property and it's the hell of a way to come back.' He turned on his heel and led the way towards The Round House once more. This time, however, instead of going up the steps to the grand portico, he looked for an entrance at ground level. 'No need to stand on ceremony,' he suggested, and opened the door without troubling to knock.

On their first visit, half an hour earlier, the house had been eerily silent. Now, by contrast, it was full of noise. Somebody was playing a piano; the sound rose through an open space above it and echoed down again from the huge dome. In another room the crying of a baby was at once fragile and piercing. Further round the circular basement another child was crying with loud sobs that racked his whole body. The two men stood in the doorway of a small room and studied the scene inside.

The woman they had interviewed earlier had put her baby down now, and instead was hugging a small boy. His face was unnaturally pale except for the purple mark of a bruise on one side of his forehead. He was beating his fists against his mother's breast in a rage of grief, so that she had to fight to prevent him from throwing himself about.

'What's the trouble?' asked the soldier.

'I want Rebecca,' wailed the child – but then he seemed to realize who had asked the question and was suddenly silent, rubbing the tears from his eyes as he stared at them.

'Who's Rebecca?'

'My big sister.'

'Big sister, hey? How old is she?'

'Fourteen.'

'Where is she, then?'

The little boy began to cry again, burying his head on his mother's shoulder. 'Leave him alone,' said the woman. 'Don't you see he's upset?'

'Let him answer and we'll be off. Where's your sister, son?'

'She's dead. She was running away from someone and she drowned in the bayou.'

'Did you see her drown?' The boy shook his head. 'Then it might not have happened. Maybe she's hiding somewhere, playing a game, ready to surprise you. Or maybe – I guess this is it – she's just gone off on a holiday for a little while.'

'No!' The single word was packed with emotion and protest. 'Rebecca loved me more than anyone else in the whole world. She wouldn't go away from me. She promised she was going to look after me always. I want Rebecca.' For a moment it seemed that he was going to cry again, but then he looked the soldiers straight in the eye. 'When I grow up, I'm going to kill that man who chased her.' He put his thumb into his mouth and began to chew it. The two soldiers looked at each other and shrugged their shoulders.

'D'you believe him?' asked the younger of them as for a

second time they set off down the track and back towards their camp.

'*He* believes it.'

'He believes what his mother's told him. Don't prove a thing. But I don't see how she could reckon to keep a kid of that age from finding out if his sister's still somewhere around. Anyhow – a fourteen-year-old girl running away! Don't sound much like an ambush to me. When the captain takes the bandages off his head and looks at the place where his eye used to be, I hope he'll think it was worth it.'

13

Mary Lee Vernon was buried two weeks and a day after the killing of the cow. Few of Loveday's friends needed to buy black for the occasion, for there was hardly a family in Natchez which had not mourned the loss of one of its members during the previous two years. As she stared blankly ahead through the service, Loveday was conscious of Thomas sobbing quietly beside her. She knew that he was not weeping for the baby, who had never been more than an intruder in his life. It was Rebecca for whom he grieved, and as the preacher spoke of the beloved daughter who had been snatched away to the promise of a better life, Loveday guessed that to Thomas he must seem to be speaking not of Mary Lee but of her sister.

Loveday herself had no more tears to shed. Within the space of only a few months she had lost her husband and two of her children and if she looked to the future she could see only a struggle against destitution and starvation. She needed no one to tell her that she must be strong, because she still had two children who depended on her alone. But it was time now for Thomas to be strong as well. For the past two weeks his tears had served a purpose, making clear to anyone who asked questions the genuineness of his grief. But he was not a baby any longer. He must control his emotions and take his place as the only man of the family.

As she walked slowly back to The Round House after the service, with the two children silently lagging behind, she wondered how much of what she could tell him he would understand. Dr Pollitt had said that he would probably never recover his memory of the two or three minutes immediately before the accident which caused his concussion, so she could choose what part of the story he should know. That was just as well, for her own knowledge of events was fragmentary – and how could she explain to a four-year-old boy exactly what was meant by rape, or make him understand the terror that Rebecca would have felt?

She waited until he was in bed that night before coming to sit beside him and hold his hand. 'I'm going to tell you a secret, Thomas. Will you promise never to tell anyone?'

'I don't like secrets.' He was thinking of Bella, no doubt.

'This is a *happy* secret, Thomas. About Rebecca. Rebecca didn't really drown, that day you bumped your head. She isn't dead at all.'

Thomas sat bolt upright in bed and looked eagerly around as though he expected his sister to step out of the shadows. 'Where is she, then? When's she coming?'

'Not for a while yet. She's gone away. If that soldier had died, you see, she could have gotten into trouble for trying to kill him.'

'But why can't she come back now? Where is she? What's she doing?'

'Do you remember Mrs Lindsay who gave you the barley sugar stick? Rebecca went off with her while you were still asleep after the bump on your head. Rebecca's going to look after Alma and when the new baby arrives she'll help look after him as well. They're on their way to San Francisco now. She'll be away for a while. But she'll come home as soon as the war's over and the soldiers go back to their own homes.'

The effect on Thomas was not what Loveday had hoped. She had expected relief – even tears of pleasure. But instead he pulled his hand away from hers and there was something cold and almost frightening in his silence as he considered what she had said.

'You told me Rebecca was dead. You told me lies.'

'Yes. I'm sorry, dearest. There was a reason for that.'

'You're telling me lies now,' Thomas accused. 'Rebecca wouldn't ever go off without me. Without even saying goodbye. It isn't true. I was the only one she loved. She wouldn't look after someone else when she promised to look after me. She *promised*.'

'It is true, Thomas. You must be glad for her. She'll be safe in California, away from the war. And when it's all over she'll come back and we'll all be happy together again. Come on dearest. Give me a hug and we'll say a prayer together for Rebecca.'

She held her arms out towards him, but Thomas did not move. He stared at her with eyes full of pain: Loveday could not guess from them whether he was hurt because Rebecca had abandoned him or because he believed that she herself was still lying to him. With a gesture of despair he flung himself back on to the bed and turned his face to the wall.

For a few moments more Loveday tried to make him speak to her. It would even have been a relief if he had cried, although only a few hours earlier she had determined to put an end to his tearfulness. She stroked the back of his head, but he pushed her hand away with a jerky movement as though she were an enemy.

Loveday stood up with a sigh of desolation and snuffed out the candle. Without understanding why, she sensed that she had lost the love of her only son. The unknown Federal soldier on the Gettysburg battlefield who had killed Wade Vernon with his rifle had robbed her of the person most dear to her in all the world, but at least he had acted without personal malice and in fair fight, at risk of being the victim himself. She could not find it in her heart to hate him. But this other soldier, the one who had attacked her children, she hated so passionately that she would have killed him if she could. Mary Lee was dead and Rebecca was far away and now Thomas was refusing to love her; and it was all because of Captain Mark Fletcher. He had not died – he had not even been completely blinded. At the cost of only one eye he had become unfit for further duty, able to escape from the dangers of war and to escape also from her reach.

She wanted him to suffer as she did. If he had children, she would like them to suffer as well. Didn't the Good Book say that the sins of the father should be visited upon the children unto the third and the fourth generation? As her finger rested for a second longer on the angry, rigid body of her little son, Loveday Vernon sent up a silent prayer that was transformed by bitterness into a curse. She prayed that one day the Fletcher family would know the same unhappiness and despair that she felt now. She prayed for revenge.

EPISODE TWO

1924

A Victim's Revenge

1

'Thomas!' Louise's voice shrilled across the basement. 'How much longer do you reckon to keep me waiting? Your breakfast's been ready these last ten minutes. I called you. Thomas! *Thomas*!'

Stooping to peer in the dimly-lit mirror, Thomas did not answer. Instead, he carefully knotted his tie for the third time, and was successful at last in concealing the worn patch beneath the knot. The tie, like his suit, was a badge of status. On his solid perambulation to work each morning his clothes, although shabby, indicated that he was a property-owning gentleman. Sitting in Ben Browning's office, with its single rattling fan, he would before too long slip off the coat and loosen the tie if – as was the case most days – no callers by appointment were expected and no property inspections had been arranged. But from breakfast until the moment when he arrived at his desk he dressed as befitted a respectable businessman.

For a moment longer now he studied his appearance in the mirror. He had put on weight in the last few years: always heavily built, he had grown stout, and it was a long time since he had been able to button the coat of his business suit. His hair had thinned, needing to be carefully spaced out before he slicked it down, and his complexion had become florid, with small broken veins patterning his nose and cheeks. But his self-appraisal was not a critical one. He was merely checking that he looked as he had always looked at the start of a working day.

He combed his already tidy hair again, just for the pleasure of showing Louise that he would come only when he was good and ready. All his life, it seemed to him, he had been dancing to other people's tunes, obeying the orders of an indolent employer, a bossy sister and a mother who became increasingly querulous and demanding as arthritis and old age imprisoned her in her dark bedroom. But although Loveday Vernon had lived to be over ninety years of age, she had died at last two years back, releasing her only son from one of his obligations. And at six o'clock on the previous evening – June 30, nineteen twenty-four – Thomas had stepped out of Ben Browning's office for the last time. At the age of sixty-four he was a free man at last, and Louise had better understand it.

Because he was hungry, however, he did not extend his gesture of rebellion beyond a tolerable limit. He and Louise had spent the whole of their lives together and each of them knew exactly how far it was possible to go without pressing one of their many quarrels past the point of no return. He had other gestures in mind to enliven this first day of his retirement from business life. One of them was already on view. As he sat down to his hominy grits – which Louise had allowed to cool just enough to remind him that he was late, but not so much as to make the dish unpalatable – he waited for her reaction. There was no need to wait long.

'For heaven's sake, Thomas, what are you doing in that get-up?' She snapped her fingers together towards his suit and tie.

'Same's yesterday.' He spoke with his mouth full.

'Yesterday you were going to Mr Browning's office, but today – I suppose you forgot that you won't be working there any more.' Louise's eyebrows, raised in exasperation, encapsulated many years of her brother's forgetfulness.

'Remembered all right. Thought as how *you* might have

remembered as well, and given me an extra egg to celebrate.'

'We shall need to cut down on expenses now, not learn new extravagances.'

Thomas snorted in protest at the word. He could not remember when either of them had last been able to enjoy any extravagances. Food was the only pleasure in which it was sometimes possible to indulge beyond the limitations of their income, because so much of it was produced on their own land. An extra egg for breakfast did not involve money going out of the house, but merely one egg the fewer in the cakes which Louise baked for the social or fund-raising occasions of the church. He knew better, though, than to fight a trivial battle when it had already been lost. 'Nothing wrong in a gentleman looking like a gentleman,' he said instead.

'You can look like the president of the United States from noontime on,' his sister said crossly. 'But in the mornings I'm counting on you to give me some help, and you can't do it dressed like that.' Louise herself, as always at this hour, was wearing a shapeless calico dress. She had three, cut to the same pattern, that had once been identifiably pink, blue and green; but years of scrubbing and bleaching by the sun had reduced them all to an identical shade of pale grey. She dressed herself in one of them at half past five each morning from Monday to Friday and wore it until she had finished cleaning the house, feeding the hens, milking the goats, working in the garden and the vegetable plot and pickling or drying or preserving its produce. Not until just before eleven did she change into a dress respectable enough for one of the many activities which went on at the church, or for entertaining any of the ladies of the congregation who happened to drop by. She had one or two piano pupils young enough to come to her in the middle of the day, but most of her lessons necessarily had to wait until school came out.

'The henhouse roof needs fixing.' Louise's tone of voice made it clear that she was carrying a long list of chores in her head. She had been keeping them for him specially, no doubt – in spite of the fact that as soon as he had finished each task she would complain of his clumsy workmanship. Thomas recognized that he was not handy. He could see in his mind how something ought to look, but his fingers seemed to have a mind of their own, always producing some effect which he had never intended.

'Not this morning,' he said.

'And the vegetables.' Louise took no notice of his interruption. 'I'm getting on for seventy years old. The work's too hard for me, and that no-good Luther stops digging the moment I take my eyes off him. The vegetables can be your work from today on.'

After almost fifty years of sitting at a desk Thomas had soft hands, as unfit for heavy work as those of a piano teacher, and he took no exercise apart from his daily walk to the real-estate office and back again. Louise's tough and skinny body was better suited than his own bulky frame to the hoeing and planting and weeding and digging needed to keep tidy the extensive plot which they had long ago helped their mother to clear from the overgrown land around the house. But he did not trouble to argue the point now. 'Not this morning,' he said again.

'What's special about this morning?'

'Got to look respectable for our company.'

'Company? Who's expecting company?'

She had forgotten, then. Thomas had thought she would forget. He chuckled happily because he had caught her out for once. 'The Englishman,' he reminded her. 'Man from London. Wants to look at the dome.'

Thomas and Louise were still living in The Round House. Neither of them could remember any other home. The house was still incomplete, for the family had never had enough money to make even one more floor habitable. They had continued to live in the basement and, after a while, because it was familiar, had come to believe that it was convenient. There was little direct sunlight, so it remained cool through the fiercest days of summer, and they had long ceased to notice the mustiness which followed any prolonged rain. Louise grumbled about the perpetual struggle to prevent clothes and bedlinen from going mouldy in the damp, and she complained even more vigorously about their lack of electricity and the need to keep the kitchen range burning however hot the weather. But she was used to it: they were both used to it.

Just as the basement was unaltered, so too was the dome. The craftsmen from Philadelphia had done their work well sixty years earlier. No roof tiles had slipped; no timbers had rotted. Seen from the outside, the golden dome still glistened above the trees like a palace waiting to be discovered in a fairy-tale jungle. But the interior of the dome was equally unchanged. Anyone making his way through the colonnaded portico and the great front door could stand on the unsanded planks of the entrance floor and look straight up to the very top of the vaulted roof. Over the years, more than one architect had asked permission to study the interior. Thomas had learned by now – because he had once been sent a copy of the article resulting from such a visit – that what caused excitement was the fact that the timbers had never been trimmed ready for the inside of the dome to be lined. Joists and rafters protruded to their full length at curious angles, showing with unusual clarity how they supported each other and the weight above them. Today's visitor, like all the others, would stare through binoculars, exclaiming with delight and amazement at this living lesson in the skills of long ago, and would request permission to set up cameras on tripods so that the details could be faithfully recorded.

Mr Lacey, the Englishman, behaved precisely as Thomas had anticipated, except that he had no camera. Instead, he scribbled in his notebook with as much urgency as if he expected the dome, after standing for so many years, to crash to the ground tomorrow. With a fine black pen he made neat drawings of joints and collars and crossings; he showed them to Thomas over coffee and one of Louise's angel cakes, still hot from the oven. Thomas, uninterested in the details, accepted the foreigner's interest with a proprietorial air. Louise, flustered by the need to spring clean the parlour and change into her best, all before ten in the morning, remained unusually silent.

'It's extraordinary!' exclaimed Mr Lacey. 'Absolutely extraordinary! Skills which must have been carried across the Atlantic in the seventeenth century seem to have survived here for two hundred years, long after the style of work had changed in England. A unique contribution to the history of architecture. And of carpentry. A fire risk, of course.' No doubt he had noticed the kerosene lamps made necessary by their lack of electricity. 'I hope you have good insurance. Not, of course, that insurance could ever compensate . . . But you should cover its value as a historic monument, not merely as a private house. You'll be well aware of that already, naturally.'

Thomas looked at the visitor with suspicion. Was he only pretending to be an architect? Was the true purpose of his visit to sell insurance? There was, as it happened, no insurance cover at all on The Round House. Premium payments of that kind came into the category of extravagances which the family had never been able to afford. But there was no need to reveal that to a stranger. Instead, his brains could be picked. 'A high value, you reckon?'

'It's unique, you see,' Mr Lacey pointed out. 'I'm not familiar with American prices. But the cost of merely rebuilding the dome if it were to be damaged would be huge. And you could multiply that by three or four times to approach its value as a piece of history. Could I presume on your patience, Mr Vernon, Miss Vernon – I may never be back in this area again – to continue my sketching? Without wishing to disturb your own routine in any way. I should be so very grateful.'

'Go right ahead.' Thomas waited until the Englishman had hurried up the steps from the basement before cutting himself another piece of cake. Then, while Louise fussed about, clearing the table, he sat back in his chair. On this first day of his unemployment – or rather, of his life as a gentleman of leisure – he had not yet established a routine which could be disturbed. But had he gone to work as usual today, he would probably have been sitting as idly at his desk there as he was at home. Inactivity was something to which Thomas was accustomed.

He had not intentionally chosen to work in a stagnating business. Ben Browning had been full of get-up-and-go when he first set up his real-estate office almost fifty years back. He needed a boy for the office and Thomas, anxious to prove himself the man of the family by supporting his mother and sister as soon as he could legally finish with school, had at first been eager to learn and willing to undertake whatever responsibilities he was offered. But it had not taken Ben long to discover that the property market in Natchez was stagnant. No one in the city could afford to move anywhere else. The old families were forced to live on in their old houses, which grew shabbier and shabbier from the lack of money to maintain them. The mansions came on to the market only when the last resident of each died.

If Ben Browning had had a little more patience, he would have realized that from now on this was likely to happen with increasing frequency. There was a whole generation of men and women in Natchez who had never married, because they could not afford to do that either. Thomas and Louise were part of that generation, but it included also the disabled veterans and the women ten years older than Louise who at the end of the war between the states had found that there were no young men available. These were the women who now, after living alone in their decaying palaces for years, had reached their eighties and were at last beginning to die.

The prospect of fresh business had arrived too late for Thomas's employer. He was seventy-five years old, and had grown tired of waiting. For many years his main interest had been gambling. Thomas was left to run the office single-handed while Mr Browning travelled from one race meeting to another, usually losing on the evening's poker game anything he might have won on the horses. Thomas's painstaking conscientiousness had made him competent to deal with what little work there was, although he had never been clever.

But at the end of May, Ben Browning had pledged his business on three kings and lost. The new owner took one look at the accounts and instructed Thomas, as the last act of his employment, to put his own office up for sale. Although Thomas had been dimly aware that he would have to retire one day, he had not considered the possibility that this might be forced on him while he was still only in his sixties. And his hopes of a small retirement pension had crashed as decisively as his employer's hopes of a killing at the poker game. Ben, apologetically, had sent a leaving present, promising other payments whenever the horses ran well – but Thomas knew that these would never arrive. He was free now to do whatever he chose; but shortage of money meant that he could only choose to remain at home.

He thought about that now, listening to Mr Lacey's footsteps above his head, and a kind of rage began to smoulder in his mind, tying his stomach into a knot of frustration. To be free, and yet still a prisoner – it was too much for a man to bear. He was only partly soothed by the sound of Louise at the piano. Although he was not normally at home to hear it, he knew that it was part of her daily routine to celebrate the moment when she had put off the clothes and dirt of a household drudge by playing a favourite piece of music. Later in the evening – after Thomas himself was at home – she would play again, this time for an hour or more. Although he rarely bothered to listen, he understood that this was her necessary release from the tedium of teaching unwilling boys and wooden-fingered girls. Today, for once, he gave the music his full attention and was unexpectedly moved not just by its beauty but by the tragedy of the woman who played it.

She had chosen a difficult, showy piece – perhaps with the wish to impress their visitor – and although her elderly and work-roughened hands had lost much of their sparkle and sensitivity, enough remained to remind Thomas how talented a pianist she had been when she was young. There had been talk of sending her to be professionally trained. Loveday Vernon, who in her own youth had never been forced into the compromises made necessary by poverty, had discussed the relative advantages of Germany and Paris before more realistically considering whether she could afford to send her daughter to New York or at least New Orleans. None of the talk had come to anything, of course; there was no money for such frivolities. After a little early help from her mother, she had been left to teach herself, and all her concert performances had taken place in the Baptist Church Hall. Thomas's rage against life flared higher, fanned by a rare sympathy for a sister who usually annoyed him. It was too late for Louise to achieve her ambitions; and if Thomas had ever been ambitious, it would have been too late for him as well. They were prisoners of the time and place in which they had been born; and it was a life sentence.

Thomas stood up and marched out of the house. He picked up a stick and began to beat it with all his strength against the trunk of a live oak. A blue jay flew indignantly out of the branches as Thomas continued to whack away his rage against life. Once, as a little boy, he had expressed resentment by sweeping crockery off the table with his arm. He no longer remembered the cause of the outburst; but his mother's face, aghast at the loss they could not afford, had made a deeper impression even than the beating she gave him. Ever since then he had learned to recognize the moment when anger, choking his throat, could no longer be controlled – and he took it out on the trees.

When he was calm again, he returned to the house and watched Mr Lacey, who was now using a theodolite to establish distances and dimensions. As the architect peered and scribbled, Thomas allowed his attention to wander and his thoughts to roam. Suppose, just suppose, that an insurance company would, as the Englishman had suggested, accept that The Round House had a value greater than the cost of rebuilding it as a home. Mr Lacey might be willing to put that in writing as a professional opinion. Suppose next that Thomas were to use Mr Browning's leaving present – which he had not yet mentioned to Louise – as the premium for a year's insurance on that high value. And then suppose that the house were to burn down. It was easy to imagine a lamp being accidentally overturned by Thomas himself, who was known to be clumsy with his fingers and should never have been asked by his sister to trim the wick of one lamp by the light of another.

The plush cloth which covered the table would burn first, and then the table itself. The flames would leap up towards the ceiling and through to the floorboards on which Thomas was standing now. They would spread across the whole ground area of the house. Then they would begin to eat their way up the exposed timbers of the walls, tentatively to start with but soon biting deeply into the old, dry wood. Thomas had never, as far as he could recollect, seen a building on fire, but it seemed to him that he knew exactly how it would sound when the first crackling, coming from all around, gave place to a single purposeful roar as the height of the dome, acting as a chimney, pulled the flames upward. All those joists and rafters which Mr Lacey was now drawing would burn as though they had been carefully stacked for a bonfire, until at last the heavy tiles of the dome would crash down to the ground. Thomas himself, and Louise, would naturally have made their escape long before this occurred. Sympathetic neighbours would give them lodging until the insurance company paid out on the whole huge value of the building. There would be no need – indeed, it would be crazy – to rebuild an unfinished folly. So for the first time in their lives they would be rich – and free.

It was as though the rage he had felt earlier were turned on its head and transformed into excitement. Thomas found himself trembling with the clarity of his vision and the urgency of his desire to set the train of events in motion. His body was unused to such an intensity of emotion. He was forced to go outside the veranda so that he could sit down.

It did not take long to rock his body into an appearance of

calmness, but his thoughts were less easily controlled. Over and over again, as though he were sitting through a day's continuous performance at the movies, he re-ran the picture of the devouring flames, shifting uncomfortably in the chair as he did so. Once or twice in his younger days Thomas had considered the possibility of marriage, but none of the young ladies whom his mother would have considered suitable had ever aroused in him the kind of excitement that he felt now.

As though she were in tune with his thoughts, Louise began to play faster and more furiously. A crescendo of crashing chords was loud enough to be heard clearly outside the house. As part of his day-dream Thomas had generously allowed that Louise should become as rich as himself; but this reminder of the real woman brought him up short, making him doubt whether his fantasy could ever be put into effect. Thomas himself felt no sentimentality about The Round House. Merely by existing and providing a home for the family it had encouraged him from ever going off to make his fortune. It was part of his imprisonment and he would be glad to be quit of it.

But to Louise The Round House represented her status in the community. It was a palace, conferring on her a rank appropriate to its size. Outside it, no reference was ever made to the hours she spent in scrubbing or hoeing, or to the fact that she was forced to give piano lessons. All the other ladies of the church which was the centre of her social life practised the same concealment of their domestic slavery and no doubt wished that they, like Miss Louise, had a talent which could be sold for money. What was important was that the big house on the bluff was recognized as being high in the pecking order of Natchez property. Louise was the supervisor of the group of ladies providing flowers for the church throughout the year, and chairwoman of the local Charity Organisation Society. Were she to move away from Natchez she would lose her dignities as well as her friends – and her brother, who knew the cash value and availability of every house within the shabby city, recognized that nothing they could buy locally would confer the same prestige.

And there were other considerations. No inducement of mere money would ever reconcile Louise to the loss of the piano which she loved more dearly than anything else in the world. And no attempt to remove it from the house on some pretext would succeed unless his sister knew why such a move was necessary. But Louise's church-going was more than merely social. She was genuinely religious and completely honest, likely to fly into hysterics at the merest suspicion of a plan involving arson and fraud. To spell out to her what he had in mind would be to finish its chance of success for good. She would rather inform on her brother to the insurance company than take advantage of his enterprise.

Little by little Thomas felt the excitement drain from his body. He ceased to rock the chair and instead slumped heavily back, tempted to succumb once more to the dullness of his life. To use Louise as an excuse for inaction was, he recognized, a kind of hypocrisy. The Round House would never burn to the ground because he, Thomas Wade Vernon, was not the sort of man who struck matches and threw them into puddles of oil.

But did that have to be true for ever? With an unusually abrupt movement Thomas stood up and began to pace up and down the veranda, his feet automatically avoiding the patches of rotten wood. Was he necessarily a prisoner of his own nature as much as of his circumstances? There must surely be some way in which he could escape from himself. He would no longer go to work in Ben Browning's office every day, but was his life, except for that, to continue along the same dull lines as for the past sixty-four years? Was nothing ever going to happen?

2

Thomas's brief vacation came to an end as soon as Mr Lacey left the house. Even Louise recognized that she would not be able to persuade her brother out of his respectable clothes, and that the henhouse roof had better wait for another day. As she rattled off a seemingly endless list of alternative chores, it seemed to Thomas that she must have spent the past fifty years deliberately accumulating repairs for him to tackle. Or perhaps it was more that he had managed to evade them for all that time. Just for the sake of annoying her, he swept every suggestion aside and instead announced one of his own. He would clear out his mother's den.

It was while he was watching the architect and visualizing the fire that Thomas had been reminded of the little makeshift cubicle. Seventy years earlier the supervisor of the workmen who built the house had constructed a small office for himself between the outer wall and the beams of what should later have become a ballroom floor, twenty feet above the entrance hall. Loveday Vernon used it as a private retreat for many years, and even when she became too crippled to climb the steep ladder which provided the only access, she had forbidden her son and daughter ever to intrude. Thomas had been up just once since her death to see whether any valuables were concealed there, but had found only a sixty-year accumulation of papers. Since then he had promised Louise several times that he would tidy it out; it was laziness rather than any feeling that his mother's writ still ran after her death which had caused him to postpone the task for two years. Now it occurred to him that he might be glad of the den for his own use, to keep him out of Louise's way.

With some difficulty, because of his weight and stoutness, he climbed the ladder and eased himself into the confined space. It seemed as though his mother had kept every bit of paper that had ever come into the house. As the first of Louise's afternoon piano pupils sat down to her scales, Thomas settled to his own task.

Most of the hoard was trash. He disposed of it simply enough by throwing it out, for the little room had only two walls. But a rusting black metal box appeared to hold contents of more importance. There were legal documents and day books and three bundles of letters tied up in pale yellow ribbon. The light in this windowless space was not good enough for him to read the faded papers; he took them down to the veranda.

The first bundle he unwrapped was of letters written by Wade Vernon to his wife while he was away fighting for the Confederate army. Thomas had been brought up on stories of what a fine and brave man his father was, but had no direct memory of him. He read the letters now with surprise that his mother had once been considered beautiful and with a kind of envy that his father should have been able to love so passionately and trust so completely. Even at the time when Thomas had vaguely considered that he was of an age to consider marriage, he had never found a woman with whom he felt safe. The girls of his own set, forty years ago – the girls who shared a hay wagon with him on church picnics or sang opposite him in the choir – were all desperate to get married and escape from mothers as hard and bitter as his own. They would have promised anything, no doubt, to entrap him, but he could not believe any of their promises.

He set aside his father's letters and picked up the next bundle. His mother had slipped a card beneath the ribbon: *From my dear sweet Rebecca*. Thomas stared at the packet uneasily, not knowing why he should feel disturbed. He had still not opened it when Louise, her last lesson done, came to sit beside him.

'Our father wrote these.' He handed her Wade Vernon's letters; but then, after a moment's hesitation, interrupted her reading. 'Louise, d'you remember Rebecca?' He had been only four years old when Rebecca died and could form no picture of her in his mind.

'How could I forget my own sister?'

'Tell me what you recall.'

Louise, searching her memory, groped for words and was upset by her failure to find them. 'Well, she was – she was here.'

'Why did she go away?'

'You know all about that. She went off with some missionary friend of Mama's, to help look after her little girl. She was supposed to stay in San Francisco, at a mission for the wild folk of California; but then when she came there the missionary society sent the family on to the Sandwich Islands. I remember . . .' Thomas saw that Louise had begun to concentrate her mind successfully on those far-off days. 'I remember Mama was more angry and weeping about that than ever I saw her before or since. She said that the Lindsays – yes, that was their name, the Lindsays – should have sent Rebecca home when they were told to go on across the ocean. But *they* said that they couldn't send a child that age alone round the Horn or back through Indian country, and they certainly couldn't leave her in a sink of iniquity like San Francisco.'

'She never said goodbye to me.' Thomas's own memory was stimulated by Louise's information. 'I thought she must have died.'

'So she did.'

'Died that night, when she wasn't there any more. She was going to look after me. I was crying one day, and she promised she wouldn't ever go away.' Suddenly emotional as he projected himself back into those distant days, Thomas found himself almost beginning to think as the four-year-old he had once been. 'And then one day I woke up and she wasn't there. Without ever saying goodbye.' He had tried to believe that she was dead then, because nothing else would explain or excuse her betrayal, but his mother had not allowed him to cling to this last consolation. He had been made to accept that the person he loved most in all the world had broken her promise and abandoned him. Later, as Louise reminded him, Rebecca had indeed died; but by that time all his tears had been shed and he had forced himself not to care.

'Still don't understand why she had to go,' he said slowly. 'We were her folks. She was supposed to care for me. Why did she suddenly take off with strangers?' He hadn't understood then and he didn't understand now. Maybe the letters in his hand would provide an explanation. Was it that possibility which made him still so reluctant to slip off the ribbon?

'I'll see these later.' Louise set down her father's letters and stood up. 'Promised I'd go down and do the flowers for Blake Whitty's funeral.'

Thomas waited until Louise was out of sight. Only then did he slip the ribbon away from the half dozen letters written by his other sister, whom he could not remember.

The first one was difficult to read, for the ink had faded and the paper had yellowed. Although the first few lines were inscribed in a schoolgirl's careful round hand, it seemed that Rebecca had become distraught as she continued, so that soon the words ran on into each other without clear breaks. Perhaps she had only been allowed one sheet of paper, for when she came to the end of it she had given it a half turn, writing the end of the letter across the lines of the beginning.

As Thomas struggled to decipher it, the writer's unhappiness throbbed its way through his eyes and into his heart. Rebecca was writing towards the end of a three-week voyage from San Francisco to the Sandwich Islands, so that the letter could be despatched as soon as she reached port. For two weeks the unfamiliar motion of the sea had made her so sick that she had been unable to keep down any food except a thin broth, and for the two days before sailing she had cried without stopping as she tried to persuade the Lindsays that they had no right to take her any farther from home. In the end they had given her a medicine to make her stop crying, and she had been carried on to the ship while she was half asleep, with no strength to run away.

Now she was angry. Almost too weak to move after her days of sickness and starvation, she accused her mother of deceiving her with the promise that she would soon be able to return home. If she had been allowed time to think about it, there must surely have been somewhere nearer at hand for her to hide until the trouble was over. As it was, she had been parted from little Thomas, whom she loved more than anyone else in the world. Was Thomas happy without her? Rebecca thought of him every night and prayed for him and longed to cuddle him again. Her mother was to be sure and tell him that.

Thomas supposed that he had been told, although he could not remember it. His mother had written at the foot of the letter the date on which it arrived – more than six months after Rebecca wrote it, almost nine months after she left home. Thomas by then would have been not quite five years old, not old enough to read the difficult handwriting for himself. If he had been given the assurance of Rebecca's love, had he believed it? It was impossible to tell whether the blank space in his memory was caused by a deliberate banishment of all thought of Rebecca or merely by the passage of time.

There was one point which his sister's letter did not explain. If she had not wanted to leave home, why had she been forced to do so? He moved on to the other letters in the hope of discovering an answer.

All of them, to judge by his mother's dating, had taken many months to arrive, presumably making the long journey round the Horn. Mrs Vernon's own letter would take just as long, and not for almost a year would she have known where to write. Still unhappy, Rebecca pleaded on each page for news of home.

In the meantime she gave news of her own. She had tried to arrange a passage home for herself on a whaling ship, in spite of the fact that, two weeks after reaching dry land, she still felt sick from the shaking-up of the first voyage. A group of sailors had promised to smuggle her on board and not tell anyone until it was too late to turn back. But the captain had discovered the plan before he sailed and had taken her back to the mission. Mr Lindsay had been angry with her and the captain had been angry with the sailors. But Rebecca promised that she would try to escape as soon as she saw her chance. Once again she sent her dearest love to Thomas.

In the third letter her tone had changed. Rebecca still longed to hear from her family, but in the meantime she had sad news of her own to report. Mrs Lindsay's baby had been born, but died within a few hours. Like Rebecca herself, Mrs Lindsay had been sick throughout the three-week voyage and it was thought that this must have affected the baby. Mrs Lindsay was weak and unhappy, unable to leave her bed, so it was left to Rebecca to look after Alma as well as nursing the invalid. She understood that she could not be spared for a little while and her own health was beginning to improve. As a result of her travels she had become very thin and – like Mrs Lindsay – had lost her strength for a while: but now she was able to eat again, and as a result was even becoming fat.

Four weeks later her temporary calm had disappeared. She was going to have a baby! Rebecca didn't see how it could be true, because she wasn't married; but Mrs Lindsay was so sure about it that she had even put a ring round the date on which the baby would be born.

It was easy for Thomas to tell that Rebecca was still not convinced; but because the Lindsays had no doubts they were making up all sorts of stories about her. She was to say that while she was still only fourteen she had married her beau, because he was just going off to the war and might never see her again, and that he had in fact been killed in battle only a week after the wedding. Since she had arrived in the Sandwich Islands as Rebecca Vernon, she had to pretend that Vernon was her husband's name and not that of her own family. Rebecca was shocked that missionaries should make up such lies, but Mrs Lindsay had explained to her what a terrible thing it was for a girl to have a baby if she had never had a husband, and what a bad example it would be to the natives who were being brought to Christ. So Rebecca had promised to say everything that she was told.

But she still didn't understand where the baby had come from.

There was more to the letter, but Thomas could not read it, for across the bottom of the page his mother had scrawled a word in thick black ink. FLETCHER. He stared at it, puzzled. Everything he had read so far had come as a surprise, but the name Fletcher was familiar to him. Over and over again in his boyhood his mother had spoken that name and told him that he must hate its owner. If ever they were to meet, Thomas must take revenge for all the evil which Fletcher – Captain Mark Fletcher, he remembered now – had brought on the family. She had not explained exactly what kind of evil it was, so Thomas had supposed that Captain Fletcher was the Yankee who killed his father and left the Vernons to starve. Because it was the business of soldiers to kill other soldiers in battles, Thomas had never completely understood his mother's obsession and had not allowed himself to be infected by it. But it seemed now that he might have been mistaken about the reason for her hatred.

There was one more letter in the little bundle, but in it Rebecca's handwriting was changed. The few tired words sprawled across the page, almost too faint to be read. The baby had been born, she wrote. A beautiful little boy, healthy and kicking. She was going to call him Thomas, after her own little Thomas at home, whom she loved as dearly as her own son. She would write more on the letter when she was less tired.

She had not written any more. Instead, across the blank space beneath the faded lines, his mother once again had scrawled a name. FLETCHER. MONSTER.

Unconsciously Thomas began to throw himself forward and back in the rocking chair, chewing on his finger nails. He had entered the period of his own remembrance of the past. It was on the morning he learned about Rebecca's baby, he recalled now, that he had swept the breakfast dishes off the table with his arm in rage that Rebecca should love another boy instead of himself and should even give his own name away to the intruder. It was only after his mother had given him a beating that she returned to the table to read the note, separately sealed, which her friend Mrs Lindsay had sent by the same boat.

Red-eyed from his whipping, Thomas had listened in silence on that day almost sixty years ago while his mother told him that Rebecca was dead. He had not allowed himself to shed a single tear more. Rebecca had promised to look after him and to love him for ever. She had broken her promise and gone away and had loved another boy more than himself. Thomas told himself that he didn't care if she was dead. He worked at the thought until he believed it and then, because the belief still gave him pain, he made himself forget that Rebecca had ever been part of his life. The passing of time, of course, had added a genuine forgetfulness to the pretence.

That moment of silence in 1865 which followed the news of Rebecca's death had encapsulated all the future pain of believing it, but five-year-old Thomas had not cried then. Now, at the end of another silence, a different Thomas – sixty-four years old, florid and stout and solitary – howled aloud with anguish. At long last the tears trickled down his face. But they were not, as they should have been in 1865, tears of bereavement. He was weeping for the little boy who had never understood his betrayal and deprivation, and for the young man who had never been able to give himself in love because once upon a time the only woman he had loved unreservedly had seemed to desert him.

It was a long time before he was able to calm himself sufficiently to glance at the third bundle of letters. The first two came from Mrs Lindsay, repeating what he had already learned. Then, after Rebecca's death, it was Mr Lindsay who took up the correspondence. The baby, he wrote, was large and healthy – so large that it had been a difficult birth, for Rebecca was not yet fully grown. And she had been weakened, before anyone was aware of her condition, by the long overland journey and her sea-sickness during the voyage. He sent his deepest regrets, but assured Mrs Vernon that she need not fear for baby Thomas, for whom a native wet-nurse had been found.

By the very next sailing – so quickly that he must have had the idea in his mind when he first wrote – Mr Lindsay despatched another letter. His wife, as Mrs Vernon knew, had lost her own baby and now could never have another. For the past four months she had kept to her bed, unhappy, but the need to care for Rebecca's baby had roused her at last from her listlessness. She had unwrapped the clothes prepared for her own child and already loved the little boy as though he were her own son. So Mr Lindsay was writing formally to ask whether Mrs Vernon would allow him and her dear friend Beth to adopt the baby into their own family.

It must have happened that way. Mrs Vernon had never told any of her friends in Natchez that she had a grandson; nor, after the first announcement of the baby's birth, did she ever again mention even to Thomas and Louise the boy who was their nephew. She might well have seen the adoption as being for the best; but her unnatural silence on the subject suggested that perhaps she could not bear to think about a child who was responsible for Rebecca's death.

None of that was important now. Thomas, uninterested in the arrangements made for this other Thomas, allowed the last letter to slip from his fingers. He still had not discovered the answer to the only question that interested him: why had Rebecca had to leave her home? He looked again at his mother's thickly-written words: FLETCHER. MONSTER. But they were not enough to give him an answer. Tipping the metal box of his mother's papers upside down so that its contents scattered untidily over the veranda, he searched amongst them for the diary which she had kept in 1863, and began to turn the pages.

Half an hour later, his eyes strained from staring, Thomas stood up, staggering a little from the stiffness of his tensed muscles. As though he were sleepwalking he crossed the vegetable patch to the shed where tools were kept and took down a sickle. Then he continued through the wood, along the edge of the bluff and down a winding track which led to the bayou. Until this point the path was beaten down with use, for Thomas himself came regularly in his free time to shoot duck or to fish in the bayou, providing food for Louise to cook whilst escaping from her nagging urge to keep him occupied.

He was wearing his best black boots and the business suit which he had put on for Mr Lacey's visit, and even in summer the land around the bayou was swampy. But Thomas took no notice of the mud which splashed around his ankles nor of the green stains of lichen which rubbed against his elbows. Instead, ignoring the indignant alarm of the bullfrogs, he began to hack at the barrier of scrub and liana which had turned a forest into a jungle.

Even so late in the afternoon the day was very hot and Thomas was not used to such exertion. He began to sweat inside clothes too tight for this activity; but rage drove him on to slash away with the same persistence sometimes revealed in his beating of the trees near the house. Even so, it took more than an hour before he finally broke through into the less heavily wooded land around the Old River Lake. His heart was beating too fast, and not quite smoothly. Panting, he stood still for a few moments, looking around.

It was not surprising that an unfit and elderly man should never have attempted to penetrate to this section of his own property – but even as a boy, he remembered, he had avoided it, claiming to be fearful of cottonmouths and moccasins. It was likely that no one had trodden this ground for the past sixty years. The Old River Lake must be somewhere very close, but it was impossible to see it for the long grass and weeds and undergrowth and saplings. The forest was moving in, casting its seeds forward to colonize the land; and each tree, as it grew towards maturity, was draped with a curtain of Spanish moss. Thomas moved a little way into the area, slashing at brambles which could not be trampled underfoot. But before very long he came to a halt, reluctant in spite of all his efforts to approach the lake.

Instead he stood still, breathing heavily and listening to the rustling noises made by birds and small animals and perhaps even the snakes whose existence he had once recognized for his own reasons. The river, too, could be heard, splashing against a rock not far away. But beneath the rustling and the splashing there was an eerie silence. A ghost frequented this place which no human being had disturbed for so long. The ghost not of Mark Fletcher, who had stumbled away, clutching his eye, to begin a new life far from the war. And not of Rebecca, who had run, sobbing, into another new life. Her death had occurred too far away to haunt this place. What had died here was the trust and happiness of a little boy; and now that boy grown old knew who was responsible.

Thomas found it hard to believe that he could so completely and genuinely have closed the door of his memory on what had happened by the Old River Lake. His mother, in her long, distraught account, had written of concussion. But there must surely be some deeper explanation, some instinct which preserved him from a memory too traumatic for a child to endure. His mother had never known the whole of what happened, but only as much as Rebecca could tell her. Standing very still, Thomas set himself to remember.

Sounds came first. The crackling of burning wood – not imagined, as in the dome of The Round House this morning, but real. Rebecca was screaming and Bella the cow was roaring and kicking in panic and Thomas himself coughed uncontrollably as the thick smoke filled his lungs. He had watched a rape, believing it to be an attempt at murder. And then . . . but now memory began to resist his probing, emerging only painfully, like a dressing tugged from a wound into which it had been packed. And then . . . Thomas looked down at the sickle he still held in his hand. And then he had picked up a knife and hurled it down.

That – not the rape or the fire, but the throwing of the knife – was the moment which Thomas had never dared to remember. Was it because he feared that he had killed his own sister, whom he had never seen again ? Or did he believe that he had killed the soldier, whose fellow-officers would take vengeance if they found out? It was impossible to say – but one thing was sure enough. He had *wanted* to kill the soldier. He had vowed to do so one day when he was old enough. But that vow, like everything else, had been sucked inside the poisoned wound which his memory had sealed up; to fester, unremembered, as the first of all the many things he had failed to do in the course of his life.

Thomas made no further attempt to find the remains of the hut in which he had sucked his barley-sugar cane while Rebecca milked the cow. Whatever had not burned would by now have rotted away, and he had no need of objects to trigger his memory further. His mother's journal had put the necessary questions into his mind and the ghost of this haunted place had answered them. He turned away and climbed laboriously back to The Round House.

Louise began to yell at him before he was even close enough to hear the words, but her meaning was clear enough. She yelled at him for leaving their mother's papers to blow about the veranda. Then she noticed the state that his suit and shoes were in and yelled some more. And last of all she yelled because he was two hours late for his supper, which had spoiled long since.

'Don't care for any supper tonight.' Thomas walked past his sister, silencing her by the extraordinariness of this statement.

When she had found her voice again, she came to the door of his bedroom. 'Thomas! You sick or something?'

Thomas did not answer, but closed the door and went to bed. Tomorrow, he promised himself, hc would set about tracking down the Monster.

3

Loveday Vernon, as her journals revealed, had done her best to discover the whereabouts of Captain Mark Fletcher after the war ended. But in her first version of events – designed to protect Rebecca when it seemed likely that the officer would die from his head wound – she had claimed that her daughter was drowned in the bayou while trying to escape from Captain Fletcher. His superior officers, noting that he had surprised an enemy in unauthorized possession of livestock, had exonerated him from blame. The motive behind Mrs Vernon's later enquiries was no doubt too obvious and the Federal army, seeing no reason why it should oblige one of the defeated rebels, protected its officer by refusing to divulge any information about him. In the end, too poor to travel and weighed down by the daily problems of keeping herself and two growing children alive, she had given up.

For Thomas, in 1924, the position was different. The Civil War had become a chapter in history books, a subject for research. Regimental archivists were no longer obstructive but instead willingly searched their records. It took a little time, but before the end of September Thomas learned that Captain Mark Fletcher had been invalided out of the army at the end of 1863. Like many another northerner in that period, he took advantage of the collapse of the southern economy to buy himself a piece of land with his Yankee dollars. Throughout the years when Loveday Vernon had been trying to find him, he had been breeding horses in Kentucky. In 1920, however, at the age of seventy-eight, he had sold the ranch and returned to his birthplace, a village in Vermont. The letter gave the address. What it did not say in so many words was whether Captain Mark Fletcher was still alive.

But it didn't say that he was dead. Four years was not too long. The man would only be eighty-two years old by now. People did live to be that age, and older. It might not be too late. On October 1st Thomas announced to his sister and his friends that he owed himself a holiday.

If his friends were surprised, Louise was startled to the point of disbelief. For as long as anyone could remember, Thomas's only holiday visits had been for the week round Thanksgiving, which he and his sister regularly spent with a cousin in the Delta.

'Only ever had a week's holiday while I was working for Ben Browning,' Thomas pointed out. 'Different now. Time to look around me.'

'So where are you reckoning to go?'

'Vermont.' He enjoyed the look of stupefaction on Louise's face. She could not have been more taken aback if he had suggested a trip to Russia or China. 'They say it's pretty in the fall,' he pointed out. 'All the trees. Red and yellow.'

'You're telling me you plan to travel all that way just to observe the scenery? Why, there's prettier things within twenty miles of here, for anyone with the eyes to see them. We can't spare the money for that kind of jaunt. Vermont!'

'I'm not asking you for anything.' Thomas was pleased with himself for keeping secret the retirement present which Ben Browning had given him. Louise looked at him suspiciously, but he was not to be drawn.

'How d'you reckon to get there, then?' she asked. 'All that great distance.'

Thomas smiled to himself again. He knew that Louise had no great opinion of his capabilities, and it was true enough that he was not accustomed to travelling. But he had had three sessions with the clerk at the railroad station, who often found time hanging heavy on his hands and had enjoyed the challenge of working out four different routes by which Thomas could travel north to New England. The first attempt would have taken him to Manchester, New Hampshire instead of to Manchester, Vermont – but Thomas, painstakingly checking every detail, had caught the mistake in time. Together the two men had compared costs and travelling times of the alternative approaches to the correct destination and made a choice: with much reference to railroad maps and timetables the clerk had written out a complete itinerary for his ambitious client in both directions.

The plan of what he would do when he arrived in Manchester was less clear than the route. There had been a few hours – first as he stood in silence near the Old River Lake and later as he tossed sleeplessly in bed – when his sixty-year-old rage, so long suppressed, had seemed to spin within his mind like a tornado, working him up to a state in which he was ready to commit murder as an act of long-delayed revenge. But with the morning, a more realistic appraisal of his own nature had brought doubts. Would he really be capable of killing a man in cold blood?

Whatever the answer to that question, at least he would not find it difficult to express his hatred in other ways. As he travelled interminably north, he rehearsed to himself what he would say and do. The man must be made to understand the damage he had done to the lives of a whole family. His children, and grandchildren if he had any, should learn that their father, grandfather, had in his youth behaved like an animal. And then Captain Fletcher must be made to feel fear. Even if Thomas could not commit murder, his victim need not know it at once. Thomas was not particularly strong, but he was large – and a one-eyed man, eighty-two years old, would surely be frail. There had to be a moment when the Monster Fletcher would believe he was about to die. Then, Thomas promised himself, he would give a last shake, throw the old man to the ground, and go.

There was a sense in which the mere act of making the journey – the taking of a decision – was enough to calm Thomas's spirit and grant him absolution for a lifetime of inactivity. To inflict a few moments of terror might not seem much of a revenge for all the parched years of his life, but it would have to do.

4

A bus brought Thomas to Manchester late on a Friday afternoon; it would return along the same route, the driver told him as he stepped down from it, in three hours' time. Holding the travelling bag that was all he had needed for the journey, Thomas stood still for a moment to get his bearings. Not far away a white church spire rose cleanly into the clear blue sky. He walked towards it, stimulated into an unaccustomed briskness by the sunlit crispness of the atmosphere.

The village seemed to consist of little more than a single wide street from which, on one side, short approach roads every hundred yards or so led to clusters of six or seven houses. On the other side the land fell sharply away into a valley. It was possible to stand on the sidewalk and look straight down to a river, and beyond that to several miles of rolling forest before the Green Mountains rose to frame the view.

The trees were certainly pretty. In the ordinary way he might not have noticed them: but Louise would ask, and so he prepared his answer. The forest foliage was as dramatic in its fall colouring as he had heard tell. Beech and birch and hickory, mountain ash and maple and black gum – and other trees that he had never seen before and could not identify – blazed in every shade from dark red to the palest gold. A few of the trees had already lost their leaves; their branches were as grey as the rings of ash on burning logs. The forest smouldered with the low red glow of sumach bushes, until its leaves were whipped up by a breeze into flames tipped by the golden heads of beech trees.

Thomas shook his head to clear the image away, but as he continued to imprint on his eyes and memory a scene which he could faithfully describe to his sister – if only to prove that he had made the journey successfully and attained his destination – it seemed to him for a moment or two that the forest was indeed on fire. The wind, bending the branches, sent the flames rippling over the foothills of the mountains –

or so it appeared. Thomas knew that the fire blazed only in his imagination; but as he followed its apparent course with his eyes, he began to hear in his head the same crackling that in his fancy had gnawed at the timbers of The Round House – and this, too, increased to a roar as the flames devoured the forest and brought the tall trees crashing down. The excitement which Thomas had experienced on that earlier occasion overcame him again now. He was forced to stand still for a few minutes while alarm and pleasure mingled in his veins – with a trace of fear as well, because his return to the Old River Lake had taught him that the memory of his actual childhood experience was an even more powerful ingredient in his fantasy than imagination.

He walked on again, but there was no escaping from the colours of fire. Wherever he looked, the sunlight danced on golden leaves. Almost every house had a sumach in its front yard, and the main street was lined with an avenue of maples which combined all the colours of flame within the leaves of each single tree. Thomas kept his eyes on the ground as he stomped on towards the centre of the village.

In a store near the church he bought tobacco before beginning to ask the questions he had prepared. Although the address of the house he sought was imprinted on his memory as well as being tucked into his pocket book, he enquired about the Fletcher household and was rewarded by an outpouring of gossip which he had not counted on finding in the unneighbourly north.

Yes, the storekeeper knew all about the family. Old Captain Fletcher had taken it into his head that he wanted to die in the place where he was born. At first he lived alone in the house on Washington Drive. But he was already an old man when he came, and a year or so back he'd had to recognize that he couldn't manage on his own any longer. His son, who'd got a good business going in Atlanta, tried to get his father to come and live with him. But the captain was a stubborn old man and wouldn't give in. In the end, it had been settled for the best when Captain Fletcher's grand-daughter came to live with him.

'Unmarried, is she?' Only an occasional question was needed to keep the information coming. Within a few moments Thomas had learned that no, Agnes was Mrs Harry Kiernan, and that she and her husband had brought their two-year-old son Alex with them when they moved in two years before. Dr Kiernan was a mighty clever man; not a medical doctor, but a university teacher. He had moved from the University of West Virginia to Williams College for his father-in-law's sake, and he must have found it something of a backwater compared with what he could have had; but of course he'd always known that his stay here wouldn't be for ever. The property was up for sale at this very moment. The storekeeper looked enquiringly at Thomas as if forming his own conclusion about the reason for all the questions.

'Moving away, are they?' checked Thomas, stowing the tobacco into his pocket.

'Captain Fletcher left the house here to his granddaughter. Only right and proper after all she'd done. He'd set his son up earlier on, when the ranch was sold. Mr Daniel's up here now, helping them to pack up, while they decide what to do next. Dr Kiernan can go back to West Virginia if he chooses, but there's talk that he's been invited to a university in England. Mrs Kiernan was never too keen on that idea, and of course Dr Kiernan couldn't consider it while his father-in-law was alive. But now that the old gentleman's dead, I've no doubt they'll have a lot of discussing to do about their plans. You feeling okay, sir?'

Thomas sat down heavily on the wooden chair beside the counter. 'Dead? When?' he asked.

'Captain Fletcher? About two months back. First week of August, as I recall.'

Thomas made no comment as he struggled with his emotions. Two months! Alive all these years, but dead for two months! If the archivist had written more promptly, if Thomas himself had not been so lazy about clearing out his mother's papers . . . Well, there was nothing to be gained by that kind of thought. 'You can give me half an ounce . . .'

he began, pulling himself to his feet – and then remembered that he had bought the tobacco already, and walked out of the store with a mutter of thanks.

Was there relief mingled with his disappointment? Thomas examined his own feelings as he paused, wondering which way to turn. For fifty years Louise had been accusing him of laziness, and he recognized that the charge was a fair one. The fault lay not so much in the indolence of his body – although in recent years, to be sure, stoutness had made him slow – but in the mental difficulty he found in working himself up to the point of action. Just for once, on this occasion, he had seemed to overcome his own failing, not only resolving to make a complicated journey but successfully accomplishing it. But still he could not help wondering what he would have done had he come face to face with Captain Fletcher. Well, now he would never know.

There was no point in going on, but no point, either, in hanging about on the street until the bus returned. Sick at heart, Thomas reminded himself that he had always known he might be too late, and allowed curiosity to take him to Washington Drive even though he no longer had any business there.

Like most of the houses in the village, the Fletcher home was a two-storeyed clapboarded building, made smarter than its neighbours by a recent coat of white paint. It had been spruced up to attract a buyer, no doubt, but there was a meticulous neatness about the property which suggested a careful owner. Perhaps Captain Fletcher, until his death, had filled his retirement days with the kind of task which Thomas had always taken pains to avoid; hammering in a nail before a shingle had a chance to work loose, or pulling out a weed before it had time to seed.

The house was surrounded by its own land. Along one side, footsteps had beaten down a track through a narrow belt of trees. The path was unfenced and he could not be sure whether it formed part of the lot or provided public access to the forested land beyond.

Thomas set down his travelling bag inconspicuously at the foot of a tree and set off to explore. If he was challenged, he could pretend to be an old acquaintance of Captain Fletcher, ignorant of the fact that he was dead. But no, thought Thomas with sudden revulsion, he would never claim to be the friend of such a man. So what was he doing here? The confusion of his thoughts suggested no answer. There was no pleasure to be gained from informing Mrs Agnes Kiernan that her grandfather had once raped a fourteen-year-old girl. Probably she would not believe him: if she did, she might not care. It was no longer a wish for revenge but rather an urge to punish himself for his own long forgetfulness that drove Thomas to inspect the pleasant surroundings in which the Fletcher monster had ended his days.

There was more land at the back of the house than its neat frontage suggested. A stretch of immaculately mown lawn led to a paddock, but the belt of trees through which Thomas was making his way was dense enough to screen him from the eyes of anyone in either the house or its grounds. He stood in its shelter, watching as a small boy was led round the paddock on the back of a pony. Thomas had little acquaintance with children and was not experienced in judging their ages; but the storekeeper had mentioned the two-year-old son who accompanied Agnes Kiernan when she first arrived to look after her grandfather, and this little boy did indeed appear to be about four years old.

The man who held the leading rein was in his middle fifties, likely to be not the boy's father but his grandfather: the business man from Atlanta, Captain Fletcher's son. He was a tall, spare man with a shock of dark grey hair. He walked with a slight limp, but appeared fit and energetic in spite of that; his clothes, although casual, looked well-made. Thomas gritted his teeth with envy of a man, of almost his own generation, who had so obviously been born to a comfortable life and could look forward to a prosperous old age.

Thomas had been watching for five or ten minutes when a woman stepped out of the house through an open glass door and strolled towards the paddock, leaning against the rail as she waited for the pony to complete a circuit. Her face was homely and her clothes were neat rather than smart, but she was happy and smiling as she clapped her hands to congratulate her son.

A door slammed in front of the house and a man's voice called out, 'I'm home, Agnes.' Only Thomas heard it. A moment or two passed, and then the owner of the voice appeared on the back lawn and called again. The little boy was lifted down from the pony by his grandfather. He ducked underneath the double rail and ran across the grass to his father, who tossed him high into the air. Thomas himself, at the same age, had been tossed up by Rebecca in just such a way, he remembered. It became easier every day to recall the long-forgotten events of his childhood, which presented themselves more vividly now to his eyes than anything which had happened in his middle years; for a few moments he turned his attention in upon himself.

When he looked up again, Agnes was welcoming her husband home with a kiss. Then the three males sat down at a wooden table which had been painted white like the house, and before long Agnes carried out a jug and glasses on a tray. Thomas could hear them chattering about the need to take advantage of the last few days of autumn sunshine before winter set in and the snow began to fall. The little boy's name, he was soon reminded, was Alex, and his shrill voice was easier to hear than the adults' softer words. But Thomas was not interested in the topics of their conversation. What struck into his heart with a poignancy that he could not endure was the happiness which visibly encircled the little family group. Alex climbed on to his father's lap; and Dr Kiernan, jogging the little boy on his knee, bent to kiss his son's head whilst Agnes looked on, adoring them both. Her own father, part of the group but holding himself a little separate from the others, watched with a patriarchal pride.

This child, Alex, would never be abandoned as Thomas had been abandoned. Captain Fletcher's great-grandson could feel beloved and secure. Thomas thought of that smaller Thomas – the boy of Alex's age – who had wept when the sister who had promised to love him disappeared without a word. It was because of that disappearance that Thomas had never loved anyone since then. But he had wanted to. Although by now he was used to the loneliness of his bachelor existence and to the shrill nagging which was the price he had to pay for Louise's housekeeping, he recognized that what he had always truly longed for was to be welcomed home in just such a manner each day, with the kiss of a loving wife and the soft hug of a contented child. Fletcher must have enjoyed that in his time; not just a wife and a child, but a granddaughter and great-grandson as well, to share his home and assure him that his line was secure. There was a special unfairness that it should be the kin of his enemy who were enjoying the contentment of which Thomas had been robbed. His bitterness grew as, unconscious of the passage of time, he stood as a spectator, observing the family scene.

There was nothing he could do now; no way in which he could revenge himself and Rebecca. Captain Fletcher was dead and to burst out with the story of his crime in front of these strangers would be to risk being thought mad. If he told the story more soberly, the fire that blazed in his heart would be smothered by the need to explain too many background details. Nor was any physical gesture possible. Thomas knew his own limitations. He lacked both the courage and the justification to attack two men who were each likely to be stronger than himself. He had failed again, as he failed in everything he undertook.

An evening breeze sprang up, disturbing the branches of the trees and bringing some of their dry, bronze leaves rustling to the ground. Dr Kiernan, perhaps feeling the coolness, glanced at his watch. 'Time for bed, young man.'

'One more ride! One more ride!'

Alex's parents looked at each other and laughed in agreement. Agnes carried the tray back inside the house, pausing in the doorway as though listening for something. Then she hurried to catch up with the two men as, swinging Alex between them, they ran down towards the fence. She had brought lumps of sugar with which to tempt the pony across from the far side of the paddock. They called and laughed; their gaiety was unbearable.

Thomas used the opportunity to move away while their attention was on the pony. His bus would be along in twenty minutes or so. At first he stayed in the shelter of the trees. But the open door of the house was a temptation. While all four members of the family had their backs to him as they coaxed the pony to approach, Thomas stepped into their living room.

The inside of the house was as neat and clean as the exterior, and as light as the basement of The Round House was dark. Agnes Kiernan had covered the chairs and sofa with flowery chintz and had edged the draped curtains and pelmets with piping and ruffles. She had embroidered antimacassars to protect the backs of the chairs and had crocheted mats to prevent vases of flowers from marking the polished tables. But what most interested Thomas was a selection of family photographs in frames of coloured glass, arranged in a row above the tiled fireplace.

The first four pictures were all of babies. To Thomas all babies looked the same, but he presumed that these showed Alex at various stages of his infancy: lying on a rug, held in his mother's arms, sitting on her lap and – as he had been today – proudly erect on his pony. There was a photograph of Agnes and her husband on their wedding day. An elderly couple beside them were perhaps Dr Kiernan's parents; Agnes's father, alone, was also represented in the display. Thomas's eye travelled along the row and focused on the picture at the far end. It was a hand-tinted photograph of a man with thick silver hair; a kindly, smiling old gentleman. He wore a black ribbon around his head, a black patch over one eye.

Thomas stretched out his hand and slowly brought the picture close enough to study. He felt no reaction at all; his mind seemed to be numb. This old man had nothing to do with him. But as he half turned to catch a better light, he noticed a much smaller portrait tucked into the corner of the frame and his heart gave an erratic jump as though it had temporarily lost its rhythm.

A handsome young man smiled out of the photograph. He wore a uniform which here was a faded sepia but in real life had been blue. He was the man who had stood in the portico of The Round House in 1863 and demanded the family's livestock. He was the man who had appeared from the woods to kill a cow and rip away the skirt of a fourteen-year-old girl. All those details which, on his frenzied return to the Old River Lake, Thomas had so painfully extracted from his memory after sixty years of repression came flooding back into his mind again. He felt once again the helpless rage of a little boy, his fingers relaxing their grip on his candy cane, which fell into the burning brushwood on the cowshed floor and was lost for ever.

There was a crash; the splintering of glass. Thomas looked down at his feet. Had he hurled the framed photograph on to the hearth, or merely dropped it? Instinctively he glanced through the open door to the garden. The pony had trotted across to nuzzle for lumps of sugar and Alex was being lifted up for his extra ride round the paddock. Thomas bent down and pulled both the old photograph and the more recent one away from the frame without caring whether his hands were scratched by the broken glass. He tore them across and across and again across. Going down on one knee, he piled the fragments on the hearth and put a match to them. A flame leapt up and then died down again, leaving grey wafers of ash to the shape of the pieces he had torn. It was all over too soon.

Captain Fletcher, Thomas remembered, had set light to brushwood and had watched the first flame flicker and die. So he had lit it for a second time. Now it was Thomas's turn. He struck a second match and held it to the curtains. Within a few seconds the whole of the ruffled edging was on fire. He picked up a child's picture book and held it in the flames until that too was well alight. Then he threw the burning book into an armchair and took a handful of gramophone records, in their paper sleeves, from the top of a cabinet gramophone to toss on to the blaze. He waited for a few seconds to be sure that the upholstery had caught. Then he let himself out of the front door of the house and picked up his travelling bag.

More briskly than usual, he made his way towards the main street. Reaching the corner, he saw the bus approaching and began to run in an ungainly waddle, one arm waving in a signal. The driver, taking pity on a breathless and overweight old man, came to a halt a hundred yards short of the official stop so that Thomas could climb aboard.

As the bus carried him away along the scarlet and golden avenue of maples and through a forest blazing with its autumn foliage, Thomas did not look back. So many backyard bonfires were smouldering under their burden of falling leaves that he would not have been able to pick out the first wisps of the smoke which soon would turn to a darker colour and rise with a more relentless roar. Instead, he allowed himself to imagine the hungry fire as it bit into the fabric of the wooden house and devoured it, just as on the day of the architect's visit he had imagined the destruction of The Round House. His body responded with the same stirrings of excitement as before, but this time they brought him pleasure rather than unease. He felt no guilt at what he had done, recalling instead what had always been his mother's favourite text: 'For I the Lord thy God am a jealous god and visit the sins of the fathers upon the children unto the third and fourth generation.' She had always used the quotation broadly, not in its biblical context, and so too did Thomas. He saw himself not as a criminal but as the instrument of God's will. Besides, his action had been merely a gesture. Agnes and her husband were already preparing to leave that house: they would reclaim its value from their insurance company instead of needing to find a buyer.

Wasting no time on pretending regret, Thomas abandoned himself to a kind of ecstasy as he imagined the fire sweeping through the house. Because he had not explored it, the details of its furnishings were all provided by his imagination. They did not include the wooden crib in a small bedroom above the living room; nor did his ears catch, above the crackling and roar of the flames, the coughing of a sleeping infant suddenly blanketed in black smoke. The store-keeper had mentioned Agnes Kiernan's arrival at Captain Fletcher's house as the mother of one little boy. There had been no reason for him to add that since then she had given birth to a second child.

INTERLUDE

1924

Reconnaissance

1

'How's it going?' From the moment when Daniel Fletcher learned that his father's house in Vermont had been destroyed not by accident but as a result of arson, he had made regular calls to the police. The killer of his grandson, little Danny Kiernan, must not be allowed to escape unpunished. Previous enquiries had been answered with a general optimism too vague to be satisfactory; but today the assurance that Daniel was waiting for came firmly over the line. 'We've got him.'

Daniel's lips tightened grimly as he listened to the details of a trail which had led the police to Mississippi. The storekeeper in Manchester had been able to describe a stranger from the south who showed a particular interest in the Fletcher household, and a bus driver recognized the description as that of a stout passenger whom he had picked up not far from the house and set down at a railroad station. The ticket presented by that passenger led the trail to the booking clerk at Natchez, who identified his customer without knowing the significance of the enquiry.

'Why did he do it, for God's sake?'

This time the answer was less revealing. Thomas Vernon, the man under arrest for the crime, had apparently made no attempt to deny that he had travelled from Mississippi to

Vermont at the time in question. He had even seemed to be on the point of admitting responsibility for an act of arson. But then the accusation of murder was made and at once he had protested vigorously that there was no one in the house when he was there. From the moment when the officer told him about the fourteen-month-old boy who had been asleep in an upstairs room the accused had refused to say anything at all.

'He's our man, though, no mistake. Let him stew in jail for a few days and he'll talk soon enough.'

'Sure hope so.' Not that talking could do anything to bring little Danny back to life. Daniel stood still for a few moments after the call ended, considering whether he should pass what he had learned on to Agnes. He decided in the end to wait for his son-in-law's weekend visit, leaving it to Harry to decide whether further discussion of the subject would increase his wife's distress.

Daniel had taken the bereaved parents and their surviving son to his home in Atlanta immediately after the tragedy. It was not a happy household. Harry had abandoned for the time being his intention of taking up an appointment in England, knowing that he would be needed as a witness if the perpetrator of the crime was found and brought to trial. After a period devoted to comforting Agnes, he had found temporary work in his old university of West Virginia, but would spend every weekend with his family. Even in normal times he was a quiet, thoughtful man, and grief had made him more silent than usual. Four-year-old Alex was confused by the sudden changes in his life and the disappearance of his younger brother and his favourite bear at the same time. As for Agnes, she could not control her distress. She had almost ceased to eat and at any hour of the day or night she was liable to weep inconsolably. It was all very understandable, but the impossibility of providing comfort to his beloved only daughter increased Daniel's own anguish at the death of the child who had borne his name.

Above all, his reaction was one of anger. Agnes might be inconsolable, but Daniel himself would find some satisfaction in seeing the murderer punished. As long as the punishment proved sufficient to fit the crime! If some spineless jury were to let the villain off simply because he claimed not to know what he was doing . . . Well, he should not expect even then to escape scot free. Daniel would make up for any deficiency in a court's decision and provide his own justice. Even as he muttered the vow under his breath, he recognized that he was using rage as his own method of controlling grief; but he knew no other.

Daniel Fletcher had not been fortunate in his family life. His mother died when he was seven, and four years later he himself was brought close to death by an attack of infantile paralysis, which had left him with a limp. There were other consequences of that long illness, less conspicuous than his disability. The weak muscles of his wasted leg left him unable to control his father's highly-bred horses, which were quick to sense his insecurity. Captain Mark Fletcher had hoped for a son who would be as much at home in the saddle as himself, able one day to take over the management of the stud. He had not wasted much sympathy on a boy who at the age of eleven had been normally healthy and energetic but found himself in his teens not only crippled but cut off from the friendship of his schoolmates by his inability to play games. Instead, Captain Fletcher had been contemptuous of his son's frequent falls when he tried to play a part in the schooling of the horses; the desperation with which Daniel was trying to regain his father's good opinion struck no responsive chord. Captain Fletcher left the boy to be raised by servants, making no secret of the fact that he was more interested in his horses than in his son.

Coldness and neglect drove Daniel from home as soon as he was old enough to earn his own living. He started his working life as a travelling salesman for the furniture business in which he was now a partner and sales director.

He had married young, hoping to establish in a home of his own the kind of warm family life lacking in his boyhood. But for a second time he was cheated. His wife, growing bored with the company of only a baby daughter while he was away on the road, had been regularly unfaithful to him. He discovered this only when she proved unable to break the habit after his promotion to a desk job in the Atlanta sales office. Seeing no reason to be gentlemanly about the divorce which followed, he had managed, after a long wrangle, to persuade the judge that his wife was unfit to bring up a daughter.

So Agnes had lived with him until her marriage. Her sweet nature had brought a reconciliation of a sort between Daniel and his father; for Captain Fletcher soon realized that if he wished to be loved by his only grandchild he would have to be polite to his son. Even after Agnes left home she had remained affectionately close to her father. When her first baby was born, and then a second, it seemed to Daniel that at last, in his fifties, he was being offered a taste of the happy relationships which other people took for granted. But now this new blow had fallen. Was it any wonder that he choked with rage whenever he thought about it! Agnes and her children were all the family he owned, and all the love of which he was capable was concentrated on them. He would do anything in the world if it would make her happy. One of the hardest facts to accept in the present tragedy was that there *was* nothing in the world which would comfort her.

For three weeks after the news of the arrest, Daniel's emotions churned in his head and stomach until at last, late in November, he could bear it no longer. A feeling of helplessness combined with a bitter hatred of the man who had murdered his grandson to drive Daniel out of his own house. Happy memories of past family reunions had made a mockery of this year's Thanksgiving. The prospect of spending the remainder of the long weekend in such a gloomy atmosphere was unendurable – and Agnes would not be alone, because Harry was with her. Daniel pointed the Packard west and began the five-hundred-mile drive towards Natchez.

Soon after he had crossed the state line into Mississippi he pulled up to stretch his legs. Only when he needed to run did he think of himself as crippled. Driving caused him no discomfort, but he knew that unless he took the precaution of moving around for a few minutes every couple of hours he would find himself painfully stiff at the end of the day. He lit a cigarette and drew on it while he paced up and down the side of the road, trying to recall what he knew of Natchez.

His years as a traveller were far behind him. He still retained his talent for salesmanship – although the semi-retirement of his partner meant that Daniel effectively ran the whole business – and his workshops continued to turn out solid furniture of old-fashioned quality, of which he could feel proud. But he rarely now visited his customers in their stores. It was more effective, he had discovered, to offer them an expenses-paid visit to Atlanta, where they could inspect all the new stock and have a night or two on the town. His salesmen, following up to take orders, would not fail to point out that such invitations were reserved for the biggest spenders.

Even in his travelling days, though, he had wasted little of his time in Natchez. The citizens of that shabby old town had acquired their furniture in the eighteen-fifties and sixties. It was made to last, and its owners had neither the cash nor the desire to exchange their substantial mahogany pieces for modern veneers. So his journey was taking him into almost unknown territory.

He had promised himself that he would wait for the result of the trial before he took revenge on Danny's murderer. Although there seemed little doubt that the man now in police custody was guilty, justice demanded that a defence should be heard and a verdict pronounced. But the processes of law moved too slowly for an impatient man. Frustration at his inability to comfort his daughter had driven him from home, and a different kind of frustration prompted him to take an advance look at Thomas Vernon's house. Once in Natchez he could form some plan of action, and then the necessary weeks of waiting would be made tolerable by the contemplation of what he proposed to do. Except where Agnes and her children were concerned, Daniel was a hard man, a man who remembered slights and bore grudges. He had not, for example, allowed the passage of twenty years to soften his attitude towards his ex-wife, but resisted all her applications for an increase in alimony payments as his prosperity increased. Although he attended church regularly, he was not greatly influenced by exhortations to 'Love your enemies.' More to the point at this moment was the thought of taking an eye for an eye, a tooth for a tooth. There could be no such exact reprisal in this case, of course; but he intended to find something that would hurt.

At the same time he hoped that his visit to Thomas Vernon's house would throw light on the man's motive for what appeared to be a motiveless – although premeditated – crime. In a general way, Daniel reckoned to understand people. The whole art of salesmanship lay in an instant perception of a customer's hidden needs, and Daniel was a first-rate salesman. He was not clever in the way that his scientist son-in-law, Harry, was clever. But he was as sharp, and had as much common sense, as the next man. Although he was bewildered by what had happened, he did not put that mystification down to his own stupidity. If any explanation for the crime existed he would be able to understand it. It was because he did not yet understand that he would have to control his anger on this first visit, in case after all there had been some terrible mistake on the part of the police, some wild coincidence which had brought Vernon innocently to the scene of someone else's crime.

As far as Daniel was able to discover, Thomas Vernon's life until October 1924 had been blameless and uneventful. He had worked for the same employer for almost fifty years, living throughout that period with an elder sister, who was a pillar of her local community and who remained firmly convinced of her brother's innocence. It seemed possible that he was not particularly intelligent, but none of the neighbours persuaded by newspaper reporters to gossip had suggested that he was mad, or even subnormal. And even were he to be certified insane, there had been such method in his madness that there must be some fact, so far unrevealed, which would explain it. The questions and possibilities disturbed Daniel's mind as he resumed his journey. Recognizing his tiredness, he stopped for the night at a hotel just outside Meridian.

A storm broke overhead as he drove on again the next day. By the time he approached Natchez, the pot-holes and hollows of the low-grade road remained dangerously flooded by standing water, even after the sudden cloud-burst came to an equally sudden end. Daniel drove through the centre of the town cautiously but without pausing. He did not need to ask for directions, as Thomas Vernon had done in Manchester, because one of the newspaper reports published after Vernon's arrest had usefully included a sketch map showing the whereabouts of the suspect's home.

The gate of The Round House had fallen off one of its hinges and stood permanently ajar, but the path which led through woodland towards the house was too narrow to allow the Packard an unscratched passage. Daniel parked at the side of the dirt road and began to walk up the rough, uncared-for approach. On either side of the muddy path, grey-green Spanish moss hung like stage cobwebs from the trees. It created a spooky atmosphere, encouraging the feeling that at any moment he might step through some invisible barrier and stumble across a skeleton or a heap of dust inside an empty tomb.

The reality was quite the opposite. The track, which had been winding upward through a steep gradient, straightened as it reached level ground. With incredulous eyes Daniel found himself confronted by a palace: as though he were not so much an explorer discovering an unmapped ruin as a prince about to awaken a sleeping beauty.

On closer inspection, the building proved to be only superficially palatial. The huge dome, glistening with the recent rain, was magnificent. But many of the windows below were boarded up, and the wooden verandas were clearly rotting. Daniel was still staring curiously when he heard the sound of running feet behind him. They belonged to a little girl, eight or nine years old, who showed no alarm at seeing him but paused, panting, to inform him that she was late for her Saturday lesson. Daniel watched as she ran on again and, ignoring the porticoed front entrance of the house, scuttled down some steps at the side. A moment or two later a young boy emerged from the same doorway. He too began to run, but with the exuberance of release rather than in a fluster at being late. Daniel waited until he had disappeared from sight. Then he moved quietly towards the house.

2

'You're late.' Louise twirled the piano stool to give it an extra inch of height. She spoke without surprise or annoyance. Christy Bainton was always late. 'Scale of F. Right hand.'

Stiff fingers thumped up the scale and down again, stumbled through another – clearly unpractised – and progressed with relief to a familiar piece, banging out a soldier's march with ferocious concentration but little musical feeling. Louise sat just behind her pupil's shoulder. In one hand she held a small stick with which she tapped out the beat, encouraging Christy to keep in time; once she used it to rap the girl's knuckles when a mistake was repeated for a third time. Occasionally she leaned forward to demonstrate how the music should be played. At such times she could see herself reflected in the highly polished wood of the grand piano: an elderly, scrawny, shabby woman with thin grey hair scraped back into a straggling bun. From time to time in the past – but not more than once every five years or so – she had recognized talent in a pupil, and then it was difficult not to study her own reflection with sadness, remembering her childhood dreams and ambitions and the fervent enthusiasm with which she had practised on this same piano. But such memories did not disturb her when she was teaching a girl like Christy, who would never amount to anything. She gave the lesson only routine attention.

Unexpectedly, her attention was distracted. Had she heard a sound more subtle than that of Christy's thumping fingers? Hardly a sound, even; merely a disturbance of the air. She lifted her head slightly, listening, and her eyes were caught by the sight of a soft film of reddish dust settling on the bass keys of the piano.

Louise looked up. In the original plan for the house, the central area in which the grand piano now stood would have been an ornamental pond, and a circle had been cut out of the floor above to provide a railed gallery. The rail had never been fitted and the open circle had proved draughty. Many years ago planks had been roughly laid across it and covered with layers of paper and scraps of old carpet. Louise never bothered to clean the top of the house, but its dirt did not as a rule trespass into her living quarters. Was there, she wondered, a rat scurrying about up there, its weight just sufficient to tilt down an edge of the makeshift covering? Louise had been waging a running battle against rats ever since she was first put in charge of the henhouse at the age of ten. She made a mental note to lay poison in the upper regions of the house that evening. But for the time being she returned her concentration to the lesson. Christy Bainton would never be a pianist, but she must be given value for her father's money.

Christy was her last pupil for the day. For a few moments after the child had left, Louise sat without moving, tired and depressed. Thomas was not much in the way of company when he was home, but his absence had brought a curious emptiness to the house. Yet *was* it empty? For a second time within the half hour she had a feeling, without being able to point to any movement or sound, that there was something or someone nearby. A snake taking refuge in the woodwork from last night's storm? Or a human intruder, holding his breath? She listened with an unusual intentness, but heard nothing. Shrugging it off, because she was not a woman to scream at shadows, she pulled a piece of music from the stack in front of her and set it up.

For a few seconds she sat quite still, collecting herself. Then she embarked on what was so much a performance that she might have been deliberately playing for the benefit of the rat or snake or whatever it was that had almost imperceptibly disturbed the atmosphere. Her head bobbed with the effort and her calloused, brown-spotted hands seemed to take on a life of their own. They crashed down in forceful chords, they sparkled and danced over the keys and then, towards the end of the work, they became peaceful again, stroking the music out of the piano with a loving gentleness.

'Louise!'

Startled by the sound of her friend's voice, Louise stopped playing in the middle of a phrase and stood up. 'Gracious, Dorothy, don't tell me it's time already.'

'I've been waiting at your gate since I saw Christy Bainton running down the road. But I know what you're like when you sit down at that piano.'

'Make yourself comfortable a minute. I picked everything we needed first thing this morning.' One of Louise's most cherished responsibilities was that of overseeing the floral decoration of the church. At this time of year the smaller gardens in the centre of the town had little to offer, but there was never any shortage of berries or evergreen foliage in the woodland which encircled The Round House. Whilst Dorothy sat down in the parlour to wait, Louise went into one of the many small kitchen cubicles originally designed for the use of the house slaves. She lifted the branches out of the deep sink in which they had been soaking and searched around for string to tie them.

Dorothy, raising her voice so that it would carry, had news to tell. ''Nother of those reporter fellows snooping around this morning. Asking about Thomas at the bank, I heard say.'

'Then Mr Bannerman had better have spoken the truth in his answering. Thomas had nothing to do with those evil things, and it's high time that all this asking and telling stopped.' Louise expressed her feelings through the vehemence with which she shook the foliage free of water.

'Sure as houses, Mr Bannerman will have told them that very thing.' But Dorothy stood up and came to stand in the kitchen. 'Don't it puzzle you, though, Louise, Thomas going all that way, and being there . . .? Don't you get to wondering . . .?'

Louise straightened up and turned to look Dorothy straight in the eyes. 'There's many a time I've told Thomas he hasn't the brains he was born with,' she said. 'He's as idle as a fat cat and all his fingers are thumbs. But he hasn't an ounce of spite or murder in the whole of his body. The day he tells me with his own voice that he set a light to that poor woman's house, that day I'll believe it. But until then . . . why, Dorothy, I couldn't stay here a moment longer if I thought he could do such a thing. Couldn't hold up my head. It will come out in the trial, the mistake that somebody's made.'

She gave one last vigorous shake and then gave the branches to her friend to hold while she put on her hat and coat. Together the two women climbed the steps up from the basement and set off down the drive. Louise did not lock the door when she left the house: it was not the custom.

3

Daniel Fletcher heard the door close as Miss Vernon and her friend left the house. For the past half hour he had been standing almost immediately above the piano, listening to the perfunctory words which punctuated the lesson and the more interesting conversation which followed. Now it would be safe to move around. To start with, he studied more intently than before the barn of a place into which he had intruded, with its lofty dome rising above a clutter of untrimmed beams. It didn't make sense, but there was no need to bother with it, for clearly this part of the building was not in use.

An instinctive sense of trespass compelled him to tread softly as he made his way down to the basement, although there was no one to hear. Smiling with a grim satisfaction to find himself alone and in control of his enemy's home, he explored the circular living quarters, looking for anything which might provide a clue to Thomas Vernon's behaviour. But the shabby rooms – with a book of daily bible readings on each bedside table – revealed only that the brother and sister were poor and devout. The sole object of any value was the grand piano. Daniel, who had spent all his working life selling furniture, recognized the superior quality of both the wood and the workmanship. But he had heard enough to be sure that the piano belonged to Miss Vernon: it could tell him nothing about her brother.

Seeking an explanation for his grandson's death was only a small part of Daniel's motive for making the journey. More powerful by far was his wish to hurt, as he and Agnes had been hurt. The smile faded from his lips as he made his way back to the higher floor and considered the exposed timber from a new point of view. It would burn. Faster even than in the Vermont clapboard house, flames would leap up the wooden walls and bring the whole structure crashing down. What a fitting revenge that would provide!

Daniel Fletcher was an unforgiving man, and prepared to be ruthless. Nevertheless, he had resolved to wait until after the trial before taking any action, and he held to that resolve. The certainty with which Miss Vernon had proclaimed her brother's innocence was unsettling. It was hard to believe that a woman who spoke so calmly and played music so peacefully could be troubled in her conscience about what had happened. The obvious sincerity of her opinion proved nothing, of course, but Daniel allowed to himself that the possibility of a mistake did exist. To take revenge against the wrong man would leave the real villain unpunished. Until he was sure, Daniel must hold his hand.

Besides, he had left the Packard where anyone could see it – not conspicuously parked, but not concealed either. Miss Vernon and her friend and her two pupils would all have walked past it. They would think nothing of it as long as the day continued uneventful, but if something dramatic were to happen . . . The boy, for sure, would have stopped to take a good look and would describe what he saw. Daniel let himself out of the house, spent ten minutes exploring its immediate surroundings and then walked slowly back to the road.

In a sense, the long drive had been for nothing; a waste of time. Certainly Daniel had learned nothing to solve the puzzle of Thomas Vernon's behaviour. He would have to hope that a spell in jail would loosen the murderer's tongue and persuade him to provide some kind of explanation, if only as a plea in mitigation. But Daniel was, nevertheless, contented with his journey. Now he knew where to come and what he would find. If the trial went as he expected, he would return. And his next visit would not be so uneventful.

EPISODE THREE

1925

A Grandfather's Revenge

1

A week after Thomas Vernon was sentenced to imprisonment for life, Daniel Fletcher kissed his daughter and grandson goodbye. 'Look after them' he said to his son-in-law, making no attempt to disguise his low spirits. He understood, in a way, why Harry had chosen to accept a university appointment in England rather than an equally prestigious post at Harvard. When the offer was first made, before the fire, Agnes had been reluctant to consider such a move, but now she was choosing to put as much distance as possible between herself and New England. For the rest of her life the bright flame colours of autumn leaves would remind her of the actual flames which had attracted attention only when it was too late; she would never be able to walk down a village street of white clapboard houses, happy family homes, without visualizing the charred ruin of her own home.

Yes, it made sense that she and Harry should want to move far away from their unhappy memories, but that was not much comfort to Daniel. He would be lucky now if he saw young Alex once in every two or three years, and then only for a few weeks. Nor was he likely to acquire any more grandchildren. Agnes, made listless by grief, had said in so many words that she did not intend to bring any more babies into the world to be the victims of maniacs.

In the four months since her son's death Agnes seemed to have aged ten years. She had lost weight, and ceased to care about her appearance, allowing her hair to hang lankly around her pale face. She had no household responsibilities in her father's home because the housekeeper whom Daniel first employed at the time of his divorce had remained with him ever since. But instead of devoting her time to Alex, depression had made Agnes so lethargic that she would sit for hours without moving, unwilling or unable to act as a mother. Daniel had persuaded her to visit a psychiatrist, but three months of treatment had not lifted her depression. He himself had felt helpless throughout that period – desperate to comfort her but unable to see any means of achieving this.

So his heart was heavy as he saw the little family on to the train and waved as it moved slowly out of Atlanta. They would spend a day or two with Harry's family in Richmond before setting sail from Norfolk; but as far as Daniel was concerned, he had lost them already. He was unable to bring himself to return at once to his empty house. Instead, angry as well as lonely, he drove for a second time to Natchez.

If there had ever been any doubt in his mind, it had been dispelled by the evidence produced at the trial. Thomas Vernon had caused the death of Danny Kiernan – but was not going to pay the full price for it. He had remained mute throughout the trial, refusing to give any information or help to his own lawyer, and the motive behind his actions remained incomprehensible. But although the prosecutor had been unable to prove any intention that the fourteen-month-old baby should die in the fire, the circumstantial evidence was so strong that the jury unanimously found the defendant guilty of murder as well as of arson. At first Daniel had been outraged by the leniency of a mere life sentence. Only when his bitterness had simmered for a few days did be begin to feel that the electric chair would have provided too easy a way out for the killer. It was better that Vernon should have years in which to undergo humiliation and hardship whilst Agnes and Harry and Daniel himself were suffering bereavement.

All the same, given the chance, Daniel would willingly have strangled the murderer with his own bare hands. But he never would have the opportunity. Thomas Vernon, behind bars, was safe from his vengeance.

Daniel's wish to hurt his enemy was as intense as his need to compensate Agnes in some way for the hurt done to her. The more impossible it appeared for him to put either wish into practice, the more sourly did his hatred and frustration stew in his stomach. As he drove towards Natchez the two problems – how to take revenge on Vernon and how to make his daughter happy again – churned over and over in his mind. Even if it were no more than a gesture, a token, something must be done to show that the mere loss of liberty was insufficient payment for the death of a child.

With Thomas Vernon out of his reach, what alternatives were there? Well, there was the sister. Not to kill, of course. Tempting though it might seem to take an exact revenge by burning down The Round House in a way which would trap the old lady inside it, that would be the choice of a madman. The possibility of setting the house on fire had suggested itself to Daniel on his first visit; but common sense reminded him that the coincidence of two fires, two deaths, would be suspicious enough to alert even the most stupid detective, and a search for motives would lead the trail straight to Daniel's door. He had no intention of putting himself at any risk by his choice of revenge; so there must be no more arson or killing. But that didn't mean that he was going to leave the house after this second visit as meekly as before.

He thought about the old lady: music teacher, flower arranger, pillar of the church. From the evidence given at her brother's trial had emerged a picture of the life which Thomas and Louise Vernon had led – a life in which poverty was kept at bay only by a considerable degree of self-sufficiency, and was made bearable by the knowledge that almost the whole of their little community had existed for more than half a century in the same straitened circumstances. Someone who possessed so little in the way of material things could be most hurtfully attacked through her reputation, but how? Daniel checked the question, because he no longer needed an answer to it. He had remembered that in that shabby basement home was one object which was not only beautiful and perhaps valuable but was also beloved. He could hurt Louise Vernon by wrecking her piano. He bore no grudge against Miss Vernon herself, but to hit at her would indirectly be an attack on her brother. In jail, unable to do anything to help or defend his sister, Thomas Vernon would realize uneasily that she was at the mercy of an unknown enemy who might break into the house for a second time to injure more than just a piece of furniture.

So that was the answer. Daniel's spirits were lightened by the mere satisfaction of having made a plan. He would wait until the house was left empty for an hour or two, and then he would smash the piano to pieces.

This time he left the Packard well away from the entrance to The Round House and took on foot what he rightly reckoned to be a short cut across the grounds. So tall were the trees, and so densely clustered, that he did not catch even a glimpse of the mansion until he was almost upon it, blinking in the bright light as he stepped from the gloom of the woods into the more open area around the house.

Even within the few months since his previous visit the condition of this cleared area had deteriorated. Weeds had surged across the vegetable plot and flower beds, smothering crops which had been left, unharvested, to rot, and strangling the rose bushes which once provided the decoration for weddings and baptisms in Louise Vernon's church.

Daniel paused, listening, before approaching the house, but he was already sure that no one was about. There was an emptiness in the air which proclaimed the house to be unoccupied. In a village street or apartment block a woman whose family had been disgraced might shut herself away from neighbours behind closed shades, pretending not to be at home in case fingers should point at her. But The Round House was too remote for such a precaution to be necessary. If its owner were here, she would be playing the piano or else bustling about her household chores. Quietly, but not furtively, Daniel went down the staircase and turned the handle of the door which had admitted him on his previous visit. It was locked.

That was a surprise. Miss Vernon had not locked it on the previous occasion when she supposed herself to be leaving the house empty. Daniel rattled it vigorously before moving with his limping stride round to the front of the house and up the wide stone steps. But the main door, behind the colonnaded portico, had clearly not been opened for many months, or even years. Daniel wasted no time on it. There was a dilapidated wooden hut at the edge of the vegetable area which was likely to contain an axe for chopping firewood. He was on his way to look there when he heard the sound of chattering voices. There was just time to step back into the woodland, with its concealing screens of Spanish moss, before a woman and two young children came into sight.

Iris Lindsay walked slowly up the unkempt approach to The Round House. Six-year-old Peter tugged impatiently at her left hand, trying to hurry her along; but Russell, on her right, was trailing behind, his short legs stumbling over the rough ground. He was getting on for two years old; in the awkward stage of being perfectly well able to walk – and in any case too heavy to be carried for long at a time, especially by Iris in her present condition – but slow, and quick to tire. For the moment, though, Iris was content to move at Russell's pace, so that her husband could catch them up when he had collected the keys to the house from a neighbour.

They rounded a bend and Peter stopped dead, his eyes widening. Iris too came to a halt, staring in astonishment at the great golden dome. Only Russell, staring steadfastly at the path so that he could see where his feet were going, continued to plod on, releasing his mother's hand as he overtook her.

'Is this it?' asked Peter.

'Must be.'

'You never told me.'

'I didn't know. Quite something, isn't it?' Everything about the trip was coming as a surprise to Iris. It was Elliott, her husband, who had received out of the blue a letter from someone who claimed to be his great-aunt. Although he was already aware that his father, Tom, had been adopted into the Lindsay family as a baby, no one had ever previously told him about his blood relations. Iris had been as fascinated as her husband by the story of the young girl who had travelled so far from home to have her baby and who had died so tragically soon after. Now, his great-aunt Louise told him, the house in which his grandmother had lived must be sold. If he wanted it for himself, he would naturally be given the first chance to buy. He might in any case, she suggested, like to take a look at Rebecca Vernon's home. Elliot had jumped at the opportunity and Iris went along with his enthusiasm because it provided the excuse for a trip from Honolulu to the mainland. Now a genuine interest quickened her pace as she moved on again.

'Are we going to live here?' asked Peter. Peter had started to ask questions at the age of three and had not stopped since. Iris hoped that it was a sign of intelligence, but she would be glad when the non-stop interrogation slackened.

'No,' she told him. 'You wouldn't find this as comfortable as the ranch. There's no pool. And the ocean's hundreds of miles away.'

'If we're not going to buy the house, why are we looking at it?'

'Because it belongs to your father's family.'

'If they're family, how come they've never asked us to visit with them?'

'We live too far away.' The true story of the child widow who had died was not for a six-year-old.

Elliott and the elderly lady who had been entrusted with the key of The Round House caught up with Iris just as she reached the foot of the stone steps. There were a few moments of introduction before Miss Price indicated that they would enter the house not through the grand portico but by a modest side entrance. They moved slowly, in a group, towards it.

'You could have knocked me down with a feather, Mr Lindsay, when I heard you were coming and who you were,' Miss Price told them. 'None of us ever knew that Louise and Thomas had any kin in the wide world save for their cousin in the Delta.'

It was even more of a surprise for us, Iris thought, but she did not speak the words aloud. She could tell that Elliott was not proposing to volunteer information to someone who might be a gossip. Instead, he asked, 'That's the cousin she's gone to live with, is it? We'll be seeing her there tomorrow.'

'There was no call for her to quit.' The neighbour spoke heatedly, allowing the key to slip back into her pocket as though she had quite forgotten the purpose of their meeting. 'Not a soul here would have spoken a word against her, or held her a mite responsible for anything that her brother did. But she couldn't bear the shame of it – of knowing that everyone knew.'

'It must have been a tough time for her. Waiting so long for the trial, and then hearing the verdict.'

'Didn't seem to worry her to start with,' Miss Price told them. 'She just reckoned for sure that her brother could never have done such a terrible thing.'

Frowning slightly at her husband, Iris interrupted the conversation. Peter understood a lot more than people expected, and if there was one thing she didn't want, it was for news of the family's link with such a crime to reach their friends in the islands.

'Peter, why don't you see if you can run right round the house on the lanai,' she suggested, using the word for the veranda with which he was familiar. Only when he was out of earshot did she indicate that the subject could be discussed further. 'So the verdict must have come as a great shock.'

'She left here before the trial ever began, so we didn't get to see how she took it. She had a letter from her brother one morning, or so I heard tell, and by the evening she was gone. Guess there must have been something he told her that wouldn't let her believe any longer that it was all a mistake. Well now, you-all don't want to stand outside here the whole day.' She went down the steps to unlock the side door; but before Iris had time to follow, Peter returned, panting, from his circumambulation of the house.

'Mom, can me and Russ go exploring? There's a shed, and a hen-house, and all kind of things.'

Iris looked around, considering possible dangers. 'Don't you go in amongst those trees,' she said. 'There could be snakes. Or you might get lost. Stay where you can see the house all the time. Keep hold of Russ. He's too little to look after himself in a strange place. And don't let him put anything in his mouth. Do you hear?' She watched for a moment as the two boys went off hand in hand. Then she joined Elliott and Miss Price in the basement of The Round House.

The air was musty, smelling of damp. Iris, who was four months pregnant, had until now suffered from nausea only when she left her bed in the morning. But the stench of decay brought a bitter bile to her mouth and she was forced to sit down for a moment, staring speechlessly at the shabby furniture, the faded wall coverings, the tattered rugs. How could Louise and Thomas Vernon have endured to spend their whole lives in such a dump!

'I'll leave you folk to yourselves,' Miss Price said tactfully. 'Louise said to tell you to take away anything you've a fancy for. She has her clothes with her, and she never wants to see any of the rest again. If you'll lock up when you've finished here and bring the key back to me, I'll have coffee and brownies waiting for you. All that travelling, you look tired.'

'Thank you,' said Iris. She waited until the neighbour had left and then moved to the centre of the circular basement and sat down again, this time on the piano stool. Ringed around by trash, the grand piano was startling in its quality; its smooth and highly-polished surface showed that many years of devoted care had been devoted to it. It seemed surprising that such a treasure should have been abandoned, as though it had no more significance than any of the rubbish, but Iris soon realized that it could not be removed from the building without breaking through a wall. She played a few bars of syncopated rhythm but then stopped, aware that jazz was somehow inappropriate to such an instrument. 'What are you looking for?' she called to Elliott, hearing the opening and closing of drawers in one of the musty rooms.

'Miss Vernon said . . .'

'You mean Great-aunt Louise said,' interrupted Iris, laughing as she wandered across to join him, because she found it as difficult as her husband to accept the idea of a relationship with these reclusive old people.

'Right,' agreed Elliott. 'Great-aunt Louise said there were some letters from my grandmother to her mother. About life in the islands sixty years ago. Could be interesting. She said to help myself; like the neighbour told us. Why don't you take a look at the china while I'm fishing around? I reckon some of this could be antique.'

'This junk!' Iris laughed scornfully. But Elliott had a point, all the same. This was just the sort of family which might have stocked a home in the years before the civil war and never thrown anything away. She took a moment to look out of the house, checking that the boys were safe and happy, and smiled to see them holding out handfuls of grass to a goat. The wary look in Russell's eyes suggested that he would be alarmed if the goat ever advanced to be fed; but the goat was equally nervous and kept a safe distance. She went back inside to see what she could find.

Iris – who would still only be twenty-five when her third baby was born – had inherited a fortune from her mother while she was still a child; and on her wedding day her father had settled on her all the land he owned in Kauai, with the promise of more property to come after his death. She had married a man, a few years older than herself, who was already wealthy from his family's trading interests. Elliott needed no help from her in earning money, so she had set herself the task of spending it to beautify their new house. Shuttled for ten of her most formative years between two divorced parents and two hemispheres, she had inherited a passion for gardening from her father in Hawaii and an informed taste and eye for artistic excellence from her mother in Paris. Even before the ranch house had been topped out, she had taken advantage of its dramatic position on the rim of the Nuuana Valley to create a landscaped garden which was maturing with tropical speed. Now she was working to make the interior of the house as interesting as its surroundings.

Left to herself, she would have built up a collection of antiques only from China and Europe; but Elliott had expressed an interest in the early agricultural and farmhouse tools and furnishings of mainland America, and she had willingly added these to her mental shopping list. She was lifting each plate in turn down from the kitchen shelves in order to look for its marks when she became aware that Peter had come silently into the house and was waiting to be noticed.

'Where's Russ?' she asked automatically.

'We were playing hide'n seek.' Peter's expression was sheepish, or even guilty.

Iris gave him her full attention, alert to a possible need for alarm. 'Are you telling me that you can't find him?'

'I found him easy enough. You know how he is about hiding. He keeps bobbing out to see if you're coming the right way. But then it was my turn to hide, and he can't find me.'

Iris frowned slightly, not sure that she understood what had happened. But the point of Peter's confession was clear enough. 'You were supposed to look after him,' she said; but there would be time enough for reproaches later. She was not seriously frightened. Russell was still young enough to be timid rather than rashly adventurous. Knowing that his mother was still inside the house, he would not wander far away. 'Come and show me where you were playing,' she said, and led the way outside.

3

From his hiding place just inside the tangle of shrubs and trees, Daniel Fletcher overheard enough of the conversation between the neighbour and the visiting family to fume with frustration. He was too late. By abandoning her beloved piano Louise Vernon had robbed Daniel of the pleasure of depriving her of it. He would have to find another way of avenging the death of his grandson.

He studied the visitors as they waited to be taken inside the house. The man, in his thirties, was well-dressed and good-looking, with thick fair hair above a tanned face. He was a big man, but solid with muscle rather than fat. A solid citizen in every respect, Daniel guessed from the clues of his polite but confident behaviour.

His wife made a livelier impression, with bright brown eyes and a wide mouth which was quick to smile. Her dark hair was bobbed and waved in the latest style and she wore high-heeled strap shoes and sheer silk stockings – not the most suitable choice for exploring such a run-down property, but no doubt the roughness of the long approach had taken her by surprise. She had a petite figure, emphasized by the narrowness of her dress, which fell straight to a dropped waistline before gaining fullness from fine pleats. But although her small, slim body revealed no visible sign of pregnancy, Daniel was nevertheless sure that she was expecting another baby. There was something about the way she walked, setting her feet more widely apart than normal, which reminded him of Agnes's gait when little Danny was on the way.

The memory of Danny made Daniel groan aloud as the little group moved down the steps and into the house. Agnes, he was sure, would have no more babies; he would never again see her eyes shining brightly with happiness and expectation, as the eyes of this woman shone. And Alex would be an only child, over-cosseted, never holding a young brother protectively by the hand as Peter Lindsay, running out of the house again, now held his brother, Russell.

How unfair it was that the Vernons and their relatives should be happy! Well, maybe Thomas Vernon was not precisely happy in his prison cell. But – safe from Daniel's vengeance – he could feel content in the knowledge that his sister was being cared for by her cousin. And Louise, it seemed, would soon be enjoying a family visit. She would take pleasure in the company of two lively little boys and look forward to the arrival of a third; whilst Agnes, whilst he himself . . . oh, it was an unfairness not to be endured. Strong though his wish for revenge might be, Daniel did not even consider the possibility of killing a child. But as he watched the two energetic boys chasing a goat and then running to explore the grounds, his whole being concentrated itself into a single channel of hatred, a desire to hurt in the way that his daughter, and he himself, had been hurt.

After a while the two boys stopped dashing about and began to play a hiding game. Peter ran up the wide stone steps which led to the portico of the mansion: he put his hands over his eyes and began to count aloud. Daniel was forced to move deeper into the wooded wilderness as Russell came trotting up to hide behind a tree on the verge. He was an attractive little boy, with his father's fair hair and the chubbiness of a toddler who had not too long before emerged from babyhood. If Danny had lived he would be now be only a few months younger than this child who was bouncing up and down with impatience to be found.

'Coming!' cried Peter; and then, as he began to prowl around the house, 'Where are you?' Daniel could hear Russell chuckling with pleasure at the game; he ran out of his hiding place, happy to be caught, as soon as the question was repeated. Then it was his turn to close his eyes. Peter, no doubt guessing that his young brother would peep, ran into the wood close to where Daniel stood, before using its shelter to conceal him as he made his way round to the other side of the house and hid in a dilapidated wooden shed.

Too young to count, Russell came after him almost at once, returning to his own previous hiding place before pausing uncertainly. Perhaps Daniel himself made a movement; or perhaps some bird, alarmed by their nearness, stirred in the leaves. Whatever the cause of the sound, it brought a look of triumph to Russell's face. Stepping carefully over creepers which lay along the ground, he made his way further into the woodland.

If he comes past me, thought Daniel, I could pick him up and take him away. A child for a child. Such a snatch would not set things right, for nothing could bring Danny back to life again; but it would relieve the bitterness of inactivity, the frustration of being unable to think of any positive action which would help his own family or hit at Thomas Vernon's. But as Russell went past him, Daniel restrained himself from stretching out the hand which could have held the boy back. There was a likeness between this child and the younger boy who had died. Nothing more specific than the softness of an unformed face, the fairness of hair which later might darken, but enough to make the idea of hurting him inconceivable. Instead, as protective as though Russell were his own beloved grandson, Daniel followed a little way behind to make sure that he came to no harm.

It had been an animal – the goat which the boys had tried to feed a little earlier – whose movement had deceived Russell into thinking that he had heard his elder brother: Daniel caught a glimpse of its rump disappearing into the thickest part of the woodland just as the little boy stepped on to the narrow path beaten down by its hooves. The path led upwards, to emerge at last into a bare strip of land which fell sharply away on the further side. The open ground was wide enough to be safe for a careful adult, but full of danger for a small child who was plodding along with his head down – no longer excited, but whimpering with anxiety, and hurrying in the hope that he would come more quickly to find his brother or parents. From time to time within the wood he had called out 'Peepee,' which was perhaps the nearest he could come to his brother's name: but now, moving more quickly with no tangle of creepers to trip him, he began to call for his mother.

Daniel came to a halt, listening to the sound of water splashing far below the bluff and aware of the danger as Russell stomped on towards it. How could he warn the child without frightening him and perhaps causing him to run even faster towards the cliff?

'Russell!' he called, taking pains to make his voice light and friendly. 'Peter's this way.'

Russell stopped and turned round, looking doubtfully at the stranger. He had been crying.

'Don't go any further, Russell,' Daniel said. 'You might fall over the edge. Come this way. I'll take you back to find Peter.' He began to move forward slowly, judging that the little boy's uncertainty would keep him rooted to the spot rather than cause him to run. Smiling, he held out his arms as any grandfather might do to welcome a grandson into his embrace. Russell did not run forward, but neither did he flinch away. Instead, he allowed himself to be picked up.

'Let's go look for Peter,' Daniel said, but he did not move at once. Without his intervention, Russell Lindsay might well have fallen to his death from the edge of the cliff. A life saved belonged, in a sense, to its saviour. Merely to return the little boy to his parents would be to display not self-restraint but spinelessness. Daniel's heart swelled with triumph as he realized that it was in his power to take a true revenge. He had resisted temptation once, but now fate had offered him a second chance.

The plan forming in his mind was inspired by hatred. He was glad to think that Louise Vernon's visitors would arrive not in happy excitement but in distress, and that Thomas Vernon would learn through letters how a family felt when it was bereaved. But love provided a motive of almost equal strength. If Daniel could find the right words, taking care not to present a strange boy as a substitute for a beloved son, Russell's very helplessness might help to break through the stiff armour of distress which since the tragedy had prevented Agnes from showing warmth even to her elder son, for fear that she might be robbed of him as well. Russell was innocent of any responsibility for his great-great-uncle's crime, but to steal him from his family would not necessarily give him a worse life: merely a different one.

Daniel made up his mind. There would be no need ever to feel guilt. Had he not been on the spot, the little boy's body might by now be floating down the river. A mother so careless of a precious life deserved to suffer loss.

'You came a long way all by yourself,' he said admiringly to Russell. 'Means it's going to be a long way back again. And I guess you're tired. How about taking a ride in my motor-car? That'll get us back faster, won't it? Come on, then, let's go find it.' He swung Russell up on to his shoulders and ran with a galloping motion which concealed his limp down a track which led not towards the house but to the road. It was all too easy.

4

By the time they reached Norfolk, Daniel was exhausted. He had not dared to take Russell on to a train, nor to book into a hotel at the end of each day's driving, for fear that police enquiries might track him down. The boy had slept on the back seat of the car, but Daniel himself dozed only fitfully.

As for Russell, he soon ceased to resemble the well-scrubbed, well-dressed son of wealthy parents who had trotted into the woodland near The Round House. In the course of the tedious thousand-mile journey he had been sick, had cried, had spilt food and drink over his clothes and had provided evidence that he still needed to wear diapers at night. It was perhaps only imagination, but unhappiness at being parted from his mother had made him within the first day look less chubby; the very shape of his face seemed to have changed. By the time they reached the port there was little danger that any police officer looking out for Russell Lindsay would recognize him in this filthy, smelly, snivelling brat.

They arrived only just in time. In the hotel room where Harry and Agnes and Alex had spent their last night on American soil, Harry was already strapping up the trunks when Daniel appeared to startle them all. 'What goes on?' he asked his father-in-law.

Daniel did not answer the question. 'How long do you have?' he demanded instead.

'Four hours before she sails,' Harry told him. 'But we can go aboard any time now.' They were booked to sail on a cargo ship which carried only a dozen passengers on each crossing of the Atlantic.

'Time for a word, then,' Daniel said. 'Alex, is there something in that bag of yours that two people could play with for half an hour?'

'He's dirty,' said four-year-old Alex, looking at Russell with disapproval rather than sympathy or curiosity.

'Right. *Very* dirty. That's another thing I'm going to ask in a moment or two, whether he could take a bath here. But do you have a picture book to show him? Or a train to run along the floor? Go and play with Alex, Dan?'

'*What* did you call him?' Agnes, white with shock, stared at her father.

'It's not what he was christened,' Daniel said. 'But it's what I want him to be called. I want you to take him with you, Agnes. You're going to be a long way away, you and Harry and Alex, and I shan't be seeing you often again. I'll be thinking of you, though: you know that. And as well as that, I want to be able to think of a boy who carries my name, even though he's not of my blood. I want to think of him happy and laughing, growing up to be a good man in a loving family.'

'You can't expect . . .' Agnes began; and then stopped, on the point of tears. 'What's he supposed to be – a kind of replacement? Do you think I'm going to forget my own baby? Haven't you understood anything at all of how it feels, Dad?'

'I understand all right. But it's not just for your sake that I've brought the boy. Now listen here while I tell you.' He had had plenty of time to prepare his lies as he drove; they rolled smoothly off his tongue. 'Do you remember Martha Nilsson?'

Agnes shook her head. It was not surprising that she should fail to recall a woman who had never existed.

'No, you wouldn't. Reckon she'd be older than you by ten years or more. Her father was a carpenter in our workshop. Dead now, though. Martha moved out to Tennessee and married a coal miner. They'd notched up three children, with a fourth on the way, when her husband was killed in an explosion. Seven men died, she said – there was gas in the mine. The company put her and the children out of the house the next day. Company house, company furniture, even company chickens. Jim had been paid in scrip to be spent at the company store, so she didn't have a cent of savings to her name. By the time the baby was born they were all starving. She left him in a church porch, to be found and taken to an orphanage, so she'd known that at least one of them would be fed and have a roof over his head. It was seeing the children hungry, that was what she couldn't bear. No one would give her a job with a toddler hanging round her skirts. She had an offer of a home with her sister for the two oldest children and herself, but they didn't have room for this one as well. Martha made up her mind that Dan would have to go for adoption as well. She'd fixed to hand him over to an orphan society. She came to see me to ask if

I could let her have the fare to her sister's. Begging for money didn't come easy to her. She'd been to all her friends for help already, and she was pretty well desperate.'

'So what did you do?' asked Agnes.

'I gave her the fare, and something to keep her going in food and clothes while she looked for a job. And tried to get her to hold on to her youngest boy until her luck turned. But she'd screwed herself up to the idea of losing him by then, and she wouldn't budge from it. So I told her, if she was sure, that I could find a home where he'd be looked after and loved. Better than being an orphanage boy. She kissed my hands, she was so grateful. If you could find it in your heart to love this boy, Agnes, it would be a Christian act. Calling him Dan is just for my sake; but adopting him would be a kindness to a stranger. And to Dan himself, of course.'

There was a long silence. Daniel had realized that his daughter's first reaction would be to feel upset. He waited until what seemed the right moment before laughing with a rueful expression on his face. 'Martha's moved on to Chicago by now,' he said. 'If you won't agree to take Dan off my hands, I'm stuck with him. Have pity on your old father, if not on the child.'

Agnes's mouth trembled uncertainly. 'I don't know . . .' she said, looking doubtfully at her husband.

'It wouldn't commit you to anything to put him in the tub,' suggested Harry. 'He stinks.'

The three adults turned towards the corner of the room. Alex, his eyes fixed on his book, was not so much reading as telling the story which he knew off by heart. But the younger boy was no longer listening. Instead, exhausted, he lay flat on his back, asleep, his chubby arms flung out above his head. Agnes stood over him for a moment, looking down. Then, without speaking, she picked him up and carried him to the bathroom.

'Didn't have a chance to ask you in advance.' Daniel realized that he owed his son-in-law an apology.

'It's a queer way of doing things,' said Harry. 'The mother, I mean. But it could be just what Agnes needs. I've done everything I can think of to take her mind off it. But it's not easy, when I feel the same myself. I'd thought of this already – adopting a child. I was going to wait till we were settled in England. And suggest a girl rather than a boy. But that's not important. I'll go along with it, if she will. Sounds like he comes from decent stock. There's only one thing that seems wrong to me, and that's the name.'

'The boy's got no papers,' Daniel pointed out. 'Nothing to show he was born, because Martha had lost whatever she had. And nothing to prove he's adopted, because there wasn't time for formalities if I was to catch you before the boat sailed. So I figured – a baby called Daniel Kiernan has had his birth registered, and he's on your passport still. There's not more than four months' difference, I'd guess. It shows now – but by the time he's five he'll just seem advanced for his age, that's all. There's no need for him to know yet awhile that he's not your own son. You're going to arrive in a new country to start a new life with a wife and two children. Everyone you meet will accept the family as they see it.'

Agnes came back into the room carrying the little boy wrapped in a bath towel. 'Where are his other clothes?' she asked – but guessed the answer from the expression on her father's face. 'For heavens' sakes, Dad, I can't put him back into those filthy rags.'

'I'm taking you shopping,' Daniel said. 'Tuck him up in bed for the moment.'

'There isn't time,' protested Agnes. 'The boat . . .'

'Get your skates on, then,' her father ordered. 'Two hours, Harry, would that be okay? Take the size, Agnes, and be making a list while I drive. We'll buy whatever he needs for the next three weeks and be back within two hours.'

Agnes pulled the bedclothes over the small naked boy who now smelt only of soap. Already he was almost asleep again. 'Momma,' he murmured as Agnes's finger stroked under his chin and tidied a strand of wet hair back off his forehead. He had cried often and bitterly for his mother during the journey north, but it seemed to Daniel that he was ready now to accept comfort from anyone who offered it with love. Agnes, too, already seemed a little less tense and unhappy as she studied the drowsy child for a moment. Then she turned back to her father, and the natural briskness which had been banished by lethargy ever since her bereavement came surging back as she accepted the urgency of the last-minute task.

'What are we waiting for?' she asked. 'Alex, while we're gone, help your daddy to look after little Dan.'

EPISODE FOUR

1940

Salt in the Wound

1

To Daniel Fletcher, lonely in retirement, half crippled with arthritis and alarmed by a recent stroke, the fall of France in the summer of 1940 came as a last straw. Ever since the outbreak of the war in Europe he had done his best to persuade Agnes and Harry that they should return home, distancing themselves from a conflict which was none of their business. But Harry, by now a professor of physics at Cambridge, refused to abandon his work, and Agnes would not leave him.

As for Alex, he had emerged from his English education as an Englishman. Against the advice of his father he had postponed going to university until after the war and instead had volunteered to join the British army straight from school. To complete the transformation, he had married an English girl on his first home leave, and Daniel could expect to have an English great-grandchild before the end of 1940.

Young Dan's attitude towards nationality was different. It was curious that the younger boy, who knew only as much of the United States as he had seen on three vacation visits to Daniel, should have chosen to remain so American. When the letter from his grandfather arrived, it was certain that Dan would vote for a favourable answer to the appeal.

Daniel knew better than to base his pleas on the danger of

bombing or the invasion of England, imminent though both these appeared to be. Instead, he confined his letter to news of his own health. 'It was only a minor incident,' he wrote of the stroke he had suffered. 'Nothing too alarming. A couple of days in the hospital, and a bit of trouble since then finding the right word when I'm talking, that's all. But it's a warning, old Doc Denniston says. Arteries furring up. I'm not as young as I was.' Agnes would know that he was seventy-two. 'I have to expect more strokes in the future. It's the third one which kills, they say, so I've one in hand still. It's made me feel lonely for you, all of you. Alex can't come; I know that. But Dan will be out of school soon, and Harry has his long vacation. Isn't he due for another sabbatical by now, to let him stay here till Christmas? I don't need looking after, but I do need your company. To say it straight out, I want to see you again before I die, and it could be that getting across the Atlantic may not be on the cards much longer. Think about it. Come if you can.' It was the best he could do. He posted the letter to England, and waited.

Agnes and Dan arrived five weeks later. Their departure date and route were subject to such wartime conditions of secrecy that they had not known the details in advance themselves. From the moment of the telephone call which told him they had arrived on American soil, Daniel sent his housekeeper hustling around the house, whilst he himself checked the guest rooms as though they had not been in readiness for weeks, and fussed about the food to be cooked or ordered. He returned continually to an upstairs window in order not to miss the earliest sign of his daughter's approach and when at last, excited, he limped with the best speed he could muster these days to open the front door himself, his heart was beating with an urgency that he should have recognized as dangerous.

Agnes came first, running to kiss him and to express her delight that he looked so much fitter than she had feared. His own happiness at seeing her contained an element of crafty satisfaction at his cleverness in persuading her to come. Only when at last she broke smilingly away from his embrace to step inside the house did he turn to welcome Dan.

How the boy had grown! Well, he was not a boy any longer, but a young man, strong and sturdy as he humped the bags from the cab to the porch. His skin was tanned by sun and wind and his hair, although cut short at the back and the sides, formed a thick blond thatch on top of his head. As he came near, grinning, Daniel's heart seemed to stop beating for a moment. He was remembering a tanned, confident, blond man who fifteen years earlier had brought his family to stare at a folly built by some megalomaniac in Mississippi. He was recalling the hatred and the desire for revenge that he had felt at that moment. And at the same time, as he took a step towards Dan, he remembered how on that same day he had stretched out his arms to a little lost boy, fair-haired and chubby and trusting, and had carried him away.

It was one of the curious consequences of that incident that the stolen child should by now be his special grandson. Alex had become a foreigner: friendly, but a stranger. Danny, the baby who died in the fire, was no longer more than a formless memory, a smudged impression of smell and sound, softness and movement. Agnes and Harry would naturally see it in a different way. But Daniel had always regarded himself as responsible for ensuring that the boy he had brought into the family should be happy, and over the years that care had grown into his deepest love. It was Dan, he recognized now, Dan even more than his own daughter Agnes, whom his letter had been designed to bring home.

So now, remembering that first encounter, Daniel stretched out his arms again: in greeting, not in enticement. He felt himself leaning towards the young man at the foot of the steps. But his head began to spin and float in vertigo and suddenly he was not leaning but falling; instead of yellow hair and a smiling face he could see nothing but blackness. He had just time enough to be angry that his weakness should be spoiling this longed-for moment of reunion before he hit the ground.

2

Daniel was not killed by his second stroke any more than he had been by the first, but he was frightened by it. In his letter he had joked about the possible fatal effects of a third stroke. Now the possibility was closer and less amusing. As he lay in bed he could feel his eyes wandering in an undisciplined manner, and there was a noise in his head as if telephones were ringing without pause. His golfing friends, dropping by to keep him up to date with club gossip, either mumbled in an embarrassed fashion or else enunciated their words with untypical clarity, as though only then could he be expected to comprehend. He was alarmed when the pastor of his church, normally encountered only on Sundays, began to pay regular visits. And the doctor's warnings were too all-embracing to be comforting. He must avoid not only over-exertion but also over-excitement. Anxiety was dangerous – but so, it seemed, was too much happiness. Agnes, competently dividing the household duties with his housekeeper, made it clear that from now on he was to lie back and take life easy.

'Will Harry come?' Daniel asked. One blessing was that on this occasion his speech had not been too badly affected, although he was quickly tired by too much talking.

Agnes shook her head. 'The British government has asked him to help out on some project; he has leave of absence from the college until the problem's cracked. It's so secret that he's not allowed to tell me about it. Something to do with finding out when an enemy plane is on the way. It could turn out to be important. Everyone over there reckons that England's going to be bombed to pieces by the Germans. Tell you the truth, Harry was glad to see me and Dan out of the way.'

'Will you put Dan into school here, then?'

'He has his own plans. I'll let him tell you.'

Dan's intention, it emerged when next he came to sit beside his grandfather's bed, was to join the U.S. navy. 'I wouldn't have left England for anything else,' he said. 'Too much like running away. Knowing I was going to train as a fighter made it feel okay, though.'

'Are you old enough?'

'I've written to ask. I could have joined the British army if I'd stayed. They have special entry schemes over there. I don't know how we do it here.'

'Why the navy?' asked Daniel curiously. If his own father, Captain Mark Fletcher, and his grandson, Alex, could be said to represent any kind of military tradition in the family, it was firmly land-based.

'I just love being on the water,' Dan told him. 'Dad bought me my own boat when I was twelve. That part of England's dull for sailing, though. I want to be out on the ocean. See the world.'

It was an ambition which was to have an unexpected consequence. Daniel was improving fast, able to leave his bed and sit in an armchair all day, when Dan came to him with a question.

'Something I want to ask you,' he said. 'Mom would know the answer, but I'm scared I could upset her.'

'So what's the problem?'

'The navy needs to see my birth certificate. I asked Mom for it, but she didn't have it here, so she got me a copy. It says that I was born in Manchester, Vermont, on the third of August 1923, and that my father was Henry Lucas Kiernan and my mother was Agnes Dorothy Kiernan, born Fletcher.'

'So?'

'Well, that's not so, is it. I mean, I'm adopted. I could have almost any other set of parents in the world – except Mom and Dad. That's what I thought, anyway. But now I'm wondering. Maybe Dad was my father all the time and had another woman and Mom took me into the family to be kind and now she might not want to be reminded of it and . . .'

'Hold it!' commanded Daniel. He spoke more sharply than he intended because this time he could recognize the danger in the erratic beating of his heart. Doing his best to impose calmness on himself, he continued more softly. 'You've seen too many movies, Dan. Every kid of your age hopes that he has a secret set of glamorous parents tucked away somewhere, but what in heaven's name makes you think you were adopted?'

Dan looked at him curiously. 'I've always known,' he said. 'Least, since I was five or six. Mom told me. The psychiatrist said she should.'

'Why did she need a psychiatrist to tell her how to bring up her kids?' Agnes had needed therapy, he recalled, after her bereavement; but Harry's reports from England had suggested almost from the start that her new responsibilities had restored her health and spirits.

Dan's face flushed to a bright red. 'I used to wet my bed,' he confessed. 'Not just when I was a baby. It went on longer than that. So Mom took me to this shrink who talked a lot of junk about me being insecure or something. Anyway, he said I ought to be told all the truth about myself, so Mom came out with the whole story. I guess she must have forgotten that herself by now. It's never made any difference. I mean, she's always been my mom.' The questioning expression returned to his face. 'You had to know all that, about my being adopted,' he said. 'You were the one who took me off my real mother's hands, Mom said.'

'Right,' agreed Daniel. 'I don't feel too good, Dan. Could you find a drink for me? Not a beer this time. Some of that chilled lime your mother makes.' He had taken a good many decisions by the time Dan came back, but before he spoke he sipped gratefully from the glass.

'I wasn't too businesslike in dealing with that poor woman,' he said slowly. 'Should have thought to ask her for papers. But she was crying and I was flustered and by the time I thought of making everything tidy she'd disappeared. She'd lost her own home and was living rough, so I never could track her down. When the time came when Harry and Agnes had to produce some sort of document for you, it must have seemed simplest . . . did they tell you about the baby?'

Dan nodded. 'Dad told me. Because there was a photograph, and I thought it was me. He said I wasn't ever to talk about it to Mom in case she got upset again.'

Daniel summoned all his strength to speak decisively. 'If the navy wants papers, give them whatever papers you've got,' he said. 'If you start being doubtful about them yourself, the navy won't want to know.' He watched the worry lines smooth away into relief. Dan had only wanted to be told what to do, not to have it all explained to him.

After the boy had left the room to complete his application, Daniel allowed himself to slump in the armchair, exhausted by his moment of alarm. These doubts and questions sprang from old events which – until the moment of Dan's arrival at the house – he had almost forgotten.

Fourteen years ago – the year after Agnes and her family had sailed to England – Daniel had returned to Natchez and looked through back numbers of the local paper. From it he learned that Iris Lindsay had been rushed to hospital in a state of shock on the night after her little son disappeared, and had lost the baby she was expecting. She and her husband had remained in the area for several weeks after her recovery, in the hope that Russell Lindsay would prove to have been kidnapped and that a ransom note would eventually arrive. But the tracker dog which was brought to the scene on the day of the tragedy led the police investigators through woodland to a point high above the river, and there lost the trail. The edge of the bluff was unstable and from the beginning it had been regarded as almost certain that the child must have fallen over the sheer drop, to be carried away by the river below. In the end, Iris Lindsay had been forced to accept the fact that Russell was dead, and returned home to Oahu with her husband and their surviving son. Their address was given in the paper, and Daniel copied it down. Later, he had looked for the note in order to destroy it, but failed to find it – and by now no longer remembered the details.

As for Thomas Vernon, he had died in prison at the age of sixty-five, only two months after he was sentenced. Daniel would have preferred to think of the murderer enduring the longest possible period of despair. Certainly the news of the death did nothing to alter Daniel's own feeling that his act of revenge had been justified. An eye for an eye; a child for a child.

All that was far in the past. It had not taken him long to put from his mind the anguish he had caused to a couple innocent of everything except their relationship to the man who had hurt Daniel's own family in the same way. His reward had been to learn through Agnes's letters, and Harry's, that his daughter had freed herself from the web of despair and lethargy and had once again become the loving, energetic mother of two happy sons. No, he had no regrets.

So it was curious and unwelcome that now, after so long, every glimpse of Dan's blond head and the sturdy set of his body should remind him of the encounter on the bluff. More even than the second stroke, it was a sign of old age that the past should unroll itself in his mind so much more vividly than the present. He fought against his memories, and then was forced to engage in a second battle to prevent the first struggle from causing turmoil in his heart. He must keep calm; the doctor had made that clear.

Calmness was more easily resolved than achieved. When Dan, straight-backed and proud in uniform, came to announce that he had been assigned to his first ship, Daniel's own pride, swelling into his heart through inelastic arteries, caused him to be packed off to bed as soon as the boy had gone. And little by little, over the next few months, he observed himself retreating from life. Because he must not become over-emotional, he soon ceased to feel any emotion at all. Only on what he recognized as his deathbed did confusion of mind break through the barriers which he had placed around his memory. Even as he rambled on, he was conscious of speaking words that he did not wish to be heard: but he was unable to discipline his tongue.

'Don't let it bother you,' he mumbled, while Agnes bent closer to catch the words. 'No way they can find out. Can't get back at you. 'Sall right.'

'What's all right?' asked Agnes, anxious and tearful. But by now a new ally had come to Daniel's aid, laying the gift of silence on his lips to prevent him from betraying himself.

3

Agnes was the only member of the family able to go to her father's funeral. Alex was somewhere in North Africa, Dan was somewhere in the Pacific, and Harry could not be spared from his top-secret work in England. Many of Daniel Fletcher's business colleagues attended the funeral, as well as members of his lodge and golf club and the congregation of his church. Nevertheless, Agnes could not help feeling lonely as she returned to the house which now belonged to her. It was more than a year since she had last seen Harry. She realized that in wartime many husbands and wives must accept separation; but Uncle Sam was not at war, and during the months in which she had cared for her father she had begun once more to feel herself a citizen of the United States.

To occupy herself, she began at once to sort through her father's papers. Everything relating to money and property had been clipped into bundles and labelled, and whatever papers referred to matters of no lasting interest must have been discarded. He had had time after his first stroke to put his business affairs in order. The bottom drawer of the bureau, though, was stuffed so full of papers that she was hardly able to pull it open. Into this, it was clear, Daniel had over a period of many years stuffed every item of family interest.

Agnes, spreading out on the floor the collection of photographs, clippings, diaries, programmes, smiled to see her own graduation class photograph, a bible study certificate awarded when she was seven years old, the local paper's report of her wedding, with lengthy descriptions of dresses and flowers. There were other records which she could not bring herself to read – accounts of her baby's death and of the trial which many weeks later followed. She sorted the papers into piles, some to be destroyed and others to go back to England with her. Before sliding the drawers back into place, she took a cloth to clean the inside of the bureau. A few scraps of paper had fallen behind the over-full bottom drawer: she pulled them out, ready to stack them in the appropriate piles. Two were newspaper clippings, but the third was a page torn from a notebook, on which a name and address was written in her father's handwriting: Mrs Elliott Lindsay, Valley Gardens House, Nuuanu Valley, Oahu. Beneath it he had added four words and underlined them: mother of Russell/Dan.

Surprised – and disturbed – Agnes stared at the note. Ten years or more ago, she remembered, she had written to ask her father whether he knew the name under which Dan had been christened. The child psychiatrist she consulted at that time had advised that Dan should be given all possible information about his birth. If, for example, he still half-consciously remembered the name by which he was called in babyhood, its sudden abandonment could have unsettled him. More controversial, the psychiatrist admitted, was his own belief that an adopted child should not only be told that he was adopted but should be given full information about his natural parents. An account of their circumstances would help him to come to terms with their reason for letting him go, and a name and physical description would enable him to form a solid impression of his background. In addition, it would convince him that his adoptive parents were dealing honestly with him by telling him the truth about himself. If it was necessary for a fact to be withheld – for example, to protect a mother who might not want her present husband to know of this child's existence – the explanation should be given instead. Even a child too young to understand the significance of what he was told would be reassured by the knowledge that his right to hear it had been recognized.

Agnes had never needed to decide for herself whether the psychiatrist's advice was sound, because her father's answer had been definite. He had never had any address for Martha Nilsson and could remember little about her appearance except that she had fair hair. He had never met her husband. He had forbidden Martha to tell him the name of her son because he already had it clear in his mind that from now on the little boy was to be called Dan.

So Agnes was forced to be content with telling six-year-old Dan the story of the coal mine explosion, the heartless employer, the debt to the company store, the desperation of a woman watching her children starve. Over and over again Dan had asked for the story until he knew it off by heart, word for word. Agnes sometimes wondered whether it was this emphasis on the first few months of his life which had made him so determined to remain American.

Yet all the time her father had known Dan's original name: Russell. She wondered what other information he had concealed or deliberately distorted. It was possible, she supposed, that Martha Nilsson had become Mrs Elliott Lindsay later in her life, had moved with her new husband to live in Oahu, and had made contact with Daniel Fletcher so that he could reassure her about the welfare of her son. Possible, but somehow unlikely. The address – unless she was only a servant there – did not sound appropriate to a history of desperate poverty. Was the story of Dan's background a fabrication? But Agnes did not allow the small problem to upset her. If her father had invented an over-dramatic story, it would have been to persuade her that she herself had no choice but to take responsibility for an abandoned child – and even if the background were not exactly what she had believed, there could be no doubt that the little boy must for some reason have been in need of a home. Her father had acted out of love for her, and his therapy had proved successful. With sad affection now she thanked and forgave him for it.

Ought Dan himself to learn that he might not have been told the truth? Her own temptation to leave things as they were helped Agnes to understand even more clearly how her father must have felt sixteen years earlier. But it was an important ingredient of her loving and secure relationship with Dan that they should be honest with each other. He was not a child any longer. Even according to his borrowed birthday he had reached the age of eighteen on the third of August, 1941, whilst in fact he was a little older than that – old enough to make his own decisions. And he was an affectionate, considerate young man. If he should choose to write to the woman who had surrendered him for his own sake – reassuring her with the knowledge that she had given him a good life, so that her sacrifice was not in vain – well, that would be a Christian act. Agnes, a sincere Christian herself, did not feel that she had the right to deprive an unfortunate mother of such a consolation, and was confident that her own bond with Dan could not be broken. In her next letter she passed on what she had learned.

She addressed the letter, as usual, to Dan's ship and not to any particular place. Agnes knew that he was in the Pacific, but nothing more specific than that. She had no idea when he would be able to read her news, or where he would be.

4

The *Oklahoma* was moored off Ford Island in Pearl Harbor when, shortly after Thanksgiving, Dan Kiernan received from his mother two letters which had been posted a week apart but arrived on the same day. Dan checked the date on each postmark and opened the earlier one first. Previous letters had prepared him for the news of his grandfather's death. Nevertheless, he was sad as he remembered the previous Thanksgiving, when his mother had prepared a feast and his grandfather, although already weak, radiated happiness in the company of the two people he loved most in the world.

'Bad news?' Whitey Nash squatted beside him with an expression of concern which made Dan realize how long he must have been staring at the letter without moving. Whitey – his name made inevitable by the plume of pure white in his otherwise raven hair – was ten years older than Dan and had appointed himself the younger man's protector during the first tough weeks of life on a battleship. He was married to a Honolulu girl, so Pearl Harbor had become his home base, and he rarely received mail of his own when the *Oklahoma* was anchored there.

Dan nodded, but did not go into details. Elderly grandfathers must be expected to die, and mourning should be a private affair. The contents of the second letter, though, were a very different matter.

Dan studied the address of his unknown mother, trying to decide what he felt. He had always known that he was adopted; there was no surprise in that. Often as a boy he had fantasized about the family into which he had been born, drawing heavily on visits to the cinema to picture the kind of life he would have led had he not been given away; but he was content with the hand which fortune had dealt him on the second round, and would never on his own initiative have asked to be put in touch with his natural mother. If the address at which he was now staring had been anywhere else in the world he would have noted it with interest, but nothing more.

As it was, he was struck by the coincidence of finding himself within a few miles of his mother at the moment when the letter reached him. He considered it for a while and then looked round for the most likely source of local information.

'Hey, Whitey! Know a place called Nuuanu Valley?'

Whitey knew. No doubt exaggerating, he painted a vivid picture of Oahu's high society living it up in million-dollar homes spaced out round the rim of the valley. He demanded to see the address in which his friend was interested and Dan showed it to him, first folding back the letter so that the reason for sending it should be concealed.

Whitey gave a whistle of mock awe. 'Lindsay, hey!'

'Heard of them?'

'Heard of them! Elliott Lindsay owns half the Big Island and his wife owns half Kauai and they have a trading business which would let them buy up the other halves any time it took their fancy. Tell you what, next liberty you get, I'll give you a lift up there. Wouldn't mind an excuse to take a look.'

Dan refrained from accepting the offer on the spot, but in the course of the following week it was several times repeated. And his curiosity was growing. At any moment his ship might sail out of Pearl and not return. So a few days later, on the first Saturday in December, he accepted his friend's offer.

'How come you know the Lindsays?' Whitey asked as they drove off the base.

'I don't. My grandfather must have known them way back. You know how it is. Families expect you to look people up if you get anywhere within a hundred miles or so.'

It was not as far as that – but it was, nevertheless, a world away from the naval base. Whitey first of all picked up his wife and daughter for a picnic in the mountains. Then he turned away from the coast and, leaving the cane fields behind, took the winding road up the valley. The child on the back seat abruptly ceased to chatter and Dan felt an increasing unease. Not that there was anything sinister about the valley except its silence and apparent lack of human life – but that in itself seemed eerie to someone accustomed to noise and bustle. He had not previously ventured inland. Earlier liberties had been spent in Waikiki, swimming and drinking and appraising the remarkably beautiful and uninhibited Hawaiian girls.

Since joining the navy he had learned to enjoy the twenty-four-hours-a-day companionship of his fellow-sailors in overcrowded conditions: he had passed the stage of longing to be quit of it. But here, it was clear that from the moment Whitey dropped him and drove on, he would be alone. If there were homes at the head of the valley, they were well hidden from sight. If families were chattering and eating and diving into pools, they were doing so behind walls of privacy. It was tempting to change his mind and stay with the picnic party. Nevertheless, when he caught sight of the archway marking the entrance to Valley Gardens House he said without hesitation, 'Drop me here.'

'I'll drive you up. Could be a mile or more.'

'No, this'll do fine.'

Whitey shrugged his shoulders and braked. 'What time they expecting you?'

'They're not.'

Whitey gave a snort of amusement. 'Hope their guard dogs don't bite, then. They could be kind of surprised to see an enlisted man standing on the doorstep. I reckon Mrs Lindsay may be more accustomed to entertaining admirals.'

The suggestion – undoubtedly correct – increased Dan's doubts. He had tried to think of some way of making his presence in Hawaii – his very existence, even – known in advance, and had failed. Playing it by ear seemed the only, although unsatisfactory, plan of action. He recalled the half-truth which he had invented to explain his original interest in the Lindsays, and elaborated it. 'You know how it is. Just because they met my grandfather once doesn't mean that they'll want to bother with me now; and I don't want to push. If no one's around, I can leave a message to say that I've been, and write home to describe the sort of place they've got here, and everyone'll be happy.' Without allowing time for further argument he checked his watch with Whitey's and fixed a pick-up time – with a back-up arrangement by which Dan could leave a note at the gateway if the family had offered to run him back to the base either earlier or later.

In case Whitey should linger to watch him, Dan set off along the private road with an energetic display of confidence. But as he had been warned, the house was a fair distance away. After five minutes of brisk walking his view was still only of the hedges of poinsettia and of the mountains rising in the background. Then he rounded a bend and stopped in disbelief.

Everything about Valley Gardens House proclaimed the wealth of its owner. It was not merely the spacious design of the villa or the extent of the landscaped garden which Dan could now see falling away from the level on which the house stood. What spoke most loudly of money was the immaculate appearance of both the building and its surroundings. It had not taken Dan long after his first step ashore on the island of Oahu to realize that its inhabitants set no great store by tidiness. The warmth and wetness of their climate encouraged trees and flowers and crops to grow and propagate themselves with tropical enthusiasm and it seemed nobody's business to trim them back. The same climate, in the residential areas of Honolulu and Waikiki, rotted wood and blistered paint and whipped dust against windows. Dan had seen no other home here whose white paint glistened with such newness, whose lawns had been shaved to such velvet smoothness. Whitey's comments should have warned him, and yet he was taken aback.

It didn't fit. How had the starving widow of a Kentucky coal miner come to finish up in a place such as this? Dan re-read the letter which had given him the address, wondering whether he had misunderstood. He had taken it to mean that Martha Nilsson, his real mother, had re-married and made her home here; but maybe she was a maid or something like that, living on the premises only as an employee. But no, that didn't fit either. Her name was Lindsay and the house was owned by Lindsays. Had the story with which Dan was brought up been a lie all the time?

It was important to know. Suppose that Martha Nilsson, or whatever her real name was, had not been poor at all, but merely desperate to get rid of a child who was an inconvenience – perhaps because her husband was not its father. It would not have been surprising if the truth – that he had been rejected in his infancy – had been kept from Dan himself while he was young; but he could take it now – because he was completely happy as the son of Agnes and Harry Kiernan.

For the first time, though, it occurred to him that a visit which could prove only mildly unsettling to himself might well shatter the life of the woman who had given birth to him. Instead of providing reassurance about the well-being of a son whom she had broken-heartedly abandoned, he might be about to disrupt her life with the reminder and evidence of some old scandal. Had he the right to take such a risk when the price of miscalculation would be paid by somebody else? No, he had not.

Ruefully wishing that he had not after all allowed Whitey to drive off without him, Dan made a half turn, ready to retrace his steps , and then stopped again, startled, as a man moved out into the road only a few feet away. He was a Japanese, dressed in the white uniform of a servant, and the silence with which he made his appearance through an apparently solid hedge was unnerving. Dan prepared to defend himself against accusations of trespassing; but, instead, the Japanese bowed politely.

'Come this way, sir, please,' he said.

5

Yawning away her siesta, Hilary Lindsay stood for a moment on the highest terrace of the garden, choosing where to spend the rest of the afternoon. She was carrying a book, but knew that it would remain unread, for the heat and her huge size combined to make her lethargic. Her baby was not due until after Christmas, but already she was enormous: an elephant. A happy elephant, though. She lowered herself carefully into a swinging chair and began to rock gently, relaxing in the rich perfume of the plumeria tree.

She was waiting for the *Enterprise* to return to Pearl; within the next twenty-four hours she would see her husband again. In the meantime, she was content to close her eyes, enjoying the December sunshine. Around her, bees moved purposefully from one hibiscus bloom to another and the fronds of palm trees whispered in the gentle breeze, but nothing else stirred.

The garden of Valley Gardens House was famous throughout the island. Iris Lindsay, Hilary's mother-in-law, who had created it, had a genius for landscape design. She had made use of the different levels of the site, with its dramatic fall into the valley on one side, and had channelled a stream which came from the mountains to twist and drop with a gentle sparkle through the grounds before tumbling at last towards the bed of the valley. She had filled the design with bold plantings of shrubs and trees so that at every turn the eye was delighted by some new contrast. But unlike most rich women in a hot climate, she was not content to leave the maintenance of her concept to servants. Her botanical interest urged her to experiment with new crosses, and the resultant seedlings needed her personal nurture. In addition, she liked to paint her flowers where they grew and not in a vase. Because there was no time of the day at which they could safely idle without being found out and reprimanded, the Lindsays' outdoor staff were far more hard-working than was usual in Oahu, and their conscientious care was demonstrated in a garden always bright with blossom.

On the Saturday afternoon of December 6th, however, Iris and her husband were watching a polo match, leaving Hilary alone in the house except for the servants. She stroked her body contentedly as she rocked, caressing the baby as much as herself and soothing it, she hoped, with her swinging.

Suddenly she opened her eyes and raised her head, her attention attracted by what was still hardly more than a disturbance of the air. The valley trapped sound, bouncing it in a fading echo from side to side, and the zig-zagging of what was almost a mountain road meant that any vehicle could be heard long before it came into sight. There were only a few, widely-scattered residences in the exclusive area at the head of the Nuuanu Valley, and Hilary could recognize the expensive automobiles of their owners by the engine noise. What she heard now had a rougher note. A delivery van, perhaps, but she was curious enough to stand up and stroll across to a point from which she could see the road. Well, it was not so much a stroll as a waddle, she thought, laughing at herself as a means of stifling her hope that Peter might have returned early. It was not likely; she knew that. Although the ocean could not be seen from the house, the carrier's return to Pearl was usually heralded by the arrival of two or three of its planes, flying ahead like the pilot fish of a shark. It was for these that she had half-consciously been listening.

The automobile drew to a halt at the entrance to the Lindsay ranch. For just one more moment, as she observed that the driver was a navy man, Hilary's heart bumped with hope. But although it was too far away to see the face of the passenger as he swung himself out and slammed the door, his uniform showed that he was not an officer.

There was a second in which Hilary's disappointment turned to anxiety. Had something happened to her husband? Even in peacetime, accidents sometimes occurred on board aircraft carriers. But no, if there was bad news, it would have been brought by an officer senior in rank to Peter. And if Dr Ennisary had told her once, he had told her a dozen times that the single most important task of a pregnant woman was to remain calm and happy. Without too much trouble, Hilary reopened her heart to happiness and watched calmly as the young man began to walk up the private road.

He turned a corner and stopped head. Hilary could guess why. He would just have caught his first glimpse of the house. There were plenty of newer houses in Oahu and some of them, although not many, were larger. But there were few which so effortlessly revealed the owners' wealth and taste. If the unexpected caller had not known in advance that he was stepping into high society, he knew now.

Even at a distance his hesitation and doubt were so clear that Hilary felt sure he would turn tail at any moment. Yet he must have had a reason for coming. Curious – and bored – she beckoned with a hand into the apparently empty garden. There was a bell beside her so that she could summon a servant to fetch a drink or anything she had forgotten, but she did not need to use it.

She had found it difficult at first, when she married into the Lindsay family, to accept that she was always watched. Peter, apologetically, had described to her the disappearance of his younger brother many years earlier. Although in the end his mother was persuaded that her son must have been accidentally drowned, she had for so long believed him to have been kidnapped that her fear of this particular crime – always a possibility where such a wealthy family was concerned – had become irrational. Under pressure from her husband – and Peter himself when he became an adult – she had agreed that the two men must be considered able to protect not only themselves but their women. But whenever Hilary was left alone in the house, one of the servants would be personally responsible for guarding her, and there was nothing she could do about it.

She had, in fact, ceased even to think it strange. Hilary had been born and brought up in England – meeting her future husband for the first time when he was crewing on his father's ocean-going yacht at Cowes. The early months of her marriage were spent in Annapolis, and she found even mainland America startling enough. But the life of the very rich in Hawaii was so far outside her previous experience that she could only laugh incredulously from time to time and settle down to enjoy it. She had a father-in-law who thought nothing of flying all the way to Oakland, California, in order to spend an hour or two negotiating a sugar contract. And she had a mother-in-law who owned a full-length sable coat and a mink in an island where the temperature rarely fell below the seventies. In such a context, living under the eye of a bodyguard hardly ranked as eccentric behaviour at all.

Today it was the Japanese houseboy. She pointed out the stranger, who seemed about to turn away, and ordered that he should be brought to see her.

He stepped on to the lawn a few moments later, whipping off his cap to reveal hair as blond as Peter's. He was either shy or embarrassed, fixing his eyes on the ground. Since it was clear that he had made a special journey to the house, Hilary concluded that he was not ashamed at being discovered, but more probably did not like to stare at a woman whose voluminous sun dress could not conceal her elephantine shape. 'Who are you looking for?' she asked.

'Mrs Lindsay.'

'I'm Mrs Lindsay. Well, one of the Mrs Lindsays.'

He risked another look at her. 'Mrs Elliott Lindsay. Older than you, I guess.'

'My mother-in-law. And you are –?'

'Sorry, ma'am.' Straightening his head and shoulders, he rattled off his name, number and ship as though she were an inspecting officer.

His name was Dan Kiernan; Hilary did not trouble her memory with the rest. She held out a hand to be shaken. 'My mother-in-law isn't here at the moment. But she won't be long.' Hilary knew this latter statement to be untrue. When the polo match ended it would certainly be followed by an hour or more of drinks at thc club. But she was bored with her own company and chatting to a stranger was as good a way as any of passing the time. 'Will you have some tea with me while you wait?' She waved a hand to indicate to him a choice of garden chairs and loungers in the sun or shade, and nodded at Endo, knowing that it was unnecessary to put the order into words. The servants, who did not need the clue of uniform to judge to a nicety the social status of any visitor, would not approve of her entertaining an enlisted man, but their impassive faces would reveal no hint of this as they brought out the trolley.

'I'm English,' she said, chattering to put the young man at his ease as she poured tea from the antique silver teapot. 'When I first came to live out here, my new family took it for granted that no true-born Englishwoman could survive without her daily ration of tea. You can't imagine the kerfuffle that went on. The choice between China and India, the discussion of favourite blends and brands, the regular order. You'd think no one in the western hemisphere had ever seen a tea leaf before. The cook was summoned so that I could instruct him in the gentle art of heating the pot and leaving it to stand for four minutes precisely, just as though the Chinese hadn't invented tea-drinking. The funny thing is that the whole family has become addicted by now. They always talk about "Hilary's tea," but then they join me. Milk or lemon?'

'Milk, if you please, ma'am.' Dan paused, and then seemed to become more at ease. 'I spent sixteen years in England myself. Born in the States but raised in Cambridge, England.'

'Go on!' The discovery made it easy to chat. Hilary was amused to notice that in her company Dan's voice even began to revert to what had presumably been his natural accent throughout his boyhood. He responded to her natural friendliness by shedding his initial shyness – until the moment when she asked him what his business was with her mother-in-law.

The question seemed so much to frighten him that she could tell he was on the point of leaping to his feet.

'I was asked,' he began, stumbling over an explanation which was patently a lie. 'A friend, on the mainland . . . if I found myself in Hawaii, he said . . . He gave me your mother-in-law's name. He said I should call and . . . and, well . . .'

'But why?'

'He told me a story. But it can't be right. He must have fouled it up somehow.'

'Tell me the story,' Hilary coaxed.

'Well, this friend of mine, he was an adopted kid, see. And he thought . . . or at least he said . . . but he must have been pulling my leg. His mother, his real mother, was too poor to look after him when he was young, that was the story.'

'And Mrs Elliott Lindsay was the name he gave you for his mother?'

'It's crazy. A poor starving widow, he said. But . . .' Dan gestured energetically at his surroundings.

'If you think that this family is stinking rich, you're absolutely right,' Hilary confirmed. 'And they have been for several generations. They were one of the early missionary families. Not the very first to arrive; but they turned up in time to profit from the great bonanza.'

'I beg your pardon?' It was clear that Dan did not understand the relationship of the early missionaries to the topics they had been discussing.

'There's a neat little story they tell in Hawaii. About how the missionaries arrived in the islands and were welcomed by the local rulers.' She put on a declaiming voice. 'And the missionaries said unto the people, "Cast your eyes up to the heavens and worship the Lord your God." So the people cast up their eyes, but when they looked down again, lo, their land was gone.' She laughed, seeing that there was still a need to explain. 'History isn't my strong point. All I know is that my father-in-law is the grandson of a missionary and that he and my mother-in-law between them own an enormous cattle ranch and acres and acres of pineapple and sugar cane plantations. Not to mention a lava field which will make them another fortune if they can ever figure out what to do with it. Land we have in this family, and money we have; but poor starving widows we don't have. What's your friend's name?'

The flush on Dan's face confirmed her suspicion that he was in fact talking about his own background. 'It was changed when he was adopted,' he said. 'He was born as Russell Lindsay.'

Until that moment Hilary had been smiling, agreeing with her visitor that someone must have been pulling his leg. But the name Russell Lindsay rang an alarm bell to check her laughter. Peter's young brother, the boy who disappeared, had been called Russell. Peter himself, who as a six-year-old had felt responsible for losing his little brother, had never freed himself from a feeling of guilt. He had told Hilary the full story early in their friendship, so that she would never discover it by chance and hold it against him. It was not a story which could have embraced an adoption. Everyone who knew Iris Lindsay as a young woman confirmed that she had never recovered her spirits after the loss of her younger son. There was no reason why she needed to give him away and no possibility that she would in fact have done so. But the name . . . If someone had indeed played a practical joke on Dan, was there a reason behind it?

One point was easy to check. 'You're talking about yourself, aren't you?'

For a second time Dan's face flushed as he nodded an admission. 'I shouldn't have come,' he mumbled. 'Sorry to have troubled you.'

'No, wait.' Hilary's abrupt movement to prevent him from leaving startled the baby into an orgy of kicking, and she found herself panting with her child's exertions. But as she lay back, trying to relax, her mind was racing. There was a time when, young and unsophisticated, she would have poured out to Dan what she knew of the family's history. But she had lived for long enough with the suspicions of the wealthy to have become cautious. It was not impossible that Dan could be a fortune-hunter – or could have been put forward by someone else, someone whose age disqualified him from claiming in his own right. Old newspaper files would have provided details of a suspected kidnapping. To approach with this cock-and-bull story of an adoption might only be the cunning prelude to pretended astonishment at hearing another possible explanation.

'I have to be going.' Dan stood up. 'Someone's fixed to give me a ride back. If I'm not waiting . . . There's a concert at Bloch Center tonight. Well, a contest more than a concert. A battle between some of the ships' bands.'

'Help me up, will you?' asked Hilary. She felt like a stranded whale in the low chair, and was determined that Dan should not simply walk away. As he carefully put his arms beneath her elbows in support, she looked into his eyes, studying his face with more care than when he first arrived. Was it just imagination, because the possibility of a relationship had been suggested, that made her see in his young freckled face a resemblance to her husband's tanned good looks? They were both fair-haired, both sturdily-built. Peter was taller – so tall that his tiny mother often wondered aloud how she came to have such a son, but there was something about their mouths . . . Hilary shook her head impatiently, dismissing the fantasy.

'My parents-in-law will want to meet you,' she said firmly. 'Even though there's obviously been a muddle somewhere, I'm quite sure they'll want to talk about it. Will you write down what you told me – your name and ship, that sort of thing. And your date of birth.'

'I've never known that exactly. I was given a day for my birthday, in 1923, but . . .'

'Just the year, then. Now, is there somewhere they can call you? Or if not, will you call them tomorrow? Sometime before five – would that be possible?'

He handed her the slip of paper on which he had written, but she could tell that he was still doubtful. 'I'm not suggesting that just to be polite,' she said. 'I'm asking a favour. Will you promise?'

'Guess so, if that's what you think they'd like.' He had begun to mumble again, his embarrassment returning after their afternoon of free-and-easy chat. 'Thanks for the tea, ma'am.'

'Thanks for your company.' A smile lingered on Hilary's face for a little while as she watched him walk away. Then, moving to another chair, she picked up her unread book.

But she had hardly time to read more than a page before she heard Peter's parents returning, far earlier than she had expected.

They came at once to make sure that she was as well and happy as when they had left. The baby which was soon to be born was almost as important to its grandparents as to Hilary herself. For the first two years of her marriage Hilary had found Iris's possessiveness stifling, but at this stage in her pregnancy she was glad to relax in the security of their solicitude. Iris disappeared as soon as she had made sure that all was well, leaving Elliott to explain.

'The admiral's invited us to join him for dinner at the Halekulani. I told him that we didn't care to leave you on your own for the evening as well as the afternoon, but Carrie heard me say it and announced that she planned to drop round for an hour or two.' Carrie was Hilary's closest friend in Oahu. 'So instead of enjoying a relaxed drink or two at the club, here we are dashing to change so that we can drive right back to the coast again.'

'Elliott, something odd happened this afternoon. I want to tell you . . .'

'Can it wait?' asked Elliott. 'We're a bit pushed. And here, if I'm not mistaken, comes your company.' Carrie's driving style involved alternate excesses of acceleration and the screaming of brakes which had just brought her to a halt. She never arrived anywhere unnoticed.

Hilary hesitated, anxious to pass on her message at once; and Elliott, who was courteous as well as businesslike, paused for her decision rather than rushing away. But it would be a mistake, she decided, to raise the subject at a time unsuitable for considered discussion, and especially in front of someone who was not a member of the family. Besides, she remembered, Admiral Kimmel invariably broke up his dinner parties in time to get to bed before ten. Although Hilary herself went early to bed these days, she would not be asleep before Elliott and Iris returned from this particular engagement. As long as she managed to prepare the ground some time before Dan Kiernan made his telephone call on Sunday, there was no particular hurry. She smiled, allowing Elliott to go. 'I'll tell you when you get back,' she promised.

6

Iris was surprised to find Hilary still awake when she and Elliott returned home that evening. 'Nothing wrong, darling?' she checked. 'Are you feeling okay?'

'Never better. I've got a message to pass on to you, that's all.' Hilary waited while Iris, smiling, sat down to hear it. 'Did you by any chance notice a young sailor leaving here just about as you came back this afternoon?'

Elliott shook his head, but Iris frowned, casting her memory back. 'We passed an automobile a moment before we turned in here, yes. There were two enlisted men in the front seats. I didn't take any great notice of them.'

'One of them had called here, hoping to see you. It can't be true, Iris, but what he said was that he'd been born as Russell Lindsay. The son of Mr and Mrs Elliott Lindsay.'

Iris held her breath. All the blood in her body seemed to drain away, leaving her head dizzy with emptiness. She was conscious of her husband coming to stand behind her, gripping her shoulders with both hands, but she was unable to take her eyes off Hilary as the tantalizingly incomplete story was repeated.

There was a long silence after Hilary came to a stop. Elliott sat down close to Iris, facing her, and took her hands in his own.

'Hilary's right, Iris,' he said gently. 'It can't be true.'

'You don't know. You want to believe it as much as I do.'

'Maybe. But I know the difference between fantasy and probability. You're not to let yourself hope. There's no way . . . Someone's telling lies, playing a cruel joke. The only way to hit back at him is not to believe it, not for a moment.'

'But why should he lie? What possible reason could he

have to invent a story after all these years?'

'Look around you,' Elliott said quietly. As a token of what he meant he stretched a finger to touch Iris's emerald bracelet. 'Think how the prodigal son was received – and he'd turned his back on his father by choice. How would you expect a wealthy father to welcome back a son who disappeared through no fault of his own. Hilary knows what I'm talking about, don't you, Hilary? That's why you didn't give anything away, right? Because you reckoned he was on the make.'

'I didn't think it was my decision, one way or the other.'

'But suppose . . .' Iris found herself stammering in an effort to force the words out. 'We can't just brush him away. What sort of boy was he, Hilary? Is Elliott right? Was he lying? Or might he . . .?'

Hilary gave a sigh which summed up both her wish and her inability to give a reliable answer. 'He was repeating a story that someone else had told him,' she said. 'As far as that goes, he was doing it sincerely, I'm sure. But he'd realized for himself, even before he began, that it couldn't possibly be true. That's what makes me feel that he *was* sincere. I could tell from his eyes. He honestly hadn't expected the people he'd planned to visit to live in such style. He would have run away without ever saying why he'd come if I hadn't sent Endo to stop him.'

'Well, then –'

Compassionately but firmly Elliott interrupted her. 'He could have been put up to it. An actor playing a part. God knows, Iris, I'd like it to be true as much as you would. But if we build up our hopes now, we could crash with disappointment. Tomorrow we'll meet him. See how far his story checks out. Maybe there'll be some kind of feeling, some chemistry, to influence us one way or the other. Or if we're only half way certain we could check it out with blood tests. But just for twenty-four hours, Iris, keep the stopper on your feelings. If you work yourself up into the kind of state when you'll accept anyone, anyone at all, just because you need to, we shall never be sure.' He helped her to her feet.

'Goodnight, Hilary,' he said; and Iris mechanically leaned to kiss her daughter-in-law before making her way to bed.

That night Elliott came to her room and, unusually, remained there after they had made love. Iris was grateful for the comfort he offered and recognized the good sense of his warnings. But she was too disturbed to sleep or to put the possibilities out of her mind. Careful not to disturb her husband, she slipped out of bed, wrapped herself in a kimono and went to sit on the lanai.

Deliberately now she re-lived the anguish of those days in 1925 when she had waited to learn her son's fate. Right from the start Elliott had feared an accident. Iris herself had clung to the belief that Russell had been kidnapped, but there had never been much to support the theory. No one except two elderly ladies had known that the family was expected to visit Mississippi, and no one in Mississippi was likely to know the extent of the Lindsay fortune in Hawaii. And although after her miscarriage Iris had remained in Natchez to give a kidnapper the chance to make contact, no ransom demand had ever been received.

So what other possibilities existed? A tracker dog had followed Russell's trail to the edge of a bluff so steep that Iris, taken to the place later, needed Elliott to hold her safe – not because she might have thrown herself over in despair, but because the sight of the swirling water so far below made her dizzy. But young children, with their softer bones, had been known to have miraculous escapes from falls. Suppose that the river, receiving Russell's small, light body, washed it up on the bank a short distance downstream. Suppose some poor woman found the child and nursed him back to life and kept him for her own – perhaps only much later realizing that she could not afford to support him. Or perhaps the woman who found him was the woman who brought him up, inventing a story of adoption so that she need not explain why she had not tried to trace his parents.

As her fancy roamed, Iris paced restlessly up and down the lanai, trying to recall the faces of the sailors she had glimpsed so briefly. They had been wearing their caps, so she could not even feel sure which of the two had the fair hair which Hilary had described. There was nothing about them which had aroused even a mild interest: certainly no instinctive reaction of recognition. Even had they met face to face, with time to stare, would she have been able to recognize in a grown man the infant she had last seen sixteen years before? Elliott had suggested, with hope rather than certainty, that the blood tie between a mother and son would somehow make itself felt. Iris wanted to believe him, but she was not sure. She poured herself a drink to steady her restless mind and sat down again.

The paper bearing the young visitor's name and navy details lay on the table near to her glass. Iris pulled it towards her and studied it. Was handwriting the creation of a teacher, or did it reveal innate characteristics which would be shared with other members of the family? Because she was staring at the way in which the letters were formed, it was a little while before her mind, and not merely her eyes, focused on the words. Until that moment she had been thinking of Russell, her son, and had extended the thought to consider the young sailor in terms of whether he was or was not Russell. Now for the first time she concentrated her attention on the name by which he was known. Dan Kiernan.

Dan Kiernan. Something pricked at the back of her memory. She had heard that name before. She puzzled over it, refilling her drink more than once. The sky was already flushing with sunrise before she at last recalled that Danny Kiernan was the name of the baby who had been burned to death by Elliott's great-uncle, Thomas Vernon. Iris had arrived on the mainland only after Thomas had been tried and imprisoned. She had never met him, nor any of the Kiernan family. But now that she remembered, she was sure: Danny Kiernan was dead.

Frowning to herself, she tried to make sense of what she had tugged from her memory. How could this new fact fit in with what had happened to her own son? Were the

Kiernans trying to take some kind of revenge for what they had suffered by sending one of their sons to claim a share of the Lindsay family fortune? But the boy called Danny Kiernan had died; would a father and mother christen another baby boy by the same name? Iris shook her head, rejecting the idea. A little at a time she groped her way towards another possibility. Suppose that the Kiernans had indeed planned a revenge – but sixteen years ago; not now.

The more carefully she considered it, the more certain she became. She had been right, all those years ago, to believe that Russell had been kidnapped. But not for money; only to cause her pain. The reason why the truth was at last being revealed was not easy to understand, but Russell himself would make it clear when they met in a few hours' time. Her darling Russell, her baby! A sound that was not quite a sob, not quite a sigh, forced itself out of her throat with every breath she expelled. Faint with emotion, she glanced at her watch. It was almost eight o'clock. On Sunday mornings both Elliott and Hilary lay in bed late, ringing for breakfast to be carried to their rooms when they were ready. But they would be awake by now, and in any case would gladly be aroused by news like this. Iris stood up, ready to shout out her certainty that Russell had not died.

It was at that moment that the first Japanese planes roared over the mountains on their way to Pearl Harbor.

7

Absorbed in her own thoughts, Iris paid no attention to the low-flying aircraft. Planes from the air base at Hickam Field often flew overhead on exercises. It was Hilary who was the first member of the family to express surprise. Peter's carrier was due to enter Pearl Harbor in the course of the day and Hilary, no doubt, had been listening for the planes which would announce their mother-ship's approach. Now she came out on to the lanai with a frown on her face.

'Those weren't the Dauntlesses. They didn't sound like anything I've heard before.'

Elliott had also been drawn out by the roaring noise, but he shrugged the matter off as he joined the two women. 'There's a flight of B-17s due in from the West Coast anytime now. Guess they were treating us to a fly-past before they land. Well, anyone else reckon it's time for breakfast?'

'Wait. . .' Iris had not been listening to the conversation about planes. 'There's something important. Elliott, look at this. Dan Kiernan. Danny Kiernan. Don't you remember?' The words tumbled out as she began to explain her theory, and she could tell from the grave expression on Elliott's face that for once he was not about to accuse her of romancing. He picked up the paper on which the name was written and began to study it with the same intensity as Iris herself earlier in the night. But before he had time to make any comment, they were interrupted by their Chinese cook, who came running from the kitchen with a pan in one hand and a wooden spoon in the other.

'Radio, sir. Listen radio.'

Iris frowned at the interruption; but Elliott, recognizing a note of urgency in the man's voice, hurried to the radio and turned it on. 'This is no drill.' The announcer's voice was urgent with alarm. 'This is no drill. Pearl Harbor is under attack. This is no drill.'

'Those planes!' Hilary remembered, and then pointed at the sky. A pillar of black smoke was rising to join the wispy white clouds of the morning. She pressed her hands on the bulge which sheltered her baby. 'Peter!' she exclaimed. 'Oh God, Peter!'

'He's not there.' Iris pushed the thought of Russell aside as she saw in alarm how the blood had left the young woman's face, leaving her white with shock and anxiety. 'He's still at sea. Whatever it is that's happening, he'll be safe.'

'They were due into harbour before dawn.'

'If he was here, he'd have called you.'

'It isn't always possible at once: you know that. And he wouldn't have wanted to wake me. I must go and see. Will you drive me, Iris?'

'Peter will want you to be here when he comes. Sit down, darling, and . . .'

'How can he come if the fleet's under attack. Iris, I have to see.'

Iris hesitated, but her own anxiety was even greater than Hilary's, for it was not only Peter who might be at risk. Whether or not the *Enterprise* had returned, the *Oklahoma* was certainly moored in the harbour. She nodded her agreement.

Elliott, listening intently to the radio whilst at the same time attempting to make a telephone call, did not stop them. 'Keep right away from the coast,' was all he said. Iris nodded again. She knew how to reach a ridge which would allow a good view of Ford Island and the harbour.

The roads were as quiet as on any normal Sunday morning. No one was dashing about in alarm or even emerging from home to exchange news with neighbours. Perhaps everyone in the island was either still unaware of what was happening or else, like Elliott, unwilling to move away from a radio. Driving steadily westward, Iris slowed for a moment as they came within earshot of the bombardment, with a fury of anti-aircraft shells punctuating the sound of explosions at sea level; then her speed increased as she made for the corniche. Sheltered by the mountain, it would be safe from air attack, but in normal circumstances provided a clear view of the fleet at anchor.

Today the view was different. Iris and Hilary walked to the edge of the road and stared in silence through the gaps in the smoke at the inferno below. The very water of the harbour appeared to be blazing as oil from shattered engine rooms covered the surface and caught alight. The two women clung to each other in shock and horror. Iris could feel that Hilary was on the brink of hysteria; her breath came in short gasps as her eyes searched the scene.

'She's not there.' Iris spoke urgently in an attempt to reassure her daughter-in-law. 'The *Enterprise* isn't there.'

'How do you know? There isn't a single ship down there that hasn't been hit.'

'You can't tell that from this distance. And a carrier – we couldn't mistake a carrier for anything else.'

'She may have gone down already.'

'That's not possible,' Iris said, but her heart was less certain than her voice as she searched the area of deep water in which the *Enterprise* would have moored. Destroyers and battleships were tipped to one side at drunken angles, or reared their sterns in the air as the bows sank under the water. One had turned turtle, so that only the bottom of her long hull was visible above the surface. And, most sinister of all, it was possible in one or two places to distinguish the masts or gun turrets of ships which had sunk at anchor. Iris blinked rapidly, her eyes refusing to accept the scale of the disaster presented to them. 'The bastards!' she muttered. 'The dirty yellow bastards!'

'The *Arizona*'s sinking.' Hilary, as a navy wife, was knowledgeable about the fleet's mooring positions. She pointed to the thickest, blackest cloud of smoke. 'My God, look at that!' Her voice was tight with suppressed panic, and Iris was infected by it. If the armour and fire power of a great battleship had been unable to protect it, nothing could be considered safe. Every single one of the planes now completing the strike and turning away belonged to the enemy. That could mean that the *Enterprise* was still far off. But it could equally mean that the carrier had been as much taken by surprise as the rest of the fleet, and that her aircraft had not had time to take off before being destroyed.

'I want to go down there,' said Hilary. 'I must find out.'

'No.' To say that it would be too dangerous was not likely to influence Hilary, but the alternative argument was equally strong. 'We would only get in the way. We must go home. Elliott will have news by now.' She would have liked to drive fast, but restrained herself in order to give the pregnant woman a smooth ride along the winding roads.

Back at Valley Gardens House, Iris hurried to help her daughter-in-law out of the automobile so that they could go together to find Elliott. But Hilary, making no attempt to move, was pale with pain, each breath emerging as a grunt. Iris herself groaned as she guessed was what happening. 'Is it the baby, darling?'

Hilary nodded, her eyes flooding with tears. 'It's too soon. He shouldn't come so soon.'

'Don't get worried. First babies never come quickly. And this will be a false alarm. You're upset. This kind of thing often happens.' She spoke reassuringly, but was far from calm herself. This new emergency trod too close on the heels of the earlier nightmare. But now she must not think about her own children: only about Hilary's.

8

Long before evening Iris was exhausted. Elliott's efforts to get Hilary admitted to the hospital had failed. The number of naval casualties was expected to be so huge that all available hospital beds had been reserved for them. In any case, it had quickly become clear that Hilary ought not to be moved. The best that could be done immediately was to obtain a maternity nurse. When Dr Ennisary was able to make his way up the valley, late in the evening, the nurse told him that the baby should already have arrived. But the young mother was too tense, refusing to let go of her child – as though she could only control the terror in her mind by locking up her body as well. Had Iris been less tired after her sleepless night and a day of emotional shock and physical strain, she might have thought of a solution earlier. As it was, when Elliott came to the door of the makeshift delivery room with a message, the news was genuine and not invented. Iris hurried back to the bedside and held Hilary's hand.

'It's all right, darling. Peter's safe. Elliott's just had it confirmed. The *Enterprise* was held up by engine trouble. She was still well away from Pearl when the attack began. Do you hear me, darling? Peter's okay. Nothing to worry about.'

It was an odd phrase to use on such a day, but it served its purpose. Hilary sighed deeply in relief and allowed herself to relax. When the next contraction came, she gave a single strong, smooth push and the baby was born as easily as if there had been no earlier problem.

For an hour longer the activity continued as mother and child were cleaned and made comfortable. Hilary was happy and affectionate as she cradled her daughter. Then she was ready to sleep, and the baby was handed over to the care of a second nurse who had by now arrived. Iris, for her part, was ready for a drink.

She had had nothing to eat all day, and her head swam dizzily as she set down the glass. But she did not forget the question she had been waiting to ask. 'Did Russell call?' One of her sons was safe; but she had two.

'Give him his own name, Iris,' said Elliott. 'He's Dan. Dan Kiernan. Until we know anything different. No, there's been no message. You couldn't expect it on a day like this.'

Iris recognized the truth of what he said. But his insistence that she should not talk about Russell made her uneasy. She set the glass down in order to interrogate her husband with a clear head. 'The *Oklahoma*,' she said. 'What happened to he *Oklahoma*?' She knew that Elliott had listened to every report which came over the air that day, and she could tell from his eyes that there had been news. 'Tell me,' she insisted.

He answered only with reluctance. 'It was hit early on.'

'Did it sink?'

'Turned over in the water.'

'And the men?' Iris's mouth was so dry that she could hardly speak the words; she did after all take another sip of her drink.

'There are casualties. But survivors as well. It's all still chaotic down there. We can't expect clear information yet.'

'He might have had a weekend liberty,' suggested Iris, clutching at the straws of hope. 'Perhaps he spent the night with a girl on land. Or with one of the families which gives hospitality.' But no, in that case he would surely have made the telephone call. 'Where are the survivors?' she asked. 'Tomorrow I could go talk with them, ask them.'

'You don't understand what's happened, Iris.'

'I *saw* it, for Chrissake!'

'Yes, but on a wider scale. We're at war! If Dan's still alive, he'll be under orders. Going wherever he's sent. But . . .' Elliott hesitated, making it clear that he had hoped to spare her the full truth. 'When I said "survivors", I meant men who weren't killed in the attack. I'm told that four hundred of them are still inside the ship.'

'You mean – under water?'

'There's air in the hull. They're still alive. Divers have been down already. They can hear tapping.'

'But trapped!' The world outside went black as Iris too successfully visualized Russell struggling to keep his head above oily water while he hammered against the *Oklahoma*'s upturned hull in the darkness. How long would the air last, with four hundred men breathing it? Russell was only eighteen. He would be frightened. Hoping that rescuers would break through to save them all, but with every moment that passed, more frightened. Incredulous that not in some wild depth of ocean, but in a calm home harbour, help should be so long in coming. He would be sick with fear, as Iris herself was now. With a hand pressed to her mouth she staggered to the bathroom, retching uncontrollably. Then she went to lie on her bed. For a little while Elliott came to sit with her, talking of Peter and Hilary and the new baby, but nothing that he said could bring her comfort. There was nothing that Russell could do to save himself, and Iris was equally impotent.

For two whole days the nightmare continued. When she was in Hilary's room Iris did her best to sound cheerful; but during the rest of the day she listened to every radio bulletin, called everyone she knew who might be able to answer questions, and drove as near to the devastated area as she was allowed – as though merely by staring she could urge the rescuers on. From conversations with workmen as they wearily left the base she learned to recognize the sound of the air-driven chisels which were cutting their way through the thick hull of the *Oklahoma*. It was too dangerous, she was told, to use acetylene torches, which might cause gas inside to explode.

At first the work continued without interruption, with one shift of workers taking over from others on the job. But when she arrived early on the third morning she was conscious of a new silence in this part of the harbour. She hurried to the gates of the prohibited area, from which on earlier visits she had been turned away, and demanded information. An officer whose face was even more haggard than her own told her that no tapping had been heard from the trapped men for the past sixteen hours and that they must all by now be considered to have died.

Iris began first to shudder and then to scream Russell's name. Her eyes seemed to detach themselves from her body so that in an extraordinary way she was able to watch from outside as she was restrained and driven to the hospital and sedated. When, later, Hilary and Peter came with Elliott to visit her, she studied the whole family group – including Iris Lindsay, who lay in bed, dull-eyed, resisting all efforts to cheer or comfort her: for by that time, a week after the bombardment, Dan Kiernan was officially reported as killed in action.

She was clear-minded enough to realize what had pushed her off balance. In time of war many mothers must expect to be bereaved. Had Peter been killed, it would have broken her heart. She would have mourned him for the rest of her life – intensely at first, but later, perhaps, in a calmer and more bearable manner. But the loss of her younger son so soon after his unexpected reappearance – for she was convinced that Dan Kiernan was indeed Russell – was a different matter. If she had had time to meet him, get to know him, re-establish a relationship of mother and son, perhaps then she would have been able to accept this accident of war as a tragedy which could in the end be borne. But to come so near to a reunion and to have it snatched away; to know that he had died, so terribly, without learning who she was or how much she had loved him; this was an anguish from which she would never escape. For the rest of her life she would hate the Japanese who had killed him, but with an equal passion she would hate the family who had stolen him.

INTERLUDE

1947

The Truth of the Matter

As soon as the war was over, Elliott Lindsay hired a private detective to investigate the case of the little boy who had disappeared from the grounds of The Round House in Natchez in 1925. One reason why he delayed setting this enquiry in train was because, according to Hilary, the sailor Dan Kiernan had been brought up in England and his adoptive parents were still living in that beleaguered island. Dan must have crossed the Atlantic Ocean at least twice in his short life, but bombs and submarines might make his path hard to follow. The other reason was Elliott's unwillingness to disturb the fragile self-control which Iris had imposed on her emotions.

Iris never, these days, spoke of her younger son, but her husband knew that where this subject was concerned she was not quite sane. She had been robbed of her child not once but twice and she would never forget or forgive it. Her silence suggested that no one else could be expected to share or understand her grief. But although he was not given to showing his own feelings, Elliott's love for his younger son had been as deep as his wife's, and he had been just as desolated by Russell's disappearance. He had protected himself from the second horror of the lingering death inside the *Oklahoma* only by closing his mind to the possibility that the boy might indeed be his son.

It was along time before a final report arrived. The

investigator needed to follow a trail which passed through Mississippi and Vermont before crossing the Atlantic to Cambridge, in England and then returning to Georgia. There were gaps in the information which would never be filled because some of the actors in the long-running drama were dead. Elliott knew already that the man – his own great-uncle – who for no known reason had burned down the Kiernans' home and killed their son Danny had died in prison and that his sister Louise had not long survived him. She was by then in her seventies, but local report had it that she died of shame at the disgrace to her family.

By the time the investigator reached England he found that Professor Kiernan was a sick man and could not be interviewed. His wife burst into tears as she described the killing of her baby and the wartime death of her adopted son, but seemed to have nothing to hide. Her father, she said, had been responsible for Dan's adoption, and she repeated the story she was told at the time. Daniel Fletcher was dead: it was amongst his papers that Elliott's own name had been found, as the father of the child. The investigator considered that Mrs Kiernan's action in passing this information on to her adopted son indicated that she had not knowingly been party to any criminal act. She had also without hesitation provided the exact date on which she first saw the little boy; it was within a week of Russell's disappearance.

The facts, then, seemed indisputable. Daniel Fletcher had stolen Russell as an act of revenge for his grandson's death. But there was still a gap in Elliott's comprehensions of what had led up to that crime. No one at the time had understood Thomas Vernon's motive for his act of arson, and neither the detective nor Elliott himself could understand it now. It was a puzzle.

Anxious not to discuss the matter with his wife until he had the sequence of events – and his own attitude to the facts – straight in his mind, Elliott read the report over and over again, spreading the copies of letters, photographs and newspaper clippings over the wide desk in his Merchant

Street office. Just as Iris, six years earlier, had gradually begun to remember that Dan Kiernan, the name on the paper in front of her, was in some way familiar, so Elliott found his eyes concentrating on a single word. Fletcher. Somewhere in the back of his mind, if only he could dig it out, was a memory of seeing that name before.

Fletcher. A common enough name for sure – although not in Hawaii. But the memory Elliott was groping for was not in any public domain but had some connection with his family history. From long ago, before he himself was born. Suddenly impatient, he stacked the papers into a file and drove home in the middle of the afternoon.

Iris had been drinking. He could tell from the way she was standing that she had heard him approach and had hastily tipped her drink away. If he were to touch the glasses on the bar counter, he would find one of them wet, if he kissed her, he would smell whisky on her breath. In the past few years they had quarrelled more and more frequently about her drinking, so that now she was carefully abstemious, almost counting the sips, when he was at home. But he knew, without having the energy to bring it into the open for another quarrel, that she was ordering her own supply of alcohol. She never became drunk in any rowdy way or made an exhibition of herself in company. But very often in the evening, when they were alone, she would begin to weep and go silently to her bedroom. He rarely, these days, followed her there.

Today she looked wary, ready to be indignant if he had come home early in order to catch her out. But Elliott, although not ready to tell her the reason for his early return, had no desire for an argument. 'I've some work to do in the library,' he said. 'Don't let anyone disturb me for an hour.'

The library was his sanctuary – a large, free-standing room surrounded by bauhinias and poincianas about fifty yards away from the main house. Half as high again as the domestic rooms, it was a private museum and art gallery as well as a library, and its own air-conditioning system worked round the clock to control the natural humidity of the atmosphere and preserve his collections. Iris, whose talent as an interior decorator was almost as great as her genius for garden design, had in the early days of their marriage shared his pleasure in fitting the room out and acquiring the furniture of his favourite period; but not for very many years now had she come to sit in it with him.

Inside an antique wedding chest were the few possessions and letters of his grandmother, Rebecca Vernon. A sad, faded photograph of her face hung in his bedroom, but everything which could be described as the family archive was here in the library. And somewhere amongst these letters and documents was the handwritten name: Fletcher.

Elliott, of course, had never known his grandmother. Even her own son, Tom, had no memory of her, for it was his birth which caused her death. But as a little boy Elliott had often heard from Tom, his father, stories of the child bride – already at the age of fourteen, widowed in the Civil War – who had travelled to the islands with a missionary family in the eighteen-sixties. Those same missionaries had adopted Tom when he was left an orphan. But although he took their name, Lindsay, he had always known that his mother was Rebecca Vernon. There seemed no room in that story for anyone called Fletcher; and yet . . . Elliott began to turn over the pages one at a time, unfolding each letter and allowing his eyes to run over it – not reading the sense, but waiting for the single word he sought to leap out at him.

He found it, more than an hour later, in a distraught letter written by Rebecca's mother, Loveday Vernon, to Mrs Lindsay. Its faint, old-fashioned handwriting was difficult to read. Although the letter was dated seven months after Rebecca's death, it was clear that the news had only just reached her mother in Natchez. Her unhappiness poured out without restraint. Only towards the end of the letter did her tone become sadly businesslike.

'Had Rebecca lived, I would have loved her child because it was hers, and would have welcomed them both back to share our ruined lives here as soon as this dreadful war is at an end. But she is dead, and I fear that I may never be able to look on her child, innocent though he is, without revulsion. Not because his birth has cost the life of my dear daughter, but because with every sight of him I should be reminded of his father, the monster Fletcher. And so, my dearest Beth, if it is truly your wish to take him into your family and bring him up as your son, I see it as God's will that his dependence may bring you comfort. He is yours, Beth dear, to name as you will and to bring up in the love of God. He need never know that he has a grandmother here, and an uncle and aunt little older than himself. I shall never forget my Rebecca, but from this day on I shall think of her always as the child I loved here in my home, and not as the unhappy victim of lust and violence.'

Elliott set the letter down on his desk and pushed back the light which he had needed to study the faded writing. He had found the name which must be the key to the story. It was certain that he would have read the letter at least once before – when he inherited the papers after his father's death – but on that occasion he must have assumed that Rebecca's husband was named Fletcher Vernon and that her mother had disapproved of the marriage. Only when Thomas Vernon wrote in 1924 to reveal the family connection which he had discovered through Loveday's cache of correspondence should it have been possible to deduce that Rebecca had never in fact been married. Vernon was her maiden name, and the dead husband must have been invented to preserve her respectability – and that of the child she was expecting – in a missionary society.

She must have been raped. Nothing else would explain Loveday Vernon's letter. And Thomas Vernon, long after the event, must have discovered what had happened.

Elliott had visited Thomas once in jail during that tragic visit to the mainland. He managed now to conjure up a mental picture of a stout, florid man, looking older than his sixty-five years, who had not spoken a single word throughout what had been intended as a friendly conversation. It was difficult to imagine such a man setting out to avenge his sister so long after her death; but revenge provided the only motive that made any sense.

How curious it was that all the little boys involved in the tragedy of twenty-three years ago – Alex and Danny Kiernan, Peter and Russell Lindsay – should prove to be descended from the same man. The blood of 'the monster Fletcher' ran in all their veins, as in his own. Well, that was not important. Elliott sat in the library without moving for a little longer, until he was sure that the sequence of events had arranged itself clearly in his mind. Then it was time to tell Iris what he had discovered.

Had he believed that she had recovered from the distress caused by the sinking of the *Oklahoma*, he might have hesitated before bringing the subject back to her mind. But although Iris never now mentioned Russell's name, Elliott was well aware of her obsession with his fate. It was natural enough, and she had the right to know the truth. He put away the papers he had been studying and went to find her.

It was not an easy conversation. For a little while Iris listened in silence as he told her everything he knew or guessed about the contacts between the two families descended from someone called Fletcher. While he was still speaking she went across to the cocktail bar to pour herself a drink. At that hour, and in front of him, defying his known disapproval, the gesture had all the coldness of a declaration of war, but Elliott kept his voice calm as he continued to detail what he and the investigator between them had discovered.

When he had finished speaking, he tried to comfort his wife. In recent years they had grown apart, but so much talk about the past revived his memories of the time when they were a young, happily-married couple, enjoying the high spirits of their two young sons. He and Iris had still been very much in love at the moment when they first arrived at The Round House in Natchez. If, from that time onwards, Iris had been less willing to show her love, he could understand it in a way. They had each suffered a great loss and had been equally hurt by it. He himself had turned to his work as a way of escaping from grief. Iris, to protect herself from suffering in the same way again, had chosen to build a barrier first of all of reserve and later, after Pearl Harbor, of coldness.

She was not prepared to relax that defence now. She shuddered as she listened to the old story, but her expression was one of anger. It was not clear whether this was directed against Daniel Fletcher, the kidnapper, or that other Fletcher, probably Daniel's father, the rapist; or even, for no good reason, against Elliott himself.

'Think of it this way,' he pleaded, trying to console her. 'For sixteen years, after he disappeared, we believed that Russell was dead. Now we *know* that he is. Nothing's changed.'

'Everything's changed,' said Iris in a low voice. 'We've been robbed of sixteen years of his life. And if he'd spent those years as our son, he wouldn't have been on the ship at that time. But you don't care, do you? You don't understand how I feel.'

'Hell, Iris, of course I care! I feel just the same. You don't have any monopoly of bereavement. Russell was my son too.' If he continued to speak soothingly he could maybe avoid another quarrel, but he was angered by her assumption that his love for their younger son was less than hers.

'So what are you going to do about it?' Iris thrust her chin forward, challenging him.

'I'm going to accept that my son is dead. He died for his country, as Peter might have done.'

'That's not *doing* anything,' she said scornfully. 'That's letting them get away with it. If you were a man, you'd find some way to pay them back.'

'They had reason to hate us; and it was when *they* started paying back that all this began.'

'From what you've been telling me, it started earlier than that. And it was this Fletcher man, *their* family, who was responsible –'

'For Christ's sake, Iris, that's past history. All the people who ought to be punished are dead. The woman who raised Russell, she never knew the truth. And she loved him. You should be grateful for that. She gave our son a happy home.'

'So you're going to leave it at that?'

'Yes,' he said. 'And so are you. You must put it out of your mind. I sympathize with how you've felt, but . . .'

'You have not the faintest conception of my feelings.' Iris shrugged her shoulders helplessly. 'I don't want to stay here, Elliott. I can't look out into the garden without remembering that Russell sat there, talking to Hilary. If we'd come home a half hour earlier that day, if we'd got him to stay for the night . . .'

'Stop playing that game,' he ordered. 'Look the facts in the eye. Russell is dead. Think how many other parents have lost their sons in the past six years. We're luckier than most. We still have Peter – and Hilary, and the two little girls.'

'They can come and live here,' Iris said. 'I'm going home.'

'This is your home, for Christ's sake.'

'To Kauai.'

Elliott stared at her, realizing that he must take her announcement seriously. Iris had been born on the small island of Kauai. An only child, she had inherited an estate there. The main house, her home as a girl, had been sold; but Iris had retained a smaller property, in the canyon, which for many years they had used as a holiday home.

'You don't have any friends there,' he began slowly; but Iris interrupted him.

'I don't have friends here any more. Alcoholics don't have friends. Only bottles. Who am I kidding? I poured a drink away when you drove back this afternoon. You guessed, right? I shall make a new garden in the canyon. And drink. But you won't need to apologize for me any more.'

There was a long silence between them while Elliott searched his own feelings to discover whether he wanted to argue, to persuade her into a change of mind. But it seemed to him that Iris was only confirming what had already taken place. Their marriage was dead. 'Do you want a divorce?' he asked.

'There's nothing you've done,' said Iris. Abruptly, as though the act of announcing her decision had swept away some of her anger, her voice seemed softer. 'Nothing that's happened is your fault. Except . . .' What she was shrugging away was no doubt resentment at what she clearly considered his spineless refusal to pursue an old feud. 'It'll be down to you. You'll have grounds. Not another man, I don't mean. But desertion. Incompatibility. If that's what you want, I shan't defend. Don't cut me off from Peter and Hilary and the girls, that's all. I shall want them to come and visit with me. I can stay sober when I choose.' She paused for a moment, perhaps needing to be sure that she had meant what she said. Then she added. 'I'd like to see the papers. What that man of yours found out about the Kiernans.'

'No,' said Elliott. Iris's talk, earlier, of 'paying them back' had disturbed him. When he wrote to the private investigator to acknowledge receipt of the report and to pay the last instalment of the fee, he must make it clear that the information should not be divulged to anyone else. 'I've told you all the facts and what I make of them. It's time to let the whole thing drop. You can take anything you want after I'm dead. But not till then.' Elliott was only fifty-three years old. There would be plenty of time before he died for Iris to forget her vindictive dream of revenge.

EPISODE FIVE

1960

A Mother's Revenge

1

Early in 1960 a tornado on its way to the Gulf of Mexico flicked its tail as it passed over Hawaii and the light plane in which Elliott Lindsay piloted himself between his various states was hurled into the side of a volcano. His widow – for they had never divorced – was naturally invited to attend the funeral.

Peter was waiting when she landed, ready to drive her to the house which had once been her own home. Had it not been a sad occasion, it would have made Iris laugh to watch the anxiety in her son's eyes changing to relief as he observed that she was sober. Two or three times – not more than that – in the past ten years there had been unfortunate incidents when, finding himself in Kauai on business, he called on her without advance warning: and on one of those occasions his three children were with him. But by now he should have learned that she had a degree of control over her addiction. She was no longer able to drink in moderation, but she could, when there was a reason for it, not drink at all.

Iris was not ashamed of her habit. In the years before she left Elliott she had become secretive and sly, telling lies to protect herself and always worried lest he should force her to abstain. But there was no cause for anxiety in her life in

Kauai, because she could pour herself a drink whenever she chose. Knowing that, she was able to be abstemious during the daylight hours which she devoted to her garden. If she needed to be carried to her bed every night, that was no business of anyone else, and no one suffered by it.

During the three days of her visit to Oahu, however, she would drink nothing but coffee or juice. Such self-discipline was made possible by the comforting memory of the well-stocked bar in the canyon house and by the fact that no one here would offer her a drink. The children, as well as the servants, would have been given their instructions. There was a third element in the situation as well; there was business to be done, and she must have a clear head to be sure that nothing was forgotten.

Elliott had made his dispositions shortly after she left him. Peter was persuaded to leave the navy in order to learn the ramifications of the business which he would one day inherit. He had returned to live in Valley Gardens House with his father. With him, of course, came Hilary and the little girls, Jess and Dinah; Howard, her only grandson, had been born soon after.

There were no surprises in Elliott's will. He had been generous to the young woman who had acted as his personal assistant for the past ten or eleven years – but then, Janine had been generous in the amount of time she devoted to him. For the rest, Elliott had left everything within the family, where it belonged.

Not, however, directly to Peter. Two separate strands had combined to create the family fortune as it was today, and what Iris brought to her marriage was even more valuable than Elliott's Lindsay inheritance. Probably one reason why he had decided against a divorce was the difficulty of making a viable financial arrangement, because Iris still personally owned the land and capital which her father had left her, but could not withdraw it without making her own estate, as well as Elliott's, insecure. Because they both accepted the realities of the situation, and remained on friendly terms after the separation, they were able to agree on the formation of a family trust. Iris, who when sober had a good head for business, took note as she studied and signed the documents that she had been effectively prevented from ever disposing of what had originally been her own property. But at the same time she could not be robbed of the use and profit of it. As long as she lived, her son – and Howard as well, when he was old enough to take his part – would need her approval before embarking on any new development.

They were not likely to quarrel. Iris loved Peter too much to be obstructive. Peter, for his part, was inclined to be nervous about his mother's behaviour, but revealed it in solicitude rather than direct criticism. At some point after the end of the war his father must have explained to him the effect which the loss and reappearance and death of her younger son had had on her life. And just as she would never subdue the implacable bitterness she felt towards Russell's kidnapper, so Peter, she knew, could not quite forgive himself for his own part in the events of that day long ago. Iris had never blamed Peter for what happened: it was entirely her own fault for expecting too much of a six-year-old. But the guilt and sadness they shared at that time had strengthened the natural bond between a mother and her first-born son. As they drove now along the highway towards the head of the Nuuanu valley, she patted his arm with her hand in reassurance. She did not intend to cause him any trouble.

Her visit passed smoothly, filled with all the inevitable routines of such an occasion. The service itself was followed by a gathering of Elliott's friends which began in an appropriate atmosphere of muted sympathy but imperceptibly developed into a party. When the guests had departed, Iris took the opportunity to talk to her three grandchildren. The two girls, Jess and Dinah, were polite but not as warmly affectionate as Iris would have liked. They disapproved, no doubt, of her way of life; and Jess, who was head over heels in love and planning a wedding, would not wish to be reminded that marriages could grow cold and die. Neither of the girls had ever particularly looked forward to their annual visits to her house in the canyon. Even with each other for company, they found it lonely, and were glad when they could return to their friends in Oahu.

Howard, her only grandson, was different. Iris tried not to love him too much, in case she should lose him one day, but she could not conceal the special feeling she had for him. Thirteen years old now, he was an outdoor boy, his naturally fair hair bleached almost to whiteness by the hours he spent in the sun. His passion was for surfing, but whenever he visited her – alone, these days, rather than with his sisters – he did not sulk at being fifteen miles from the ocean. Instead, he was happy to enjoy the canyon, enjoying the contrast between the rocky ridges which rose into the clouds and the tropical forest below. Like Iris herself, and unlike his sisters, he was a loner. As a small boy he had climbed trees or waterfalls, or searched for pots of gold at the feet of the rainbows which rose almost daily from the canyon. As he grew older, his expeditions became longer; he tracked steams to their sources or searched the rocks for petroglyphs or climbed the steep side of the gorge. Iris had always insisted that he should draw two sketch maps of the route he planned to take and should leave one of them with her, in case he had an accident. Humouring her whim, he would devote a whole evening to the maps, checking the scale for accuracy and adding thumbnail pictures of the landscape. He had never discovered that wherever he went, his grandmother's bodyguard would be silently following.

Nor, even while he was illustrating his route maps, had he discovered that he had a talent for art. If Iris had told him this, he would have dismissed the idea with scorn. So when she asked him to paint one of her orchids, or the feathery red blossom of a lehua tree, or a waxy anthurium, it was always as a favour to herself, to provide a record of some special display in her garden. And when she suggested that he should sketch his friends on their surfboards, it was with the excuse that it helped her to imagine Howard himself in action. She kept everything he gave her. One day, when he was older, she would use them to show him that he was an artist.

That thought put an idea into her mind when, on the last day of her visit, she went into the library which for many years had been locked against her. She had been there for only a few moments when Howard followed her in.

'What are you looking for?' he asked, ready to help.

Iris looked up, startled. 'Family papers,' she said, forcing her fingers to move more slowly, as though it hardly mattered what she found. Had Elliott, she wondered, destroyed the only documents she wanted to read? Or instructed Peter not to let her have them? Without thinking, she found herself lying to Howard in case he had been sent to spy on her. 'There should be a portfolio of my mother's drawings somewhere hereabouts.'

'I don't know about your mother.'

'Don't know a lot myself,' Iris said briskly, pausing in her search. 'She ran away to Paris when I was only five. To be a painter.'

'Was she French?'

Iris shook her head. 'American as apple pie. She just took it into her head that France was the only country where you *could* be a painter.'

'She'd have to speak French all the time, though.' Howard's comment revealed his own attitude to foreign languages.

'It comes easier when you live in a country.' She laughed as he pulled a face. 'We'll have to get you over there sometime. A couple of months in France and you'd be jabbering like a native. I was sent to Paris myself in 1914, to stay with my mother and learn the language.' She laughed again at the memory. 'Not a great success. My mother and her friends didn't know what to do with a girl my age. And before they had time to find out, the war began. So they packed me off back home to my father in Kauai.'

'Did you ever see her again?'

'No. After the war there was a flu epidemic in Europe. Millions of people died. She was one of them. Her friends sent all her work back for me to have. I left the drawings here when I moved out because of the air conditioning. You know how it is in the canyon. Everything goes mouldy. But I like to look at them from time to time. Would you fetch me a jug of orange juice, dear? It's thirsty work, sorting through papers.'

Even as her fingers moved fast and methodically through Elliott's folders she was able to register, as though from outside herself, an astonishment that she should have waited so long and patiently for this moment. Elliott had forbidden his own investigator to pass on any information to her, but there were other detectives. At any time she chose she could have hired her own man to cover the same ground again – as she would do now if she found that the original report had been destroyed. But she had taken a deliberate decision to wait: her intention to take revenge one day for the terrible wrong she had suffered provided a deep satisfaction which increased with the passing of time. The family who would one day be her victims knew nothing about her or her hatred. One of them – the woman who had raised Russell as her own son – would once long ago have seen a name and address on a piece of paper; that was all. They would be living calm, ordinary lives, not dreaming that a Damoclean sword was about to fall. Iris would have preferred them to be living in fear, but as a second best she took a spiteful pleasure in stretching the period in which they could remain unsuspecting.

That period had not yet ended. Even as her eyes brightened at the sight of the folder she sought, Iris recognized that the information in it would need to be brought up to date. Daniel Fletcher had been dead for twenty years already, and by now his daughter and son-in-law might also have slipped from between her fingers. It wouldn't matter. Iris herself had been wholly innocent of any responsibility for a family feud when she was robbed of her son, and she felt no qualms at the prospect of punishing the innocent in return.

The report was already folded into her large handbag

when Howard came back to the library, carrying the orange juice, and prepared to share it with her. As she thanked him, a plan was already germinating in her mind. And there would be a place in it for her grandson.

2

'Why me?' asked Howard of the family at large. There was something odd about the invitation which had arrived in the morning mail, a year after his grandfather's death. Or perhaps the oddness was in the way that his parents were waiting for his reaction. He could work out that bit of it. His grandmother would have cleared it with them first, to make sure that Howard himself would not get excited about a holiday which he was then forbidden to enjoy. So they had known what was in the letter before he opened it and they were not sure whether they wanted him to agree.

Would he enjoy it, he asked himself. A trip to Europe sounded exciting in a kind of way. But it would mean a whole summer away from the ocean. Whatever treats Paris and Rome and Venice and Athens and London might provide, they were unlikely to include the sight of huge combers gathering themselves together and roaring towards a beach. And although he enjoyed his visits to his grandmother's house in the canyon, where he could go hiking or fishing or climbing, it might not be so good being cooped up with her for weeks at a time, living in classy hotels and trying to understand people who didn't speak English.

Maybe that was the answer to his question. The invitation had come his way to get him speaking French. That settled it. No *sir*.

Just as he provided one answer, his mother offered a quite different one. 'There's not much choice,' she pointed out unflatteringly. 'Dinah's already fixed to spend the vacation in California and Jess won't be going anywhere this summer.'

Howard recognized the truth of this. His elder sister had married six months earlier and was already expecting her first baby. 'But Grandmother doesn't need any of us,' he said. 'Not if it's just for looking after her. She's bound to take Yung Chang or Serge.' He knew that her Chinese cook and her Russian driver took it in turns to act as her bodyguard, or nurse, as required.

'She called up to tell us about the trip,' his mother said. 'She's going mainly to buy some antique statues to put in her garden. But on top of that, it would give her pleasure, she said, to watch you discovering Europe. She plans to show you things. Buildings. Pictures.'

'You mean she's going to drag me round museums and art shows. No thanks.'

His mother, who usually laughed all the time she was talking to him, even when embarking on one of her sustained sermons about his unspeakably bad habits, looked serious for once. 'We're big fish in a very small pond here, Howard,' she reminded him. 'We have a good life, but it's not the only life. The time's bound to come when you'll want to explore a wider world. Iris is offering you a taster. Picking some of the plums out of the pudding. Think about it before you decide.'

'Think about something else on top of that.' Howard knew at once from the tone of his father's voice that he had doubts about the invitation. 'Your grandmother. Reckon you could cope?'

Howard knew what he meant. 'She never drinks in front of me when I stay in the canyon,' he said. 'After I'm in bed, maybe, and she doesn't get up for breakfast. But she's always okay for lunch.'

'You've never visited with her for more than a couple of weeks at a stretch. She might not be able to keep up the act over three months.'

Howard took the point seriously. But it seemed to him that if his grandmother wanted to slosh her way around Europe she would take care not to have any member of the family at hand to be ashamed of her. He had not been completely truthful in suggesting to his father that he had never seen her under the influence of whisky, but that very fact was reassuring. He knew that she did not sing or shout or act in any similarly embarrassing way. Either she fell asleep or else she passed out – suddenly, silently, falling straight to the ground. But she was such a tiny woman that he could handle that situation. And if his father had sounded doubtful over the telephone, Iris might now think that her grandson was turning down a marvellous offer only because he was ashamed to be in her company. Howard, who loved her, would not like her to believe that. Although not prepared to show positive enthusiasm until he had thought the matter through, he was careful not to close the door on the idea.

'Could be kind of interesting,' he muttered. 'Don't know yet, though. I'll think about it, okay?'

3

When Howard accepted his grandmother's invitation, she produced a detailed itinerary with a promptness suggesting that she had taken his agreement for granted. They would be away for ten weeks, she told him. The journey was so long that no shorter period would be worth while. But she did not intend to hustle around in the manner which gave American tourists in Europe such a bad name. They would visit only a few important places. Serge would hire an automobile in each city and drive them around so that they could explore thoroughly and without hassle. Serge could speak French, too, so that it would be entirely up to Howard to decide whether he wanted to practise the language himself. The trip would be fun, she promised him – and when the time came, she kept her promise.

The last stop on the tour was London – and London, it soon became clear, was to be approached differently from the other cities they had visited. To begin with, there was a surprise in the form of a family connection. Howard's maternal grandparents had died before he ever had a chance to meet them, and his English mother had been an only child. But the two children of her first cousin had, it emerged, been lined up by Iris to take charge of Howard during his stay.

'Our instructions are to give you a good time,' said Biff. He and his twin sister, Jinx – Howard never discovered what they had been christened – were both nineteen, studying at Sussex University but at present on vacation. They were almost indistinguishable, for Biff's hair was as long as his sister's, whilst Jinx – in spite of a summer heatwave – wore fly-fronted black leather trousers which fitted over her slim hips like a second skin. Their enthusiasm for enjoying themselves was infectious and Howard surrendered to it without a fight.

'Starting,' said Jinx, 'with a party tonight, so that you can get to know a few people. Your grandmother warned us that she'd be too tired after the journey from Greece to indulge in any night life herself, but she's staked us for a gig. Nothing but the best for her beamish boy, she said, although not exactly in those words. So the champagne will be flowing tonight, instead of our usual plonk. And we've got Monday with Melody.'

Howard could see that he was expected to react to this in some way. It was indeed Monday, but . . . Biff observed his hesitation.

'Obviously you don't know about Melody,' he said. 'The female of that name, not the generic word for a good tune. Have you heard of the Beatles?'

Howard shook his head and Biff turned to his sister in mock dismay. 'Our provincial cousin,' he said sadly. 'Out of the swim! Never mind, Howard. When you get back to Hawaii, you'll be the one who knows what's going on in the big wide world.'

'But what do beetles have to do with melody?'

'The Beatles are a pop group,' explained Jinx. 'They

produce a noise called the Mersey Sound which isn't quite like anything that's happened before. They have an adoring audience consisting of every female in the country under the age of twenty, which screams in the aisles whenever they appear. That's because they're blokes. There has to be a female equivalent to keep the chaps happy, and Melody is it. She doesn't strum a guitar like the Beatles, but when she sings it's electric. Well, you'll see tonight. Monday is the name of the group she sings with. It's playing at The Scene this week, but they have one night a week free for private gigs. This evening, we're it. Your grandmother said that you'd be having dinner with her at half past seven, so we'll pick you up at nine.'

Howard promised to be ready. He was startled – but pleased – by the sudden change in the nature of the trip. Up to this point it had been heavy with culture. Pictures and palaces in Paris, pictures and churches in Rome, pictures and canals in Venice. The relentless pace had begun to slacken while they were in Greece, with leisurely journeys to ruined cities and free time for Howard while his grandmother shopped for antiques. Now it seemed to have come to an end altogether.

To his surprise, he felt a slight regret. When there was no escape from Iris's sightseeing timetable, he had found himself coming to identify different kinds of painting and to like some better than others. And he had been bowled over by palaces. The Iolani Palace in Honolulu – the only once-royal residence he knew – was no more impressive than his own home, so the sheer scale of Versailles and Fontainebleau had opened his eyes wide with amazement. Iris had delivered one of her many lectures to him at Versailles; this time on the relationship between buildings and the lifestyles which went with them. Howard's first thought on that occasion was that it must be fun for an architect to design a building which exactly suited his customer's requirements. But Iris's lecture prompted a further idea which she had not mentioned – that it would be even more fun to design a building whose shape forced people to live in a way they would not have thought of for themselves.

It was another of the surprises of the trip to discover how much his grandmother *knew*. During holidays in the canyon, conversations tended to be about food or plants or school or the way he had just passed or planned to spend the day. He had been vaguely aware that she had an interest in antiques, but he had not expected her to be able to tell him so much about cities and paintings which she had never seen before, or to express it with such enthusiasm that he found himself sharing her excitement.

Over dinner in the Connaught, however, her lecture was on a different topic. 'Biff and Jinx,' she said, pronouncing the names with a degree of disbelief. 'You're five years younger than they are. Remember that. You'll want to act as though you were their age, and that's okay up to a point. A glass or two of champagne never did anyone any harm. But drugs are a different matter. There's a lot of that sort of thing going on in London. Boys like to experiment, I know that. But I'm responsible for you while you're away from home. I want you to promise me that you won't let yourself be tempted to try anything. Not even nicotine. Once you start smoking, it's hard to say no to a marijuana joint if it's passed round casually. I'm asking for a no-exceptions promise. No drugs. No tobacco, grass, snow, speed, coke, pot – whatever they have, whatever they call it, you say no. Right?'

'Right,' agreed Howard, and Iris smiled at him in an invitation to kiss her.

'I haven't come the heavy grandmother on you too much, have I?' she asked. 'Off you go, then, and have a good time.'

He had a good time. Jinx and Biff, inviting mainly their fellow-students, must have suggested that brothers or sisters of Howard's age might be brought along. But although everyone was friendly and most of the girls were pretty, from the moment that the group of musicians appeared Howard had eyes for no one but Melody.

Everything that Biff had said about her was true. Her vitality crackled round the room like electricity, drawing sparks from everyone it touched. She belted out the words of her songs with too much energy to be truly musical, but Howard felt that every pulse in his body was throbbing in time to its beat. The most wonderful thing about her was the movement of her body, so rhythmically strong that it was as much a part of the music as the frenzied percussion of the drummer. She wore a low-cut catsuit which clung to her skin so tightly that had it not been black it would have seemed transparent. A frill, too short to be described as a skirt, encircled her hips; and this and a narrower ruff across her breasts were stitched with sequins which sparkled in the coloured lights.

In the first break, to Howard's delight, Melody came over to join him, accompanied by a lanky young man whom she introduced as Colin, the group's manager. Howard found himself being thanked for choosing them to appear at his party and was reluctant to explain that the choice had actually been made by Biff and Jinx.

'Let me get you a drink.' That was the polite English thing to say. Within the space of half an hour he had become a different person. When he walked into the room that evening he had been a schoolkid and a foreigner. Now he was a young man of the world, entertaining a pop star. Melody, to his delight, while agreeing that she was panting for something to drink, sent Colin off to fetch it.

Seen at close quarters she was even more exciting than when she was clutching a microphone. Her dark, curly hair was dusted with something which made it sparkle like the Milky Way and her elaborate eye make-up, too, glistened with gold and silver. And yet there was nothing artificial about her smile when – perhaps still surprised that an American should have known enough about the group to choose it – she asked Howard what his favourite music was. 'What records do you listen to?'

Howard considered whether to tell the truth. Should he confess to Ray Charles, or was there some other name which would impress Melody with the fact that they were soulmates?

He needn't have worried about his choice. Melody sighed in sympathy. 'When I was younger,' she said. 'I used to pray every night that I'd grow up to be large and male and black, with a voice somewhere down here,' she pressed her hands against her diaphragm, 'so that I could spend my life singing the blues. But I've got the wrong sort of body and the wrong sort of voice; I've had to make the best of what I was born with.'

'You've got a perfect body and a marvellous voice.' If Howard had said that to any of the girls he knew in Hawaii he would have blushed, but tonight it seemed the easiest thing in the world to pay a compliment to a beautiful woman.

The evening passed in a haze of happiness. Perhaps it was due to the champagne, or maybe it had something to do with the music, which increased in volume and frenzy as the night wore on. But secretly Howard knew the real reason. He had fallen in love with Melody.

Only one thing was needed to make the party perfect – and Melody provided it when – as the group dismantled its amplification system and packed away the drums and guitars – Howard went to thank her and say goodnight.

'We're at The Scene till the end of the month,' she told him. 'If you find yourself in that part of the world, drop in and say hello. Colin will give you a card.'

'I sure will,' said Howard. 'Gee, thanks.' Now he was talking like a schoolkid once more and his cheeks flushed with the realization of it. But it didn't matter. He was going to see Melody again.

4

Until they arrived in London, Howard had been impressed by the businesslike efficiency with which all the arrangements for their trip had been made. Flights and railroad seats and hired limousines were all reserved in advance and hotel suites booked for a precise number of nights. But suddenly now he found that everything was flexible. If Iris had decided on the date of their return home, she did not trouble to mention it. Howard's school term would be starting soon; but if his grandmother was not bothered about it, nor was he.

Another difference was that Iris had given up educating him. That was not because he had rebelled against her lectures on pictures and buildings, which as a matter of fact he found interesting. She had decided, it seemed, that her own interest in England was in its gardens. Every morning, with Serge driving cautiously on the unfamiliar side of the road, she embarked on an expedition to Kew or Sissinghurst or Stourhead. Howard could accompany her if he wished, but she assumed that he would prefer to choose a destination from the list of tourist sights prepared by Biff and Jinx. More surprisingly, she showed no sign of disapproval even when his choice was for Carnaby Street rather than the National Gallery. Nor did she seem to mind that he was out every evening, returning to the hotel only in the early hours of each morning. Only once did she reveal by a comment that she knew what was going on.

'Every young man falls for a showgirl some time in his life,' she said. 'If he never gets close enough to know her, it fades away and there's no harm done. It will be tougher for you, if she's being friendly. You have to remember that you and she have two very different lives. And that she's six years older than you. That's a big gap between two people when one of them's only fourteen. Try to keep it in the back of your mind that there's no future in it. Don't give her your address. She wouldn't write anyhow, but this way you can tell yourself that it's because she doesn't know where you are. Protect yourself, that's what I'm saying. Keep reminding yourself that she must have been dating someone before you came along, and she's still dating him now. You probably think that you've fallen in love, but there's good sense in that young head of yours. You don't need me to tell you that it's just infatuation.'

'It's not either of those things,' protested Howard. 'She's a great singer, that's all.' Then he spoiled the effect by adding, 'She's invited me to a party on Monday. A private party. In her own home.'

'Birthday?' asked Iris.

'Nope. A send-off for Colin. He's the group's manager. They're all going off to the States for a tour in a month's time, and he's flying over in advance to see that all the arrangements are right.'

'And where is her home?'

'She has a basement flat in her parents' house. Not really big enough for a rave-up, she said. If it's a fine night we can spill out into the garden. If it rains, we'll have to spread up into the house.'

'I shouldn't have thought a colonel would take kindly to having his home taken over by a pop group.'

'What colonel?' asked Howard, puzzled.

'Didn't you tell me that Melody's father was in the army?'

'I don't know anything about her parents,' Howard said, and smiled as Iris tutted at her own muddled memory.

'It must have been one of Biff's friends. Anyway. I take it you don't want me to book our flights home for Sunday!'

'You got it!' Howard didn't mind his grandmother's teasing. He was too excited by the prospect of the party.

Monday, when at long last it arrived, was wet; all afternoon the rain poured down with a steadiness which reminded Howard of the rainy season at home. There would be no question of using Melody's garden; and he soon realized that the party was private only in the sense that no one had to pay for admission. The pleased surprise with which each new arrival was greeted suggested that the group had simply let it known that they would be at home and then waited to see who turned up. Within the first hour the basement was bursting at the seams. 'Time to spread ourselves,' said Colin, fishing in his pocket for a key.

Howard went with him up a short flight of stairs.

'We act as caretakers when Mel's parents are away,' Colin explained, unlocking a door. 'Open and close the curtains from time to time. To make it look lived in, you know.' He moved through the rooms, switching on every light. Other guests were beginning to follow. Any potential burglar tonight would certainly get the impression that the house was occupied.

'Gee! They have enough to read!' Howard looked curiously round a room almost completely lined with bookshelves. To judge by their titles, all the books were scientific.

'Mel's grandfather was a professor,' Colin told him. 'When he died, no one liked to throw his books away. And Colonel Kiernan – that's Mel's old man – is a boffin-type soldier, if you know what I mean. An expert on missile systems. That's what he's doing in Australia now; testing things in the desert.'

'I didn't realize . . .' began Howard slowly. He was about to comment on the odd business of Melody's father being a colonel, just as Iris – who could not possibly have known that – had said by mistake. But Colin took the comment in a different way.

'Not what you'd expect, is it, a family like this producing a girl like Melody? She's their only kid. When she was born they christened her Melanie and I don't suppose their big ambition was to see her at Number One in the hit parade one day. Any more than they'd have fancied someone like me for a son-in-law if they'd had the choice. But I have to hand it to them; they're not as stuffy as you might expect. As long as nobody's sick on the Persian rug, they won't mind us being here.'

As though the risk had prompted its own solution he rolled up the dark red rug which was spread out in front of the fireplace and propped it against the wall. Speechless with shock, Howard stared at him. What had Colin just implied? That he was married to Melody? It was impossible. Wasn't it? Howard checked back over the words, trying to persuade himself that he had misunderstood. But the longer he thought about it, the more occasions he remembered on which Colin – and even Melody herself – had said 'we' in a context which had seemed at the time to refer to the whole group but perhaps meant only the two of them.

Sick at heart, Howard turned against the tide of guests who were surging up from the basement and made his way with difficulty down the stairs. He wanted to take another look at the apartment. Was it the home of a married couple? Naturally he had noticed that Colin's luggage was stacked next to the door; but since he would be going straight from the party to the airport there was nothing surprising in that. The bathroom would provide an answer. The contents of bathroom cupboards and shelves were bound to divide themselves between male and female owners.

A familiar figure emerged from the bathroom just before Howard reached the door: Serge, his grandmother's driver and bodyguard – a huge, square man with hair cropped short, as though by a barber in jail. At the time when he jumped ship from a Russian whaler, many years before, he had spoken not a word of English. He had been taught the language by Yung Chang, Iris's Chinese cook, so that his manner of speaking was as individual as his appearance.

'I looking for you,' he said now before Howard had time to ask him what he was doing. 'Mrs Lindsay say come back quick.'

'What's wrong?' asked Howard. 'Is she ill?'

'Tomorrow going back home. Now getting ready.' He turned as though to lead the way out at once.

'Hold on,' said Howard. His grandmother surely would not have expected him to leave the party so early, when she knew how much he had looked forward to it. It was only a moment or two past midnight. Yet the sick feeling in his stomach reminded him that his pleasure in the occasion had already been killed by Colin's casual remark. Iris had warned him. And even without being told, he had known. Even though he might refuse to accept that his adoration of Melody was mere infatuation, there was no chance that she could ever have thought of him as anything but a kid. Had he been making a fool of himself all this time? Had Melody been secretly laughing at him? No, she was too sincere and unaffected for that. There was no reason why he should feel ashamed. And so he need not – *must* not – walk out now without a word. 'Wait outside,' he told Serge. 'I'll be with you in ten minutes.'

He climbed the stairs for a second time. By now the whole party had moved up, leaving the basement empty except for a few late arrivals coming through the open door. It took him a moment to find Melody and catch her eye. She danced across the library floor towards him, her hips twisting in time to music which was playing at full pitch in another room. She was happy. Howard could see that her eyes were shining, and her lips twitched with the effort to keep a smile under control.

'I have to go,' he said. 'A message just came through for me. We're leaving London. I shan't get to see you again.'

'What a shame!' exclaimed Melody. 'And our party hasn't got going yet. It's been fun meeting you, Howard. I'm sorry our tour won't be taking in Hawaii.'

'Me too. But I'll watch you moving up the charts. You deserve to make the big time. It's been . . .' He hesitated, but could not prevent himself from speaking the words in his mind. 'I didn't know that you and Colin were married,' he said.

'Perhaps that's because the last time you saw us, we weren't. It only happened today.'

Howard was, if possible, even more surprised. 'You mean Colin's taking off for New York the first day you're married?'

Melody's grin refused to be confined any longer. 'You could say that we've had the honeymoon already. How did you know, though, about us being married?'

'Something Colin said.'

'He wasn't supposed to. It's a secret. Keep it to yourself, there's a love. It does terrible things to anyone's ratings, being married. The kids all like to feel that they're in with a chance.'

'Well, if no one's going to know, and if you've . . .' Howard spluttered over the words and failed to pronounce them. 'I mean, what's the point of getting married at all?'

Melody did not answer at once. But her eyes were still shining, and at last she leaned her head close to his. 'This is even more of a secret, and if anyone gets wind of it in the next four months, I shall know you're the one who sneaked,' she said. 'The reason we got married is because I'm a petty bourgeois at heart. Sex without a marriage certificate is okay. Babies without a marriage certificate are not okay. Hence this morning's quiet ceremony. But pregnant pop singers are a laugh. We'll be back from the tour before anything shows, and it will make commercial sense to spend time in the recording studios after that, not out on the road. So it's all going to be fine and dandy. As long as Colin keeps his mouth shut. And you. I can trust you, can't I?'

'Yep. Sure.' It was less of an effort than Howard had expected to make his voice sound off-hand. He could hardly bear to look at her and think how her body had been stirred around. From the way she was still leaning forward, her black curly hair close to his cheek, he could tell that she would not mind if he kissed her goodbye. For three weeks he had been dreaming of ways in which he could pull her into his arms, but now he did not want to touch her. 'Well, 'bye then,' he said. 'Thanks for everything. And good luck. With the tour. And with the baby and all.' He turned away and hurried outside to look for Serge.

5

In the sitting room of their Connaught suite his grandmother was waiting for him, alert and wholly sober. Her hands clasped each other on her lap; and her back, not needing the support of the chair, was so straight that she gave the impression of being ready to walk straight out of the room to start the journey home. But instead of that, she smiled at Howard as he came in. 'Good party?'

'Hardly got going yet.' He saw no reason to reveal that his pleasure in the evening had been spoiled even before Serge's arrival. 'Why did I have to get back so early?'

'Our plane leaves at seven tomorrow morning. We need to be away from here by five. I suggest you pack now. Then you can sleep for an hour or two.'

'What's the rush?' asked Howard. 'I mean, why didn't you say yesterday that we'd be going back?'

'Why didn't you tell me yesterday when you were supposed to start school?'

Howard was as sure as he could be that she had known the date. 'It's not important,' he mumbled.

'Your father thinks it is. Find Serge and tell him I want a word with him, please. I'll fix for him to wake you early.'

Howard shrugged his shoulders and did as he was told. As he packed his bags he could hear the murmur of voices, too soft for him to catch the words. And a little later, as he turned out the light and prepared to sleep, a faint tinkle from the telephone extension in his room told him that his grandmother was making a call. Half past one in the morning was an odd time to be calling anyone. But maybe she was letting his parents know when to expect their return. He tried to think what time it would be in Hawaii at this moment; but before he could work out the answer, his eyes closed in sleep.

6

Howard sat next to his grandmother in the first-class cabin of the plane. Every few minutes since they left Heathrow the air hostess had offered them something to drink, and Iris was accepting every offer. Soon, if she continued to drink at this rate, she would fall asleep, snoring slightly as she always did when she was drunk. The other passengers would turn round and stare: it would be embarrassing.

Still, there had been less of that particular embarrassment during the past ten weeks than Howard had secretly expected. In fact, when he came to think about it, Iris had not been drinking at all during their stay in London. Perhaps from time to time she liked to prove that she could stop whenever she chose. And now, with her test – if that was what it was – successfully completed, with no more sights to be appreciated or travel arrangements to be made, she could afford to relax and enjoy herself. Besides, the drinks were free. Howard had been brought up in a family which could afford to buy anything which took its fancy, but that had never spoiled his pleasure in the feeling of getting something for nothing. He accepted another glass of champagne and orange juice, and turned his thoughts to more important matters.

Iris was sober enough to notice the frown of concentration on his forehead. 'Penny for your thoughts,' she said.

'I was thinking about Melody.' For once he did not blush at the mention of her name. His infatuation had been cured, it seemed, with Melody herself providing the antidote. 'I ought to have taken something to the party.' Almost all the other guests had arrived carrying bottles, as Howard had guessed they would. He had turned up empty-handed only because he had intended to send flowers, dozens of flowers, on the morning after. But in the rush of departure there had been no time to make such arrangements, or even to consider what, in the changed circumstances, might be a more suitable gift.

Last night he had felt jealousy and disgust at the thought

of Melody's body swelling with Colin's baby. This morning, though, he could think of her with a new maturity. His grandmother had been right to warn him that a sophisticated twenty-year-old woman, with her own life and career, could not have been expected suddenly to change direction just because a fourteen-year-old American kid drifted on to the scene. She was beautiful and talented and one day she would be a big star. It should be enough for him that she had been friendly: kind without being patronizing. There was no reason why they should not remain friends at a distance.

So as soon as he arrived home he would send off a gift to thank her for the party. That would provide an opportunity to enclose a letter, and his address, and would oblige her to write in return, if only to thank him for the gift. But when he began to explain this to his grandmother – omitting all mention of the letter and rephrasing his true thoughts so that they emerged like a quotation from a book of etiquette, she shook her head briskly.

'No call for that. Didn't Serge tell you? I knew you'd want her to have a keepsake, so I gave him something to take round when he picked you up last night. For you to give to her.'

'I didn't see it.'

'He must have misunderstood and given it straight to her. But she'll know who it's from.'

That wasn't the way for a gift to be presented, thought Howard with a trace of sulkiness. And it would be quite the wrong thing. How could his grandmother know what someone in the swing like Melody would like? 'What was it?' he asked suspiciously.

Iris pointed to the crocodile skin handbag which lay beside her seat. 'I fell for this in Rome,' she told him. 'So I bought two. The second one was to be a gift for someone very special. When I saw how much you liked your singing friend, I reckoned she was special enough.'

Howard studied the bag more critically than when he had first been shown it. He knew that it was very expensive, and there was no doubt that it was elegant as well. Not the sort of thing that went with the group's singing gear, of course. But although Melody had rebelled against the stuffiness of her parents' life, he had noticed the stylishness of her street clothes and the smart decor of her flat. The bag would not be unsuitable.

But it wouldn't be *his* gift, because he hadn't chosen it. He had already decided on something different, something which would give Melody pleasure. He would send her the Ray Charles records which she could not get hold of in England. She would like that and every time she listened to them she would be reminded of Howard. There was no need to tell his grandmother that. She had been generous on his behalf, in this as in so many other ways. 'Thanks,' he said. 'Thanks for the whole trip. It's been great.'

Iris smiled at him with her eyes half closed, like a satisfied cat. Soon she would be asleep. 'Yes,' she agreed, patting his knee with her thin hand. 'I think we may say it's been a success.'

EPISODE SIX

1985

The Final Revenge

1

As he drove himself from Kona airport in the spring of 1985, Howard Lindsay tried to imagine how the approach to his new hotel would seem to someone arriving on the Big Island of Hawaii for the first time. Mauna Loa, the still-active volcano, had erupted regularly over many centuries to send red-hot rivers of lava flowing down towards the ocean; and these had cooled into a desolate expanse of black rock in which no seeds took root. It was through this lava field that the road had been cut.

To Howard himself the apparent bleakness was exciting, because he knew what it concealed. He had walked for miles along the ancient royal roads, his eyes alert for petrographs carved into the rock by spies sent out by the old kings to report on the armies of their tribal enemies. He knew where to find the caves which had sheltered those old travellers; and even where there were no secrets to be discovered, his trained architect's eye took pleasure on noting the curious shapes which had been formed by the lava as it cooled.

Vacationers, though, could not be expected to appreciate such details. They might well find the black bleakness unattractive. No matter. Their doubts would last only for twenty minutes or so as they were driven from the airport.

Then they would turn into the side road which led to the new development – and gasp.

Howard braked his own car to a halt and studied the transformation he had effected. On either side of the approach road stretched a golf course, the grass of its sweeping fairways appearing almost unnaturally green in contrast to the outcrops of lava which had been allowed to remain as natural hazards. The course sloped gently down to the coastline, drawing the eyes towards the new hotel. The design of the building was severe, but softened by the tropical blossom which even in this first season had begun to cover the walls. There was more blossom in the landscaped gardens surrounding the hotel, and the graceful palm trees which provided shade had been planted almost fully-grown. Howard tilted his head in approval as the beauty of this peaceful oasis made its effect even at a distance. The new development would bring more tourist money into the family business, but a man who had always been wealthy could genuinely claim not to care about that. The satisfaction he felt on every visit came from the knowledge that his own imagination and professional expertise had created a garden of Eden out of a rocky desert. Pleased, he drove on, leaving his car in front of the hotel for the porter to park. He had ten minutes to spare before his meeting and used it to stroll through the gardens.

On the narrow bridge which crossed the royal fishponds – a genuine survival of the island's history – a fashion photographer was at work. Howard nodded approvingly to himself. The development was so new, and so far from any other tourist complex, that he had deliberately encouraged its use – with full credits – by magazines and advertising agencies and film companies. They in turn appreciated the effects to be obtained from such a dramatic mixture of black rock and grass, tropical trees and flowers, waterfalls and ponds, and a bright sunshine guaranteed in its season. For models and technicians from the mainland, a trip to Hawaii at a client's expense was a bonus. This provided a good example of an arrangement which suited all parties equally.

To judge from the number of swimsuits clipped to hangers on a rail, today's session must be for a catalogue. A canvas shelter had been rigged out of shot behind the camera, and from it now a young woman appeared, wearing only the bottom half of a bikini as she dangled the top over her arm. Howard watched for a moment as with professional speed she stretched herself out on a slab of rock, tipped a straw hat over her face and bent one knee at an angle which showed the slimness of her long legs to advantage. There was the usual flurry of activity as the bikini top was spread out to create a precise impression of casual disregard, the straw hat was readjusted a millimetre at a time and the whole of the model's body was sprayed with water.

It was a beautiful body, slim and long-backed, with small but perfect breasts. But long-legged blondes with glossy tropical tans were two-a-penny in the islands. A divorced millionaire like Howard, still on the right side of forty, could find himself a gorgeous companion at the drop of a hat. In practice, though, he dropped his hat only in front of women who were intelligent as well as glamorous. A glimpse of a stranger did not tempt him to give even a mental wolf whistle.

Only as he turned away did he realize that the photographer and his army of assistants were themselves about to be put on film – and that he would become an involuntary extra unless he moved. The presence of a film crew would be good for the bar profits! Howard was in a good mood as he joined his fellow-directors to report progress on the next stage of the development: a shopping mall next to the hotel.

Because he was the supervising architect as well as representing the family trust which provided the finance, Howard was closely involved in every detail of the three-hour discussion. He felt the need of exercise and relaxation when at last the meeting broke up, so instead of drifting towards the bar with the others, he went off to change into swimming trunks. Strolling past the pool and through the gardens, he reached the sandy beach and stood still for a moment, enjoying the early evening light as he filled his lungs with fresh air.

He was not alone in the bay. Most of the hotel guests would by now be enjoying the Happy Hour, but one of them, a girl in a black and white swimsuit, was struggling with a windsurfer. He watched without moving as she gradually hauled the sail out of the sea. She was doing everything by the book, taking care to tip the water off the sail a little at a time, but the unsteadiness of her legs and the tense concentration of her whole body revealed her as a beginner. Her back was towards the land, so Howard kept still, not wanting to startle her. A little at a time the red sail rose into position: the young woman straightened herself and began to turn the windsurfer to catch the wind. But at the very moment when it began to glide away, something seemed to disturb her concentration. She lost her balance and, as though she had been shot, flung both hands in the air before falling backwards with the sail on top of her.

Howard took a running dive into the water and swam rapidly towards the windsurfer. By the time he reached it, the girl had extricated herself from beneath the sail. Her long black hair floated behind her as she spluttered and rubbed her eyes.

'You okay?' he asked.

'Yes, fine, thank you.' She smiled at him, revealing beautiful teeth in a beautiful face. 'I was distracted for a moment.' She pointed out to sea, where glistening black bodies were moving in graceful curves across the mouth of the bay. 'Are they dolphins? Or porpoises? They look enormous.'

'Whales,' Howard told her, putting a hand on the windsurfer to hold himself close. 'They come here to calve. Then they hang around till the calves have put on enough weight to tackle the swim back to Alaska. Five hundred pounds a day. A weight-watcher's nightmare.' As though to illustrate his identification, a spout of water erupted into the air, followed again by the stately arching of a glossy black back. 'Can I help you to get going again?'

She shook her head. 'Thanks a lot, but that's enough for a first try.' Her voice was British. Later he would ask her why she had chosen to come so far for her holiday, for such information was important to the development's publicity strategy. But first he volunteered to sail the windsurfer in for her.

Accepting the offer with a smile, she swam back to land with a strong racing crawl and was already sitting on the beach when he came to join her.

'There's not enough wind at this hour,' he said, dropping down beside her. 'At seven in the morning you could find it more exciting.'

'I have only limited ambitions,' said the English girl. She laughed. 'I'm an actress. And when an actress signs on with an agent, she has to fill in a form designed to put all her talents on record. Tick "well", "fairly well", "not at all". To such questions as "Can you drive, ride, ski, play the piano, swim?" And so on. Naturally one claims with enthusiasm to do absolutely everything well. Later on, panic sets in. It seems wise to put in a little practice just in case one's actually asked to demonstrate the various skills. And learning to windsurf in England means putting on a wet suit before falling into the icy water of a flooded gravel pit. So I thought I'd use any opportunity which might present itself in a warmer climate – but without actually aiming for an Olympic gold medal. Luckily, this particular skill, or lack of it, doesn't figure in my current script.'

Howard had been staring at her as she spoke. 'Did I see you earlier?' he asked, his question expressing some doubt. He was almost sure that he recognized the long back and even longer legs of the photographer's model who had stretched herself out in the garden that afternoon; and although she was wearing a one-piece swimsuit now, it was cut low enough to reveal breasts which swelled with the same firmness as those which had been exposed to the sun as well as to the camera. But this girl's long hair was black, not blonde, and her skin was so pale as to seem almost translucent. 'What happened to your tan?'

She burst out laughing. 'It all came off under the shower. My skin won't take an instant tan. Unless I work up to it gradually, I blister. And anyway, we're shooting out of sequence. By the end of the week I shall be in Waikiki as a pale new arrival. It's easier to apply bronze from a jar than white.'

'So you're not a regular model?'

She shook her head. 'An actress playing a model. And the model is actually a murderess, so *she*'s playing a part as well. It's all very complicated.'

'Do I know your name?'

'No. Nothing I've done so far has crossed even the Atlantic, much less the Pacific. This is my first starring part. A serial for British TV. You've probably already deduced from my cute English accent where I hail from.'

'My question,' said Howard, 'was intended as a subtle way of finding out what your name *is*.'

'Sorry.' She laughed again. 'Joanna Blythe.'

'Glad to know you, Joanna. I'm Howard Lindsay.'

Joanna's eyes opened wide in mock awe. 'The great white chief in person? I heard the message going round the hotel this morning, that Mr Lindsay would be arriving at two. The effect was pretty startling to someone brought up to believe that all Americans think of themselves as equals. There was an unmistakable note of deference.'

'Don't let our propaganda fool you. Democracy is strictly for politics. In any corporate body, hierarchy is the name of the game.'

'And you're at the top of this particular hierarchy.'

'Strictly speaking, my grandmother holds the purse strings and my father is in executive control.'

'And less strictly speaking, *you* had the idea of developing this good-for-nothing land and *you've* designed this splendid hotel. I had half an hour to kill while the crew was setting up this morning. I've not only studied the model of the whole development – I had time to read the credits as well.

She turned to smile at him in a way which made Howard's

heart skip a beat. Earlier that day he had recognized the blonde model as being beautiful, without allowing himself to be stirred by the recognition. His wife – his ex-wife – had also been blonde and glamorous, but that had not prevented the marriage from being shipwrecked on a rock of boredom. This girl was more than good-looking. She was articulate and lively, and he suspected that she was intelligent. Having cleared that in his mind, he was able to appreciate her looks after all.

Even without make-up, the shape of her face survived the unflattering flatness of the wet hair which framed her cheeks. It was a long face, with a strong forehead and high cheekbones. Her nose was thin and straight, her mouth small and rosy in repose, but generously wide when she smiled. Her eyes, in unexpected contrast to her black hair, were a clear blue, and her pale skin was very faintly flushed. Perhaps that was because he was studying her too intently. He let his eyes drop to her slender body and laughed silently as he realized what it was that most attracted him. He found it easy enough to ignore the kind of local flattery which was inspired by his family's wealth or social position, his sporting prowess or the tanned fitness of his body. What was irresistible was that a girl from thousands of miles away should put a finger of admiration straight onto the professional skill of which he was proud. He believed himself to be a good architect. Without gushing about it, Joanna was managing to exude the impression that she thought so too. She would say it in so many words if he gave her the opportunity. 'How long are you here?' he asked.

'According to the shooting schedule, we have two days here in Hawaii and three in Waikiki. We all have to be available for a sixth day in case of problems – and there always *are* problems. After that, the crew flies home. But I've made an arrangement with Rick the director. I'm staying on for a couple of weeks. I couldn't ever afford to fly all the way out here for a holiday at my own expense. But having had the transport provided, it seems silly not to take advantage of it.'

‘Where do you plan to go?’

‘I haven’t booked anything in advance. I’ve read a guide book and I have some ideas. But I thought I might as well wait and see how much time I had for exploring during this working week. And I want to take advice from local people about the best sights to see.’

‘I’m a local person,’ Howard pointed out, grinning.

‘Then I shall look forward to hearing your recommendations. But not here, because I like to write things down.’

‘Over dinner?’ Howard had not planned to stay the night, but a suite was permanently at his disposal.

‘I’ll have to ask Rick,’ Joanna told him. ‘I’m under director’s orders for eighteen hours a day. But I’ll ask him very strongly. I’d love to have dinner with you, Howard. Thank you very much.’

2

Treading water as he waited for a comber, Howard wondered whether Joanna was watching him. It was easy for him to pick her out on the beach, because she was wearing a wide-brimmed red straw hat as she sat in the dappled shade of a feathery kiawe tree. But to her – unless she had kept her eyes fixed on him as he swam out – he would be only one of a distant line of tiny bobbing heads until the moment came when he could rise up on his board and ride in through the surf.

It was impossible not to laugh at himself for this blatant exhibitionism. He knew what he was doing: did she? In the ten days or so since their first meeting she had made no attempt to disguise what seemed to be admiration. But it was a curiously cerebral form of admiration. While clearly taking pleasure in his company and appearing to be interested in his work, she seemed almost to be unaware that a man might desire her body – unaware, even, that this very unconciousness of her own beauty was provocative.

Howard was not in the habit of making passes at vacationers. As a rule he moved slowly into a new relationship. Even if he did not expect it to last, he needed time to make it begin. The urgency he felt now was inspired as much by the shortness of Joanna's stay in the islands as by her apparent assumption that he only wanted to talk to her.

It was this urgency which had prompted him to bring her today to Makaha beach. As he rode in on a forty-foot-high comber she would see that he was strong. For the first time, she might take an hour off from discussing his views to look at his body. Howard was not vain, but he knew that he was good-looking. He had lost the lanky thinness of youth long ago, but his smooth, tanned skin enclosed a muscular fitness. He wanted Joanna to notice, to touch. He wanted to feel the tingle of electricity which would before too long bring their bodies together.

What he felt first was a trembling in the ocean, a tension which made the surface almost as hard as rock as it drew itself together, ready to be sucked up into a huge wall of water. It was time for Howard to concentrate on what he was doing. He had been surfing as long as he could remember, so that his skills were instinctive – but he must not, nevertheless, allow himself to be distracted by looking towards Joanna. He turned his board into position and prepared to unfold himself until he was standing, confident and steady, beneath the curling froth of surf.

With the roar which never failed to excite him the comber bore him back to land. Zigzagging gracefully he swooped and soared on the vertical surface as his board responded to the pressure of his feet. For a few moments he forgot why he had come today, and enjoyed the experience for its own sake.

Yes, Joanna had been watching. As he ran across the beach towards her, carrying the ten-foot board, she greeted him with a silent handclap.

'Come out into the sun,' he commanded her. 'You're allowed more than forty minutes today.' Now that the camera crew had finished its work and flown home, Joanna had made a cautious start on acquiring a tan. He held out a hand to pull her to her feet.

'That was marvellous!' she exclaimed as they spread their beach mats side by side on the sand and sat down together. 'I was terrified for you all the time, but it was beautiful.' Howard's heart bumped as she put a hand on his thigh. She had never touched him in this way before. He had hoped that his demonstration would have just such an effect, and was excited by its success. 'You must have terrifically strong leg muscles to control a surfboard like that,' she said.

'Right.' Howard grinned at her. 'Superman in person.'

'Anyone who can slalom like that on a moving cliff of water would be a natural on a snow piste. Have you ever ski'd? On snow, I mean, not water? You should come over to the Alps some time and try it.'

'Who needs the Alps?' asked Howard. 'There's a whole continent of ski-slopes between me and the Alps. And why do I need to travel anywhere at all when I can ski on the slopes of Mauna Kea most winters?' He laughed at the surprise on her face. 'You're like all our visitors,' he teased. 'Grass skirts and hula and leis and palm trees and tropical sunshine. That's Hawaii in the vacationer's cliché book, right? But we can also offer not only the wettest place on the face of the earth, but the highest active volcano in the world. Complete with snowfields. Do you ski, Joanna?'

'Yes.' She lay back, stretching herself full-length in the sun but tilting the red hat so that it continued to shade her face without covering it. The change of position brought her leg close to his own. From knee to hip he could feel her warmth glowing onto his own still-wet skin. He kept still so that she should not notice the contact as she continued to talk in the lazy voice of a sunbather. 'It's one of the few genuine ticks on my agency form. I was brought up by my grandparents; so when my grandfather became a military attaché, I went with him. And emerged from the period with fluent German and a ski-school diploma.'

'What happened to your parents?' Howard asked. She had, when he thought about it, talked mainly of Hawaii and himself since their first meeting. Once or twice she had discussed the TV serial which was the reason for her presence in the islands, but had not volunteered any personal details about herself.

'They divorced when I was two,' she said now. 'My father walked out even earlier than that. I'm not sure whether he ever saw me. If he did, he lost no time in beating a retreat. And my mother . . .' There was the hint of a tremble in Joanna's voice and she paused, perhaps to bring it under control. 'My mother died. Soon after the divorce.'

'That was tough.'

'My grandparents were very kind. They're both dead now, but they were father and mother to me until a couple of years ago.'

The determined cheerfulness of her voice touched Howard's emotions. It was as though until now he had seen her only as an actress, allowing her profession as well as her beauty to obscure the fact that she was as vulnerable in her private life as any other young woman. He turned his head to look at her and felt himself lurching out of control. With one finger he moved the red hat out of the way. Then his lips pressed down on hers; and his excitement grew as she returned his kiss, twining her slender arms round his shoulders. He twisted round until he was lying half above and half beside her, one hand mapping the contour of her breast while the other groped for the fastening of her bikini. He was brought back to earth only by the realization that Joanna had ceased to embrace him and was instead trying to hold him off.

'Howard. Darling. This is a public beach!'

'Right. Sure.' She was younger and less experienced than he had thought if she believed that his desire for her could be switched off as easily as a kettle on the boil. But she was right, of course, to check him. He slid a little away to lie face downwards on the sand. 'Talk to me,' he said after a few moments of struggling with his frustration. 'So I can hear your voice. Talk about anything you like.'

'Anything I like. Well.' Her voice considered the

possibilities. 'We were talking about the Alps. I was, at least. Have you ever visited Europe, Howard?'

Howard still needed a moment before he could answer. Then, with his body once more under his control, he turned on one side so that he could see her as he spoke. 'Just once. A long time ago – more than twenty years.' He laughed. 'Maybe it's time I planned another trip, now I know what attractions are to be found there.'

'Where did you go?' asked Joanna, ignoring the flirtatious note in his voice. 'What did you see? I suppose the idea was to study European architecture, was it?'

'Hell, no, nothing so serious.' Howard laughed at the thought and then, considering it, spoke more seriously. 'I guess maybe it worked the other way. I wasn't interested before I went. But when I was in Greece I worked out for myself a theory that a lot of people had invented before me – but I didn't know it. Something to do with scale – the relationship between the size of a man and his surroundings. The landscape of Greece is on a human scale. Mountains and seas round there aren't too big or too small. And then, when I was in France, some of those palaces opened my eyes, that's for sure. Versailles! No one asks an architect to build a palace these days. But there are other uses for space – other ways to fill a need on a grand scale.'

'That shopping mall in Honolulu,' said Joanna. 'I went to see it. Is that the sort of thing you mean?'

'You went . . .!' Howard did not disguise his amazement. 'Even my own sisters have never bothered to set foot inside it, because their favourite stores are someplace else. Why. . .?'

'I went to see it because you designed it,' Joanna told him. 'There was a list of your work in the display for the hotel development. When I meet someone, I like to find out how he spends his time, what he's good at. It's interesting. But you were telling me about your European trip.'

'Before I started, I didn't have much idea what I was going to do with my life. Maybe, just maybe, some of the architecture rubbed off on me and pointed me in the direction of that career. But if so, I wasn't conscious of it at the time. It wasn't the reason I went. When a fourteen-year-old's offered a vacation trip, he takes it as just that, not as education.'

'Fourteen!' exclaimed Joanna. She made no attempt to hide her astonishment. 'Are you telling me you were only fourteen when you went to Europe?'

Howard looked at Joanna with as much surprise as his remark had apparently caused in her. She had abandoned her lazy sunbathing position and was sitting up with her hands clasped round her knees, staring at him as though she could still not believe what she had heard. Her astonishment seemed unreasonable to Howard. He had never said anything to give her the impression that his travels had come later in his life.

'I told you, this was more than twenty years ago. Twenty-three years, to be exact. How old d'you reckon me to be now, then?' Her answer seemed likely to be unflattering, so he gave her no chance to speak. 'I'm thirty-seven.'

'Sorry,' said Joanna, obviously reading his thoughts. She lay back again, as though her sudden movement had been only part of a change of position, exposing a new section of skin to the sun. 'It's just that you seem to have achieved such a lot in your career already. Fourteen seems very young to be let loose in a strange continent. But I suppose you didn't go on your own.'

'Right. It was my grandmother's trip, not mine. She fixed the programme and made the bookings and then invited me along for company.'

'Did you visit London?' Joanna asked.

'London came at the end of the trip. I'd had enough of rubber-necking by then. If anyone were to invite me back now . . .' he raised his eyebrows as he smiled at Joanna – 'I'd take a closer look at all your Georgian crescents and squares. At the time, I guess I was really shocked by all the holes in the ground – bomb sites left undeveloped since a war that ended before I was born. And from what I've read since in the architectural reviews, I don't get the impression that the British are world leaders.'

'The man who designed the Pompidou Centre . . .'

'Had to get it built in France.' Howard finished the sentence for her. Not for the first time, though, he was interested that a young actress should possess even a sketchy knowledge of his own field. 'Anyhow, when we reached London at the end of the grand tour, Grandmother Iris handed me over to some young British relations. They'd hardly heard of the Tower of London but boy, did they know their nightlife! You're too young to remember, but London in the Swinging Sixties was the capital of the world.'

'I had heard.' Joanna grinned at him. 'So you swung with the rest of them.'

'Right.' He smiled at the memory. 'It was kind of exciting for a fourteen-year-old. The Beatles hadn't hit America then, but they were so big in England that you could tell something had to burst. Seemed like every kid in England was playing a guitar and aiming for the big time. Some of them were going to make it. They bubbled their way up to the top and put a fizz into every part of society. That's how it felt, anyhow.'

'Did you meet any of them?' asked Joanna. 'Not the Beatles, I don't suppose, but any of the up-and-coming pop stars?'

'There was one,' Howard admitted. 'Melody, she called herself. She sang with a group.' For a moment he was silent. He hadn't thought of Melody for years, but just the mention of her name was enough to revive the memory of his boyhood infatuation. No, it had been more than that. Only a genuine attack of first love could have delivered him into such agonies of desire and despair. But it was a long time ago. He could laugh at himself now.

'Did she ever become famous?' Joanna asked.

Howard shook his head. 'She must have been one who didn't make it. I never heard her name again after I left London.'

'You really knew her, did you? Or were you just one of a thousand fans?'

'She invited me to a party in her home.' This time Howard laughed aloud. 'That was when I found out she was married. To the group's manager. He was flying off to the States to set up a tour. The others were to join him in three or four weeks. It came as a nasty shock to see her cuddling up to another man.'

'Did you hate her for it?'

'Hate her? Christ, no. I adored her. I just felt suicidal, that's all. You know that sick feeling you get when you go overboard for somebody: you can't imagine not getting what you want and then you find out that someone's got there first and you never were more than one of the crowd. Has someone got there first with you as well, Joanna?'

In the silence which followed it was hard to tell which of them was the more startled. Howard had had no intention of asking such a direct question, or even of probing casually. It was as if for a moment or two he had felt himself to be face to face with Melody again, but this time with the chance to test the ice before he stepped on to it more firmly. As for Joanna, she looked almost pale with shock.

How much of his difficulty in understanding Joanna, he wondered, was due to the fact that she was a foreigner. On the very first evening of their acquaintance she had accepted his offer to show her the highspots of his home state with a quick enthusiasm. A brasher man than Howard might have persuaded himself that she was a pretty girl looking for a wealthy lover. But in fact he had been sure – and was sure still – that it was not calculation but a lack of sophistication which had inspired her eager friendliness. He had not, in other words, judged her by the standards of the American women he knew, but as a stranger whose behaviour was governed by slightly different rules.

Events had proved him right. For the past few days there had been a kind of restraint behind the friendliness in Joanna's manner – almost too slight to be noticed, but enough to make it clear that she was not setting her cap at him. But he had taken pains to interpret this restraint also in the light of her Englishness. It was her upbringing, almost certainly, which caused her to repress her emotions. Englishwomen had a reputation for being cool – or, at least, less warmly out-going than their American cousins. Once again, reading her character, he had reached the conclusion that her restraint was a concealment of her true feelings rather than an indication that she felt no warmth towards him. In this, too, he had just been proved correct by her passionate acceptance of his embrace until the moment when a British sense of propriety alarmed her into holding back. Almost as clearly as if she had said it in so many words, she was telling him that at another time and in a more private place she would shed any remaining inhibitions.

Up to this point, therefore, Howard was confident that he was reading her. It added a certain satisfaction to the chase that his quarry should be of a breed with which he had until now been unacquainted, but that he should be able to follow her through any checks and evasions. Her apparent reluctance to answer his question came into that category. Why should she hesitate?

The silence itself became important. In waiting for an answer to the question he seemed to be repeating it.

'I'm not married, if that's what you mean,' Joanna said, speaking more quickly than usual as though to cover up her pause. 'But of course I have friends. A life of my own in England.'

'Of course.' Howard smiled at her but, for once, her clear blue eyes avoided his. When she spoke, it was with a rush which seemed intended to prevent him from pressing the point.

'You were telling me about . . . about Melody,' she said. 'How did you show your adoration? It must have been difficult for a fourteen-year-old. Did you shower her with presents?'

'Right.' Howard answered without bothering to consider whether he was speaking the truth. His eyes were still fixed on Joanna, who had pulled the red straw hat back over her eyes. He had not yet decided whether or not to take the conversation back under his own control. The subject of an unknown pop singer could not possibly be of interest to his companion. There must be a reason for her curious insistence on continuing to discuss it. He would think of the reason soon, and add another dimension to the satisfaction of getting to know her.

'What sort of thing?' she asked. 'Dozens of red roses?'

'Candies, mostly. It was the fashion those days to be skinny, and Melody was skinnier than most.'

'But you gave her something for that farewell party you went to, I suppose?'

Howard, neither remembering nor seeing any need to remember, crumpled his forehead in concentration. 'It's more than twenty years ago,' he reminded her. 'I don't recall . . .' But even as he spoke, a picture of himself as an infatuated teenager flashed before his eyes. The whole scene presented itself so clearly to him that he laughed aloud at the quirks of memory.

'I was snatched from that party to fly home,' he said. 'So I didn't get to give Melody anything of my own choice. But my grandmother . . .' He laughed again at the oddness of it. 'My grandmother sent along a gift as though it were from me. An expensive Italian handbag. Crocodile skin, as I recall. Very fashionable. But not my own choice. After I got back here, I sent Melody some discs. Ray Charles. All my own favourites. I hoped . . . She never even acknowledged them. Well, why should she? I was only a kid, after all. A kind of fan – luckier than most because I got to speak with her. She'd probably forgotten all about me before I'd been gone five minutes.' As he, although more slowly and painfully, had forgotten about Melody until today.

'Did you – or your grandmother – put anything inside the crocodile bag?'

'Why should she want to do that?'

Joanna shrugged her shoulders as though she were not sure herself why she had asked; but then explained. 'In England, anyone who gives a handbag or a wallet as a gift always puts something inside, even if it's only a penny. A kind of superstition. "May your purse never be empty."'

'I've never heard that. I wouldn't know what my grandmother did. I never saw the bag she gave. I don't know why we're talking about crocodile bags, Joanna.'

'We're not. We're talking about your European trip. And your generous grandmother.' Joanna smiled up at him. She looked happy – and even younger than her twenty-two years. 'She's still alive, you said, didn't you?'

'Alive and well and still with her fingers on the purse strings. But that trip in 1962 was kind of a last fling for her. She leaves all the business to my father. She has a home in Kauai and the most beautiful garden in the world around it, coaxed out of the wilderness. I guess she knows every flower petal and blade of grass there by name.'

'Is that the Ola Pua garden? I've got that on my list of things to see.'

Howard looked at Joanna curiously. Just as she had surprised him by her mention of the Pompidou building and her visit to his shopping mall, so he found it unexpected that she should be sufficiently interested in a tropical garden – even one which figured in guide books as a tourist attraction – to carry its name in her head.

'Ola Pua is open to the public,' he said. 'My grandmother's garden is very strictly private. She's terrified of kidnappers, so she'll never let a stranger come within miles. If you want to see *her* garden, you'll have to ask me to take you along.'

'I'd like to take you up on that. Would you really? Kauai is the next island I want to visit while I'm here. The garden isle, it says in my guide book. I'd planned to go to Ola Pua. But a private garden would be far more fascinating – especially if your grandmother would be willing to take me round it herself.'

'We can go this afternoon if you like,' said Howard. The same wish to impress which earlier had driven him to demonstrate his skill in the surf now prompted a different form of display. 'I have my own plane. Ready whenever I want it. The flight doesn't take more than half an hour. I could give Grandmother Iris a call before we leave.'

'Howard! Just like that?' The amazement in her eyes as she clapped her hands was exactly the reward he had hoped for. She threw off her sunbathing languor and leapt gracefully to her feet. 'Would there be time for me to swim first? I'm roasted.'

'It's a surfing beach,' he reminded her. 'But as long as you stay in your depth and hold tightly to your personal life saver you should be okay.' The excitement which he had only just succeeded in controlling earlier in the morning took him in its grip again as he ran hand in hand with her down to the ocean. The day was going well.

3

Joanna had spent more than a year waiting for the opportunity to travel to Hawaii and planning an eventual meeting with Howard Lindsay. She had expected to open her campaign when the film crew moved to Oahu at the end of the three days' shooting on the island of Hawaii. Mugging up on modern architecture with the same concentration which she normally applied to studying a new role, she intended to present herself as a journalist planning a series of articles on 'Building For Leisure.' Whether or not she proved able to sustain the pretence was hardly important, as long as it provided the opportunity to bring him face to face with a beautiful woman who would make no secret of her admiration for his work. Her mental picture of Howard – which in the event proved inaccurate – was of a middle-aged playboy. She had felt confident of her ability to develop the situation from a first meeting.

Playing it by ear, though, she was quick to take advantage of their earlier encounter in the Big Island – and this was not entirely fortuitous. When she discovered in the course of her research that Howard was involved in a hotel development, she had passed on the illustrated brochure to the director of the television serial at a time when he was making his location plans; as she had hoped, the unusual black lava fields had proved irresistible. Howard's visit to the hotel on the very day they started shooting was a bit of luck; but even without that serendipity she had been confident that soon after the holiday part of her trip began she would have succeeded in attracting his attention.

He proved to be a more serious man than she had expected. Almost all the Americans she knew in England were connected in some way with show business. The majority were gay, but almost all the others were uninhibited in their approach to an actress. If a girl was good looking and appeared to be unattached, they moved straight in. She had never needed to learn how to attract them, but only how to fend them off. Right from the start she had realized that Howard's attitude was different. Whether or not her looks succeeded in catching his eye, he would not want to pursue her acquaintance unless he thought her interesting as a person. It had been the matter only of a moment to adapt her approach, establishing a careful balance between shyness and earnest gush.

Not all her self-restraint had been acting. In surprising her, Howard had also attracted her. She had not expected to like her prospective victim: it was definitely not part of the plan. To pretend a warm interest in him when she actually felt it but must not allow herself to admit the feeling required continual self-examination and self-control. There were times when she could have done with Rick, her director, to steer her along the right course. There were also times – and this morning on the Makaha beach had provided one of them – when the situation seemed to be swinging out of her control. But now, as she jumped down from Howard's private plane and walked towards one of Howard's cars, she was moving in the right direction.

'Do you keep a car on every island?' she asked, laughing.

'In Oahu because I live there. In Hawaii because I work there. And Kauai because I visit here. That's all. Hold on to your hat.'

Joanna took it off instead, enjoying the wind in her hair as they sped along the coastal road. Kauai was more than merely an island which contained beautiful gardens: it was itself a garden, lush and green – a refreshing contrast to both the black lava fields of Hawaii and the urban density of Waikiki and Honolulu. Blossom cascaded from vines which twined round trees already brilliant with colour. Joanna had no great knowledge of flowers and no special interest in gardening; but as Howard drove her between flaming hedges of poinsettia she could hardly fail to be impressed by the exuberant vegetation.

The road curved to avoid an outcrop of rock and she gasped with surprise as the change of direction revealed a double rainbow ahead of them, bright and seemingly very close.

'Didn't I tell you we can offer the wettest place on earth?' Howard pointed up to the cloud into which the rainbow disappeared. 'Mount Waialeale has about four hundred and fifty inches of rain a year. While the sun keeps on shining all around.'

Joanna knew from the map she had studied that Kauai consisted of little more than a single mountain. Only a narrow ribbon of land around the coast was flat enough to be habitable. 'Where does your grandmother live?' she asked.

'On the side of a canyon.' Howard pointed straight ahead. 'At the foot of the rainbow.'

The pot of gold, thought Joanna – but in the context of Howard's family the words might come too near the truth to be spoken aloud. In any case she was too tense to chat. With every mile that they covered her nervous excitement increased.

Twenty-three years ago someone, anonymously, had given a crocodile-skin handbag containing three grams of cocaine to a young singer: a pretty, vivacious girl with her life before her and the world, it seemed, at her feet. A larger supply of the same drug had been left in a bathroom where anyone seriously searching for a drug-pusher's store would be sure of finding it – and a telephone call to the police had made sure that the search would be made.

The only possible clue to the identity of whoever had acted with such apparently motiveless spite had arrived out of the blue too late to help its victim. Almost twenty years had passed before Joanna stumbled across an unopened box and an unread letter and became curious enough to explore a chapter of past history. Until a few hours earlier, that letter had seemed to prove without a shadow of doubt that it was Howard Lindsay who had been responsible for planting the drug and presumably also for the tip-off. But the conversation on Makaha beach that morning had thrown a new light on the events of twenty-three years ago. Joanna was convinced that Howard – not even realizing that he was under interrogation – had been telling the truth when he disclaimed responsibility. She believed him – and that meant that she could admit to herself how attractive she found him – and even, if she were honest, how easy it would be to fall in love with him. But there was no time for that now, and probably there never would be; because Howard, unconsciously absolving himself from blame, had shifted the responsibility for what had happened squarely on the the shoulders of his grandmother.

Why had Iris Lindsay acted in such a way? Well, in only a short time now, the question could be put, and Joanna did not intend to leave without an answer. The plan by which she had intended to make Howard pay for destroying a life could not be turned against an old lady; but Joanna promised herself that she would think of something else.

For all her determination she was nervous; frightened of what she might do if anger caused her to lose control of herself. She was surprised to sense, as they drove at speed along the coastal road, that Howard was nervous as well. Was he concerned about the impression his grandmother would make on her – or about the impression which Joanna herself would make on Mrs Lindsay? Either way, the implications were interesting.

* * *

The sides of the snow-capped mountain sloped almost to the sea, so that few roads led from the main highway into the interior of the island. They had been driving for an hour before Howard turned along a wide new road which zig-zagged steeply upwards, its camber and deep curves showing that it was designed for coach traffic.

'The Waimea Canyon is the great tourist attraction of the island,' Howard told her. 'This road runs along the edge, further along.'

'Is that where we're going, the Waimea Canyon?'

'We shall turn off the road before we reach the best look-out point.' But when they had wound their way up to the beginning of the ridge he stopped the car and opened the door, offering her at least a half-way view.

'Goodness!' exclaimed Joanna. A mere three steps forward were enough to take her to the edge of a precipice. She retreated again in order to stare down from a safer spot and her eyes widened in surprise at the scale of the vista. The word 'canyon' had suggested to her only a single steep gorge, but below her now was a complete landscape of deep valleys. There were mountain ranges within the valleys and other, higher, valleys cutting through these mountains. Waterfalls tumbled down the heads of each valley to feed streams which, like the outstretched fingers of a hand, converged into a single strong artery. Above the forested lower slopes, the rocky sides of the canyon were almost as brightly coloured as the rainbow now fading into the mist around the invisible mountain peak. Clouds passing overhead changed the colours of the rock by their shadows in an ever-moving kaleidoscope. There was no sign of human habitation, no possibility that anyone could penetrate the canyon without a demanding trek on foot.

'Down there.' Howard pointed into a seemingly impenetrable forest. 'That's where Grandmother Iris lives. It can't be reached from the coast road because there's no bridge across the river there. This is the only way in.'

It was an impossible way, thought Joanna as they returned to the car and began to drive – more cautiously now – down a steep track which had perhaps purposely been allowed to deteriorate near its junction with the tourist road in order that no stranger should be tempted to see where it led. After half a mile the surface improved, but the steepness and narrowness of the track made it still a nerve-racking drive. By now they must be almost down to sea level again. They were approaching a narrow bridge which spanned a fast-moving mountain stream. At each end of the bridge was a metal gate.

With the bonnet of the car almost touching the gate Howard took what looked like a small calculator out of the glove pocket, pointed it towards a half-hooded electronic screen and punched out a series of numbers. There was a brief pause, and then both gates silently opened. Joanna twisted in her seat as they crossed the bridge and within a few seconds saw both barriers close again. 'There's no one there,' she said.

Howard laughed at her surprise. 'We'll pass the gatekeeper later on. He lives close to the house. Every member of the family has a personal code to announce his arrival. As long as we've announced in advance that we're coming, we can get straight through. There was a phone back there for anyone deciding to drop by on the spur of the moment.'

'I can't imagine that anyone is ever just passing,' Joanna exclaimed. 'Is this part of a burglar alarm system?'

'The house has its own security. The gates are an extra, for the general discouragement of intruders. An old lady living in such an isolated spot gets nervous, I guess. Not of robbery. I mentioned before, it's the thought of being kidnapped that terrifies her.'

'Surely . . .'

'It could happen,' Howard said seriously. 'Grandmother Iris is one of the wealthiest women in the state, and that's saying something. Anyone who got his hands on her could reckon that the family would have to buy her back. Hawaii may be a paradise for vacationers, but it has its fair share of native crime. And she's not . . .' he laughed at his own difficulty in finding the right phrase . . . 'she's not the kind of sweet old woman whom everyone loves and no one would want to harm. I'm her favourite grandchild – her only grandson – so I don't often get the sharp side of her tongue. But she's made enemies in her time.'

Yes, thought Joanna, exulting in the thought that one of them had now passed the barrier. There was no point in wondering how she would get back again until she had discovered what was going to happen to the little old lady whom nobody loved. 'But there must be other approaches to the house,' she said.

'Depends what you mean by approach. Sure, you could hike along the track and cross the stream in knee-high water on shifting stones. A thief could get away with the petty cash that way, maybe. Not that she keeps much in the house. But any ambitious villain would need wheels. Tell you the truth, it wouldn't even occur to anyone here to make a plan that depended on trekking. Well, that's what Grandmother Iris reckons, and I'm not about to worry her by arguing. Here we are.'

Joanna blinked in the bright tropical sunshine as they emerged from a stretch of woodland whose tall trees formed a tunnel over the track. There was more than the contrast between shade and light to widen her eyes when she stepped out of the car. Instead of bare rock or dense forest she was confronted by neat lawns. Instead of a limitless and inhospitable panorama, a series of carefully-tended gardens led into each other, taking advantage of the slope of a small valley and undulating around a low outcrop of rock. And on that rocky platform was one of the most extraordinary buildings she had ever seen.

The house was completely round, walled at ground level almost wholly in glass, with only the necessary minimum of support, and surrounded by a wide lanai. There was nothing surprising about that: from the moment of her first arrival in Hawaii Joanna had admired the adventurous domestic architecture, with its emphasis on open-air living. But from the centre of that low circle rose a huge dome covered in gold mosaic tiles. It would have fitted suitably and without any change of scale on top of a cathedral in Rome or a mosque in Jerusalem, crowning a building whose other proportions were on the same massive scale. But here, in such a secluded spot and with the base of the dome raised a mere fifteen feet from the ground, the effect was ludicrous. It could only represent the whim of a megalomaniac. Joanna glanced at Howard, not wishing to offend him. 'Did you design this?' she asked cautiously.

'Christ, no!' The snort of indignation with which Howard greeted the suggestion made clear his own opinion of the building. 'She had it built for her long before I had any thought of qualifying.' He hesitated, and then took her hand. 'Sit down a second. I'd just like . . .' Again he hesitated, choosing his words.

Joanna sat down on a grassy bank and waited. They had come to a halt in a water garden and the splashing of a tiny stream lulled her into a kind of serenity as it tumbled over a miniature cliff and bubbled its way between pebbles into a lake. Howard took a deep breath and began.

'My grandmother,' he said. 'There's been one big tragedy in her life. I wouldn't want you to ask her anything about the house, in case it reminds her . . . Talking about the garden is fine, of course.'

'What kind of tragedy?' asked Joanna, since it seemed that he did not intend to go into details.

'She had two sons. One of them was kidnapped.'

'That's sad. I suppose that explains all the security measures, does it, and why she's frightened of being kidnapped herself?'

'Maybe. But fear of being snatched is reasonable. It could happen. The rest – the dome – is something different. The little boy was kidnapped on the mainland, while the family was visiting some kind of ancestral home. A round house with a dome.'

'I wouldn't have thought she'd want to be reminded of that time,' Joanna said.

'There was a sequel. My grandmother never talks about

it, but my mother told me. The boy wasn't killed by his kidnappers. And years later, when he was in the navy, he came to Hawaii. But he didn't know that he belonged here. My grandmother only found out about the visit when it was too late. He died in the attack on Pearl Harbor. So she never saw him. She has this obsession – that if only there'd been something to remind him of the place he was snatched from – a round house and a dome – he would have made contact. And then he might not have been killed.'

'But if he's dead . . .'

'There's nothing rational about the shape of this house,' Howard said. 'On this one subject my grandmother is – well, crazy. Not about anything else. Sharp as a needle in business. But whenever she remembers the son she lost . . . I just wanted you to know so that you don't ask the wrong sort of question.'

'Thanks.' Joanna stood up, eager to meet this tragic tyrant. Howard was still holding her hand as they walked towards the house. Who, she wondered, was reassuring whom?'

'I'll just go ahead and remind her that you're here with me,' he said.

For a minute, as she watched him disappear, Joanna was tempted to laugh. Could they have seen him now, the staff of the hotel complex where she had first met him would hardly have recognized the confident developer whose instructions they obeyed with such respect. But this was a serious moment. As an actress – and she had been acting from the first moment of her arrival in Hawaii – she was about to take on a more dramatic role: and she would have to play it without a script.

He had left her in the orchid garden, and for a few moments she wandered aimlessly beneath a pergola which provided a broken shade for the plants. She stared at the graceful sprays which arched from hanging baskets of moss or the forks of tree branches, but without seeing them; and after only a short time her impatience drew her closer to the house. She had almost reached the door when Howard emerged with a grim expression on his face.

'Sorry,' he said. 'Guess my grandmother's not up to showing you round today. Another time, maybe.'

'How do you mean, not up to it?' Incredulous at the possibility that after coming so near she might fall at the last hurdle, Joanna struggled to make her voice express social disappointment rather than the anger she actually felt. 'It's only a couple of hours since you spoke to her on the phone. Surely she would have stopped us making the journey if she wasn't going to let us in.'

'She's a very old lady.' Howard spoke apologetically. 'She may have been okay a couple of hours ago, but now she's sick.'

'Well, let me at least go and meet her, and say how sorry I am that she's not feeling well. I won't stay long.' She took a step forward, but Howard gripped her arm.

'No,' he said. 'We'll come back another day.'

'I may never be in Kauai again.'

'I'll see to it that you are.' He smiled at her flirtatiously, but she refused to soften her mood in response.

'Are you ashamed of me, Howard?' she demanded. 'Ashamed of letting your grandmother see me?'

'Ashamed of you! When I called her this morning, it was to tell her that I wanted her to meet the most beautiful girl in the world. I love her, Grandmother, I said, and I want you to love her too.' He was breathing fast now, as though the possibility of a quarrel had thrown him into a panic. 'You don't believe I brought you here just because you're crazy about gardens, do you? I haven't come here in company since I divorced. You're here because you're special.'

Joanna should have been softened by the admission: Howard had never said directly that he loved her. But she refused to be distracted from her single-minded purpose. Her face registered disbelief. She stared at him stonily until he gave in.

'It's her, not you, that I have to apologize for. Well, okay then, if you don't believe me.' He stood back to allow her through the door and gestured towards one of the rooms which opened from the circular hall. Joanna took one step inside and came to an abrupt stop.

4

So suddenly did Joanna halt that Howard, behind her, was unable to check himself. His hands gripped her waist as he pressed against her from behind, and he looked over her shoulder at his grandmother as though seeing her for the first time.

The shades were down, and after the brightness of the sunlight outside, Howard's eyes took a few seconds to adjust again to the dim light. Iris was sitting in a straight-backed chair, her tiny figure held upright by cushions packed on either side, and her feet supported on a stool. But her head was lolling to one side and she had begun to snore, dribbling from the corner of a half-open mouth. Her thin grey hair, which was always dressed around a hairpiece before she allowed anyone but her staff to see her, hung lankly round her shoulders. An empty bottle of Scotch showed all too clearly how she had passed the previous two hours. She must already have had her first drink of the day before Howard's call came through. He knew that once she started she could not stop.

'Mrs Lindsay,' said Joanna, her voice challenging rather than sympathetic, as though she did not believe the evidence of her eyes.

'It's no good, Joanna. She'll be out for hours.' He crossed the room to take the glass out of his grandmother's hand and set it down on the table. Then he turned back to face Joanna. 'I'm sorry,' he said.

'Does this sort of thing happen often?' Joanna was staring at the old lady as though she were photographing the scene on her mind.

'Guess so. Bad things have happened in her life. She kept a grip on herself while she was living with my grandfather.

But sometime after the war she moved out here and, well . . . She made that one trip to Europe with me after my grandfather died. After we got back, she signed the ranch – our family home in Oahu – over to my father, and has lived here as a recluse ever since. She's still head of the family trust and she calls up on the telephone most mornings to talk business. She's always sober then. I hoped today, if she knew we were coming . . . But she's old and tired. If she feels she hasn't got much to live for except a drink, I've never reckoned that it's for me to interfere.'

'Doesn't she ever leave the island?'

'Last time, as I recall, was when one of my sisters got married again. That must be six or seven years ago,'

Joanna let out her breath in a deep sigh. Howard found himself excited by her obvious disappointment. A girl who wanted to meet the other members of his family must, he reasoned, be interested in him in a serious way. As recently as a week earlier he would have been alarmed by the thought that someone might have her eyes on him as a possible husband. It was crazy that a few minutes on the Makaha beach should have made the idea not so much terrifying as enticing. Well, maybe that was going too far. But every moment he spent in Joanna's company made the idea that he might never see her again after the end of her holiday visit seem more and more unbearable. Overcome by his desire for her, he pulled her into his arms and began to kiss her as passionately as earlier on the beach, pressing his lips against her mouth, her cheek, her neck.

Joanna did not hold him at a distance; but neither did she allow herself to melt into his arms. It was his grandmother, he quickly realized, whose presence was inhibiting her – even though the steady snoring from the tiny figure made it unlikely that she would suddenly become a voyeur.

'Come on,' he said abruptly, tugging Joanna by the hand out of the room, out of the house. 'Let me show you the garden.'

'I'm not really interested.'

'Good.' The realization that she had never cared about

seeing his grandmother's garden, but had used it merely as an excuse to become better acquainted with him through his family, increased his delight and confidence. He began to run with her down an avenue of fan palms to the sunken garden before tumbling her onto the grass. Now he could kiss her seriously, lying on top of her while with one hand he unbuttoned her blouse. She wore nothing beneath it.

He buried his face between her breasts, identifying traces of salt and coconut oil before reaching the warm, tingling taste of Joanna herself. After a little while he was able to be more gentle, stroking his mouth over her skin. Joanna too seemed to have surrendered herself to the moment. Her eyes were closed, while her fingers moved sensitively over his face and neck and shoulders. But when he turned on one side, feeling for the fastening of her skirt, her reaction was unexpected. 'No,' she said.

For a moment Howard did not believe her. He had found the bow which tied her wrapover skirt, and tugged at it. Joanna twisted herself from beneath his shoulders and sat up, retying the sash. 'Sorry, Howard,' she said. 'But no.'

Even then he did not take her seriously, but presumed that – as in his grandmother's room – she felt a lack of privacy. He would not have expected an actress to be a prude, but because he loved her, he spoke reassuringly.

'No one can see us here,' he said. He had used the sunken garden as an outside bedroom more than once in the past, although he had more tact than to say so. But Joanna was shaking her head.

'It's not that,' she said. 'I'm sorry. I shouldn't have let you . . . I should have stopped you earlier.' She shook her head again, this time in protest at her own incoherence.

'You don't have to stop me at all,' Howard told her. His hand returned to stroke her breasts, but he made no other move which might alarm her. 'I love you. You know that. You love me. You know that too.'

Joanna made no attempt to deny it. 'That doesn't make any difference,' she said.

Howard stared at her in bewilderment. If she were simply

a tease he would have recognized it at once. Instead, one of the qualities which attracted him had been a kind of shy gravity, a cautious control of her feelings – if only because this had contrasted so vividly with the laughing happiness which revealed her enjoyment of her holiday. But, his recognition of her fundamental seriousness had made it possible to feel sure, in the few moments when her self-control slipped, that beneath the surface lay a passionate nature and that she longed to reveal it to him. It was possible that she was as much taken aback as himself by her own behaviour. Checked now in his certainty, he allowed his hurt disappointment to show on his face.

'I suppose I'm old-fashioned,' she said, taking hold of his wandering hand in order to control it, although showing no embarrassment at her semi-nakedness. 'I told you, didn't I; I was brought up by my grandparents. Elderly Christians with strict morals and a stern line in discipline.'

'No touching without a marriage licence, is that what you're getting at?'

'I'm not as old-fashioned as *that*,' Joanna admitted. 'It would be different if I were going to stay on here. Or if you were coming to England. You're right. I do love you. I want you to love me. There's nothing I'd like better. But in a few days I shall be back in London, on the other side of the world. We shan't ever see each other again. So something which would be marvellous if it were part of a long relationship will be – oh, I can't think of the right word. Cheap, almost. It would be just a kind of one-night stand. I should be ashamed instead of happy. I don't think it's right to start any kind of affair without love. Real love, I mean, not lust. And I don't want to break my own heart by letting myself fall in love with you and then having to say goodbye almost at once.'

'You don't have to fly back so soon,' Howard pointed out. 'Why not stay on as my guest?'

'I have a contract to honour. It's a thirteen-week serial we're making. I've been lucky to get even this much gap between the location trip and the studio work. It wouldn't be fair to extend it.'

'Then I could visit you in England.'

'You could. But you won't. It's too far. This is nobody's fault, Howard. Geography's against us, that's all.'

'But suppose I did come to England.' The plan was forming in his head already. 'I have to be in Canada in a few weeks' time. After I've finished there, I could take a side trip.'

'Some side trip!'

'There are people I'd like to see in London. But they wouldn't be more than excuses. I should only make the trip if you invite me.'

Joanna's blue eyes stared steadily at him for a long time. 'I invite you,' she said at last.

'Then I accept the invitation. So . . .' He freed the hand which he had been holding throughout the conversation and prepared to start again from the point at which he had been checked.

Yet again Joanna shook her head. 'In England,' she said.

Howard hesitated, reluctant to give in so easily. He prided himself on recognizing willingness in a woman even before she might be aware of it herself. There was a sense, he knew, in which Joanna was ready to be over-ruled. Were he to be rough she could kid herself that she had no choice, and in the end they would both be happy. But in a curious way her repeated prohibition increased his desire for her. To extend the anticipation of pleasure for a few weeks would be not so much a sacrifice as a heightening of the excitement he already felt. He put a finger to her lips as though he were testing the sincerity of what she said.

'The Atlantic is a lot of water,' he pointed out. 'I wouldn't want to fly all the way and find no one waiting. Or some new reason why it has to be some other day. I'd be looking for a warm welcome. Could you promise me that?'

Joanna opened her mouth to suck in his finger. He felt her teeth close on it gently before she let it go with a kissing sound. 'Promise,' she said.

5

As she poured herself a drink Tamsin Trent caught the sound of a police siren. It was distantly faint at first, but with every second that passed its wailing approached with an urgency which might have induced panic even in someone whose conscience was clear. Had she not already realized from the rapid approach of the sound how fast the car was approaching, she could have deduced it from the screaming of brakes as it drew to a halt, making her jump with alarm as she recognized that she was indeed the quarry. Car doors slammed. Heavy footsteps approached. The doorbell rang and, at the same time, there was a peremptory hammering on another door. Tamsin's eyes flickered with anxiety, stared incredulously, looked round in desperation for a way of escape and widened in terror as she realized that she was trapped.

'Lovely, darling.' Rick's voice came over the loudspeaker from the glass-walled monitor deck.

Joanna emerged from behind Tamsin's face and grinned mischievously. 'Twenty-three seconds of drama school audition material: listening and reacting.'

'Then you've passed. You could let the glass drop from your nerveless grasp if you like. But it's up to you. The knuckle-clenching bit was very effective. Hold on. I'm coming in.'

'Would the police really approach so noisily?' asked Joanna as he joined her in the rehearsal studio. The answer would not make any difference, for the outside scenes had already been shot. 'I'd expect them to creep up so that I wouldn't have time to run for it.'

'Running for it might be what they wanted. Evidence of guilt. Straight into the arms of the two bobbies who arrived silently half an hour earlier.'

'Rick, oughtn't I to look guilty?' This was a more important question. 'After all, this is the moment when I realize that I've been found out.'

'You've committed a murder,' Rick reminded her. 'Long

enough ago to make you hope that you've got away with it. If it had been an unpremeditated murder, almost an accident, then yes, you'd feel guilt. But the guilt would be caused by the fact that you didn't really mean to do it. And in that case you'd have been showing signs of remorse all the way through. But you killed your woman deliberately and cold-bloodedly. Someone who sets out to commit a crime with that attitude must have started off by persuading herself that there's a sufficient reason for whatever it is that she's going to do. Conscience is the first casualty of the crime. I don't think you know what guilt is. You're horrified at being found out and terrified of the punishment you'll have to take – and you're getting it over beautifully. Right; break for lunch, everyone.'

He caught her up as she reached the canteen. They moved slowly together along the self-service counter and sat down at the same table.

'You're too good for me, you know that, Joanna?' Rick said, dousing his fried fish with tomato sauce. 'I mean, I know precisely what effect I want to achieve and precisely how to achieve it – and I can do it by telling everyone in the cast what to do one at a time and second by second. You give me just what I want – I'm not complaining. With some of the others, that's all they've got to give, and without me they'd be lost. But you could do it without being told. You can act.'

'So I should hope,' Joanna laughed – but she knew what he meant. 'I like to dig deep, that's true. Until I know what makes Tamsin tick, I can't be sure how she'll behave. It's one of the problems about television work.' Rick knew that this was her first major part for the small screen, so there was no need to pretend to more experience than in fact she possessed. 'When I was training, I was taught that an actress should always be conscious that she's acting – and there's no other way to tackle this kind of serial. But the way I really like to work is different.'

'How?'

'I like to think myself into a character. To *be* that person.

It's easier with stage work, where you can switch over and stay in character for a whole evening.'

Even in the theatre that's a dangerous principle,' Rick warned her. 'It's how actors go mad or fall in love with unsuitable people, because they're putting too much of themselves into a part. Just as well, anyway, that you don't apply it to the character of Tamsin Trent. You couldn't feel yourself to "be" a murderess, I imagine.'

'Certainly I could, if the script presented her as a rounded character and not just a cardboard cut-out.'

'This script didn't give you a face-to-face confrontation with your victim, of course.' In order to keep the viewing audience in the dark about the murderer's identity throughout most of the serial, the death which sparked off all the subsequent action had been artificially contrived to appear an accident. 'Suppose you'd been asked to strangle her with your bare hands . . .'

'You'd have needed someone ready to pull me off.' Joanna grinned at him, but she was not entirely joking. 'If the script gave me – Tamsin – a proper motive, I could have worked myself up to *feel* hatred, not just show it. I mean, it would be the feeling that would show.'

'All the same.' Rick was interested in the discussion. 'You wouldn't be able to go through with it, even if no one stopped you. It's like hypnosis. I'm told you can't make someone commit a crime under hypnosis that he'd disapprove of if he were awake. Perhaps you'd push it deeper down than some actresses, but somewhere at the bottom of your mind you'd know that you were really Joanna Blythe and not Tamsin Trent and that you couldn't kill.'

'You have to be right,' Joanna agreed. 'Otherwise the death rate amongst members of Equity would be appalling. And no one would ever agree to work with me.'

'I don't know about that. Depends on the relationship of the two characters involved. At this moment, in a manner of speaking, Chief Superintendent Margrave is speeding along the motorway in the expectation of spending a passionate weekend with Tamsin Trent. If Peter is acquainted with your theory of total immersion, he may be entertaining hopes of that kind himself.'

They laughed together at the thought, both well aware that the actor who played the ardent lover was gay.

'Since there's no way in which I could be cutting him out, tell me what your actual plans are for the weekend.' Rick's voice was casual but his meaning was clear.

Joanna looked down at her plate, stabbing with a fork at the salad as though she had lost interest in it. 'An American friend of mine is coming over for a few days. I've promised to show him round in any free time I have.'

'A close friend?'

Joanna flushed and hesitated. 'N-no.'

'There, you see! You couldn't possibly commit murder if murder is something you disapprove of, because you can't even tell a convincing lie.'

'It wasn't a lie. I don't know what the truth is.' It was odd, Joanna thought suddenly, reverting to the earlier topic of her conversation with Rick. It was not only the character of Tamsin Trent with which she had tried to identify herself. She was playing another part at the same time – the part of a woman who shared her own name, Joanna Blythe, yet was not herself. She had acted out a set of emotions for this other Joanna, but was in danger of feeling them to be her own.

'I get it.' Rick gave a dramatic sigh to show her that his hint of an approach had not been serious. 'Tamsin Trent has been handed a complete script of thirteen episodes, with all her own lines under-scored in red. But Joanna Blythe has been less well served. She's only seen the pilot episode of her new adventure. She doesn't know yet whether the tall dark handsome stranger on the first page is a non-speaking extra or whether he'll turn out to be the hero – of the play of her life.' Rick looked at her quizzically. 'Or it could be a tall blond handsome stranger, of course. Not a Hawaiian-type American friend, by any chance?'

Joanna flushed again. Howard's admiration for her had not gone unobserved by her fellow-actors during the week of location work in Hawaii; there had been a good many teasing comments on the speed with which she had found herself a new dinner companion.

Rick did not need a more specific answer. 'Well,' he said, 'I hope the weekend performance will go well.' He leaned across the table to put a finger under her chin, forcing her head up so that he could look into her eyes. 'You're nervous,' he said.

Joanna forced herself to smile. 'I'm spoilt,' she suggested instead. 'By a certain Rick Nelson. For the past eight weeks I've been acting under instructions. I haven't needed to choose what to do, what to think, what to say or how to say it. I've never had to decide for myself whether the character entering stage left is a goodie or a baddie. It's all in the script – or if it isn't spelled out, you've been there to tell me. But now – well, you're right, Rick. I don't know how to tackle the role of Joanna Blythe. I'm waiting for someone to give me my lines.'

Rick laughed in a friendly fashion as he pushed back his chair and stood up. 'It'll be all right on the night,' he said. 'After all, there are more methods of acting than just the two we've been talking about. There's a very respectable school of thought which believes in improvisation. All I ask is that you'll give me three more hours of Tamsin Trent before you start working on the character of Joanna Blythe. See you at two. Sharp.'

Joanna made a moue which combined apologies for all past sins of unpunctuality with promises of perfection in the future. She sipped her coffee thoughtfully, glad of a few moments to herself. There was more at stake than Rick could have realized, but this summing-up was correct. She was very nervous indeed about the coming weekend.

6

The reunion was to take place in Scotland. Joanna, who was working in a Newcastle studio, was glad for more reasons than one that she would not be meeting Howard in London, where she owned a flat. It was Howard who had chosen Edinburgh as the venue. He had considered her convenience – but also, he told her, he had been required as a student to make a comparative study of half a dozen new towns designed in different periods. Edinburgh New Town was one of them – but he had never visited the city. Joanna found the reason surprisingly sentimental. No doubt, though, it was her own attempt to construct a mental image of Howard as a tough man which caused her to be startled by every reminder that his nature was in fact loyal and affectionate.

All the arrangements for the meeting had been set down in the torrent of letters which passed between them after Joanna flew home from Hawaii. She had not expected him to be so effusive: Americans, she had thought, communicated by telephone rather than through the mail. But then, she had realized early in their acquaintance that Howard was not a typical American or else – more probably – her definition of 'typical' had never represented more than a caricature. In conversation he had surprised her by being quiet and sparing of words. Equally surprising was his willingness to expose his feelings on paper; she received a letter from him almost daily.

Sandwiched between expressions of endearment, the letters had set out a precise schedule for Howard's visit. He would fly overnight from Vancouver to Prestwick, arriving early on a Friday morning. Since Joanna would still be at work, he would take the opportunity to inspect the gallery designed to house the Burrell Collection and to meet a fellow-architect for lunch in Glasgow. He would check in at the Caledonian Hotel in Edinburgh, where their rooms were reserved, at about five o'clock, and would wait impatiently for Joanna to join him as soon as she could – at the latest, in time for dinner at eight.

Perhaps because she had mentioned her plans to Rick, he allowed her to leave early, devoting his last hour of studio time to the searching of Tamsin Trent's cottage by the policeman who was in love with her. Joanna, who had taken her weekend suitcase to the studio already packed, ran for a taxi and was able to catch an earlier inter-city train than she had expected.

Panting slightly from the scramble to board the train only a second before it moved out of the station, Joanna tried to laugh at herself. Anyone would think that she was a lovesick girl dashing into her long-lost lover's arms instead of . . . but the thought had to remain unfinished, because she did not truly know what she was or what she expected. The nervousness which had been kept at bay first by work and then by hurry returned to unsettle her stomach as the train sped through the empty Northumbrian countryside. Normally she would have enjoyed the view of moors and valleys and rivers, but today she could think of nothing but Howard.

She had never intended to like him, much less to love him. He was too old, for one thing; fifteen years older than herself. Age was not important in itself, but such a gap highlighted their different levels of sophistication. As an actress Joanna was well able to pretend sophistication in her private life – it was expected of her and it was a part she found easy to play. She was young and good-looking and knew how to make the most of herself, dressing smartly and keeping up-to-date in make-up and hairstyle. In London she was never short of invitations to the latest nightclubs or the most fashionable restaurants. At film premières and at the presentation of awards of film and television work – occasions which were themselves shown on television – she was in demand as a companion who would catch the camera's eye; and this too she took in her stride.

But Howard's worldliness was of another kind. Joanna could appear to fit in with any social situation, but Howard was a man confident and experienced enough to create whatever social situation he chose. He had authority, that was it: the authority of a man who had a solid reputation in his professions and was in charge – well, almost in charge – of an important section of his family business. A strong, healthy man who had always been rich. It was unlikely that many women had said *No* to Howard Lindsay. Recognizing that in terms of self-confidence the two of them were in different leagues, Joanna wondered uneasily whether she was wise to tangle with such a man.

Unnerved by doubts, she was put out to discover, when she reached the hotel, that Howard had not yet arrived. She unpacked and changed and checked once more by telephone that he had still not registered. Then she sat down by the window and tried, while she waited, to enjoy her view. The huge rock which was crowned by Edinburgh Castle rose vertically only a hundred yards away. On one side where the ground fell steeply but not as a sheer cliff towards Prince's Street, she could see a footpath zigzagging through the gardens; and somewhere out of sight the Royal Mile must be providing access to the castle at a gentler gradient. But seen from the hotel room, the stone walls looked grim and unassailable, as though the building behind them had been carved out of the living rock rather than erected on top of it.

What would Howard, the architect, think of such a building, she wondered. Would he approve of the fitness of the plan for its purpose and feel interest in it as a historic curiosity? Or would his eye be so accustomed to clear lines under a blue sky that he would find it difficult to appreciate this brooding castle in the clouds?

At the thought of Howard, Joanna's earlier feeling of near-panic returned. At any moment now there would be a knock on her door or the telephone would ring, and she was still not sure how she would greet him. Writing letters had been easy. Hawaii, in a different way, had been easy as well. On its tropical beaches Joanna and Howard had acted out the first chapter of an old-fashioned romance: millionaire meets beautiful girl; beautiful girl claims to be virtuous;

millionaire becomes enamoured; circumstances part them. It had been possible there for Joanna to think of Howard almost as a fellow-actor feeling his way into a predictable role.

That pretence could no longer be sustained. She would be dining tonight not with an actor and not with a cardboard character but with a real man, solid and heavy, forceful and passionate and as well able to show anger as love. Joanna had deliberately led him on and Howard, equally deliberately, had made clear to her why he was coming. He had asked her to promise that she would not disappoint him. She had given him the promise and was here, waiting to greet him. As far as that went, everything so far had proceeded along the lines she had mapped out before she ever met him.

That was the trouble, of course. It was only several days after their first meeting that she had discovered it was not – as she had previously thought – Howard himself but his grandmother who should be confronted and punished for the crime of wrecking a young singer's life. The extreme difficulty of approaching Iris Lindsay had forced Joanna to turn back towards Howard; but no longer with the clear-cut motive for revenge which led her to approach him in the first place. She shook her head at her own uncertainty. How ridiculous it was that at this very last minute she should still not be certain of what she wanted.

The thought of the last minute prompted her to look at her watch. She was startled to realize how long she had been sitting by the window. The light was fading. She could hardly now distinguish the outline of the castle and already the time had passed at which she and Howard had arranged to dine. In the course of their correspondence Joanna had pointed out that she might unavoidably be late if her working week failed to end at the scheduled time; but Howard knew that it would be easy to travel from Glasgow to Edinburgh and had been confident that there would be no delay on his part. With a twelve-hour margin, no flight delay could explain his non-arrival. Frowning to herself,

Joanna phoned down to reception to be told again that Mr Lindsay had not yet registered. And no, there was no message for her.

Her first reaction was to laugh. Could it be that after all her soul-searching it was to be Howard who failed to keep his promises? Only a moment earlier she had been recognizing how deliberately she had encouraged him to fall in love with her. Was it possible that all the time it was Howard who was making the running, picking her up in the hope of a holiday romance and shrugging her off at the first sign that she might prove hard to get? But if that were true, he would not have bothered to keep in touch after she left Hawaii. He could have no possible motive for encouraging her to fall in love with him and then dropping her flat on her face. Unless, of course . . . but Joanna, indignant now, straightened her shoulders as she walked back from the telephone to the window and stared down at the street four storeys below.

'I am not in love with Howard Lindsay,' she said out loud. 'Therefore I don't care a damn whether he turns up or not. And I'm starving.'

That third statement at least was true enough. A cup of coffee was all she ever had for breakfast, and at lunch that day she had found herself without appetite for her salad. In the hotel dining room she asked for a table for two, not really because she expected Howard to join her now but because women eating alone were always tucked away in the corner with the worst service. She delayed ordering and then lingered over the meal – not of course in the hope that she might yet look up to see him standing in the doorway but because she had no other plans for the evening. Telling herself that a good night's sleep was just what she wanted after working with such concentration during the week, she went early to bed.

But sleep did not come easily. She was not truly tired, but alert and eager for stimulation. Her mind, disconcertingly aware of her body, raced out of control through a jumble of disconnected thoughts. Behind them all lay the hope that there might still be a ring on the telephone, a light tap on the door. Fidgeting in the bed she was forced at last to recognize that she was angry. More than that, she was disappointed. Most surprising of all – for the first time now she admitted it to herself – she was in love. 'Damn!' said Joanna vigorously to herself, and at last fell asleep.

7

It was raining in Vancouver. Howard couldn't recall that he'd ever been in Vancouver when it hadn't rained. That was one reason why he had chosen to clad part of his prize-winning building in mirror glass which afforded exciting reflections of the clouds as they scudded in from the ocean and were lifted by the wind to surmount the immediate barrier of the Rocky Mountains.

The plane had the same problem as the clouds; like them, it climbed steeply into the air immediately after take-off. As it circled over the city, gaining height, Howard stared down. Amongst the unimaginative skyscraper cubes in the downtown area his own distinctive design stood out as clearly from the sky as on the ground. He looked forward to describing it to Joanna. To have told her in Hawaii that he had won an architectural competition three years ago would have been boasting, but now that the building was complete and open for business he could reasonably reveal his pride in it.

The mere thought of Joanna made him smile, and the feeling that he could discuss his work with her was an additional pleasure. One of his early delights in her company had been the discovery that she was interested in architecture. It was a bonus to meet a pretty girl who could not only talk knowledgeably about Nash, Vanbrugh, Adam and Inigo Jones but was sufficiently aware of present-day British architects to compare their achievements. That she was less well-informed about the American scene was hardly surprising. How many American girls in their twenties would recognize the names of Stirling, Siefert or Rodgers?

He could happily have devoted the whole flight to thoughts of Joanna, remembering the time they had spent together in Hawaii and anticipating the greater pleasures to come. But his attention was abruptly called back to his present surroundings as the plane gave a sudden lurch and seemed for a few heart-stopping seconds to be dropping straight down to earth. Automatically Howard checked that his seat belt was still fastened. But the engines continued to roar in a reassuring manner, and frequent trips between Honolulu and San Francisco in storm conditions had made him familiar with the effects of air pockets or sudden gusts of a following wind.

Five minutes later the lurching was repeated. Brief gaps in the heavy clouds revealed that the plane was steadily approaching the great black wall of the Rockies. There was a feeling of unease in the cabin and stewardesses smiled more brightly than usual as they offered refills of champagne to the first-class passengers. Howard asked for orange juice. If the plane was going to bob up and down like this he could do without any other form of effervescence.

Half an hour later they were above the mountains and also above the clouds. The first sunshine he had seen that day gave hope that from now on the ride would be smoother. But the plane continued to bump up and down – not as dramatically as on the first two occasions, but almost continuously. Looking down at the jagged peaks thrusting upwards from what looked at this height like a layer of cotton wool, Howard realized that there must be some fault in the stabilizer which automatically corrected any unplanned variation in the plane's altitude. The pilot, presumably, had been forced to take manual control. Clearly he was out of practice; but the process should be safe, if bumpy.

This guess was confirmed before too long by an announcement that the plane would be landing briefly at

Calgary for a minor mechanical adjustment to be made. Howard sighed to himself and concentrated on his book to avoid irritation, knowing that such stops were never brief by any normal definition of the word. Only when they at last took off again did he look at his watch and see that he and the other passengers had been cooped up in the stationary plane for more than three hours. Quickly he calculated the effect on his plans – but he had allowed himself plenty of time in Glasgow. Although the Burrell Collection, and the gallery which housed it, might have to wait for another day, he would not be late for his rendez-vous with Joanna.

Before long it became clear that the mechanics at Calgary had failed to correct the fault. Once again the plane began to pitch, with each correction in height as jerky as the rise or fall which preceded it. Howard was not bothered. He spent enough time travelling between the islands in his own small plane to have a feeling for the effects of weather and to know what was dangerous and what was not. Every throb of the engines was carrying him nearer to Scotland; that was all that mattered. He enjoyed his leisurely first-class meal and was settling back in his seat to watch the film when a crackling in the loudspeaker above his head heralded another announcement.

First of all the captain admitted the failure of the repair and apologized for the resulting discomfort to passengers. But that was not all. He regretted to announce that there was another and more serious fault. The inertia navigational system was malfunctioning and so it would be necessary for the plane – now approaching its point of no return over Hudson's Bay – to turn back to Vancouver.

A groan went up from the passengers. Howard, dismayed, was the first to summon the stewardess. 'Why the heck do we have to go right back to Vancouver?' he demanded. 'There must be airports nearer. Toronto. Or even Calgary again; it's the right side of the Rockies.'

'Toronto closes for the night at ten o'clock local time, sir. As for Calgary – this is a brand new plane on its first commercial flight. Calgary has no experience of handling it.

No spares.'

'You don't mean we're going to be kept sitting around again while a couple of mechanics tighten all the screws!'

'No sir. There'll be another plane prepared for take-off as soon as we land at Vancouver. That's another reason for returning there. We'll have you on your way to Prestwick as soon as we possibly can.'

The reassurance did little to comfort Howard as the plane made its unsteady way back across the continent. The bumping which had been just bearable as long as it carried him nearer to Joanna was intolerable now that they were travelling in the wrong direction. When at last the landing procedures began he struggled with a tired brain to work out what the delay had done to his timetable. The second take-off from Vancouver could not possibly be less than twelve hours after the first. The whole of the time he had allowed himself in Glasgow and for the train journey had disappeared and there was no chance of making his rendezvous in Edinburgh on time. He had not seen any need to give her the number of his flight and she would be more likely to fear a rail accident than to think of checking on the plane. Or would she, instead of being alarmed, believe that he was not coming, had never intended to come? Perhaps she would walk out of the hotel after she had eaten her lonely dinner, thinking that he had deliberately let her down. Somehow he must get a message to Edinburgh. As soon as the passengers were released from the rogue plane he demanded, fuming, to be shown to the first-class lounge so that he could make an international call.

There were no facilities in this area of the terminal, he was told, and no time. The second plane was waiting for them.

'Don't tell me you can shift our baggage in less than half an hour,' Howard protested. 'There must be some way . . .'

'If you'll go to the special communications desk over there, sir, and leave the name, address and telephone number of anyone you'd like to be notified of the new arrival time, it will be dealt with while you're on the way.'

Howard joined the line. Weary and frustrated, he was tempted for a moment to call the whole thing off. He could get a good night's sleep in a hotel and fly back to Hawaii next day. But then, of course, he would never see Joanna again. No woman with any spirit would put up with that kind of treatment, even when there was such a good reason for it. Well, did he care? Even though it had taken place on his own home territory, their brief acquaintance had been only a holiday romance – and he had not even been allowed to become as romantic as he would have liked.

The answer came more positively than he might have expected. Yes, he cared very much indeed. There was something special about Joanna. It was not just that she was beautiful: he knew plenty of beautiful women. It was not just that she had class: he realized that what presented itself to him as a stylish elegance and good manners might be explained by her British upbringing. Foreigners were always socially interesting simply because their rules of behaviour were different, making them less predictable.

What most of all attracted him was the contrast between the passionate warmth which he had briefly been allowed to glimpse and the calm, restrained temperament which disciplined it. Joanna allowed her eyes to speak for her but kept her words under control. Even when her enthusiasm for something was clear, she did not gush. As a young man, and again since his divorce, Howard had learned to recognize the insincerities of women who claimed to adore him when what they meant was that they would like to take their place in Hawaiian society as Mrs Howard Lindsay. Howard was convinced that Joanna genuinely loved him – had he not believed it, he would never have embarked upon this appalling journey. But instead of smothering him with her love, she seemed to be fighting it – either refusing to acknowledge her feelings even to herself or else, more probably, believing that there were so many practical obstacles to a love affair that for her own sake she would be wise to hold back.

She was right that there were obstacles. Ruefully, as he

took his seat in the replacement plane and began another eight hours of flying, Howard acknowledged that distance was the greatest of them. But it was also the problem most easily solved. If Joanna agreed to marry him . . .? Howard paused, wondering how long he had known that this was what he wanted; this was why he was travelling to Scotland.

He put it to himself another way: *would* Joanna agree to marry him? He was sure that she was not a gold-digger. She must have realized how wealthy he was, and how powerful was his family's influence in their home state; but the prospect of marrying into such a family might alarm rather than tempt her. Still, she was an actress. Until the new way of life became second nature to her, she could play it as a character part.

Was that another obstacle, that she was an actress? Guiltily Howard realized that he had made no serious attempt to find out how ambitious she was, how dedicated to her vocation. A great many beautiful girls whose looks gave substance to their expressed hopes of working on stage or screen, pursued their careers more as an adjunct to their social lives than as a serious way of earning a living. Was Joanna one of these; or was she the rarer bird who intended to be famous and so would not willingly move too far from London or New York?

There was only one way to find out, and that was to ask her. And there was only one way to be sure of eliciting the right answer. Howard allowed himself to fantasize, visualizing in explicit detail how he would sweep her off her feet. In imagination he enjoyed her surrender, her energy, her delight. As though she were already in his arms he allowed himself to sink through ecstasy into sleep as the plane roared steadily over the continent and ocean.

8

Two separate rooms had been booked in the hotel for the weekend. Accepting his own key, Howard was at the same time given the note which Joanna had left at reception to tell him her number. As soon as he had tipped the bellboy who showed him to his room, he hurried along the corridor. A door opened just as Howard raised his hand to knock on it and Joanna, dressed for walking, stared at him in silence. Then, with a laugh of incredulity, she ran forward into his arms.

'That's the welcome I was hoping for,' said Howard when at last their frenzy of kissing had exhausted itself. He stepped inside the room so that the door could be closed. 'But I was bothered that you might have given me up, decided I wasn't coming.'

'And so I did.'

'Were you angry?'

'Very.'

'Disappointed?'

'Very.' Joanna kissed him again. 'What happened? Why didn't you let me know?'

'There's a message sitting in your pigeon hole at reception. I guess it arrived in the middle of the night – it doesn't seem to have occurred to anyone that you might care to know. I'll give you the blow-by-blow story later on. Other things have priority now.' His arms were still around her; he used both hands to pull down the long zipper at the back of her dress.

'The chambermaid –' began Joanna; but Howard interrupted her.

'Can be kept at bay by a *Do Not Disturb* notice.' He looked at her seriously. 'You invited me, remember?'

There was a moment in which Joanna, inexplicably, appeared to hesitate. Then she nodded and Howard's brief anxiety turned to elation. 'Even the most ardent lover needs to take a shower after sweating for twenty-four hours in a crowded plane,' he said. 'Stay right there.'

By the time he returned Joanna was lying in bed. Howard looked at her bare shoulders and the shape of her long, slender body, revealed rather than concealed by a single sheet. It was so exactly how he had visualized their reunion that for a moment he could hardly breathe.

'Aren't you tired?' she asked.

'Why don't we find out?' Howard threw off his robe and slipped into bed beside her. No, he was not tired – and even had he been, loving Joanna would have revitalized him.

She was as strong and as passionate as himself, and her energy sparked against his until they fused into a single body, sharing a single emotion. 'Christ!' he said, unable to find words which would adequately express his feelings. 'Christ!'

For a little while he lay beside her without moving, tempted to spend the whole day in her arms – tempted, even, to accept that he was indeed tired, and to sleep. But the pleasure of returning to bed could only be bought by leaving it, and there was a dry stuffiness in his head which demanded the open air, a gusty wind, exercise.

'Shoes for walking,' he commanded as they dressed.

'Are we going to explore the Georgian New Town?'

'Not today.' Later, no doubt, he would be appalled at the shortness of the time which Joanna would be able to spend with him before returning to work, but for the moment it was enough that there should be tomorrow as well as today. 'Arthur's Seat.' He laughed at her look of surprise. 'You're not the only one who can read a guide book.' He took a tight hold of her hand, as though she might run away if he were to let her go, and led her out of the hotel.

The hill was steeper and higher than he had expected. They took the path which ran along the cliff edge before striking across the grass to arrive, panting, at the summit. Admiring the view provided an excuse for them to catch their breaths again.

'Which is Holyrood Palace?' asked Howard.

Joanna gave a rueful laugh. 'I hoped you'd only want me to point out the castle. Even I could hardly mistake that.

You have to remember that I'm just as much a foreigner here as you are.'

'No Scotch blood?'

'Scottish,' she corrected, and then shook her head. 'I don't know anything about my father's family, but I assume he was English. My maternal grandfather – the one who brought me up – was actually an American.'

'You didn't tell me that before.'

'No one would have guessed it to speak to him. He was brought over to England as a child, swimming against the tide of immigration. *His* grandfather came from Ireland, I think. So I can't claim Edinburgh as part of my cultural heritage. Your New Town must be over there, the other side of Princes Street from the castle. Do you ever wish you could get a commission like that – to lay out a complete city, or at least to house a community, from scratch?'

'It was something that hit me early in life.' Howard lowered himself to sit on the grass and, because he was still holding Joanna's hand, she was pulled down beside him. 'That time my grandmother took me round Europe when I was fourteen. I began to work out this theory that the building you live in determines the way in which you live . Mostly an architect has to work the other way round. The client gives instructions. If it's for a private home, he describes his life-style and expects a house which will cater for it. With bigger schemes, though, you can say that the lay-out will have specific social consequences. So it's important to have a clear idea of what society wants, and then to get the plan right. Sounds pretentious, I guess.'

'It sounds good sense. And I suppose you're in a better situation than most architects because you can work for your own family business. Presumably you don't have to wait for a commission. You can think of a development you'd like to design and put the idea up to – well, to yourself.'

'Right. Well, I need to get the okay from my father and grandmother. But I can usually persuade them to put up some risk money. It's always paid off so far. That doesn't mean that the rest is plain sailing, though. There can be political obstacles. Corruption may be too strong a word – or maybe it isn't – but private interests certainly have to be fought. That hotel complex you came to with your TV people. We – the family – owned the land already, and it was dead land. Unusable. Nothing but solid black lava. Well, you saw it. Nothing to spoil, no agricultural value to be lost, no beautiful view to be ruined. Just the prospect of more employment and more tourist dollars. But if I were to show you the file of our fight to get permission! Simply because two gentlemen on the legislature had their own hotel on the Big Island and didn't fancy the competition. Something I have in mind, and soon, is to move into politics myself. I'm already working on the right contacts. Eventually' – he grinned at her – 'I reckon to be President of the United States. And with a touch more probability I see myself as Senator for the State of Hawaii. But as a starting point, I guess I shall have to cut my teeth on local politics.' He checked himself abruptly. He had not intended to mention his political ambitions to Joanna just yet. He had his own timetable for this weekend, and it was important that she should not be over-awed by his future plans until she had agreed to more immediate suggestions.

The next item on that timetable was necessarily the continuation of their walk. By mutual agreement they abandoned any thought of lunch and covered the whole distance back to the hotel on foot, dawdling up the Royal Mile and exploring the castle before running down through the gardens to the hotel. A bath and drink brought them with high spirits and good appetites to an early dinner. After it, Howard was just about to propose the next appointment of the day when he noticed Joanna looking at her watch.

'I wondered whether you might like to watch television,' she explained.

'TV!' expostulated Howard. He had other plans for the evening's entertainment and Joanna could hardly pretend not to know what they were. But just in time he noticed the amused glint in her eye and checked himself. 'Is this the programme you were making in Hawaii?' he asked.

Joanna shook her head. 'That serial isn't scheduled to be screened until the autumn,' she told him. 'We haven't finished making it yet. What's on tonight is the repeat of a play I made a year ago. I've only got a small part. But it attracted a bit of notice. It was because of this play that I was offered the lead in the serial. I just thought perhaps . . .'

'You thought right.' They settled down, very close together, in front of the television set in Joanna's room. The next hour came as a revelation to Howard. Joanna had told him that she was an actress. It was her profession – and his first glimpse of her had come while she was at work. It was totally unreasonable that he should be astounded by the discovery that she could act. No doubt his surprise had something to do with the number of his female acquaintances who devoted their whole attention to their personal appearance, perfecting tans around Hawaiian pools and announcing in loud clear voices that they were actresses – but rarely doing anything to substantiate their claims. Howard did not precisely despise them, but they did not attract him. His early interest in Joanna had grown in spite of her career and not because of it.

Now he understood what in a sense he had always known; that she was serious. And at the same time he learned that she was talented. She was playing the part of a sixteen-year-old girl, shy and vulnerable until the moment when she broke out into a passionate rage against her father, blaming him for the fact that her mother had deserted the family. So delicate and so sincere was the portrayal that it was hard to accept it as being created by the same actress who had also been the glamorous, tough-minded model stretching out her long limbs beside the royal fishponds of Hawaii.

'Christ, you're beautiful!' he exclaimed as the final music died away. There had been no commercial breaks to interrupt his concentration and he was amazed at the speed with which the hour had passed.

Joanna's smile combined pleasure at the compliment

with a trace of amused warning. 'Be careful,' she said. 'The most dangerous thing that anyone can do is to fall in love with a screen image.'

'But that's what's so great! I have the luck to know you in the flesh.' Unexpectedly he remembered that he had enjoyed the same feeling once before. His first love, Melody, had thousands of fans but he, briefly, had been invited within her circle of friends. Why should he think of Melody at this moment? It could only be because he felt young and head-over-heels in love now, just as he had been then. 'Will you marry me?' he asked.

Joanna's smile broadened. 'I thought you were never going to ask.'

Howard gave a laughing gasp of pure exhilaration. 'I couldn't be sure –' He lifted her hand to his lips.

'I told you in Kauai that I had a strict upbringing,' Joanna reminded him. 'This weekend wouldn't have happened at all if I hadn't been clear in my mind that I wanted to marry you. If you should happen to ask me.'

'Today,' said Howard. 'Why don't we go out right this minute and get married? Make an honest woman of you, isn't that what they say?'

'You can't do that sort of thing in England. Outside the permitted hours and without notice. Even a special licence –'

'We're in Scotland,' he pointed out. 'What's that place with the blacksmith's forge? Gretna Green, right?'

'Not any longer, I'm afraid. Even Scotland demands three weeks' residence now, and I do have to finish my contract period. Anyway, Howard –' She paused, as though needing to search for words. 'Getting married in a rush would make it seem a hole-in-the-corner affair. I want to look forward to my wedding. Do it properly. And I want your family to welcome me. They might not be too pleased if you simply turn up with a wife in tow.'

'They'll love you,' Howard assured her. 'And this may not come as a complete surpise to them. I dropped a hint or two when I explained why I wouldn't be flying straight home from Vancouver.'

Joanna was considering some new point. He waited to hear her thoughts.

'Why don't we get married in Honolulu?' she said. 'I know it's usual to choose the bride's home. But in this case – I haven't any relations at all who could come. Not a single one. It would be ridiculous to bring all your family half-way across the world when they'd make up almost the whole congregation. Your grandmother, for example. I take it she'd want to come to your wedding, but an old lady like that couldn't be expected to face such a long journey. It would be much simpler for me to be the only one to travel. Don't you agree?'

'Right. We could be married in my parents' home.'

'In a *house*?'

'It's usual,' he assured her, but she continued to look doubtful.

'I'd prefer a service in church, unless you're very much against it. That day when I wandered around looking for the Merchant Street building you designed, I came across a cathedral. St Andrew's, wasn't it? Not really too big. Someone was going to be married there that afternoon, and it looked so pretty with all the flowers and ribbons.'

Howard saw the advantage of her suggestion at once. He had not expected her to be a churchgoer – but she had surprised him so often by her unfrivolous approach to life that he ought to have considered the possibility. A cathedral wedding would be appropriate to the family's status in society. His grandmother, in particular, would approve – and an occasion like this would induce her to make one of her rare visits to Oahu.

For a few seconds he was content with the picture of his grandmother and his parents, his sisters and their families, sitting in the cathedral as a radiantly beautiful bride walked with graceful elegance down the aisle. But almost at once his imagination began to spread itself more widely. Naturally he would invite his friends, and perhaps one or two business contacts who would like to be regarded as friends. And some of his father's colleagues, wealthy and important, members of the generation which ran the state. Judges, senators – but to his amazement, Joanna had reached the same point almost before him.

'You were talking this morning about going into politics one day,' she reminded him. 'A wedding is always a big party as well as a church service, isn't it? The sort of party to which people accept invitations just because it's happening, without wondering whether the host had any ulterior motive for asking them. It would be a good opportunity to invite people who might be able to give you a helping hand.'

'You wouldn't mind that? If it became a big social occasion.'

She shook her head. 'It's one of the things I shall want to do, once I've settled down – to find a way in which I can use my time constructively and help you in your career. If the most useful thing turns out to be socializing, that's fine. As far as the wedding is concerned, I'm used to performing in front of an audience. Anyway, there's no need to decide anything yet.' She leaned against his shoulder in a way which made it clear that the present was more important than the future. Howard needed no second invitation.

Their first love-making that morning had been perfect, but this was even better. Some indefinable new element made itself felt. Joanna, whilst just as passionate as before, had become subtly submissive, accepting him more as master than as equal partner. It was almost too much to bear, the thought that such delight should be his for the rest of his life. He tasted, and rested, and spent himself in an outpouring of body and spirit which left him temporarily drained.

Lying beside her afterwards, breathing so deeply that he almost groaned with the effort, he thought again about the wedding. There were practical matters to be considered. Undoubtedly documents would be needed before he could make the arrangements; he tried to recall what he had had to do before his first marriage. There was a moment in which he regretted that he had been married before – but the regret was mainly in respect of his age. He wished he were in his twenties again, that was it, so that he could be half of a young couple just starting out, discovering married life together.

The thought was easily dismissed. It was as a result of that first marriage that he had learned what it was like to live with a woman who had nothing but a beautiful body to offer, and whose self-indulgent pampering of that body and attempts to conceal its gradual ageing had quickly become intolerable. Without that experience he might never have been able to appreciate the depth of Joanna's personality. She was quite as beautiful as Donna, in a different way, but was made far more attractive by her superior intelligence and depth of character. He would never grow bored with Joanna.

Returning to practicalities, he puzzled over the question of a sample of her blood. Would a British certificate be acceptable? Was there a consulate in Edinburgh where he could find out? Perhaps it would be simplest to call the embassy in London and check out all the details. One thing, though, was certain. He pulled himself a little up in the bed, plumping a pillow behind his shoulders as he looked down at Joanna. 'Business,' he said, his fingers exploring the hollows round her neck. 'I shall need your birth certificate.'

Joanna gave a gasp of mock horror as she too pulled herself up to a sitting position. 'My guilty secret!' she exclaimed. 'If ever you find yourself wondering whether I do truly love you, you can tell yourself this: I'd never let any man see that bit of paper unless I was absolutely crazy about him.'

'What's it going to tell me? That you've been kidding me about your age? You're an old lady of twenty-four?'

'Not that, no. It's my name.'

'Well, let's have it,' said Howard, amused, when it appeared that she was not ready to confess. 'Guess Joanna Blythe's just a stage name then, right?' The possibility had not occurred to him earlier, but he was not particularly surprised by the information. A good many actresses tailored their names to fit their personalities – or simply to make them more pronounceable.

'More than "just", if you see what I mean. Thousands of people have the surname that I was born with. It's a very ordinary name – nothing odd about it at all. But I've always hated it. So much that I left it behind on the day I left school. If anyone were to call me by it now, I'd think he was talking about a stranger. Sometimes, even, I feel as though I'm acting my own life, because Joanne Blythe is a different person from the schoolgirl who inhabited the same body for seventeen years, but had a different name.'

'You're stalling,' said Howard severely. 'What were you christened?'

'Joan Blunt.' She watched to see his reaction. 'Have you ever heard anything so ugly? I suppose the Blunt couldn't be helped; but I sometimes think that my mother tacked on the Joan specially to stop me from ever considering the stage as a career.'

'Poor little Joanna. What did your mother work at herself, to be so much against the stage?'

'She was only twenty-two when . . .' Joanna's voice sounded strangely subdued. 'My age now. She didn't have time to do anything.' Howard could tell that she was upset, but with a determined attempt at cheerfulness she changed the subject. 'You've never told me anything about *your* mother.'

'Didn't you get to meet – no, I guess she was in California with my sister all the time you were over. She's British by birth, so you'll have that in common. You'll get on fine with her. And she'll be all over you because –' Howard stopped dead. He had not yet discovered what Joanna's views on having children might be. Donna had refused to consider the possibility because she could not bear to be ugly even for a few months. Would Joanna have the same attitude? It must have been a subconscious fear of that which had prevented him from raising the subject before, lest the very possibility should lead her to turn him down. 'She's longing for more grandchildren,' he confessed. '*My* children in particular. And to tell the truth, I favour the idea myself. I don't know how you feel . . .'

'I feel that whatever you want, you should have,' said Joanna without hesitation. 'Not for the first year, perhaps. I'd want to get used to coping with a husband before taking on a baby as well. But after that you'd only need to ask.'

'Darling!' He looked at his watch. 'Twenty after eleven. Time to go to bed,' he suggested solemnly, as though they had not been lying there for more than an hour already. 'Tomorrow we'll look at the calendar and fix a day for a Honolulu wedding.'

9

Iris Lindsay, with two hours to go before her grandson's marriage to the English girl, sat in a straight-backed chair in the Royal Hawaiian Hotel. The hat she would wear lay on the bed, but except for that she was ready to leave. She had asked Howard to reserve a day room for her in the hotel where the wedding reception was to be held, so that she need not drive from the airport to the ranch before returning to Honolulu for the wedding.

Now she could rest after the flight from Kauai – but not relax, because her mind was fretful. Had she been at home she would long before this have poured herself the first drink of the day. But there must be nothing to spoil the occasion for her favourite grandchild. Howard had not in so many words asked her to arrive stone cold sober at the cathedral – he had never said anything to suggest that he was aware of her weakness. But there had been a trace of anxiety in his smile as he reminded her that everybody who was anybody in the state of Hawaii would be watching her as she took her place in the front pew. He was confident that she would look her very best.

So she had brought nothing with her. Certainly not a

bottle; not even the slim silver flask which fitted no so neatly into her bag. She had seated herself at the furthest possible distance from the telephone which would summon Room Service and had resisted the temptation to open the ice-box and inspect its mini-bar. The best way of keeping her mind off what she was forgoing would be to doze off in the chair. There was no danger that sleep would make her late. Hilary, who would be picking her up for the short drive to the cathedral, had promised to arrive early enough to help her with the hat. Iris could no longer easily lift her arms above her head.

A tap on the door momentarily alarmed her. After some thought she had decided that she would not need a bodyguard in Honolulu. The Lindsay wedding had naturally attracted a great deal of publicity. The importance of the groom's family, the distinguished guest list and the unknown bride who was reputed to be stunningly beautiful but had not yet been glimpsed by even the most tenacious paparazzi – all these factors had provoked social gossip, much of it in print. Any literate burglar might very well decide that this would be an afternoon on which the private houses of the Lindsay family could safely be entered. So Iris had left all her staff on duty in Kauai.

'Who is it?' she called in answer to the knock.

'Joanna.'

Iris stood up, steadying herself before she moved towards the door. A visit from the bride was unexpected, but a girl whose wedding would not be attended by a single member of her own family might be feeling the need of someone in whom to confide – or even, if Howard had not thought to send her a maid, to help her with her gown. But as Iris stared carefully through the spyhole before fumbling with the chain and bolts, she saw that her visitor was wearing a simple sleeveless cotton dress.

'Gracious, child, shouldn't you be getting yourself ready by now!' Iris exclaimed as she opened the door – quite forgetting the compliments more appropriate to the first glimpse of her future granddaughter-in-law. 'I suppose you actresses think nothing of slipping into a new face and a new gown – but on such a special day . . .'

'There's plenty of time yet,' said Joanna. Iris noted with approval that she was shooting both bolts and refastening the chain on the door. 'I thought it would be nice if we could have a little chat first. I'd hoped to meet you when I was here before, but you were ill when Howard took me to call on you.'

Iris remembered the day, and the memory increased her craving for a drink. She closed her lips on the thought and pointed to a chair as she herself sat down again.

As though she were a mind reader, Joanne produced a bottle of whisky from the bag slung over her shoulder. 'I've come to offer you a drink,' she said, looking round for glasses and finding them on a shelf above the ice box. 'We need to get our courage up, don't we?'

'Not for me, thank you, dear. I never touch a drop before sunset. Well, today, of course, I look forward to toasting the happy couple in champagne, but until then . . .' Her eyes followed Joanna's movements as the young woman poured a generous half tumbler of the whisky and set it down within reach. Joanna probably did not realize the temptation she was offering, but Iris knew her own limitations. If she were to taste a single drop, she would not be able to resist taking another. And another.

'You may not make it to the reception, Mrs Lindsay,' her visitor said. 'I suggest you do have a drink, even though the sun hasn't set yet. We have a lot to talk about, you and I, and you may not enjoy the conversation.'

What an extraordinary young woman! Iris stared in astonishment at this far-from-blushing bride. Howard had explained that one reason for celebrating the marriage in Hawaii was to make it possible for his grandmother to attend, and Iris had approved of Joanna's consideration. She was prepared to like the English girl. Hilary and Peter had already reported favourably on their future daughter-in-law. Visiting the ranch after her arrival in Honolulu thirty-six hours ago, Joanna had, it appeared, combined a polite and pleasing demeanour with a firm efficiency in checking over the wedding arrangements. But now, instead of ingratiating herself with the family matriarch, as would have been proper, her voice was cold and her stance almost threatening.

Iris felt the tumbler pressed into her hand; her fingers were closed around it. Automatically, because she was bewildered by what was happening, she raised it to her lips and took a sip. The sudden clarity of mind which always followed the first drink of the day enabled her to struggle with her own inclinations and set the glass down. Joanna's hand grasped her wrist and raised it again. 'Drink!' she commanded.

'What are you trying –' Outraged by such behaviour, Iris turned her head away, knocking the glass as it approached her lips so that some of the whisky splashed on to her dress. Then she felt the rim of the tumbler pressing against her teeth. She was forced to swallow in order that she should not choke, and gasped a little as the fire of the neat Scotch hit her throat. It gave her a momentary illusion of strength. 'I don't understand,' she said. 'Everyone will know that this is your fault. I shall tell them. You can't hope to get away with it.'

Even as she spoke, she realized that there were circumstances in which she might not be able to explain to the rest of the family who it was who was at this moment pouring out a second tumbler of whisky. Iris felt her throat go dry with fear as she stared up at the young woman. Joanna's black hair framed a face that was not so much pale as white with anger, and her eyes were shining not with the radiance of love or the excitement of her approaching wedding, but with hatred. Was she mad? What motive could the woman whom Howard loved have for behaving in such a threatening manner? Even if she knew that Howard would have access to a great fortune as soon as his grandmother died, Joanna was surely sensible enough to see that she would not need to wait long for an eighty-five-year-old woman to release her hold on the family trusts – and

Howard was already wealthy in his own right. Yes, she must be mad. But even if she had taken leave of her senses, she would not dare to risk Howard ever finding out. Iris fumbled for the glass, not daring to take her eyes off Joanna's face. 'You'll be caught out,' she said. 'Howard will realize –'

'I might not care about that,' said Joanna. She topped up the whisky and then looked around the room, perhaps to satisfy herself that the telephone was out of reach. 'I have an old score to settle with you, Mrs Lindsay. For a crime you committed years ago. When someone has to wait a long time to take revenge, it can become an obsession. Then the prospect of punishment doesn't matter any more. Just as long as the criminal has been made to suffer.'

'Criminal? Crime? What are you talking about?'

'I'm going to tell you.' Joanne's voice was coldly calm as she pulled up a chair and sat down to face Iris. Howard had been right to describe his fiancée as beautiful, but she wore her beauty now like a mask, to conceal her feelings.

'In 1962, Mrs Lindsay, you flew into England at the end of a trip round Europe with your grandson. In your luggage you had a large tin of talcum powder. Except that it didn't contain talcum powder, but cocaine. You also had an expensive crocodile-skin handbag. Italian. For some reason that I don't understand you arranged for the tin of cocaine to be left in the bathroom of somebody's flat. Somebody who had never done you any harm – who didn't even know that you existed. Then you telephoned the police, anonymously, tipping them off that it would be worth their while to raid the flat. And just in case its owner tried to persuade them that she'd never seen the talcum powder tin before, you made sure that the crocodile bag, which you also left in the flat, should be punched with her initials and should contain a few grams of the same batch of cocaine. Is it coming back to you now?'

A pain that was almost too sharp to bear stabbed across Iris's head, behind her eyes. There was a moment in which the room became dark and she could see Joanna only as a shadowy figure bending accusingly towards her. Yes, indeed it was all coming back to her, the old story which no one could possibly link to herself, the secret which had been safe for more than twenty years. If Joanna had somehow stumbled on the truth then it was not madness which had brought her here. Nor could it have been love which had drawn her to Howard in the first place. Iris licked her lips nervously as with increasing horror she realized how deliberately this whole nightmare must have been contrived.

'What does it have to do with you? She asked in a last despairing attempt to brazen it out. 'So long ago – you can't even have been born then.' She put out her hand for the whisky, but this time the tumbler was deliberately moved out of her reach.

'Later,' Joanna said. 'When I've finished my story, you're going to finish the bottle. You can be looking forward to that. But first of all I want you to understand what I'm telling you. Or asking you. Here's a straightforward question to start with. Why? Why did you do it? What had a twenty-year-old girl called Melody done to make you hate her so much?'

'It wasn't her in particular. Her family. I hated her family. I couldn't get at her parents. They'd gone off to Australia unexpectedly and weren't due back in England before I had to leave. So it had to be Melody.'

'But –'

'I'll tell you what her family had done.' Iris could feel the whisky warming her body without yet having had time to cloud her mind. She spat out the words in fury. 'Melody's grandmother and her great-grandfather, between them they stole my son. My sweet little Russell. All because of some old quarrel that had nothing to do with me at all. I never saw him again, Russell, but for sixteen years he was alive. That's what I can't bear, that he was still alive, and I didn't know. Don't you understand that? They were wicked, wicked, wicked.'

The tears streamed down her face as she rememberd the years of heartbreak and the hours of hope and the days of horror and despair. As she dabbed at her eyes some of the cloudiness cleared and she could see Joanna staring at her with no trace of sympathy.

'I don't know anything about what happened before,' Joanna said. 'But if you understood how it felt to suffer as an innocent party, how could you bring yourself to inflict the same kind of suffering on someone else who'd done nothing to deserve it?'

'The same kind of suffering? What compares with losing a child? How would a girl like that suffer from a drugs charge? A month or two in jail, maybe, but that was part of their lifestyle in those days. London in the sixties. Swinging London, they called it. A singer like that, with a group like that – they'd all have been stoned out of their minds twenty-four hours a day. Cannabis, LSD, cocaine, heroin. Whatever she got, it was less than she deserved.'

'Melody was pregnant at the time when you did your informer act,' Joanna told her. 'She may have had her wild years in the past; I wouldn't know. I expect she smoked the odd joint in her time. But from the moment she knew that the baby was on the way she didn't drink and she didn't smoke. She had no drugs in her possession until you put them there.'

'Maybe so, but –'

'I'll tell you how she suffered.' There were tears in Joanna's eyes, but she was making no attempt to hide her anger. 'To start with, she was sent to prison. You were so generous with your supply of coke, it had to seem that she was pushing it, not just keeping a little for her own use. Once she had a criminal conviction she was refused entry to the United States. Her husband was over there already, setting up a tour. The rest of the group had joined him by the time Melody came out of prison: she had to stay behind. Because they needed a singer, they took another girl instead. Do you remember hearing about Monday with Maggie? They had a sensational tour, all over the States. Their album stayed in the top ten for thirteen weeks. Everyone who knew both girls said that Maggie wasn't a patch on Melody. Melody ought to have been part of that triumph. Instead, she had to sit at home and read about it – and no other group would take her on because she wouldn't be able to get an American visa. Her husband never came back to England, not even to see his baby. He got a job with a record company, promoting American groups, and took up with another girl. The day the divorce came through, Melody jumped out of a window. She meant to die, but she didn't quite make it. Broke her back instead. Do you know what it means to be quadriplegic? She's spent the rest of her life in hospital. And all because of you. I hope you're satisfied.'

Iris felt herself trembling. If the girl was mad, she was dangerous, because the anger of madness could not be diverted by an appeal to reason or a fear of consequences. And if she was sane, Iris knew herself still to be in danger. Joanna was in complete control of the situation – in control even of her own fury. Clearly she had made a plan, and nothing Iris could do could prevent her from carrying it out. It seemed all too probable that there was to be a sacrificial victim, balancing one act of revenge with another.

'It's not right,' Iris whispered, her voice frail with tears and terror. 'I've been the victim once already. My whole life ruined. I was never happy again, not truly happy, after I lost Russell. I don't deserve –'

The words choked in her throat as Joanna slowly rose to stand above her; too tall, too close, menacing in her silence. Iris tried to scream, but no sound emerged. Instead, as she shrank back into the shelter of the chair, she heard herself beginning to whimper. Her throat bubbled with sobs and the muscles of her mouth went slack, so that she could feel herself dribbling. Was she to be murdered by the girl she had expected to welcome into the family with affection? Terror turned the whole of her body into water as she waited.

Joanna stood very still. Only her hands moved as she first clenched her fists and then slowly unclenched them and stretched out her fingers until they quivered with the effort.

Iris closed her eyes. The dark silence was broken by a sigh of bitterness.

'I didn't come here to kill you, if that's what you're frightened of,' Joanna said. 'I understood a long time ago that death is peace. The easy way out. It's life which allows time for punishment. Sometimes life *is* the punishment. I wanted you to understand, that's all. You can finish your drink now.'

The glass was pressed back into Iris's hand. For a moment she forced herself not to move, but when she opened her eyes and saw Joanna staring down at her she knew that she had no choice.

'That's right. Drink up. I want them all to see. The bishop and the governor and the senators and all the rich snobs from the country club – let them all see the bridegroom's grandmother rolling down the aisle, dead drunk at three o'clock in the afternoon.'

It would not take very much more whisky to achieve the result which Joanna had planned. Already Iris could feel her tongue tying itself in knots as she tried to speak. 'So long ago,' she managed to say. 'How –?'

'You covered your tracks very nicely.' Joanna stepped back a little. Her outburst seemed to have come to an end and now she turned away and spoke almost as though she were bored with the subject. 'On the night of that party, no one knew how the drugs came to be in the flat. No one admitted to owning the crocodile bag. It had Melody's initials on it, and she was the owner of the premises, so the police didn't bother to look any further. How could Melody prove that she'd never seen the bag before?'

'So how –?'

'Round about the time she had her accident, a parcel arrived from Hawaii. The letter inside was from Howard Wade Lindsay. He was sending her some records, some jazz music, because he thought she'd enjoy them more than the crocodile-skin bag. Melody herself never opened the parcel. It was stored with all her other possessions when her parents packed up her flat, after she first went into hospital.

A couple of years ago I unpacked all the crates and read Howard's letter. I told Melody about it. That was when I heard the whole story – or at least, the part of it that she knew.'

It was too late for Iris to deny her own involvement. In any case, she could no longer think coherently enough to argue. 'Howard,' she began, but at once discovered that she did not know how to continue.

'It took me a year to search back and find out who Howard Wade Lindsay was,' Joanna told her. 'And another year to set up some way of getting out here. I didn't have enough money simply to buy a ticket and fly out. To start with, of course, I thought it was Howard who had been responsible. I hadn't realized, no one had told me, that he was only a boy at the time. That it was you. You.'

There was a long silence in which Iris's terror returned. Joanna might not have come to the room with the intention of committing murder, but how could she afford to leave a witness to the scene which was being played out now? Had the whisky bottle itself been chosen as a murder weapon? Although Iris drank steadily in her home in Kauai, she was not accustomed to drinking so much whisky in such a short time, and she did not normally take it neat. Was she to be found collapsed on the floor, dead of alcohol poisoning for which no outsider could be blamed? She felt her heart beating erratically; the throb of a pulse against her ear drums almost prevented her from hearing her own question: 'What are you going to do?'

'I came here to take revenge on behalf of somebody who hasn't the strength to do it for herself.'

'How?'

'Well, I have choices, don't I?' Joanna looked straight at Iris. Her face was no longer a frozen mask. Instead, the animation had returned to her eyes. She even seemed to be amused. 'What do you love most in the world? We mustn't forget that there's a wedding arranged for this afternoon. As Howard's wife, I'd be in a good position to dissipate the family fortune, wouldn't I? All those funds you've been hanging on to so grimly. You can't live for ever, Mrs Lindsay.'

What did she mean by that? Iris put down the glass and began to stand up. But her head was spinning – or else it was the room which suddenly seemed to be turning upside down. If she were to move away from the support of the chair, she would lose her balance and fall. The violent pain which she had experienced a few moments earlier returned, as though she had been struck on the head. For the second time Joanna became a shadowy figure whose edges dissolved in an unnaturally fading light. Iris tried to step forward, to reach the telephone, but her legs refused to accept the instructions of her brain. For a moment or two she stood precariously still, holding on to the chair. But there was no strength in her grip, and her legs would no longer support her. She pitched forward on to the carpet.

'Right. I'm through.' Joanna's voice came from a long way away. 'I told you before, I don't intend to lay a hand on you. I wanted to explain to you exactly what damage you'd done in the past. And as for the future – every time you think of Howard's wedding day I want you to feel humiliated, knowing that he's ashamed of you and everyone despises you. I've hired someone to take you to the cathedral. He'll be here well before you're expecting your daughter-in-law. He'll help you right to your seat in the front pew, and he won't let you fall more than twice. You can get up now, Mrs Lindsay.'

Iris could not get up. Nothing in her mind or body seemed to be functioning correctly. There was no strength in any of her muscles and she could not work out how to move her arms or legs. She tried to speak, but even this effort was beyond her. With her face pressed into the carpet, she waited for Joanna to realize what had happened.

10

For the occasion of Howard Lindsay's wedding, St Andrew's Cathedral in Honolulu had been turned into a flower garden. Tiny posies peeped from each knot of the looped satin ribbons along the aisles, while the apse was filled with huge formal arrangements. There were flowers on pillars and flowers on window-ledges, flowers in the pulpit and flowers arched over the west door. Almost all of them were white, but the sun, streaming through the stained glass of the cathedral's west wall, dappled them with bright splashes of red, orange and yellow. As the guests poured in between the open bronze doors to take their seats, each of them paused for a moment to appreciate the effect and enjoy the almost over-powering scent.

Only Howard, anxiously checking that everything was proceeding according to plan, had no eyes for the floral decorations. Part of his uneasiness was due to the stipulations which Joanna had made in respect of the wedding arrangements. She had particularly asked to stay in a hotel between her arrival in Honolulu and the wedding service, rather than in one of his family's houses, and he had made the reservation without demur, recognizing that it would add to the strain of preparing to be married in a foreign country if she had to adjust to unfamiliar servants and the curiosity of assembling relatives. She had shaken her head when Howard, showing her to the suite he had booked at the Royal Hawaiian Hotel, looked hopefully at the huge double bed, but the warmth of her embrace and the passion in her kiss had reassured him that she, as clearly as himself, remembered the delights of their time together in Britain and looked forward to renewing them. Although he had been disappointed, he could in a way sympathize with the wish of a bride to approach her wedding chastely.

Less easy to accept was her refusal to be given away in marriage. Howard had offered to find one of his male relations to play this part in the service, since Joanna had no father or brother. But she had turned the offer down indignantly, pointing out that she was nobody's property; he had to be content with her agreement to accept the arm of a senator for her walk down the aisle. Most frustrating of all was her refusal to let him see her on the day of the wedding until the moment of her arrival at the cathedral. It would bring bad luck, she said – with support from his own mother. It was harder to argue with a superstition than with some rational point.

Nothing that Joanna had said or done could be considered unreasonable, but the effect was to leave Howard feeling that his bride had slipped out of his control at precisely the moment when he needed to feel confident of her movements. If any problem were to arise . . . But why should there be a problem? Howard straightened his shoulders and tightened his lips. He had not expected to find himself so jittery. After all, he had been married before – but that had been a more intimate affair, at the bride's own home in California. It had been his own choice to turn today's ceremony into something akin to a state occasion. His edginess was directly related to the importance of the guest list.

There had been no need to divide the seating between the friends of the bride and the groom in the usual way. Joanna, when suggesting that the wedding should be on Howard's home ground, had pointed out that even in England she could not have produced any relatives. As for her friends – an invitation to take such a long and expensive journey would seem merely to be a request for a wedding gift: she had been definite in her wish to send an announcement after the event, rather than before it. So all the guests were Howard's and – as Joanna had encouraged him to do – he had used the occasion to plant a marker which would be remembered when he first of all stood for the state legislature and later on planned his move to Washington.

The governor, by arrangement, would make his entrance only a few moments before the bride was due to appear; and the bishop would process down the aisle with the clergy and choristers at precisely the moment specified on the timetable. By now, ten minutes before the appointed time, most of the state's judges and legislators appeared already to be in their seats; Howard's personal friends and colleagues were sitting in a convivial group towards the centre of the cathedral; and the presidents of companies which had already commissioned work from him or might do so in the future were still arriving. Journalists and photographers were busy scribbling and snapping and checking names.

It was too soon yet for Howard to start worrying whether Joanna would be late, and he and his best man between them had tried hard to discount this particular anxiety in advance. All brides are late for their own weddings, Bret had assured him, and Howard was already aware that a tendency to unpunctuality was the only flaw in his fiancée's otherwise perfect temperament. He hoped that she would regard her wedding as a kind of theatrical performance, and would ensure that she was on stage when the curtain went up, but he was almost reconciled to the fact that this was unlikely. What bothered him now was that his mother and grandmother had not yet appeared. For the fifth time in five minutes he looked at his watch.

The governor arrived and shook hands with Howard before taking his seat in the front pew across the aisle. During the rustling and turning of heads occasioned by his presence Howard's mother slipped more unobtrusively into her place. Howard waited impatiently while she knelt in a pretence of prayer.

'Where's Grandmother, Iris?' he whispered. 'You were going to pick her up.'

'She won't be able to come, darling. She's sick.'

'Christ!' With an effort Howard kept his voice low. 'Couldn't she hold off the booze for just one day?'

Hilary put a finger up to her lips as the organist brought a prelude and fugue to a precipitate end and the congregation rose for the arrival of the bishop. Two or three minutes elapsed before she bent her head close to his again. 'She's truly sick, Howard. I wasn't going to say, in case it spoiled the day for you. But I don't want you to feel angry, imagining . . . She was being carried out of the hotel to an ambulance just as I pulled in. Someone had called from her room to say that she needed a doctor. Maybe she felt it coming and made the call herself just in time. She isn't able to speak now. She's had some kind of stroke.'

'Is it bad? Ought we –?'

'You don't know.' His mother, although still whispering, spoke firmly. 'She's been taken to the hospital and she's in good hands. You can't do anything for her – and you can't call off something like this at the last minute. So you don't know. I haven't told you. Don't think about it any more for the moment. Think about Joanna.'

Howard leant over to kiss his mother's forehead. If the whole congregation was watching, they would put it down to the normal emotion of the moment. Then, as she had instructed, he thought about Joanna, who should at this very moment be stepping out of the car. He glanced round. His two nieces, who were to act as flower girls, were waiting beside the fountain outside. As from now, the bride was late. Howard set himself the task of not looking at his watch for five minutes, and succeeded in restraining himself for three. The organist had gone back to the beginning of the prelude and fugue and was giving a virtuoso performance. It would be a shame if he were to be interrupted again. Howard, who had no interest in music, forced himself to listen to every note. As a result of such unusual attention he was able to recognize the point at which the organist went back once more to the beginning.

'When do we start getting nervous?' asked the best man, teasingly.

'I'm nervous already.' Howard did his best to grin as he spoke, glancing yet again at his watch. Now she was fifteen minutes late, and the governor was looking across the aisle as though some reassurance was needed. The bishop, however, showed no sign of impatience, so Howard could only hope that what felt like a hitch was normal practice. He heard a sigh of relief at his side.

'Senator Morse is just stepping out of the car,' said Brett.

The senator – an old friend of the family – had accepted the role of escort, promising to collect the bride from the hotel and ride with her to the cathedral before leaving her to stand alone beside her bridegroom. No doubt he had been as much put out by the delay as Howard himself. Sharing his best man's relief, Howard stood up and heard a rustling and fidgeting behind him as the rest of the congregation followed his example. The organist allowed his recital to meander into vagueness as he pulled another sheet of music into place. The bride would approach the altar to the accompaniment of the *Wedding March*. There was a moment of silence as he waited to begin.

The moment lengthened. Howard tried to visualize Joanna standing in the doorway, shaking the creases out of her skirt, smiling at the flower girls, nodding at the senator that she was ready. Unable to bear the suspense any longer, he turned his head and saw Senator Morse walking towards him down the aisle. Alone.

'I don't like to say this, Howard. But it looks like she's skipped.' He spoke in the same quiet tones as Hilary earlier, keeping a smile on his face so that no one should guess what he was saying. 'I've got a note for you. Can we go –'

For a moment Howard was too stunned to move. Then he led the way to where the register was waiting to be signed with the record of the marriage.

'I asked the clerk to call her room to say I'd arrived,' the senator told him. 'When there wasn't an answer I reckoned she was in the bathroom, and waited five minutes to call up again. Still no answer. Went up to the room; no joy. Got the maid to open up in the end. Not a sign of anyone. No suitcases packed and ready to go, no clothes lying around. Except that a wedding dress was laid out right over the bed. And on top of it was this note, addressed to you.'

Howard opened the envelope. It was not even sealed – had Senator Morse read it?

'The dress is yours. I hope your next bride will fit it.' He stared at the words, unable to believe what he was reading. Rage and humiliation were fighting their way to the top of his emotions, but both were smothered by incredulity. It wasn't possible. It just was not possible. He was as certain as any man could be that Joanna loved him. If for some reason she had taken fright at the prospect of an over-elaborate ceremony in a strange country he might just have been able to make himself understand. But she must have spread out the dress as a deliberate gesture, and such a heartless note was intended to hurt.

It had succeeded. There was a moment in which he feared that he was going to throw up. Such a let-down, following the strain of the waiting period, could hardly be endured. All the self-control he could summon was needed to keep his anger out of sight until he had done whatever he could to prevent himself from becoming the laughing stock of Honolulu.

'There's been a family crisis,' he said. He would have to hope that either the senator had not opened the envelope or, if he had, that he would not wish to admit the fact by broadcasting its contents. 'Joanna's got her priorities wrong, I'm afraid. From the best of motives. But an unwise decision. I guess she didn't know how to get in touch with you at the last minute. But she ought to have left a message. I'm sincerely sorry to have put you into this situation. Will you excuse me – there'll have to be an announcement.'

The chatter of voices was abruptly silenced as Howard appeared in front of the curious congregation and strode straight across to speak earnestly to the bishop. Returning to the front pew, he went down on his knees and buried his head in his hands. No one now could see the shuddering of his body as he tried to come to terms with what was happening. Above his head floated the bishop's calm, sonorous words.

'Dear friends, it is with great regret that I have to tell you of the sudden illness of Mrs Elliott Lindsay, whom so many of you here assembled know and love. At the very moment when she was due to leave for her grandson's wedding, she was taken instead to the hospital. All our hearts must go out to Howard in his anxiety as he waits for news of her condition. In this emergency, Mrs Lindsay has been comforted and supported by the beautiful and caring young woman who is about to become her granddaughter. And so it has become necessary to alter the timetable of today's events as a result of the changed circumstances. I am asked to tell you that the reception at the Royal Hawaiian Hotel will take place in ten minutes' time, as previously arranged. But the marriage between Howard and Joanna will be celebrated privately at a later date, hopefully when the news of Mrs Lindsay's condition is encouraging enough to disperse the present cloud on their happiness. I ask you all to join me now in prayer.'

Howard made no attempt to listen as the bishop prayed first for the recovery of his grandmother and then for the future happiness of Joanna and himself. Had it worked, he wondered. The story was the best he could produce on the spur of the moment. Would it keep the inevitable gossip under control? The senator, whether or not he had read the unsealed note, must have realized that what he saw in Joanna's room did not indicate an unexpected emergency; but the senator was a friend. If Howard's grandmother were to die, a further postponement of the wedding would be accepted as only correct; and when sufficient time had elapsed it would perhaps not create too great a stir when he let it be known that he – he, and not Joanna – had called off the marriage.

Realizing that for his own convenience he was almost hoping that his grandmother would die, Howard hated himself. Besides, even that would not be enough to silence unkind guesses. All the journalists who had earlier been scribbling details of names and hats and dresses were doubtless already working up a new story. The hospital details would check out, and if he moved fast he could lean on the hotel to be discreet. But when had Joanna gone? Assuming, as he must, that she had already flown out of the island, was it on a last-minute impulse? Or would her name be found, by anyone who enquired, on a list of passengers who had booked their flights in advance?

For a few seconds Howard allowed his attention to divert from the need to be practical whilst amazement and incomprehension swept over him for a second time. What could possibly have happened to make Joanna behave in such a way? Only twenty-four hours earlier she had stood at his side in this same cathedral as they rehearsed the ceremony. She had looked pale and nervous – but then, she was naturally pale and a little nervousness was to be expected. And it was less than three hours since he had called her at the hotel to check that there were no problems; she had given no hint of her intentions then.

Close beside him his mother knelt down so that she could speak without being overheard. 'What's happened, darling?'

'She's walked out on me, Mother. No one else is to discover that. But I want your help in covering up, so you need to know what you're covering.'

'Are you sure? Could something have happened? An accident? An abduction, even?'

Howard shook his head. If there had been no note, his own imagination would have been running riot long ago. But the cruelty of those few written words left no room for doubt. Whatever had happened was deliberate.

'What would you like me to do?' his mother asked.

'Receive the guests, will you? Tell everyone I've gone to sit with my grandmother. If you're pressed for details, say that she's had a stroke and that things look bad. But then make it clear that the reception isn't a wake and try to get a party spirit going.'

'Do you expect to be back at the hotel before the party breaks up?'

'No, said Howard. 'I couldn't face it. Keep mentioning Grandmother's illness. And tell anyone who asks that I'm too upset.'

It was true, he recognized as his mother squeezed his hand and slipped away. He was indeed upset. His body rocked convulsively forward and back within the narrow pew as he buried his head within his hands. Nobody could tell for sure that he was weeping. Only he was aware of the tears trickling between his fingers. The shock of Joanna's betrayal – and the humiliation of fearing that for the rest of his life he would be remembered as the man who had been left at the altar – formed only a small part of his distress. He was upset because he was in love with Joanna. He hated her, and would never forgive her. And yet he still longed to possess her body again, to hear her laughing with him, to see her clear blue eyes smiling into his own. He was upset because he loved her more than anyone else in the world and because he had lost her. And most of all he was upset because he could not understand what had happened to make her go.

THE END

1985

The Winner and the Loser

As Joanna packed her luggage into the car she had left at London Airport, she was tempted to drive straight home and collapse into bed. Almost twenty-four hours had elapsed since she left the Royal Hawaiian Hotel. Even at the best of times she did not find it easy to sleep on a plane, and this had been the worst of times, as action replays of her conversation with Iris Lindsay endlessly rewound and re-ran themselves in her mind – interrupted only by memories of Howard's fingers touching hers as they rehearsed the wedding ceremony in St Andrew's Cathedral, of Howard's eyes looking into hers as they kissed. By now her body ached for sleep and her mind for oblivion.

But the hospital was not far from the airport. It would make sense to pay her visit while she was in the area. Then she could go home and sleep the clock round. Driving carefully, in case exhaustion had made her accident-prone, Joanna made her way to the institution for the incurably disabled in which her mother lived.

The room in which Melody Blunt had spent the past twenty-one years would remain her home until she died. An elaborate system of slings and hoists and overhead tracks made it possible for her to be transported to a bathroom or to be wheeled, when the weather permitted, into the grounds. But such efforts were made only infrequently. For most of every day she lay immobile in bed. The position of her helpless body was regularly changed, either automatically by a machine which tilted the mattress on a time switch, or more radically by a pair of nurses: she herself had no control over her arms and legs.

She could still move her head, and with a stick gripped between her teeth was able to control a variety of electrical gadgets. As she touched squares on a sensitive panel the television set turned itself on or off or changed its channel, the video player presented a film, the cassette player embarked on a concert or a talking book: any silent moments could be filled by the radio. Melody no longer listened to the pop music which had once promised her fame and fortune. Her own brand of rock'n roll had gone out of fashion and later come back in again, but she had confessed to her daughter that she found it unbearable to listen to a familiar beat knowing that she would never again be able to move in time to it. Instead, she had deliberately taught herself to enjoy classical music – but had discovered that this too, in many cases, was designed to set feet tapping to a strong rhythm. So she had come in the end to appreciate a generation of composers whose names, like their music, were unfamiliar to Joanna. The harsh half-tones of Kelly, Hamilton, Birtwhistle seemed to give Melody pleasure – and perhaps their irregular silences aroused a special sympathy in someone whose own life had such a long pause written into the score.

Joanna supposed that over the years her mother must in a manner of speaking have become content with her way of life, but electrical entertainment could not wholly make up for a lack of human companionship. The nurses were friendly, of course, and a period of chatting to each patient was included in their daily timetable. Also, Melody's control panel allowed her to converse through a microphone with other patients in the hospital wing. Nevertheless, Joanna knew that her own visits were her mother's red-letter days. That was why, when she arrived at the hospital, she took the time to refresh her make-up before approaching her mother's room. And that was why, as she glanced through the glass spy-hole before announcing her arrival, she set a vivacious smile on her face. What was the use of being an actress if she couldn't be cheerful to order?

Very often during these visits a kind of rage would sweep over Joanna as she compared her mother's helpless middle-aged body with the photograph which hung on the wall of her own flat – the picture of a vital young singer, seeming even in two-dimensional black and white to crackle with electricity. Today, though, she felt curiously calm. Less than thirty hours earlier, as she phoned from Iris Lindsay's room for a doctor to come, she had seen Howard's grandmother caught in almost the same trap as her one-time victim – unable to move her body, but with sufficient mental capacity to hear what was said and understand what was happening to her. It was not the precise revenge which Joanna had planned, but its appropriateness held a satisfaction of its own.

But there was one difference between Melody and the old lady in Honolulu. Iris Lindsay had been robbed of speech by her stroke, and her age made rehabilitation unlikely. Even if she lived, Howard would never know – but Joanna tried to shut her mind to thoughts of Howard. It was time to celebrate the difference between the two stricken women and allow Melody to exclaim with pleasure because she had a visitor.

Only later, after they had talked about television programmes and the new student nurse and the death of the patient who played chess by telephone and the daily visits of the robin to the bird table outside the window did Melody pause in her chatter to stare into Joanna's eyes.

'I know this is the one thing never to say to a beautiful woman, but you *do* look tired, darling. Are you getting enough sleep?'

'It's travel tiredness.' Joanna forced a grin on to her face. 'Since I last saw you I've been back to Hawaii so that one of the scenes I did there could be retaken. Twenty-four hours each way for the journey and three days' hard acting in between – yes, you're right. I'm whacked.'

'Rick took you all that way just to re-do one scene! The television company must be made of money.'

'There were special circumstances. A volcano has come to life on the Big Island of Hawaii. It's tremendously spectacular. Have you seen it on telly? A curtain of light. Red-hot lava shooting up and falling along the whole ridge of the volcano.' Joanna had seen the news item herself on her hotel TV set in Waikiki and so was able to describe it with confidence. 'That kind of effect is produced quite often, apparently – but it wasn't on offer when we were there before. Rick decided that it would make a perfect back-drop.'

'You'd think with all their technical know-how they'd be able to add a background to what they've already filmed, without needing to drag you back there.'

'Rick changed the scene from day to night so that he could show my face lit up by all those lights in the darkness. Very dramatic.' Just in time Joanna remembered that her mother would watch every moment of the serial when it was finally screened. 'Of course, it will probably turn out in the end that they didn't use the right kind of film or that the lenses were clogged up with volcanic dust, or something.'

Never before had Joanna lied to her mother in such a deliberate manner. She could feel herself sweating. But she had made a firm resolve not to reveal the true reason for her return to Honolulu. Her sweet-natured mother had never understood the reason behind the first disaster which precipitated all the others and ruined her life, but she had come to terms with her fate without attempting to put the blame on anyone else. To tell her a story of spite and vengeance would be unsettling and cruel. Right from the start Joanna had been clear about one thing; it was for her own sake only that she was going to take revenge on the stranger who had framed a young singer twenty-two years before. Were she to boast, or even to confess what she had done, she would inflict on Melody not satisfaction but distress. The constraint, combined with her genuine exhaustion, made it difficult for Joanna now to smile.

'Joanna. Darling, look at me. You're not just tired. You're unhappy. What's the matter, sweet?'

Joanna dropped her gaze, lest Melody should be able to read the truth in her eyes. From the helpless woman in the bed came the sound of a groaning sob.

'I remember,' Melody said, as tears began to trickle down her cheeks. 'I remember the very first time when I realized what a terrible thing I'd done. My father brought you to see me in hospital. You hadn't been allowed to visit me before and you didn't understand why I couldn't play with you. You began to cry. And I tried to stretch out my arms to hug you, to lift you up on to the bed, to comfort you in your unhappiness. Of course, I couldn't do any of those things. And I can't do them now. However much I long to hug you, I have to wait until you hug me.'

'Mother!' Joanna enclosed Melody in her arms, lifting her shoulders in order to embrace her more closely. 'There's nothing – it's all right, truly.' But she could not disguise the misery in her voice. For a few moments she was silent, burying her head in Melody's shoulder. Then, pulling herself together, she found a tissue to dry her mother's eyes.

'Tell me,' said Melody softly.

Joanna shrugged her shoulders and attempted to laugh. 'The usual thing. A love affair that went wrong. Not important now. I shan't ever see the chap again.'

'I can't believe that any man in his right mind would walk out on a lovely girl like you.'

'Everything that's happened is entirely my own fault.' This time Joanna spoke briskly, perhaps because she was telling the truth. 'I led him on. Quite deliberately, to teach him a lesson. I was going to be the one who did the walking out. But then I made the mistake of falling in love with him.'

'Why did you need to split up? Whatever it is that's gone wrong, can't you explain it and make up?'

Joanna shook her head. 'No,' she said. 'There are some things that can't ever be forgotten or forgiven. The best that can be said is that perhaps he and I are equally hurt. All square, you might say.'

Without warning she burst into tears. It was the first time since her meeting with Howard that she had allowed herself to cry. Even when she laid out her wedding dress on a hotel bed in Waikiki, knowing that in acting the part of a jilt she was breaking her own heart, she had managed to stay dry-eyed, forcing herself to scribble a note which would close the door on any hope of reconciliation. It had taken her two years to make her plan of revenge, to adapt it to new circumstances as she discovered them, and to bring it to fruition; no weakness of her own must be allowed to spoil it. Only now, when neither regret nor hope could change what had happened, did she admit to herself how much it had cost the real Joanna to play the part of this other Joanna, so unrecognizably cold and cruel.

'I loved him,' she said through her sobs, clutching one of Melody's pillows to her face and rocking backwards and forward in her distress. 'I love him so very much. But . . . but. . . ' She took a deep breath to calm herself and crossed the room to the washbasin so that she could splash her face with cold water. 'But there's an impediment,' she said. 'A permanent one. So we won't talk any more about it.' Melody would take that to mean that the man was already married and, because of the seclusion in which she had spent the past twenty years, would be more likely than most people in the modern world to accept that there was nothing more to be said.

'Do you think you'll be able to forget him?' she asked. The tone of her voice revealed that she was puzzled, as well as being anxious on her daughter's account.

'That's the only thing to do, isn't it?' Joanna spoke briskly and turned round to smile before leaning nearer to the mirror to repair her make-up. It was time to remind herself again that she was an actress. In the past few weeks she had successfully played two quite separate parts at the same time: Tamsin Trent, the sultry murderess and Joanna Blythe's alter ego, the shy charmer and passionate lover. Now it was time to return to the role of the real Joanna Blythe and play her as she had always been played before – as a beautiful young woman, competent and contented in her private life and increasingly successful in her profession. It was with a jaunty air that she stepped out into the corridor to see whether the tea trolley was on its way; and the gaiety in her eyes as she returned with a tray and set it down would have deceived anyone except her mother.

'Yummy, yummy!' she exclaimed. 'Chocolate cake. They must have known I was coming. And until I phone my agent tomorrow to report that I'm back and waiting for work, no one will care if I grow fat.' She set a curved glass drinking tube between her mother's lips. But while shc waited a few seconds for the tea to cool she looked straight at Melody with eyes which were still smiling but now very serious.

'It's all over,' she said. 'Never to be mentioned or thought of again. It was a complicated affair. But it's finished.'